A Ship A Gale A Mermaid Tale

A Story of a Father's Love

A Ship A Gale
A Mermaid Tale

A Story of a Father's Love

Larry P. Buckingham

CITIOFBOOKS, INC.
3736 Eubank NE Suite A1
Albuquerque, NM 87111-3579
www. citiofbooks. com

Hotline: 1 (877) 389-2759
Fax: 1 (505) 930-7244

Ordering Information:
Quantity sales. Special discounts are available on quantity purchases by corporations, associations, and others. For details, contact the publisher at the address above.

Printed in the United States of America.

ISBN-13: Paperback   979-8-89391-405-4
          Hardback   979-8-89391-487-0
          eBook   979-8-89391-406-1

Library of Congress Control Number: 2024921864

Dedication

This book is dedicated to my father, who unfortunately passed before it was completed. In addition, I must express my undying gratitude to my darling Darlene, for without her patience, insight and contributions, this book would never have been. Also, I would like to thank Kathy for whose ideas, opinions and understanding were invaluable.

TABLE OF CONTENTS

Chapter 1
"Homecoming"

Soft puffy clouds, high in the sky, were beginning to adorn themselves with the early morning hues of orange, pink and red as the sun slowly made its approach towards the horizon to herald in a new day. The morning crew of the ship was already on deck and in the rigging, making the necessary preparations to get the ship ready for daytime sailing. The year was 1622 and it was an unusually clear summer morning for this part of the Atlantic.

It had been over two years since the ship, the *Galaunt*, a three-mast galleon, constructed after the East India Dutchman pattern and possibly the finest ship of her time to ply the open seas, had set sail for the East Indies. Now it and her crew were, finally, coming home. She was coming under full sail and was starting to glide across the open water as if she was sliding across the surface of a frigid frozen lake. Her sails billowed out, catching the strong, steady morning winds coming from astern. Her crew was hoisting all the canvas her masts and yards could hold, stretching the rigging lines taunt until they sang with vibration. Her flag, the English Union Jack, and pennants were straight out, flapping in the wind. Today, it was as if she were alive and more than eager to reach the port that she called home and was anxious to deliver the cargo stored in her holds and bring her crew back to their home and families.

Captain Nathan Roth, master and commander of the *Galaunt*, was standing on the wheel deck watching his crew go about their tasks with excitement and happiness and the anticipation of finally returning home.

Roth was very similar in nature to that which the name of the ship implied. He was brave, noble, high-spirited and adventurous, he stood just a shade over six feet, with broad shoulders and dark blue eyes that seemed to be able to see into your soul when you caught their gaze. His hair was shiny black, long, very wavy and uncut since leaving port over two years ago. His size and burly manner, most often, gave people the impression of someone to avoid if possible. That was just the way he liked it, but his friends and especially the crew knew a different Nathan Roth. They knew he was a man that, almost to a fault, was honest and fair. It was very rare indeed that he ever had to more than slightly raise his voice to have his orders carried out. They also knew he was a man that would shell out discipline, as they had seen on those rare occasions, and show a great deal of compassion when the need arose, as they had also seen on more than one occasion.

Roth saw the first rays of the sun touch the topmost tip of the main mast and he could follow its rise by watching a line of orange as it slowly crept down the sails. He watched until the sails and the seas around him appeared to be a fiery pool of molten lava as the first arc of the sun itself, peeked above the horizon. He knew that it was going to be a great day for a homecoming, something that he, as well as his crew were eagerly looking forward to. With no visible signs of a storm on any horizon, it meant they would have clear sailing all the way to port.

When the sun fully cleared the horizon, he was distracted from this view by a flashing glint from a light coating of gun oil applied to the cannon. Roused from his reverie, he took the time to look around the ship and was very proud of what he saw. The *Galaunt* was a fine vessel and she had weathered this voyage with her grace and style mostly intact. She had received a few scars nevertheless, for this had not been a completely mundane voyage. Sometimes the voyage had been very perilous and the ship and crew had to fight for their very lives against both enemies and the weather itself. You could easily see the repairs to the deck planking of the bow and a section of the starboard railing, near the bow, was held together with rope and the mainmast main yard was a good thirteen feet shorter on the starboard side. He could easily remember every scar the ship had received during every battle they had to fight. Ultimately, they were able to emerge victorious, thus enabling him to bring his ship and crew home safely. He was very proud of this ship and very proud of the men that manned her.

Standing beside Roth was his first mate, a man, tall and lean, deeply tanned complexion, with a mass of unruly blond hair bleached almost white by the suns of many years at sea. He had shrewd, watchful brown eyes, the chiseled nose of his Roman ancestors and an even smile. He carried about him an air of authority, as rightly he should, for he was Edward Berkshire, First Mate and longtime friend of Captain Roth. Roth turned to him and said, "Tis gonna be a very good day for sailin'. The wind should stay steady and strong all mornin'. Keep her on this course and we should be sightin' land about midday."

Berkshire, while respectfully delivering a salute that showed the familiarity of their long friendship, replied with, "Aye Cap'n, it will be this course and none other that we be sailin' this mornin' you can mark me words on that." Turning towards the helmsman, he said over the sounds of the vibrating ropes, "You heard the Cap'n, steady as she goes."

With that and one last look around his ship, Roth said, "Mister Berkshire, come to my cabin when land is sighted."

"Aye Cap'n," his first mate replied, delivering a sharper salute.

Roth chuckled to himself as he returned the salute and turned to descend the stairway from the starboard side of the wheel deck to the main deck. As he stepped upon the main deck, he took a few seconds more to once again cast his gaze around the ship and up into the rigging where he saw most of his crew scurrying around making things fast. He remembered his days in the rigging with a touch of melancholy and maybe even a touch of envy for the men that were still able to do the chores that the masts and yards called for. As he watched, he could hear the sounds of the men talking amongst each other, as well as the sounds of laughter, singing and whistling. Indeed, his crew was showing a great exuberance of returning home. He chuckled again to himself as he headed off towards his cabin.

His cabin was located under the wheel deck, accessible through a door, which was offset from the center of the ship, which opened onto a short hallway. This hallway contained five doors, two on each side and one at the end. The doors on the port side, the wider side, led to the cabins occupied by the first and second mates. The doors on the starboard side led to the cabins generally used by passengers, but for now used as additional storage space, crammed full of the more valuable cargo taken on board during the long voyage. Roth's cabin was behind the door at the end of the hall. His cabin was as wide as the ship and slightly less than half the length of the wheel deck. The stern wall held five long and narrow windows, affording ample light to brighten the room. Two of those windows, however, now consisted of planking used to close up a hole caused by a cannon ball that had ripped through his cabin into the adjacent cabin used for storage. As was true for the entire ship, items hung from the ceiling beams and other items were crammed anywhere there was empty space.

On a long drawing table, that took up most of the portside hull, were the charts and maps that Roth had drawn depicting the parts of the world he had visited during this voyage. Next to the table were the racks of maps that he had obtained from various sources, including those seized from defeated opponents. The bed and wardrobe took up the starboard side hull. His wood crafted and ornately carved desk, also confiscated from a rival ship, dominated the center of the cabin. It was not an overly large desk, but large enough to hold the charts and maps when he needed to look them over and certainly large enough to write in his log. The latter was something that he did daily but not something that he enjoyed at all. He did not relish the time spent in his cabin, his was a life in the open, feeling the sun on his face and the wind blowing in his hair. He much preferred being topside with the crew, ensuring that the ship was being sailed as he, himself, would sail her.

Upon entering the cabin, Roth moved to his desk, took his seat, and removed the log from its drawer. As he began making the final entries in the ships log about the long voyage they had just made, he began to reflect on events that had happened during the long and arduous voyage they were just completing.

It was his first voyage while in command of his own ship and his first voyage to the East Indies. He was very glad that it had turned out to be as successful as it had, although, it had not been without much hardship and loss of life.

The ship had originally sailed with a crew of thirty-five, including himself, and now it was returning home with only twenty-four of the original crew and five others they had rescued from other ships he had encountered. The Portuguese and the Dutch had a solid hold on the lucrative East Indies trade and they did not look favorably on other nations, especially the British, intruding upon their waters. So, the ship and its crew fought many times, losing friends and shipmates. It was because of the unique design of the *Galaunt* that they were able to fight their way out of trouble so successfully and finally to make the trades that they had come so far to make.

The *Galaunt*, by design, was actually an armed merchantman, built for speed, agility and especially the ability to fight, when necessary, to make trades in the East Indies. She differed from the more commonly used Spanish type Galleon in that she had no castles fore and aft. Her forward and main masts each held three sails and the aft mast carried two along with the boom that held the stern spanker sail. She had two jibs on her forward bowsprit and there were staysails on all the masts. This sail design enabled her to gain greater speeds, granting her the ability to maneuver, quicker and faster, into better firing positions for her sixteen cannons. Captain Roth, early on, had learned how to gain the most out of her unique capabilities and turn all encounters with foreign vessels into victories for the *Galaunt*.

When they first arrived in the East Indies, it had not taken them long to realize the broadcloth they were carrying was not a very good item for trade. It was much too heavy to use in that climate for clothing. The people who inhabited that region, preferred a much thinner and cooler cloth. However, with the small amount of bullion they carried with them from England, he was able to purchase spices and teas from some of the smaller islands they encountered from time to time, but he soon came to the realization that they were not going to be very successful at this rate. He knew he needed to secure a different assortment of goods to trade. He and Mister Berkshire had many conversations regarding how to resolve this dilemma.

One day they happened upon a Dutch Galleon that had evidently been in a battle recently. From the looks of her, a battle she had lost. Her mainmast and mizzenmast were both mere stumps, jaggedly jutting above her deck and her foremast had lost its top third. The torn and tattered canvas left in the rigging was barely enough to give her forward headway. As the *Galaunt* approached, Roth observed that the Dutch crew was manning and preparing their cannon, making ready for battle. Reaching the point where the stricken ship was within range of his own cannons, Roth ordered that two shots be fired over her bow in the hope that he would not have to fight with this already grievously wounded ship. He was very pleased when the Dutch commander lowered his countries flag and raised a white flag in surrender.

The *Galaunt* quickly moved in and in short order the Dutch vessel was alongside the *Galaunt* and completely under the control of Captain Roth and his crew. Roth hurriedly made it known to his crew, show no further harm or disrespect towards the Dutch. With this assurance, the Dutch crew showed obvious relief.

Roth sought out the Dutch Captain and courteously invited him to join himself and Mister Berkshire in a cup of wine in Roth's cabin. The Dutch Captain graciously accepted and followed Roth as they both made their way across the gangplank used to span the short expanse between the two ships. When the Dutchman set foot upon the deck of the *Galaunt*, he looked around and was very impressed with what he saw, obviously glad that he had made his decision not to try to take her on.

As they entered his cabin, Roth gestured for the Captain and Berkshire to take seats and rang for his cabin boy to bring wine. After all three took their seats and while waiting for the wine to arrive, Roth started to question the captain. He was very interested to find out what had happened to his ship. As it turned out, a Portuguese Galleon had attacked his vessel, late in the afternoon, some days earlier. Her Captain went on to tell them that they had been sailing northward with a cargo of Indian cotton, when the attack came. She had fought a running battle with the Portuguese ship for two days before she managed to fire two cannon shots, hitting the Portuguese amidships below the waterline. The Portuguese abandoned their attack and turned about before they sustained further damage, but not before firing off one last devastating salvo. This was when the majority of the damage to the masts had occurred. The Dutch were nearly helpless in the water but were still able to make slight forward headway. Roth doubted, from the description of the damage, that the Portuguese would be able to follow without major repairs and felt safe for the time being.

Satisfied with the tale of the battle, Roth inquired as to why they were sailing north. The Dutch Captain replied that they had been sailing northward toward the Orient with hopes to trade the Indian cotton for gold and silver jewelry, silk, teas, and jade carvings. Mostly silks, however, for that seemed to be what the islanders desired most of all in trade for their spices. Roth inquired further about the Indian cotton. The Dutch Captain told him that they had acquired the cotton at a port on the eastern coastline of India in trade for the grains and lumber they had brought with them from Portugal.

At this point, the Dutch Captain asked Roth what his intentions were concerning his ship and crew. Captain Roth assured him that he would allow the ship to proceed on her way, only after a trade of his broadcloth for the cotton and other cargo that the Dutch ship carried. This would be a beneficial trade for both vessels. The *Galaunt* needed different trade goods and the Dutch needed a stronger cloth to fashion some sort of a sail, otherwise they would not make it to a port before they sank.

The broadcloth, from the *Galaunt*, was loaded onto the decks of the Dutch galleon, while the cotton and other Dutch cargo was safely secured in the holds of the *Galaunt*. Roth said farewell to the Dutch Captain, a man that he found to be pleasant company, and watched as the Dutch crew immediately set out on the task of sewing the broadcloth into a useable sail. After a few moments of thought, he gave orders to his crew to set course north for the orient.

Now loaded with a cargo of fine Indian cotton, the *Galaunt* made her way up the Asian coastline, where Captain Roth and the crew were able to make several good trades. It was a very exciting time for the captain and his crew. Everywhere they went, they experienced new sights and sounds. They were even beginning to acquire a taste for Oriental foods. Soon they found themselves becoming very heavy with the silks and the teas they had been able to trade in abundance for. The jewelry and the jade carvings, alone, would make them all rich if they could get it home. Captain Roth figured that now was the time for them to make their way south to the islands and start trading the silk for spices, after all, wasn't that what they had come for?

The trip south, as it turned out, proved more difficult than the trip north. On the third day, they encountered a heavily laden Portuguese galleon. Instead of turning away as they were prone to do, they turned directly towards the *Galaunt* with the obvious intention of fighting. It proved to be no match for the armed merchantman. The *Galaunt* was able to move around the galleon at will and soon the opposing Captain lowered his flag in surrender. The Portuguese, as the Dutch, were loaded with silks, a small chest of jewels and some jade and jade carvings. The Portuguese galleon was in bad shape after the short battle. The *Galaunt* had all the silks they could carry, so the only thing salvaged after this altercation were the jewels and jade. Captain Roth then ordered the Portuguese crew into their longboats and torched the ship. He felt unusually satisfied with this small victory because the Portuguese were not friends and if the battle had gone the other way, would not have done the same and probably shot his crew as well. That is the very reason why the British trading was so difficult.

On three separate occasions while continuing to the islands, they subsequently came upon two more Portuguese and one Dutch vessel they had to fight and defeat. After removing all valuables from all the ships, the Dutch being heavily damaged and in no shape to sail far, sailed away, the Portuguese ships were destroyed.

Once in the islands they found trading went very smoothly. The inhabitants of the islands eagerly sorted through the beautiful treasury of silks and happily took all they could carry. They were able to make many successful trades for the spices they sought and soon found themselves with cargo holds stuffed full of spices, the remainder of the silks, cottons, teas, and jewelry and jade. Captain Roth was satisfied the mission had been more than successful, made the decision to head for home.

At that time, it was early spring and the perfect time to start the voyage home. This would mean that they should have smooth sailing around The Cape of Good Hope. The Cape had claimed many fine ships over the years because of the massive storms that engulfed the region during the winter months. Roth knew it would be better to sail in the spring and summer or not sailed at all.

While deep in thought, a tapping at the door startled Captain Roth. "ENTER," he bellowed, resentful of being interrupted. Mister

Berkshire stepped into the room. Seeing his friend, Roth's resentments quickly waned.

"What is it that I can be doin' for you, Mister Berkshire?" Roth asked in a soft and friendly way.

"Cap'n, we come within sight of land and will soon be roundin' the point and enterin' the mouth of the river. The crew and I are awaitin' your orders sir."

"Finally," Roth replied with a deep sigh, "I never thought this voyage was ever goin' to end!"

"Aye Cap'n, it has been a long one at that. I am anxious to be seein' my family again myself. I am lookin' forward to a long beach rest without wind blowin' all the time."

"Aye Mister Berkshire, it will be good to be on land again." As he picked up the bell to ring for his cabin boy, Roth inquired, "Would you care to join me in a cup of wine Edward?"

"I would be enjoyin' that," Berkshire answered.

The cabin boy arrived with the wine, Roth relieved him of it and set the tray on his desk. Picking up the two glasses, he offered one to his friend and said, "We learned a lot on this trip."

"That we did," Berkshire replied with a smile.

Roth, moving back behind his desk to take his seat, commented, "Next year, with the knowledge we have gained, we should be able to make this same trip in a lot less time".

"If we can obtain our cotton from the same source as the Dutch, the rest will be easy," Berkshire stated.

"I agree, that is one of the problems that we will face, but I believe that we can be persuasive enough to acquire what we need," Roth said while finishing his wine.

Berkshire finished his wine and said, "I should be headin' back topside sir."

"Aye Edward, let me finish with this log and I will join you shortly."

"Aye, aye Cap'n," Berkshire said as he departed the cabin, closing the door behind him.

After his friend had left, he proceeded to make the last entry into the log and stood looking around the room that had been his home for over two years. Usually strewn with charts and maps he had made during the voyage, he was amazed at how the cabin boy had kept the cabin livable. His thoughts turned to home and the comforts he had come to miss more and more. He could picture his home in his mind and realized that it would not be long before he would be there. He anxiously donned his coat, grabbed his hat and headed out onto the deck.

Roth chuckled to himself as he made his way to the wheel deck. He saw men were already in the rigging, anticipating his orders. They were obviously as anxious as he was to get home. This made him smile and think to himself that this was a taut ship with a happy and loyal crew. The crew was more than willing and able to follow his orders and meet his commands. They had been hand picked, chosen from sailors Roth had sailed with before or else had come highly recommended. They were all gathered here on the *Galaunt* to sail one of the finest ships ever to ply the East Indies trade routes. As he stepped onto the wheel deck, Mister Berkshire gave him a crisp salute and said, "Your orders Cap'n?"

"Let us let her fly a bit longer Mister Berkshire, let us show them a real sailing ship as this proud vessel rounds the point," Roth said beaming with pride in his ship and crew.

"Aye Cap'n," Berkshire replied. He then yelled to the crew, "tighten those mainsails and topsails lads, we are goin' to come round the point at top speed with the wind blowin' up our tail. We will show them landlubbers the full glory of a Far East trader returning home to port, after a successful voyage!" A loud cheer arose suddenly from the crew. They were delighted to show off their ship and prove that they were indeed the best crew sailing the finest vessel on the open seas.

Under full sail, the ship made great haste coming around the point and sailed into the mouth of the river. The captain knew the ship would be sighted soon and easily recognized as soon as it rounded the point. The owners and dock crews, probably already alerted to make ready for their arrival.

As the port town came into view a short distance up the river and its docks coming into sight, Roth gave the order to Mister Berkshire to have the crew start lowering the main sails and secure the jibs. They left topsails to provide the needed forward momentum to enable the ship to maneuver alongside the docks.

As the ship neared the dock, Roth could see people gathering along the wharf. He sensed they were aroused with excitement and anticipation. News of what ship coming into port must have traveled faster than he had expected. This was the first successful voyage from the East Indies, and undoubtedly, the richest these people would ever witness. Roth knew the people would want to hear all about it firsthand from the crew members. He also saw a small group of men standing off to one side, these men would be the owners, those aristocrats of society, obviously trying to avoid any unwarranted association with the riffraff that usually hung out around the docks.

As the ship docked, Roth saw the owners making their way amidships, not wanting to wait for the gangplank, where they could be hoisted aboard. He also noticed that all three of the *Galaunt's* sister ships were anchored in the river. With the ship secured, Roth gave the order to rig a boson's chair and bring the visitors aboard. The first hauled on deck was Lord Jarvis Creed, his position was head of the company that owned the *Galaunt* and the cargo she carried.

Creed, a short, balding man, very much on the portly side, had a look of gaiety about him, but if you looked into his eyes, you would immediately know this man was not as he appeared. He had the eyes of a man that was used to giving orders and having those orders promptly carried out.

Next on board was Gerald Raynerd. He was the opposite of Creed in that he was tall and lean to the point of being called skinny, with a look of suspicion perpetually on his face. Roth knew he was also a man not to cross. His job was to take the orders from Creed and see them carried out, without question. Of the two, Roth would much rather deal with Creed.

Captain Roth hurried to greet the men. Creed offered his hand and in an almost friendly way said, "I would like to offer my congratulations Captain Roth on the success of your return home." With a slight smile, he added, "And with a full load of cargo, I presume, from the looks of how low the *Galaunt* is riding on the water." Raynerd said nothing and simply nodded towards Roth. Two other men, introduced as cargo inspectors, also came on board. Roth led them all to his cabin where he could brief them on the voyage.

After Creed and Raynerd found a seat, joined by the inspectors taking up positions by the door, Roth took his place behind his desk. Once seated, he rang a small bell to signal his cabin boy, a boy of about fourteen, to bring them all some wine. The cabin boy returned almost immediately and proceeded to pass out the cups of wine.

"First of all," Roth started, "let us dispense with the pleasantries and get right down to the purpose of this meeting," as he removed some papers from a drawer in his desk.

With obvious excitement, Creed mumbled, "Agreed," as he raised his cup for a sip of the wine. "I am very anxious to hear of your voyage and learn what you have brought us."

Roth, glad for that, starting again said, "As you all know, we have been in the East Indies for over two years and during that time we have had the fortune to learn how to do trade in those parts. It was not an easy task and after you look the ship over you will see that we had to do our share of fighting to learn those lessons." At this point Roth went on to tell them the story of the voyage, the lessons learned and the battles the ship and crew had incurred.

Raynerd broke in to ask, "Is the ship badly damaged, and will it require much repair?"

Roth stopped to answer, "Not badly enough to keep her from sailing if the need should arise, but she does surely require some minor repair that should be completed before any lengthy voyage is attempted". This was a relief to Raynerd.

Creed, starting to show impatience, demanded, "What about the cargo, Captain? I would like to hear a little more about the cargo."

"Ah yes, the cargo," resumed Roth as he spread the papers out on his desk for them to examine. "Our holds are full of reams of the finest oriental silks, gold and silver jewelry".

An obviously interested Creed interrupted, "You found gold over there?"

"No, we did not find gold ourselves, what we have we traded for with the Orientals or from defeated enemies," answered Roth, inwardly annoyed at the interruption.

"Do they have a lot of gold?" inquired Raynerd wistfully as he stood and began pacing the room behind the others.

"We did not see a lot being worn by the people. They do not seem to be much in the way of body ornaments, though rumored, the rulers of the countries have amassed a large quantity for their own uses and religious idols. What we traded for was offered as that, trade, the Orientals do not hold gold in the same esteem as we do," replied Roth, leaning back in his chair, folding his arms.

"I see," Raynerd said quietly. It was obvious that he was deep in thought about the gold, the riches it meant, and undoubtedly would have more questions later.

Roth began wishing that Raynerd would retake his seat, his pacing was beginning to irritate him. He hesitated with his narration and reached for his pipe. He resented the interruptions and wanted to get on with the meeting.

Creed finally broke the silence by asking, "What about the rest of the cargo? Is she as loaded as she looks?"

"I think that you will be very pleased by the cargo that we have brought home." Roth, lighting his pipe, went on to say, "There are over one hundred barrels of spices stored in the holds below, containing peppers, cinnamon and a vast variety of teas. Also there are bolts of Indian cottons, not as strong as our broadcloth but finer and there are several pieces of carved jade"

"Jade, you say, that should bring a good price," Creed acknowledged wringing his hands in delight.

"Yes Lord Creed, the jade, gold and silver alone should more than pay for the costs of the voyage," Roth added, taking a slow draw from his pipe. "The spices and cloth will bring in a hefty profit for all of us."

Raynerd again spoke, having stopped his pacing to listen, "Yes m'lord, the value of those spices is at a high right now. This was a very fortuitous arrival indeed, especially under these circumstances." Raynerd mused to himself, yes indeed!

"Well then, gentlemen," Lord Creed said, "Let's see what we can do about getting this ship unloaded so that we can find out just exactly what it is we have."

"Agreed m'lord, let me show you to the main deck and instruct the crew to start unloading," Roth said as he arose from his seat. He gathered the papers into a neat stack, then walked around his desk and handed them to one of the cargo inspectors. He was relieved that this meeting would soon be over and these men would be gone.

Roth led the small party out onto the main deck where he was pleased to see that the crew had already lowered the gangplank to the dock below.

"Ok then Captain, we will be getting in touch with you very, very soon," Creed said not even offering his hand, as he turned on his heals and quickly marched down the gangplank with Raynerd close at his side whispering something into his ear.

As Roth watched them depart, he wondered what it was that Raynerd was saying to Creed. A feeling deep down in the pit of his stomach was telling him it was not going to be something that he would like. He hoped, however, that it did not have anything to do with him.

As his thoughts returned to the ship, he saw wagons and dock hands already starting to line up on the dock to begin hauling the precious cargo to the warehouses for storage and eventual sale. He turned toward the wheel deck and saw that his first mate was deep into conversation with the ships cargo master and the cargo inspectors.

"Mister Berkshire," he called from his spot on the main deck, "how are preparations for unloading comin'."

"Ah, that is what Smitty and I were just discussin' with the cargo inspectors Cap'n," Berkshire called back. "We are ready to begin on your orders sir."

"Very well Mister Berkshire, you have your orders. If you would, start with the chests and the carvings. Have them taken straight up to Lord Creed's office for storage," Roth said as he turned towards his cabin listening to Berkshire.

"Aye, Cap'n," Berkshire replied. "All right men, enough of the lollygagin', lets get this ship unloaded," he shouted at the crew and men waiting to start hauling the cargo onto the dock and into the wagons. The crew immediately started unfastening the cargo hatches and rigging up the pulleys and ropes that would be needed to lift the heavy barrels from below decks as the men from the docks began filing aboard the gangplank in hopes of work. "I need twenty strong men," the first mate said, and started to pick out the strongest that he saw. "Mateys, you four go with the cargo master. Bring out the chests and crates of carvings and load them onto that wagon, pointing to the wagon at the front of the line. "You will have to follow the wagon so that you can unload them at Lord Creed's office. All right?" he questioned and watched one of the workers nod his head in acknowledgement. "Then get a move on it lads, the lord is not to be kept a waitin'. The rest of you lads go help with the unloadin'."

Roth chuckled to himself as he entered his cabin. It was twenty-two years ago and Roth was just seventeen years old when he first set foot aboard a sailing ship as part of the crew. Life aboard a ship in those days was not very pleasant and he had a hard time getting used to it. Had it not been for the fact that he met and befriended a wise and hardened sailor, with one voyage under his belt as Berkshire had informed him, he might not have made another voyage. They became close friends and shipmates by the end of that first voyage and have remained so since.

Berkshire was amazed at how quickly Roth learned the tasks required aboard a ship and soon it would be hard to keep up.

For the next eighteen years, the two steadily advanced up through the ranks until they had earned the positions of first and second mates aboard a ship sailing to the Americas. The voyage turned out to be a huge success, bringing home a cargo hold full of furs.

It was on this return that Roth took command of a new ship, to be finished in a little over a month. Lord Creed, himself, made the offer and Roth accepted almost immediately and asked about the crew. Creed told Roth he could pick his own crew from any of the sailors currently in port, however, not those preparing to set sail soon. Then he learned the mission of his ship would be East Indies trade. This made Roth stop and think. The British had been trying to break into the East Indies trade for several years and had not been able to gain a foothold. It would only be by force if the British hoped to succeed and the ship he was to take command would apply that force. Chosen for this task, he felt a sense of excitement knowing the future of East Indies trading would rest upon his shoulders. A feeling of foreboding followed at the prospect of possible battles with the Portuguese and maybe the Dutch.

When he finally began picking his crew, Roth's first choice, of course, was Edward Berkshire. How could he think of sailing anywhere without his friend and confidant at his side? When word got around that Roth made captain, sailors started to line up to volunteer to serve under him. Roth and Berkshire then proceeded with the task of choosing the crew. It turned out not to be too difficult a task to select the best men available, for Roth and Berkshire chose only those they knew or those that were known to have a good reputation. Captain Roth could not think of a finer and more loyal crew than the one he had now.

For the next month, under orders from either Roth or Berkshire, the crew helped, as they could, around the shipyard, trying to get the ship ready for launch.

It was March 18, 1620, the day for the christening of the *Galaunt*. She carried a bold name for the bold voyage she and her crew were undertaking. On that day when she completed her maiden fitness voyage, Roth knew that he had, under his command, a ship and crew more than ready and able to tackle any task set before them.

That had been only a little over two years ago, but to Roth it seemed much longer.

He heard Mister Berkshire bark another command and thought about how fine a captain Berkshire would make with own ship. Roth would hate to see him leave but would not begrudge him the right of his own command. He had no way of knowing that Berkshire had sometimes also thought along these same lines, but for now, his only desire was to be right where he was, serving as first mate for whom he thought of as the finest captain ever to sail the high seas.

Roth went first to his desk where he opened the log for the final entries of this voyage. Finishing, he closed the book and as he opened a drawer to put it away, he noticed the small cloth pouch that had been stored there since their time in the orient. He picked up the pouch and held it in his hand, feeling the small object inside. He hoped that it would mean as much to his daughter as it did to him as he carefully placed it in an inside pocket of his coat. The thought of his daughter made him more anxious to get home so he could see her again. He had no doubt that after his two-year absence, she had turned into a lovely young woman.

He hurriedly gathered the few remaining items that he would be taking ashore with him, stuffed them into his sea bags and went topside where he encountered a flurry of activity as the men and crew hurried to offload the ship. "Mister Berkshire, a moment of your time if you would," he shouted over the din.

"Down here," he heard Berkshire call, "in the cargo hold sir."

Looking first to make sure he was not going to interfere with the offloading, Roth moved to the edge of the hold and peered down. There he saw Berkshire doing what he thought a good leader should do with all the orders given and the work underway, helping the workers, showing them that he was willing to do anything that he asked of them.

"Mister Berkshire," Roth said. "See to it that the offloading is completed on time and that the ship is taken care of before you release the crew."

"Aye Cap'n, it will be done. Are you to be leavin' the ship soon sir?" inquired Berkshire.

"I am departin' the ship now, and will be leavin' the ship under your care," he replied.

"Aye, aye Cap'n, she will be offloaded on time or before. In addition, any crew spared for repairs are already seein' to the needs of the ship, sir. Now you be movin' on and go and hug that daughter of yours," Berkshire said with a wide smile.

"Aye, that is what I shall surely do. I hope that you are able to leave the ship soon and be with your family also," Roth said with a sense of fondness for his friend. "The command of the ship is yours, Mister Berkshire," he then said, changing his tone to one of authority and quickly turned to leave his beloved ship.

As he walked down the gangplank and onto the dock, Roth noticed how the men moved to the side to let him pass. He chuckled to himself, he would have gladly moved for them because they were the ones doing the work, not him. When he finally reached the end of the long dock, he turned and took in one last look at his beloved *Galaunt*. He paused for several minutes, took in the lines of the ship, the rake of the bow, and admired the rigging and the tied down sails. He was, indeed, very proud of her and with a sense of pride, turned away and proceeded on his way home to his beloved daughter, Kathryn.

Chapter 2
"Gift"

Liverpool was located on a piece of land that, looking from the river, gives the impression that a giant hand had smoothed away the steepness and roughness of the cliffs into a gently sloping incline jutting into the Thames River. King James the First had originally designed it as a Royal Dockyard because the Thames River around London was gradually filling with silt, making it harder and harder for the larger ships to find a safe passage into the ports of London. The original dockyards were still there, but over the years, private shipyards had taken up residency. Eventually, all the shorelines became docks and a trading city sprang forth.

The port city of Liverpool is very much like any other port city in the world, arranged as if in layers. First, you have the docks and that is the area with the most activity. This was the place where all ships, big and small, were both loaded and unloaded. Large warehouses came next, where all the cargo stored was being either readied for shipment or just unloaded. Then there are the shipping and warehouse offices, this is where they keep cargo records, filled orders and itemized cargoes. The shipping owners keep their offices amongst these. They are easily recognizable as being a place of importance, usually a big ornate building where they can buy or sell large quantities of cargo and fortunes could be made on a daily basis. The merchants form the next layer. There are several types of merchants, catering to both the town and the shipping companies. The townspeople's homes are next and they occupy the area between the shops and the bluffs. The wealthy, the owners of the shipping companies, the larger merchants and of course, the royalty inhabited the bluffs.

Captain Roth's home was located on the southern outskirts of the city and it did not take him very long to reach it. The cottage, a two-story rock dwelling, was located on a small rise overlooking the river. The rise is high enough to give a spectacular view of the docks to the north and south, far enough to afford a grand view of the river. Roth remembered the first time he and his fiancée, Mary Elizabeth, had come to this place, many years before. The son of a minor lord had originally built it as a summer cottage, so it had plenty of windows for ventilation and lighting. Mary Elizabeth fell in love with it at first sight and the next day Roth started making inquiries about the purchase of the property. It turned out that the minor lord that owned the cottage had recently fallen into hard times and was more than willing to part with it for a reasonable price.

On their wedding day in 1604, Seaman Nathan Roth and Mary Elizabeth Roth moved into their cottage by the sea. Called to sea shortly after their marriage, it had been up to Mary Elizabeth to turn the cottage into a home. It turned out to be a rather lengthy voyage of over two years with Roth not being able to arrive home until late fall of 1606. He was able to stay at home until the early spring of 1607. During this time, Mary conceived. This was a very distressing thought for Roth, it was going to be his first-born and he knew that he would not be at home with Mary Elizabeth during her time of need. Roth went and talked with Lord Jarvis Creed about the possibility of being able to remain at home, but to no avail. He needed to be at his post when the ship sailed. When it came time for departure, a very pregnant wife saw Roth off. Knowing her husband was very worried, Mary reassured him, with that all too familiar smile and that special look of love in her eyes, that everything would turn out to be all right and not to worry. They embraced each other strongly, clinging to each other, neither of them wanting to let go. Mary kissed him softly on the lips, caressing his cheeks with her hands. As he noticed a tear rolling down her cheek, he wiped it away gently. She smiled and softly whispered to him, "Just think, when you return, you will be a father." Somehow, this eased Roth's reluctance to leave and he felt almost comforted. With this, Roth turned to board the ship trying not to look back because he knew that if he did, he would not be able to leave her.

It was not until 1609 when Roth returned home, only to hear the distressing news that his beloved wife, Mary Elizabeth, had died giving birth to a healthy baby girl. Roth, devastated by the news, hurried to his cottage to find his mother-in-law, Beth, living there attending to his two-year-old baby girl. Beth was surprised to see him not knowing that he had returned. She could see that he was distraught and full of many questions. She offered him some tea and told him that the baby was napping. "This must be a very difficult time for you. I have much to tell you. It is better that we talk while the child sleeps," she said. Roth, grief stricken, removed his coat and hat and found that he put them away automatically in their proper place. He felt as though her voice was an echo and that he was moving in slow motion. He sat down in his favorite chair and waited for her to return with the tea. After Beth had settled herself in another chair, she told him that Mary had lived long enough to hold their daughter and name her Kathryn. She also told him that she at been at her side during the entire time. "Nathan, Mary told me to tell you that she will always be with you and her love will shine through the eyes of your beautiful daughter." Listening to Beth, his thoughts returned to when he had left Mary on the dock where she had been reassuring him. He could not help but think of how his precious wife offered her tender smile and comforting words. He knew he had her love to the very last moment of her life. Tears began to fill his eyes.

Beth interrupted his thoughts when sounds began to emerge from upstairs, signaling that his daughter had awakened from her nap. He felt a quickening of anxiousness wondering how he would be able to look upon the daughter that he had never seen without a great deal of emotion. He knew that she would be a constant reminder of the love that he had lost but also a symbol of the love that they had shared. Beth said, while hurriedly moving up the stairs, "I am still a little fearful of the stairs even though that feisty little toddler had climbed them several times without difficulty. Kathryn is a very rambunctious child and she is always persistent at trying to do everything herself, much like her mother or for that matter her father too!" Beth soon returned, pulled along by a very impatient little girl. When Kathryn reached the bottom of the stairs, she saw someone sitting in one of the parlor chairs. She looked up at her grandmother and said, "No!" Beth smiled and glanced at Roth. He was in awe of this beautiful child, his daughter. Kathryn looked just like her mother. He immediately fell in love with her. Again, his eyes moistened with tears that he quickly wiped away. He stood up and walked over to where his daughter stood. As he neared her, he saw that she shyly stepped behind Beth. He knelt to look her in the eyes and said, "Hello." Smiling, he asked softly, "What is your name?" Kathryn looked up at Beth as if to get her approval.

Beth said, "You can tell him your name."

Kathryn slid further behind Beth and said in a very soft voice, almost a whisper, "No."

Roth could not help but smile as he said, "Beth I think I am going to have to take this a bit slow." He returned to his chair and continued, "I am guessin' that she has not been around many menfolk. I think I may have to let her get used to my presence here."

Beth replied, "Yes, I think that would be a very good idea. I always thought my daughter picked a good husband and now I am almost sure she picked a good father. Kathryn is quite independent and I think in no time her curiosity will get the best of her and she will soon be following you around like she does me."

Roth, still trying to recover from all that had happened since his arrival, felt a delight in what she had just said to him and proceeded to sip his tea.

At first, his lovely little girl was fearful of the big bushy man that had come suddenly into her life and spoke to her. It was not long, however, before she looked upon him as a kind and gentle man that would swing her about and play games with her all day long. Sadly, however, the time came for Roth to leave for the sea once again, it was a very hard goodbye. He had come to love this little girl more than life, knowing he would miss her dearly.

Kathryn was already five and very near her sixth birthday, when he returned home. She could barely remember him, but again, it did not take much time to get her to warm up, and soon, once again, gain her confidence and love. Roth was able to stay at home through the winter and he and Kathryn were seldom apart. It was a wonderful time and they grew to love each other as only a father and daughter can do. Winter turned into spring and again it was time for Roth to say goodbye to his daughter to return to his job at sea. Kathryn begged her father to let her come with him, but she was too young he told her, "Maybe when you get a little older and I get command of my own ship it might be possible to bring you along."

Finally, upon returning three years later, Roth found to his amusement, a little girl of nine going on nineteen. Gramma Beth, as Kathryn called her, was starting to have trouble getting around as she had been able to before. More and more she found that she had to rely on Kathryn to help with the day-to-day chores. Kathryn thought this to be a glorious arrangement, now she could play house all day long in a real house. He could see that his little girl was indeed growing up.

His next voyage only kept him away from home for two years and he was able to return just before her twelfth birthday. It was also, at this time, he received command of his first vessel, the *Galaunt*. Kathryn reminded him of his promise the last time he was home about taking her with him when she was older and he was in command. Roth explained to her the nature of the voyage, and she reluctantly agreed with him that she should wait and once again, he left her to go to sea.

Returning home from this latest voyage, he was walking towards his cottage thinking about what had incurred during the trip. Suddenly the front door burst open followed by the excited voice of his daughter. "Father, you are home!" Kathryn screamed delightfully, as she ran towards him.

Roth immediately saw that she was no longer the little girl of twelve he had left behind two years ago, now she was a young woman of fourteen, going on fifteen. Her long auburn brown hair was flowing out behind her and her blue eyes were wide with excitement. When she smiled, his heart melted as he realized how much he had missed as she grew up.

When she reached him, she flung her arms around him and said, "Father, oh father, I have missed you so very much."

"I have missed you as well Kathryn," he said in return, swallowing hard as his emotions welled up.

Together they walked arm in arm the rest of the way to the cottage, with Kathryn asking many questions about his voyage faster than Roth could answer them. Inside the cottage, Kathryn took his sea bag, led him to his favorite chair by the fire, and sat him down still holding his arm as if he needed support. With that Roth declared to her, "be careful there young darlin', I may be a captain, but I am certainly not an *old* captain," he said with a chuckle and a gleam in his eye.

"Yes father," she came back with, "for a sea captain I guess you would be considered young." She giggled teasingly. At that, Roth could do nothing more than shake his head and grin.

After a few moments, Roth inquired, "How is Beth?"

Kathryn paused briefly before replying sadly, "Father, I believe you have come home at the right time, the doctor was here yesterday and told me that it could be any day now and she will be gone."

"I did not know that she was sick, let alone that she was dying," he stated with heavy concern.

Kathryn looked at him as if she were suddenly realizing that Beth was indeed dying. With obvious sadness in her voice she whispered, "She seemed to be getting better right after you left, but this last winter was very hard on her and she started to decline very quickly."

"Maybe I had better look in on her," he said as he reluctantly gazed toward the stairway leading to the upper floor that contained the bedrooms.

"Yes father, she would like that but don't be surprised if she does not recognize you at first, if at all. Her mind has been failing as fast as her health."

Roth climbed the stairs and with each step he took, more dread crept into his mind. As he entered Beth's bedroom, not sure of what he would find, he was shocked to see that she was nothing more than skin and bones and did not even appear to be breathing. On closer inspection, however, he saw that she was indeed breathing but taking very shallow breaths. Kathryn was right, Beth was considerably worse since he was home last. She was obviously sleeping, and not wanting to disturb her, backed out of the room and quietly closed the door behind him so as not to awaken her.

Returning downstairs, he found his daughter staring out the front window towards the river. "What is it really like out there father? I mean what is it about the sea that draws men like you, time after time, into her clutches willing to face any danger that she throws at you?" she asked solemnly without turning.

Roth moved to her side, lightly placed his hand on her shoulder and said, "To me, I guess it is the adventure, seeing new places and different things all the time. Sometimes even being the first to sail someplace."

Kathryn turned to him and with a hopeful look on her face she asked, "Father, are you ever going to take me with you, maybe on the next voyage? You could not even count how many times I have stood in this exact spot and imagined that I was out there, on the water, with my father facing the dangers and sharing the adventures."

"Kathryn," he started to say, but was immediately interrupted.

"Before you say anything father, I want to tell you that I have been learning how to sail for the last two years. A friend of mine has been teaching me and I am getting really good and have even sailed out along the river to the ocean," she said with her chin defiantly stuck out.

Roth had to smile at that. Kathryn reacted by putting her hands rebelliously on her hips and declaring, "Do you not think it is possible that a girl can learn to sail as good as any man can?"

"It is not that, young darlin', I know that you can learn to sail and if you say you have, I believe that and would someday like to go sailing with you. It is more the life aboard a ship. It is not easy, there is no privacy, you are cold and damp almost all the time and the food is usually less than palatable. And of course, the work can be very arduous and dangerous at times," he said as he peered out the windows at the river.

"Yes, you are probably right" she said sighing. "Anyway, who would be here with Gramma Beth if I were to go gallivanting off to sea?" emphasizing gallivanting. "Well enough of that," she said. Changing the subject, she added, "I bet you have not eaten since last night, have you?"

Roth replied, "As a matter of fact, no."

"You sit down and rest, it will not be but a minute to fix dinner." As she bounded up the stairs, she said over her shoulder, "First I have to check on Gramma Beth."

He turned to watch her. He could not believe how much she had matured in the last two years. It was obvious that she was running the house and apparently had been doing so for quite some time. Musing to himself, he thought about how her mother had been similarly independent. If there were something important needing to be done, then she would make certain it was completed in a timely manner.

Roth was now alone in the parlor. Arranged around the room, he saw all the things that he had brought home over the years. Beth had carefully placed these on the mantle, shelves and tables that furnished the room. It added a sense of warmth and coziness. Each item brought back memories of the places he had visited. He chuckled to himself, as he thought of how disappointed Kathryn and Beth would have been if he had not brought home something to show he was thinking of them in his absence. Each present had its own story and he enjoyed sharing the details about them.

Kathryn returned a short time later and not saying anything, went straight to the kitchen to start dinner. He followed her in and asked, "How is she doing?"

After a moment Kathryn, holding back a sob, replied, "She is not doing very well at all. I could barely rouse her long enough to give her the medicine the doctor had left."

"I will go into town, myself, tomorrow and see if there is anything I can do," Roth told her.

"There are only two doctors in town and they were both here for the last visit. They did not know when you would return, so they told me that they both agreed, there is really nothing that can be done except to keep her comfortable and asked if I thought that I needed help. I said no to that and told them I could manage." she stated sadly.

After that, he returned to his chair and watched as his daughter moved efficiently around the kitchen preparing the evening meal. Beth had obviously taught her well. Roth had never been in doubt that Beth would raise Kathryn just as well as she did her daughter, Mary Elizabeth.

As it turned out, Kathryn was right when she said it would not take long for dinner. Almost before he knew it, she had set the table and set out the food. Roth was hungrier than he thought and the food was very good. After more than two years of eating nothing but galley food, anything would taste good, but this dinner was unexpected. "When did you learn to cook like this?" he asked with an obvious tone of admiration in his voice.

"Gramma Beth started me cooking when I was old enough to be in the kitchen. I have been cooking for both of us for over a year now," she answered with pride.

"Well, I have to say that this just might be the best food that I have ever eaten. Your mother was a very good cook also, she had the same teacher," Roth stated.

They ate the rest of the meal in silence, both with their separate but similar thoughts of Beth.

Roth finished eating, excused himself from the table and returned to the parlor. Kathryn started to clean up. He sat and studied his daughter as she went through her chores and thought of how proud he was of her. She was a young woman that any father would be proud to call their own.

Brushing a crumb from his jacket, he felt the lump in his pocket. Reaching in, he pulled out the small cloth bag and thought about where he had acquired it. His mind drifted back to the second time the ship stopped to trade in the Far East.

Roth had been wandering around the village looking for something unusual that he could give to his daughter when he returned home. He was walking down a back alleyway when he passed by a large box. On the other side, he saw a very old and crippled man sitting on the ground behind it, dressed in shabby clothing that was torn in several places but still, barely, clinging to his body. He almost rushed on past the man because there was a stench in the air smelling of old rotting fish. Something, however, caught his attention causing him to stop, turn around and closely observe him. His hair was long, white and very scraggly, more noticeable were the eyes. They were clear, the bluest that he had ever seen, portraying a very wise and intelligent appearance. Looking at him it was impossible to identify his nationality. It was obvious that he had not taken a bath for several weeks, if ever. The man raised his head and spoke in a low gravelly voice saying, "Can ye spare a little somethin' for an old sailor, too old for the sea?"

"Aye, you miserable old wretch, I can spare a little, but I will have you know that I did not come all the way here to give things away, I came here to do trade," Roth said sternly.

"Ah, that is very kind of you. If it is trade you want then I might have something that will interest you," he said as he pulled a small object from the tatters.

Roth took it from the old man. It was a small clamshell carving, about six centimeters in length, of what appeared to be, possibly, a mermaid that hung from a thin leather thong. He was amazed at the intricacy of the carving. The coloring of the shell itself was very special, giving the effect of having an iridescent tail. It was a very pretty piece, not quite what the captain was looking for but still something that he thought would make a nice gift. "Well old man," Roth inquired, "if I decided that this is something that I would like to have, what would you take for this?"

"Now that is a question all by itself, considering what I had to give for it," the old man replied.

"What was that? Surely it could not be much, it is just a piece of carved shell," Roth ventured.

"No, you are right, it is not much. My life has not really amounted to much, so I guess you would be right that my life was not much to give for it," he said with no show of emotions.

"Your life, you say? How can that be, I can see you sitting right in front of me. I think, however, this might be a tale worth hearin'," Roth added skeptically.

"You think you be a wantin' to hear about it, huh? Well maybe it is that I do not wish to tell you or even to remember it," the old man stated flatly.

Roth quickly spoke, "I will hear the tale, or I will seek trade elsewhere."

"Very well, it has been a long time and I will tell it the best way I can," the old man started again, "We were caught in a storm, the wind had ripped our sail to tatters and broken the mast. We could do nothing without a sail and soon found ourselves at the mercy of the sea. It was not long before a huge wave capsized our small boat and I found myself in the water. The only thing that I could find to cling onto was a small piece of planking that was drifting nearby. I called all through the night for my shipmates but heard nothing. When morning arrived, I found myself alone in the sea. No one and nothing were anywhere that I could see. I have no idea how long I was adrift before I could no longer hold onto the planking. I remember slipping into the water and trying to regain my hold and then things became hazy. I awoke next, feeling as if I were being pulled through the water. I think I can also remember seeing what I thought to be an iridescent tail of a large sea animal swimming alongside me, before I passed out again." The old man paused at this point, and Roth wondered if he would be able to continue. "When next I regained consciousness, I was on a sandy beach surrounded by people who were just standing there staring at me. No one offered any help or even came near me. As I sat up, I noticed that around my neck, was hanging the carved piece of clamshell that you now hold in your hand. At that time, it was hanging from a gold chain, but I had to part with that many, many years ago. It turned out that the village people recognized the carving as an evil omen. They did not like mermaids, who were forever stealing fish from their nets. Now here was a man, come to shore, with the sign of the mermaids. What would you expect them to believe? Me, I always thought it was a great tale myself, but still, I must wonder, how did I make it back to shore and where did I get the carving?"

"I think that you are right about the tale part," Roth snorted. "It was a good one at that. I will give you one small piece of gold for this trinket, far more than it is worth but worthy of such a story." Roth did not believe the old man for a second, but he did feel sorry for him and decided that he deserved a little happiness.

"Done!" the old man cried.

Kathryn broke into his thoughts, "What do you have there, father?"

"It is something I acquired for you while in the Far East," he said as he stood to place it around her neck.

Kathryn turned and pulled her hair aside while Roth placed the carving, once again supported by a delicate gold chain, around her slim neck.

"It is beautiful father, what is it?" she asked.

"It is something that I acquired for you, trading with the Orientals," he said. "There is quite a story behind it also," he thought about telling her the story of the pendent but leaving out the acquisition of the chain that he had found in the small Portuguese chest.

"Oh, father please tell me, I so love it when you tell me stories of your travels," Kathryn said beaming.

Roth started out by telling her the story of the wretched old man that he had originally gotten it from.

He went on, "After I left the alley, I was walking down the street looking into shops and displays the merchants had set up. I stopped at a shop that had some fine pieces of jewelry hanging on racks in front of the shop. I had been holding the shell craving all this time thinking about what the old man had told me. A very short and very old oriental woman came out speaking surprisingly good English, suspiciously inquired if there was something that she could do for me. I told her that I was looking for something to give to my daughter when I returned to England. She took my arm, the one holding the carving and led me into her shop. "Do you mind if I take a look at what you have in your hand?" she asked. Her voice had changed, it was obvious that she was very curious about the piece.

He replied, "No, why would I mind?" adding, "Of course you may," and handed her the carving, wondering why it had caused such a sudden change in her attitude toward him.

After carefully examining the shell for a long time, she looked at Roth, trying to hide an obvious mounting excitement. "Where did you get this?" she asked.

Roth repeated the story of the old man to her and she immediately grabbed his arm once again, dragged him out of her shop and demanded he show her where the old man was. When they finally reached the place where he had made the deal, the old man was now nowhere in sight. The place looked slightly different this time. Where the old man had been sitting, there was now a barrel containing old fish parts, rotten by the smell. How could that be, he thought to himself, this barrel was not here before or I would have surely noticed it. The smell filled the entire pathway.

"Just as I thought," the old merchant said.

"This was where I met him, it was not more than ten minutes ago," Roth said with puzzlement in his voice, thinking she was questioning his truthfulness.

"Yes, that would be just as it is foretold," the old woman said. She went on to add, "This must be the talisman that is mentioned in the legend."

"What legend are you talking about, old woman," Roth asked with relief. "This is just an old piece of sea shell that someone carved up in the shape of something from old sailor's tales."

"You really do not know what you have here, do you?" she said in surprise.

"No, maybe you can tell me," Roth probed.

"Come, I will make us some tea and then tell the whole legend to you," she said leading him by the arm back to her shop.

Once they were back inside, the old merchant went about the task of preparing them some tea. Roth had become accustomed to the stronger teas of the orient. He would even go as far as saying he preferred it to English teas.

As the old woman served them, she asked, "Would you consider selling it to me?"

"Before I would consider such a thing, I must first hear about this legend that you spoke of," Roth replied.

"I do not think that you will part with it after hearing the tale." She started out saying, "You have probably noticed that I can speak your language."

"Yes, and quite well in fact," he complimented her.

The old woman paused for a moment, clarifying in her mind what she was about to say, "I was raised by a missionary that taught me how to read and write several languages, he also taught me ciphers, but that is not all that I learned from him. He was a great teller of stories. Having traveled all over the world, he had heard hundreds of tales. One in particular had stirred his interest because he had heard the same story, with slight variations, from several storytellers almost everywhere he went. It is a story about a sailor and a mermaid."

"A mermaid you say," Roth questioned, "I thought they were just an old sailor's myth."

"Did you not just claim to have met a very old sailor in an alleyway a short time ago?" she looked at him. "And did he not tell you a tale about a myth?" she inquired.

"Well, yes I did and yes he did tell me a tale and what a tale it was," a chuckling Roth, replied.

"How is your tea?" she asked, changing the subject.

"It is very good indeed. Oriental teas are brewed much stronger than English tea," he said anxiously, "but what about this legend you were going to tell me."

"Ah, the legend," she paused for a few moments gathering her thoughts once again. She then proceeded, "What I am about to tell you is as it was told to me, as best as I remember it."

"Centuries ago, no one quite knows how long ago exactly, when men were making their first ventures out upon the open seas beyond the horizons. One man in particular, with a crew of two, would sail his small craft further than anyone else would. His village held him in high esteem for his courage. After a short time, finding that they could only sail so far out and back during daylight, they decided it was time to go out for one full day, turn around and sail back during the night to return home the next morning. This was unheard of at the time and some of the villagers pleaded with him not to go. The man would hear none of this and made the decision to start the next morning.

"The sea was very calm that morning when they set sail and the man and his crew felt certain that they would be back in the village this time tomorrow. The village people were still trying to make the men change their minds, but the man and his crew pushed their tiny craft into the water and set sail for the far horizon, followed by the shouts of foreboding from the villagers.

"Towards midday, the crew noticed a storm growing in their direction of travel. The storm was obviously approaching them head on so they made the decision to turn around and head for home. They were sailing as fast as they could go but the storm, moving much faster, quickly overtook them. The storm tossed and turned them for several hours tearing off the sail and breaking the mast before finally, capsizing and sinking their vessel.

"The man found himself alone in the water, far from land, with nothing but the clothes he was wearing, clinging to a piece of the boat. After floating like this for several days, the man finally succumbed to the elements and sank slowly down below the surface of the water. A mermaid, swimming in the area, noticed an object sinking and went to investigate. When she neared the object, she saw that it was a man and immediately went to his side and pulled him to the surface where she breathed a breath of oxygen into him to clear his lungs, which started an instinctive reaction to breathe on his own. She saw that he did not regain consciousness and she swam for shore." At this, the woman paused for a sip of tea.

When she resumed talking, she remarked, "Maybe I should first explain to you about a mermaid so you might better understand what happened to the man.

"A mermaid is a warm blooded mammal that has lived in the sea since the beginning of remembered time. Once there were a great many mermaids roaming the vast oceans of our world. Mermaids were dedicated to helping all living things in the seas and those that might fall into the sea. Humans soon ventured out in their crude boats and would occasionally fall overboard. Mermaids would rescue those that they found and take them back to shore. Mermaids found men to be fascinating, so much like them, but men were able to walk upon land with two legs. Mermaids were gray in color with the upper torso of a woman for the females and strong arms and chests for the male. Both had long flowing hair and deep blue eyes, but instead of legs, they had long slender, iridescent colored tails. Their tails were very powerful and could propel them through the water faster than any fish in the sea. Over the years, however, mermaids began a gradual change towards a form better equipped for life in the water, losing the upper torso that resembled man and becoming more like a fish with a long gray snout but still liked to be around humans.

"Mermaids lived a very long time, a few of them even lived long enough to see the final change take place. In the legend, one of these few remaining mermaids found a giant clam that had died a short time before. Breaking off a small fragment of its shell, she began to carve a replica of herself. Upon completion, she enhanced it with the very essence of mermaids and hung it about her neck on a long delicate gold chain that she had found.

"It was at this time that she came upon the man. Breathing the essence of life back into him, she took his body and swam towards shore with strong and powerful kicks, soon arriving at a sandy beach where she left him, but not before she placed the carving and the chain around his neck. According to the legend, the people who inhabited a neighboring village, came upon him the next morning. Seeing the carving around his neck and being very superstitious, they mistook him for a mermaid that had decided to walk upon the land. The villagers were not people who ventured out upon the distant waters. They had a limited knowledge of mermaids. This knowledge was limited to what they had experienced and seen. To them, the mermaids were nothing more than a creature of the sea, destroying their fish traps and releasing fish from their nets. He was taken and presented before the village elders, where he told his story. They in turn, not being fond of mermaids, found his story to be disconcerting. They had not been able to envision this creature as anything more than a nuisance. In the eve of the night, they would hear songs of the creatures and knew their traps would be empty. They would hurry down to the shore only to find their nets and traps, indeed empty, with occasional glimpses of a man like creature, with an iridescent tail, slipping below the surface of the water. They were mystified and perplexed over what to do about this problem.

Now here before them stood a man, claiming not to know how he arrived on their shore wearing this carving, claiming not to know what it represented. One of the elders whispered to another, "I think this man is definitely mad."

"I agree," the other elder replied, "but how do you explain his being here and found on our shore alive wearing that pendant shaped like one of the creatures."

The first elder answered, shaking his head, "I cannot venture to explain, my thoughts are cloudy. I think we need time for further discussions and thought. It may be he is confused or even mad as you say, after his so-called ordeal. The few days required for this will be favorable for us all. He can get his much needed rest so that he may recover his senses and regain his memory so that maybe we can find out the truth behind his arrival. At that time, we will make our decision."

With that, the villagers led him to a small hut that contained food and a bed. He ate very little and soon gave way to sleep. When he awoke, he found fresh food and being very hungry, he was glad for this. After he ate, he tried to move around a bit. Restless, he went outdoors, only to find that the people from the village would back away as if he had a terrible disease. Doing this routine every day saw that within a few days, he had regained his strength.

One day the elders summoned him and they questioned him more as he retold his story. After hearing the tale again and not hearing any difference, the elders again quietly conferred amongst themselves. After a short period, the elder that had spoken the last time stated, "It has been decided that you are to be set free, as you have not shown yourself to be a threat, but it has also been decided that you must leave this village never to return."

The man was unsure as to why they had come to this decision but honored it by turning on his heal and walking away from the village never to be seen in that part of the world again." The woman stopped here for another sip of her tea.

After a short time, Roth asked, "Is that the end of the tale, old woman?" His interest at this point had now peaked.

"No, there is more," she added with tiredness in her voice. "Over the centuries, it has been told, the man, now a very old man, would appear to some folks and, somehow, as in your case it was a trade, get them to take this carving from him. As the story goes, he appears to select people and when he does, it is for a reason unknown to them. Most people never have a use for the powers but they have always experienced good luck in one form or the other and in the end, the charm always disappears and somehow finds its way back to the old man. Now for some reason he has given it to you and only you will discover why."

After a short period of deep thought, Roth replied, "That is a fascinating tale, good woman, but how will I know why it has come into my possession?"

The woman smiled and said, almost in a whisper, "In the times to come, you will be made aware."

With that the woman asked, "Now that you have heard the legend, is there anything else that I may be of service to you? I have some things that may be of interest to you for your daughter, many fine pieces of jewelry that will surely look good on her."

Captain Roth, clutching the carving in his hand, turned to her and said, "No, I thank you for all you have told me, but I think that I have all that I need for now. Can I at least pay you a small sum for the tale?" The woman declined his offer and after thanking her once again, he strode out of the shop.

"Father," Kathryn, with excitement in her voice said, "That was the most beautiful story I have ever been told. I love this and will never take it off."

Kathryn moved to her father and sat down on his lap, nestling her face between his neck and shoulder. "Father, I love you so much and have missed you more than you could ever know."

"Aye, but I do know young darlin', I have always been feeling that same way," Roth softly returned. "Now it is getting late and you had better check on your grandmother."

Kathryn moved from his lap after another tight hug, told him goodnight, proceeded up the stairs to Gramma Beth's room to check on her, and on to her own bed.

Roth took a deep sigh, rose from his comfortable chair and thought about the day and all that it had produced as he moved off towards his room. In the night he heard what must have been Kathryn checking on her grandmother. He wondered how difficult her life must have been, never knowing her mother and having a father that was continuously absent for years at a time. He was thinking that somehow, in some way, he would try to make it up to her. Right now, she was taking care of this household and caring for her grandmother in her last days. He felt completely helpless, knowing she would again feel the grief of losing someone she loved.

Chapter 3
"Summons"

A few days later, a knocking at the door awakened Roth. He hurriedly threw on some clothes and rushed downstairs to answer the door before whoever it was woke up the whole house. As he opened the door, he saw a well-dressed young man who said, "Lord Creed has dispatched me to inform you that your presence is required at his office just as soon as you can come."

Roth replied, "Tell M'lord Creed that I will be along as soon as I can get properly dressed," trying to stifle a yawn.

The young man nodded and hurried off to make his way back to Lord Creed's office.

Roth returned to his room, somewhat perplexed, having had an emotional day yesterday, he had been resting very well. He proceeded to change into something a bit more appropriate for his visit to the lord's office, but he was definitely not looking forward to it. Having dressed, he returned back downstairs. There he found his daughter waiting for him. She greeted him with a hug and a smile and then asked, "Who was at the door this early in the morning father?"

"He was a messenger from Lord Creed. It seems that I am wanted for some kind of a meeting," he answered. "I don't think that I should be gone too long. It has probably got something to do with the cargo we brought back," he added. "To be entirely honest with you, young darlin', this mornin' I would rather have slept in." He grinned at that.

"Alright father, I will have breakfast ready for you when you return," she said as she wrapped her arms around his neck to give him a soft kiss goodbye, on his cheek. Roth returned the kiss and left the cottage to make the short walk to Creed's office.

As he started down the hill towards town, he noticed his ship tied up alongside the dock. Roth thought this strange, by now he thought the ship should be completely unloaded and safely moored out in the river with the other ships waiting to sail on their next voyage. The *Galaunt* should not be getting ready for another voyage until next spring when he supposed he would be heading back to the East Indies to test the trading knowledge he had gained from the last trip. He also noticed the stream of activity around the ship and there seemed to be a lot of movement. He could hear the sounds of hammers and saws and knew that repairs were being made. Perhaps the repairs that were being made are why the ship was still at the docks, he reasoned to himself. Roth could also see men moving around in the rigging, they did not seem to be securing the ship for the winter, but rather they appeared to be preparing the ship for sailing or maybe they could just be inspecting the sails. Then he saw that there were men loading crates and barrels aboard. What was going on, he wondered, that should not be happening? Now his curiosity was peaking. He was sure that he and his crew were not going to be leaving any time soon. He dismissed those thoughts as he drew nearer his destination. He figured that he would know soon enough.

As he reached the building occupied by Lord Creed and his shipping company, the largest such company in Liverpool, he saw that there was a lot of activity there also. Men were running in and out of the building, coming and going from the docks. It was then that he saw that his was not the only ship being prepared for sailing. Two others tied to nearby docks were receiving the same type of attention. They were the *Princeton* and the *Noble*, two of *Galaunt's* sister ships. Roth was beginning to feel a bad omen was in the air.

Roth climbed the short steps and made his way through the crowd, to the second floor where Creed had his private office. He entered the outer office and was greeted by Creed's private secretary, "Ah, Captain Roth, m'lord has been expecting you."

"What is going on around here? I see several ships being loaded. It is surely too late in the year to be preparing to set sail," he inquired, knowing before he asked, that he would not get any answers to his questions from this man.

"Lord Creed will answer all your questions when you meet with him. Go right in. He and the others are waiting," was the response Roth received.

Roth opened the door to Creed's private office and saw that he was not the only captain to be summoned on this morning. In the office, off to one side stood an obviously perplexed Captain Pringle, he was the captain of the *Princeton*, standing next to him was Captain Holmes, who was in command of the *Noble*. They made up two of the other three-armed merchantmen christened in the year 1619. Roth greeted both men with a nod and turned his attention to Lord Creed. Creed, with his back towards the other men, was deep in conversation at the back corner of the room with his chief advisor Raynerd and did not seem to notice that Roth had entered the room.

Before Roth could make his presence known, there came a knock at the door. "Come," Creed called as he turned toward the other men in the room.

"Ah, Captain Connery, you finally made it. Now that I have all of you here, let us be seated and get down to the business before us." Creed said with obvious impatience.

Connery, Captain of the *Royale*, the other ship christened that year, was the last to take a seat.

Roth could not help but wonder why all the Captains of Creed's prize fleet were here this morning. Then he remembered that ill feeling he had after the meeting they had aboard ship upon his return. He was beginning to feel very uneasy once again.

With all the men seated, Creed finally spoke, "You have all been brought here to discuss a venture that I want you to undertake. As you have undoubtedly heard, the recent return of the *Galaunt* was far more profitable than we had first expected and further congratulations to Captain Roth are in order."

Roth accepted the handshakes and slaps on the shoulder from the other Captains with ambivalence. It did nothing, however, to relieve that ill feeling that was still growing inside him.

"This has prompted me, and other investors, to believe that an immediate return to that area will be more than in our best interests. Right now, the market is crying for spices, and the royalty bought up the silks before we even had a chance to show them. The teas alone, repaid all the expenses of the voyage. The profit from the spices will enable me to invest in at least two more ships and possibly three. All of this comes from just one voyage. You can see now gentlemen that it is imperative that we set sail at once on the return voyage to the East Indies," Creed announced with pride.

"M'lord, you must rethink this, it is near impossible to return during this time of year. The Dutch and the Portuguese do not attempt the Cape in the winter!" stated Connery, who had made more than one unsuccessful trip to the Indies.

"It is not winter. If you make the voyage now, you will have plenty of time to round the Cape and make it to the safer waters in the north," Raynerd interjected.

"How can you expect us to get our ships ready in time? We will have to leave within the next two weeks. The *Galaunt* is in need of many repairs," Roth replied with concern.

"The ships can be made ready, we have already hired extra men and the task of repairing your ship has already begun and will be completed in time," Raynerd stated flatly.

"It still cannot be done," Captain Pringle interposed, "our crews are scattered all over and you cannot even dream of finding them all in such a short notice."

Creed said, "I have already sent out messengers to post notices and to round up as many of your crew as possible. As for the ones not being found, we will replace them from the extra hands we have hired."

"My first mate is in London," Holmes said.

"So is mine," Connery added.

"There are several fully qualified men in our employee to replace anyone not able, or for that matter, unwilling, to make the voyage." Creed said impatiently. The underlying message of that statement was not lost on any of the men standing before him.

"My crew needs a rest, m'lord, they have been at sea for over two years and have just returned. I think that they have earned this time off. I am sorry, but I think that for the sake of my crew, I must refuse." Roth said apologetically.

"Let me put it to you this way!" Creed raised his voice to a tone that implied nothing other than anger. "The *Galaunt* will set sail in two weeks' time, with or without you in command!" For the next few moments, there was a deafening silence.

It was obvious to Roth and the other captains, that any further argument would be fruitless.

Roth said at this point, "Very well, m'lord. However, I must ask that you allow me to delay my departure for a short period. My daughter's grandmother is gravely ill and as I leave you this day, I will be contacting her physicians to learn the full extent of her illness. I cannot leave until arrangements are in place for my daughter's welfare, in the event that her grandmother dies. I implore you sir to give this request your consideration or I may be forced to withdraw my services."

This caused Creed to turn his back and walk away to the window thinking that he needed Roth more than any of the others. He was the only one that had the knowledge and experience to make this voyage successful. After all, this Captain was the one that made him aware of the potential for the riches to be gained from the East Indies. With this thought, he turned back to Roth, nervously clasping his hands behind his back. He did not want to show how desperate he was to have him leading this voyage. There was not a sound as the two men stared into each other's eyes, both of them not knowing how far they could press the issue. Creed finally broke eye contact. He said, "I will allow you to do whatever it is you think you must do, but the ship must sail on time."

Captain Roth glanced at his fellow captains and lowered his head. "Aye m'lord, I understand. We both have some thinking to do regarding this matter, so I suggest that we meet again later. Perhaps in three days' time I will have made my decision."

Creed, reluctantly, dismissed the other three captains with a wave of his hand, and asked Captain Roth if he would mind staying a bit longer.

As the three captains filed out of the room, each one gave a sympathetic look towards Roth.

Now that they were alone, Creed said, in a much calmer tone, "I can sympathize with your problems, and I am sure that you understand the need for a quick departure. I will expect your decision in three days' time."

Roth replied, "Aye, m'lord, I will not know what decision I will make until I have had a chance to consult with the physicians. Now sir, may I be excused to get to the matters I must attend to?"

Creed, glowering, replied, "Yes, I suggest that you proceed promptly. Also, keep in mind Captain Roth, that if you do not sail with the *Galaunt* on this voyage, you will never sail an English vessel again."

"With all due respect, m'lord, I feel any further discussion at this point will lead us nowhere and should again be taken up in the future," Roth stated with all the patience he could muster. He knew that if this conversation continued, it would only lead to a useless argument. He despised threats and he knew that Creed's greediness was shading the issue and that he was not at all as sympathetic as he proposed himself to be. Arising from his chair and preparing to depart, Roth took a deep sigh and quietly left the office. As he stepped outside the office door, he cursed softly under his breath, "This man is without heart!" He had known Creed to be a reasonable man, and he had served him well. How could he put his greed above all else? Did he not deserve the respect of this man as well as his sympathy and understanding? After all, Creed knew that Kathryn was all he had left in this world. She was the reason that he had given so much of his life in the employment of a man such as he, in order to provide her with the comforts of life he so dearly wanted for her. Almost aloud, he angrily said to himself, "Damn him for his threats! I shall do what I must do, despite him!"

Roth returned home, to find Kathryn filling a basin with cool water. He could tell by her flurry of movements that she was nervous. She turned to him and said, "Father, I am so relieved that you are home. Beth has a very high fever and I am about to try to cool her somewhat."

"Is there something I can do to assist you, Kathryn?" Roth asked.

"You must summon the physician, father. I fear the pneumonia may have gotten worse," she replied in a somber voice.

"I stopped by his office on the way home and he told me that he had already planned on making a visit this morning. It is good that the physician is coming. It will afford me the opportunity to consult with him," Roth said with his voice trailing off as he realized she was going upstairs to Beth.

He thought to himself how efficiently his young daughter was handling the situation. Just then, a knock came from the door. Roth turned to answer it, knowing it must be the physician. Opening the door, Roth was surprised to find not one, but both town doctors standing on the porch. "Please come in sirs, I am afraid that Beth may have taken a turn for the worse."

"We were afraid of that and that is why we had already made the decision for both of us to follow up on her condition this morning," the eldest of the physicians stated, and hurried off up the stairs with Roth close behind him.

When they entered Beth's room, they found Kathryn applying a damp cloth to Beth's forehead to cool her. "Oh Doctor Waite, I am so glad that you are here. Gramma Beth was burning up with fever, I managed to cool her some, and now she has slipped off to sleep."

Doctor Waite suggested to Roth, "Captain, it would be better if you took Kathryn and yourself out of the room, so that we can examine Beth and assess anything we may be able to do to make her more comfortable." Roth took Kathryn's hand and led her downstairs.

"I have an urge for a cup of that new Oriental tea I brought home, would you like to share it with me?" he asked Kathryn as he led her towards a chair.

"Allow me to get it for you father, I do so need something to do while we wait and I have never prepared an Oriental tea and so I too am eager to try it," she said.

"Aye, my darlin', we will prepare the tea together," Roth said with a smile.

Kathryn responded with her beautiful smile. As they walked arm in arm into the kitchen, Roth was thinking how sad it would be when she is told of her grandmother's death, he hoped it would not be soon. "I must warn you, Kathryn, that this tea is of a different taste and much stronger than what you are used too."

"Father, I am sure that if you like it, I will like it also," she said playfully.

"Well, young darlin', we shall soon find out." Now seated back in the parlor, he was sipping his tea awaiting his daughter's reactions. After watching her take a few tentative sips, he asked, "Is it to your liking?"

Kathryn stared at her cup a long time before replying, "It is rather pungent, and definitely stronger, tasting of an herb that I cannot place. I think that I could, however, develop a taste for it, but perhaps with a bit of sweetness."

Roth chuckled and told her that he had heard the Orientals sometimes would add a squirt of lemon to enhance the taste and add flavor.

Kathryn laughed back, "But that would make it sour, father. Why would they want it like that?"

"All I said was just a squirt, not the whole lemon. You must remember they are different people than we are, young darlin' and have different tastes. I have found in my travels, there are many foods and beverages that our people have not been able to try. I have found most of it very palatable even to the extent of makin' our dishes seemingly bland. I have an idea, let's try lemon and add some honey and see how it tastes then."

Kathryn arose and started for the kitchen, saying as she moved, "I believe that we have a lemon and I know that there is honey, so why not try it now?"

With a gleam in his eyes and a big smile on his face, Roth replied, "I think that would be a fine idea." He thought to himself, she was being polite, wanting to like the tea, so he was far more than willing to let her experiment with it.

Waiting for her to return, his thoughts turned to what was happening upstairs. Was it possible that Beth was indeed dying or, as Kathryn thought, just sleeping? He was uneasy with his impatience and his dread of what was possibly about to happen. His thoughts, of course, mainly lay with his daughter. She had already lost a mother that she had never known. Now it was probable that she was going to lose her grandmother, the one person that had always been there for her, caring and loving her as though she were her own. For this reason, he had always been so thankful for Beth. He could go to sea knowing that his daughter would be well cared for at home. This had particularly become known upon this last return. He had come home to find his young daughter, striving to take care of herself as well as an ailing grandmother. She had done a fine job, but it was obvious that she would not be able to go on alone. She would need further love and support as well as guidance, before being able to make it on her own. Roth, at this point, knew what decision he would have to make. He could never leave Kathryn alone. He would have to give up his life on the sea.

Kathryn, taking a sip of her doctored tea, squealed with delight. "Father, come and taste this," she called.

Roth picked up his cup and started to walk towards the kitchen, only to meet her in the hall leading to the kitchen. She exclaimed, "I like the tea this way, the lemon does indeed bring out a flavor that was hidden, and the honey makes it delightful. Taste it father," she said as she handed him her cup excitedly.

Roth took his own tentative sips and swirled it around in his mouth before he replied, "Kathryn, this tea is just as though I thought a young miss would like it to be."

"Then you like it?" she asked eagerly.

"Daughter, I have to admit that it is very tasty, but maybe a bit sweet for my liking, perhaps the lemon, but not the honey. Remember, as a sailor, not having honey on board ship, I got used to a more pungent taste." He gave her a hug and a light kiss on the cheek reminding her that young people have a history for liking sweets, whenever and wherever they could get them.

"Yes," she replied, "I admit I like sweets and I understand that old, rough and tough sailors may not."

Roth, beaten at his own game, responded lamely, "be easy with that old stuff young darlin'." At that moment, they both hugged each other and laughed.

Later that evening, the doctor called from upstairs, "Captain Roth, can we please see you up here for a moment?"

"Aye, on my way," Roth called back. Turning to Kathryn, he said firmly, "Wait for me here, I will not be long." As he made his way up the stairs, he found himself knowing, in his heart, what the summons was.

Doctor Waite met him just inside of Beth's room, "I am sorry to have to inform you that Beth has passed on. Doctor Metts and myself were unable to do anything more for her and are very surprised, I must add, that she made it this far. Her heart had been giving way for some time and we knew that without movement the pneumonia would set in. She was not physically strong enough to fight it. I must tell you that Kathryn has done more to keep this woman alive than both of us combined may have been able to do. Without Kathryn's love and constant care, Beth would have died months ago. We, as physicians, are not capable of providing the love our patients need. Though we try, we can only show compassion. Only someone very close, can provide the love and support that they require on a daily basis. Beth often spoke of her concerns about what would happen to Kathryn if she were to die before your return. I truly believe that her fear for Kathryn's welfare helped keep her alive until you did return. I will report her death to the Magistrate and trust you will make all the rest of the necessary arrangements."

After thanking the physicians for all they had done and tried to do, Roth bade them goodbye, assuring them that he would take care of everything. He led them to the door. Kathryn appeared asking of her grandmother and Roth's heart sunk. He summoned her to join him in the parlor. "Kathryn, it is with a grave heart that I must tell you…"

"No father! She cannot be! I made her cool again and she was resting well," she said, her voice broken and her eyes welling with tears.

Roth tried to calm her but she broke away and ran up the stairway before he could comfort her. "Kathryn!" he called after her, "you must not go up there right now." Witnessing her grief was overwhelming to Roth and he found it difficult to swallow, much less talk.

When he got to Beth's room, Kathryn was lying beside Beth holding her lifeless body, sobbing almost hysterically. "Gramma, you cannot leave me! How will I go on? I only have you. Oh please," she was pleading, "I do not want to lose you." She laid her head on Beth's shoulder and started weeping uncontrollably.

"My darlin' Kathryn," he said, as he gently laid his hand on her shoulder, "Let me to take you downstairs." When she did not respond, he gently tried to take her hand.

"NO! I will not leave her! Let me be, father," she said sounding almost angry.

"Kathryn, I know you may not be able to understand this right now, but Beth is not in pain any longer or enduring any suffering. She is at peace, at last." He said helplessly. "Please Kathryn, I cannot let you endure your grief and the heartbreak you are feeling alone. I feel your pain as though it were my own." His voice was broken and his eyes moist with tears as he stood helplessly over his daughter, trying in vain to console her, knowing in his heart, he could not possibly say or do anything that would make her feel any better at this time.

"Father, do not weep. I just need some time alone with her. Please, just leave me for a time and soon I will be able to terms with this." She looked into her father's eyes, pleading for him to understand.

Roth knew what it was she needed. He had felt the same way when he had learned her mother had died. He decided to respect her wishes and left Beth's room. On his way down to the parlor, he found himself thinking of how Kathryn had said that Beth was all she had. Did she not know how deeply he loved her and that she would not be left alone? He knew that he was going to have to be there for her, even more now that Beth was gone. He vowed to himself never to leave her again.

Now he must arrange for Beth, but he dared not leave home until Kathryn was ready. He brewed some more tea and sat alone in the parlor for what seemed like forever. His mind clouded with many thoughts of Elizabeth, how angry he was that she had died giving birth to their child, and he had not been there. Beth reminded him that he had a part of Elizabeth in Kathryn. It seemed of little consolation at the time.

After all, had he not lost the most important person in his life, the one person that he had so loved and treasured more than life itself? He was bitter and alone. It was only after the short voyage that he had made after her death, when he returned to find this delicate child. He took one look at her as he held her, his heart had melted with love. She was so perfect. Yes indeed, Elizabeth had left him part of her love and being within this child. He had realized that Kathryn was a gift, to be treasured forever. It was not of any great surprise that his darling daughter would be angry. Beth had been the only person that had been a constant in her life. Beth was the only mother, she had ever known.

She was always there for Kathryn. "Now, I will always be there for her," he found himself saying aloud.

Kathryn quietly entered the room. He had not heard her move down the stairs.

"What were you saying father?" she quietly asked.

"I was voicing my thoughts aloud darlin." Roth spoke quietly, "I made a vow that I will never leave you again! I will always be here for you."

"Then you are not angry with me, father?"

"Why would I be angry with you, Kathryn?"

Moving close to her father and taking his hand, she explained, "I did not mean to push you away."

"Oh, do not let those thoughts worry you, young darlin'. I fully understand why you behaved as you did. I acted in that same manner at one time in my life."

"Was that when you lost mother?" Kathryn asked tears welling up in her eyes once again.

"Aye darlin', that was the hardest loss of my life. She left me with a gift of love though."

"Oh father. What was that?"

Roth bent down to look into her eyes and whispered, "You, my love."

"Father, I love you," she said with a sigh and laid her head on his thigh.

"Are you sure that Gramma Beth is not suffering any longer?" she questioned with concern.

"Aye young darlin' she is with your mother and they are happy and well for all time."

Kathryn drifted off to sleep lying on her father's leg, he gently picked her up and carried her to her bed. As he covered her, she was still whimpering. She had wept herself into exhaustion and he knew that she would sleep soundly for some time.

Leaving Kathryn, Roth went into Beth's room to prepare the body for burial. While doing so, Roth was pondering in his head as to what he was going to do. He could not leave Kathryn alone, where would she go, what would she do. This left only one choice, a choice that he knew he would have to accept.

Completing his duties to Beth, he placed a clean white sheet over her body and quietly left the room, closing and locking the door securely behind him. Roth then went to his room to prepare for bed. Sitting on the bed, he was drawn towards thoughts of his wife Elizabeth. He remembered the times when both she and her mother were together. Those were happy times, times that now seemed so long ago. His thoughts turned to Kathryn. In his mind, Kathryn was a piece of both Elizabeth and Beth, the better part of each one. With these happy thoughts on his mind, he lay down upon his bed and drifted away into a troubled sleep.

The following morning, Roth awoke to the smell of cooking bacon and steaming coffee. Hurriedly dressing, he went downstairs to find Kathryn busy in the kitchen preparing breakfast.

"I was beginning to wonder if you were ever going to get up this morning. I got up early to get breakfast started because we have a very busy day ahead of us," Kathryn said as she moved about the kitchen preparing the meal.

Roth was caught a little off guard by his daughter's attitude. Leaning against a countertop, he looked at her before he said, "are you all right young darlin'?"

"Oh yes father, I had a talk with Gramma Beth last night and she said that everything was all right. She said she was happy and not in pain anymore."

"You went to her room? How did you get in, I locked the door?" Roth inquired.

Kathryn smiled at her father and replied, "I did not need to go to her. She came to me. She had another woman with her, a woman I have never seen before. She came and assured me that everything was fine now. She was where she needed to be and not to worry about her any longer, she was happy."

"She came to you, in your room, with someone else? Are you sure you were not dreaming darlin'?"

"No father, this was not a dream. She came with the other woman and sat right on the edge of my bed. Beth and I had a long talk, at first, I was very scared, but the other woman began to hum a song and I calmed right down. There was something very familiar about the tune but I cannot place it."

"What did it sound like?" Roth asked.

Kathryn then proceeded to hum the song that she had heard last night in her room.

"What did this other woman look like Kathryn?" Roth asked already, seeming to know the answer.

Kathryn paused for a while to examine the progress of her cooking before she replied, "She was quite pretty, with long, wavy brown hair. She had blue green eyes and a very warm smile. She reminded me very much of Gramma Beth, only younger."

Visibly shaken, Roth took a seat at the table and put his head in his hands.

"What is it Father? Have I said someone to upset you?"

"Oh no my darlin', you said nothing to upset me. It is just that you described someone very dear to me."

"Who father?"

"The lady you described was your mother and the tune that you were humming is a tune that she used to hum all the time when she busied herself around the house or outside in her garden when she was pregnant with you." Roth replied, hanging his head in sorrow, not wanting Kathryn to see his tears.

Kathryn walked across the room and sat down on her father's lap. Wrapping her arms around her father's neck, she said, "Could she really have been my mother? I have often dreamed about my mother. Beth used to tell me about her, what she was like when she was my age. I never imagined that she was so beautiful."

"Aye young darlin', she was indeed a beautiful woman." Roth returned. More tears were starting to form in his eyes.

"Do not cry father, she seemed to be very happy. She said to me, 'be not afraid, my Kathryn, your father is a good man.' What did she mean by that father?"

"She was telling you that things will be all right in your life, that you will never be alone again, I am with you," Roth managed to say, wiping away the tears.

"I am sure that things will be all right, we are together and I will take good care of you. Now let me finish your breakfast before you waste away to nothing," she said as she kissed her father on the cheek and rose from his lap.

Watching her move back to the stove and back to her cooking, Roth could see his wife Elizabeth standing there. This young girl was the monument to their life together. He knew he would never be able to leave her side again.

As they were finishing eating their breakfast, someone knocked on the door. Roth rose to answer the knock. Opening the door, a short thin man dressed entirely in black, greeted him and introduced himself as Torrence Hinds, the undertaker. He told Roth that Doctor Metts had stopped by his shop and informed him that there had been a death in the family and he decided to save Roth the trip into town and brought a coffin out with him.

Roth was very grateful for this gesture of friendship and invited him in for coffee. Mister Hinds reluctantly declined, stating that he had one more stop to make. Roth helped Mister Hinds unload the coffin and bring it into the house.

Kathryn and Roth cleared off the table and placed the coffin on it. Roth then went upstairs to Beth's room, brought the body down, and carefully placed it into the coffin. Kathryn carefully rearranged the sheet and neatly folded it down exposing Beth's face. Kathryn then ran upstairs and returned with a brush that she immediately put to work on Beth's hair. Satisfied with her job, she remarked, "There, now she looks just as pretty as she did last night."

Roth, still amazed at the profound transformation in his daughter, replied, "Yes, she looks very good. She would be grateful and proud of you right now." He walked over to his daughter, drew her into his arms, and gave her a big hug.

It was not long after that when people from the village started to arrive to pay their last respects to Beth and offer any service they were able to give.

Roth greeted each one at the door and Kathryn led them to her Gramma Beth. They were all told that the burial would be tomorrow. They were going to lay her to rest alongside Elizabeth on the knoll behind the house. It turned out that Beth was a much-respected person in the village, judging by the number of people that came. Mister Berkshire and most of the crew also came.

Roth took his old friend, Edward, aside and said, "It looks as if I am goin' to have to give up the sea now and stay home to care for Kathryn. I am goin' to recommend to Creed that you be given command of the *Galaunt*. I am of firm belief that you will command her well, if not better than I have done."

"That is a hasty decision Cap'n, darn't you think you should be a givin' that a bit more thought?"

"I have given it plenty of thought, my friend. The day after tomorrow, I am to meet with Creed again and I plan to give him my note of absence. Creed told me at our last meetin' that if I did not go on this next voyage, he would replace me. That is why I am recommendin' you. I can think of no better person to take over command of the *Galaunt*."

Berkshire lowered his head and thought this over. After a long pause, he looked up and said, "Nathan, I beg you to reconsider, I would not feel comfortable at sea without you. I have thought often about what it would be like to be in command of my own ship and every time I come to the same conclusion. You are my captain, but foremost, you are my friend. It would not be the same, sailin' the seas, without you by my side givin' the commands for me to carry out."

Roth stared at his friend for a long time, wondering what made men like him so loyal to another.

"Maybe you are right. Maybe it is time to give up the sea. I have five kids that do not even recognize their father when he comes home. I have enough set aside to live on for quite a while so maybe you are right." Edward added.

"That would be a great loss to England. You would be a good captain and you would open up the East Indies." Roth said, trying to dissuade his friend.

"Maybe so or maybe not, but I think I will be a givin' this a lot of thought over the next two days." With that, Berkshire walked back into the parlor and the other members of his crew.

Roth could see that his friend huddling with them and was sure that he was telling them of his possible retirement. He was roused from his thoughts by a hand on his shoulder. Turning, he saw that it was his daughter.

"Father, why do you look so concerned? What did your friend say to you?"

Roth looked at his daughter for a long time trying to find the right words before replying, "He told me that he was considering givin' up the sea."

"Why would he want to do that?"

"Because I told him that I am givin' up the sea," he said flatly.

Kathryn stood straight up, stared her father directly in the eyes, and with all the sternness she could muster, said, "You are not going to give up the sea. It is your life."

Roth, feeling more than a bit humbled, replied, "I have new responsibilities now in my life that prevent me from bein' gone for long periods of time."

"Do you mean me? Are you giving up the sea for me?" Kathryn relaxed her posture and went on, "There is no need for that, Father. I will come with you."

"That would be impossible young darlin'. The next voyage could be and most certainly will be, very hazardous and I could not even consider takin' you along. Besides, the ship leaves in thirteen days and I could not possibly make the needed arrangements for your care in that time."

"That is even more reason why I should come with you. We can watch out for each other," Kathryn stated with a smile.

Roth, not wanting to cause his daughter any more grief, said, "We will continue this discussion after the burial tomorrow. Right now, we have guests to attend to." Roth gently took Kathryn's arm and led her back into the parlor.

The next day was much the same as the day before. People started arriving early in the morning to follow Beth to her final resting place. Six men from the village entered the cottage and lifted the coffin for the march up the knoll.

The knoll was located about five hundred yards behind the cottage. It rose slightly higher than the rise on which stood the cottage and afforded a grand view of the town and river. Elizabeth and Roth had spent many hours there and it was Elizabeth's favorite spot. It had steep sides but was relatively flat on the crest. A lone sycamore tree grew off to one side of the top giving ample shade during the heat of the day. The only other thing to occupy the surface of the knoll was a stone cross marking the spot where Elizabeth rests for all eternity. Now however, there was a large hole next to Elizabeth. This would be Beth's final resting place.

A path led from the cottage to the knoll and along this path, the people of the village were now marching on a sad procession towards the knoll, led by the six men carrying the coffin.

After everyone had gathered around the coffin once again, the pastor asked for silence and opened his bible. "Friends and neighbors, we are gathered here on this mournful day to say goodbye to Beth Adams, beloved friend and grandmother. Hers is a memory that will live forever in our hearts. She was a woman who gave of herself selflessly and freely, asking nothing in return. Hers had not been an easy life. She lost her husband, John, and son, Jason, in our war with Spain and shortly after that, lost her daughter, Mary Elizabeth, while giving birth to a beautiful baby girl, Kathryn Jean. Beth took that baby girl and raised her as her own until she was no longer able to do so. Now she has gone to be with her family, sorely missed by those of us remaining behind. Let us have a moment of silence in honor of Beth,"

After a few minutes had passed the pastor once again spoke, "Father in heaven, please have mercy and look kindly upon this lady before you. She was of good heart. Beth Adams, be at ease and forever rest in peace. Amen."

"Amen," chorused the gathering.

The coffin was slowly lowered into the ground and Roth and Kathryn walked to the edge of the hole. Gathering a handful of earth, they each tossed it into the hole, said their final, silent, farewells, and moved off arm in arm down the knoll. The rest of the mourners followed and slowly filed past Beth's final resting place, adding their handfuls of soil with silent prayers and goodbyes.

Roth and Kathryn remained at the bottom of the knoll to receive their condolences and thank them for their attendance. With everyone gone, Roth and Kathryn climbed back to the top of the knoll and walked over to the grave. "I am glad she is with her family but I will still miss her," Kathryn said sobbing quietly.

"As will I darlin'," Roth returned, putting his arm around Kathryn giving her a reassuring hug and his support.

Neither spoke after that and soon started down the path towards the cottage.

It was later in the day, before either of them spoke to one another again, Kathryn that broke the silence. "Well Father, what have you decided?"

"Decided what Kathryn?"

"You know what," Kathryn said turning towards her father showing obvious signs of irritation. "What are you going to do? You must let Lord Creed know your answer tomorrow."

"I have already told you what I am going to do," he said sternly, not wanting to get back into this conversation.

Kathryn moved across the room and took a seat directly in front of her father. Leaning forward with her elbows on her knees and her hands clasped, she solemnly said, "Father, I do not want you to give up your life at sea. I know how much it means to you and how much it has cost you. I want to be with you for sure but not like that. You would never be happy again and in return neither would I. I do not want to go on knowing that I was the cause of your unhappiness. Do you really think that is fair for either of us?"

Roth leaned back in his chair and stared at his daughter, thinking this over. "What would you do if I were to leave?"

"Accompany you of course."

"I told you yesterday that it would be impossible."

"Gramma Beth told me that nothing was impossible if you were only to try."

"Gramma Beth has never sailed around the Cape in the winter. There will be storms down there the likes of which you have never seen. It is far too hazardous."

"Father, you said that you would be leaving in twelve days. That would put you at the Cape during September. That is well before the winter storms should hit."

Roth, smiling and wondering where Kathryn had gained all this knowledge about the Cape, leaned forward, took her hands in his and said, "Kathryn, I cannot do it. Now let us forget this and move on, we have other things to worry about."

Pulling her hands away from his and sitting up straight, Kathryn defiantly said, "No, I will not forget it! This is my life that you are talking about also and I will not go through it watching the only person left to me, suffer."

He could only smile at his daughter, "That sounded just like somethin' your mother once said to me when I talked of givin' up the sea before. You must carefully think over your decision Kathryn. Life aboard a tradin' vessel is not very pleasant."

"Father, what do you think I have been thinking about all my life? It has always been my dream to go to sea with you. There is nothing more to think over, I want to go with you and what safer place could I be than with my father?"

Roth said, "Those have been my thoughts also from time to time," he hesitated and realized she was right, he had not given any thought to Kathryn's feelings, he only thought of his own. In her youthful exuberance, she would of course deny the perils of the voyage in exchange for being with her father. Acknowledging these thoughts, Roth said, "I will have to sleep on it and will give you my decision in the mornin'. Now it is getting late and we have had a very long day so I think it would be wise if we went to bed. We can continue this conversation in the mornin' when we are well rested."

Kathryn, obviously disappointed that he had not made the decision now, abjectly lowered her head and said, "You are right father, I am getting rather tired."

Roth rose from his chair, gave Kathryn a kiss on the cheek, and ruffled her hair saying, "there is no need for worry young darlin', and things will be all right." With that, he strode from the parlor towards his room, leaving Kathryn with her thoughts.

When he reached his room and closed the door, he sat down on the edge of the bed and rehashed what he and Kathryn had been discussing. On the one hand, she had been right about him not being happy with having to give up the sea. On the other hand, she had no idea of what her life would become if he did decide to take her along on this voyage. He knew that it would be very dangerous in the Far East this time and he knew that there would be several battles. With Kathryn to worry about, how was he going to lead his men? The more he thought about it, the more he came to realize that it was not going to be possible for her to accompany him and therefore it left him no choice but to give up the sea.

Chapter 4
"Preparations"

The following morning, Roth arose again to the smell of cooking downstairs. He marveled at how well his daughter, at her tender age, was able to continue with all that was happening around her. He donned his clothes for the day and made his way to the kitchen where a very wide-awake and undoubtedly excited young girl greeted him. "Good morning father, I hope that you slept well. Breakfast is ready and if you take a seat, I will join you so we can eat together before it gets cold." Kathryn was thinking to herself that her father must recognize her abilities and he should start thinking of her as a capable young woman.

Roth knew immediately what she was up to, and it just made him love her even more. He pulled out a chair at the table and sat down. It suddenly dawned on him that Kathryn was not dressed in her usual dress today, instead, she was wearing clothes more fit to the outdoors, perhaps, in her eyes, fit for the sea. He almost laughed aloud.

Kathryn turned to bring him his breakfast and Roth, who could contain himself no longer, broke into a loud fit of jolly laughter. He laughed until tears rolled down his cheeks.

"What is so funny?" Kathryn asked starting to laugh herself at the sight of her father's glee.

Roth managed to say between laughs. "Young darlin', do not be thinkin' that I do not know what you are up to."

Kathryn, placing his plate before him, asked ever so innocently, "What do you mean father?"

"Alas young darlin', I be a thinkin' that you are tryin' to show me how much of a sailor you could be." He stated with a chuckle and a smile.

"Well, I was only making myself ready for when it was time to go to the ship."

"Just what makes you think that you will be goin' to the ship today young lady?" He asked in a jokingly manner.

"How could you possibly even think about leaving a sweet young thing, such as myself, behind, alone in the world, defenseless, having to make her own way in life?"

Roth broke into another burst of laughter. "Are we beginnin' to get a wee bit dramatic here?"

Returning his laughter, Kathryn sighed, and asked, "Well?"

"Aye my young lass, you are giving a compelling argument and I did think on it last night. You will be sailing with me when I depart if it is to be allowed by Lord Creed."

Kathryn excitedly wrapped her arms around his neck and joyously hugged him very tightly saying, "Oh father, you do not know how long I have waited for this moment. You will never regret this decision, of that I promise."

"Hold on a minute young darlin', the final decision has yet to be made. Lord Creed will have the final word."

"I am not worried father, I know that you will convince him that this is how it must be."

"I do hope that you will not be too disappointed if he says no."

"He will not say no. This I am sure of," Kathryn stated matter-of-factly.

"Well, we will soon know. Let us finish our breakfast and I will go to town and meet with him." he said as he returned to the meal, managing to eat between chuckles.

Roth said goodbye to Kathryn and left the cottage. His mind was in turmoil. Why did Creed have to put him in this position? Did the man not have any sense left in him? Had the greed driven it all out? He was not ready to give up his life on the open seas, he was still young, but he would if need be. What would he do if he were forced to give that life up? He would have to reason with the man and try to dissuade him from ordering this voyage now. It would be better undertaken in the spring. It would give them more time to plan and prepare.

It was not a long walk to the village and Roth was happy that it was not raining. The port town seemed quite busy this morning. Word must have gotten out that the four ships would be sailing soon and the merchants were busy preparing their wares for transport to the docks. Lord Creed's offices were located just beyond the shops.

For the second time in three days, Roth made his way to the second floor office of Jarvis Creed. He was greeted by Creed's secretary and led into the inner office.

Roth was not surprised to see that Raynerd was also in the office with Creed. "Ah Captain Roth, we have been expecting you." Creed rose from his desk, walked over to greet him with a handshake, pointed out a chair and invited him to sit.

"I think that I would rather stand if you do not mind m'lord," Roth said declining the offer. He laid his coat and hat on a table by the door and moved over to the window where he had a clear view of the docks. He could see that all four ships had been brought together for easier loading. The *Galaunt* was closest and he was able to make out the activity on and around his ship. He knew that Edward would be aboard and wondered what he and the rest of the crew were thinking.

Creed made his way back to his desk and sat down. "Have you come to a decision yet?" Creed was not sure if he really wanted to hear what Roth had to say.

Roth turned from his musings at the window and slowly started to speak. "I feel that I must press you again, m'lord, to make use of your better judgment and reconsider this venture you are asking us to undertake. This is not a good time to be startin' on a voyage around the Cape. The storm season will soon be upon us and the chances of failure will increase with each passing day."

"Then maybe we should move up the schedule and plan to set sail earlier," Raynerd suggested as he moved across the room and faced Roth.

"You still do not understand, do you? You are risking the loss of four of your newest and finest ships because of your greed," Roth shot back, facing Raynerd squarely now.

Raynerd withdrew a step, somewhat intimidated by Roth's size and obvious anger. "I think the only thing I am beginning to understand, by your reluctance to accept our offer, is that maybe you have lost your stomach for danger."

Roth quickly closed the gap between them. Now standing face to face with Raynerd, he said threateningly quiet for Raynerd's ears only, "I have not lost anything, and I am still not afraid of anything or, I might add, anyone."

Raynerd quickly moved away from Roth and took a place behind Creed. "Are you sure that you are ready to give up your employment here, for that is what you are doing by not accepting our offer. On top of that, I will personally see that you will never set foot on another ship for as long as you live in England. Not even as a dock worker!" Creed said, trying to protect Raynerd.

"As I am sure that you are aware, I have suffered a death in the family. This has raised the issue of my daughter. There is no one to care for her and nowhere for her to go. I simply will not leave her behind without a soul to care for her. I will captain your ship if I am allowed to take my daughter with me and only under those circumstances."

Raynerd bent down and whispered in Lord Creed's ear. Creed nodded his head and returning his attention back to Roth, replied, "I do not care who you take with you as long as you captain the ship, but if your daughter is to sail on one of my ships, she will earn her way. I do not give a free ride to anyone."

Roth could barely control his anger. He could not believe that anyone could be so callous. He wanted to shout at Creed, expose his greed, but "I cannot leave her behind," was all that Roth said. He returned to the window to await Creed's decision and once again looked longingly upon his ship.

"Ok then, it is agreed. You will lead the voyage from your ship. Raynerd will be in overall command and will sail with you to carry out negotiations with the local leaders."

"No, that is not part of the agreement. I will not have someone on my ship that undermines my authority."

"My dear Captain Roth, you obviously do not understand," Creed said in his patronizing way. "Raynerd will not interfere with the running of the ship. That will remain your duty. He is merely going along to make trade negotiations."

"In that case, let him ride on one of the other ships. I will have enough to do gettin' this small fleet around the Cape safely without havin' to worry about your man here." Roth turned and glared at Raynerd, as if daring him to respond.

Raynerd returned the stare from the safety of Creed's back. "As you wish Captain, it is not my desire to upset the voyage," he responded with a tone resembling a hiss.

The two men continued to stare at each other, neither wanting to show any signs of weakness. Creed broke the spell. "Raynerd, you will sail with Captain Connery aboard the *Royale*. I do hope that meets with your approval, Captain Roth," Creed said with a look of contempt and disdain.

"Yes m'lord. Now if you will excuse me, I have a ship to attend to and preparations to make." Roth took up his coat and hat and started to walk out of the office.

"One more thing if you please. Your ship will be loaded and repaired in four days' time. Be prepared to sail then," adding insult to Roth's obvious injury. "Yours will sail first, to be followed in two day intervals by the *Royale*, the *Princeton* and the *Noble* in that order. After you are clear of the Cape, you are to wait in calm waters for the arrival of the other ships. I prefer not to lose all of my ships at the same time, if I must lose any at all."

Roth could not believe what he had just heard. Creed, just as much as admitted, that he expected to lose one or more of his ships and was still willing to proceed with this venture. The men under his control were mere pawns to be used in acquiring the wealth he so desired. He slowly managed to regain control of his emotions. "Yes m'lord," he said calmly. He then turned and left the through the crowded corridors and stepped out onto the street. Roth looked back at the second story windows of Creed's office and thought to himself, 'Someday this will all catch up with you'.

Roth made his way through the bustle of the docks to the gangplank of the *Galaunt*. Stopping to gaze up at his ship, he noticed that the main yard had already been replaced and the men aloft were busy rigging the block and tackles and tying off the sail.

Hearing his first mate shout an order, Roth made his way past men, carrying crates and barrels up the gangplank, to seek him out. Attaining the main deck, he was surprised at the frenzy before him. Creed was obviously sparing nothing in order to get this ship ready for sailing. Roth noticed the repaired starboard railing was shining with its new coat of paint. There were several carpenters onboard, busily repairing the battle damage the *Galaunt* had sustained on her last voyage. He recognized a few of them as being from the Payne Brothers Shipyard, where the *Galaunt* had been built. These men were experts in the art of shipbuilding and he knew that when finished, the repairs would not be noticeable.

Berkshire barked another order to the men in the rigging and Roth saw that he was standing under the mainmast, supervising the activity in the sails. Alongside him were the captains, Connery and Holmes, also watching the activities.

Berkshire saw his captain moving towards him, tendered up a very crisp salute, and said, "Cap'n, it is good to see you onboard again. Things are comin' along nicely and we should be ready to set sail when the time of our departure arrives."

"It is good to be back onboard Mister Berkshire."

"Does this mean that you will be a sailin' with us?"

"Aye, that it does Mister Berkshire, you cannot get rid of me that easy," Roth said with a smile while appreciatively patting his hand on his friend's shoulder.

Turning to greet the other men, Roth offered his hand first to Captain Seth Connery, a big man, much like Roth himself. Connery had been born into power and taken over his first ship when he was just twenty-five. He had a reputation of ruthlessness and ran his ship with an iron hand, dealing out punishment for the slightest infractions. He was also very petty and Roth knew that when he found out that Roth would be in command of the voyage, there would be trouble. Connery and Raynerd were two of a kind and they would get along quite well during their trip to the Far East.

Offering his hand next to Captain Thomas Holmes, he smiled. Before him was a man of short stature, Roth had to bend down to take his hand. Holmes was the exact opposite of Connery and he ran a happy ship. His crew was very loyal for they knew that this captain was fair and just, much like Roth himself. Of the two captains before him, Roth knew that it would be Holmes, that he would be able to rely on in times of trouble. Holmes may be a small man, but there was fight in this man with no quit and that would be in much demand before this voyage was over.

"We heard a rumor that you might not be makin' this voyage and we came over to find out what the story was. James was here earlier but he got called back to his ship. He will be returnin' shortly as soon as he solves the problem," Connery said, removing his hat to wipe away the sweat with his handkerchief.

"Aye, that was the rumor," Roth said staring towards a first mate that was grinning sheepishly and shrugging his shoulders. "News travels very fast through the crews, it would seem," he added with a smile and a nod to Berkshire.

"The curs should learn to hold their tongues when it comes to the doin's of their betters," Connery said with arrogance. "On my ship, my men would see the lash for spreadin' a rumor about me." Only Roth noticed the look of anger Berkshire shot towards Connery. It was a good thing that Connery had not seen it, if he had, more than likely, he would have introduced Berkshire to the sharp end of his saber.

"If you would excuse me sirs, I need to get back to the yardarm," Berkshire said disgustedly.

"First, would you seek out the cabin boy and tell him to bring our finest wine to my cabin?" Roth asked, glad to see Berkshires willingness to leave the conversation. "Also, would you watch for Captain Pringle and escort him to my cabin when he arrives. I would like to have you join us at that time if you can free yourself."

"If it is all the same to you Roth, I would prefer a mug of ale, wine is a little too sweet for my tastes this early in the mornin'," Captain Holmes said.

"You heard that Mister Berkshire, now be off." Roth wanted him out of there before Connery noticed the way Berkshire was glaring at him. Berkshire would be no match for the talented Connery in a fight with sabers. Connery had been trained in the proper use of a saber long before he rose to his current position.

"Aye, aye Cap'n," Berkshire said as he saluted crisply. He was also relieved to be out of the presence of Connery.

"Well gentlemen, should we retire to my cabin, I am sure it will be warmer there." Roth stretched out his hand offering to let them lead the way.

Connery replaced his hat and moved towards the door leading to the captain's cabin. Holmes turned and looked at Roth, shook his head and followed a few steps behind. He looked up, and to no one in particular, said to himself 'Why me?'

Roth did not notice that Berkshire was standing by the door, talking with Brian, the cabin boy, until he heard him say, "Here, let me get that for you. We wouldn't want you to be a soilin' your hands on that knob, it ain't been polished yet today." Berkshire took out a rag from his back pocket and set to polishing the knob, making the brass gleam brightly in the sunlight. "There ye go Cap'n, not even ye could object to using it now," Berkshire said insolently.

"How dare you speak to someone of my rank, like that?" Connery stepped back and began to draw his sword. "I should kill you for that!" he screamed.

"There will be no killin' onboard my ship today," Roth shouted, as he stepped between Connery and Berkshire barely in time to prevent Connery from drawing his saber.

"Step aside Roth, I will accept no insult from a man such as the man before me," Connery demanded.

"I am the man standing before you and I have issued no insult. I will take care of him," Roth said as he moved toward Connery, and placing his hand upon Connery's sword, pushed it down to point at the deck. "I need this man for this voyage."

Connery replaced his sword in the scabbard and pointing at Berkshire said with a snarl, "Today you live, but when this voyage is over, you are mine." He reached down grasping the doorknob and flung open the door in anger.

Roth turned to Berkshire and said, "what on earth did you think you were doin'? That man would have killed you where you stood. You are not even armed. Now get back to work. Also, it would be wise if you did not join us when Pringle arrives."

"Aye, aye Cap'n," Berkshire said turned and moved off, chuckling to himself.

"That is quite the man you have there Roth, he showed no fear, at all, of Seth. He looked as if he would have been more than willin' to fight, even unarmed," Holmes remarked with a twinkle in his eye and a smile on his face.

"Aye, that he is and he would be in command of this ship if I were not goin' to be makin' this voyage."

"Well I, for one, am glad that you are. Things will go much better for all of us." Holmes entered through the doorway and made his way to Roth's cabin, with Roth close behind.

As both men entered the cabin, Connery immediately started, "I require the satisfaction of knowing what punishment you plan to hand out to that insolent sailor and demand to be present when that punishment is carried out."

"You will make no demands aboard my ship Captain Connery, me, and only me, will determine what is to be done about this incident. As far as punishment is concerned, this trip might prove to be punishment enough. If you would please be seated, we will wait for Pringle." Just then a knock came from the door, "That must be him now."

Connery cut Roth off as he moved to open the door, "This is not over yet. I will get my satisfaction!"

Roth brushed him aside and opened the door, standing outside was the cabin boy and Captain James Pringle of the *Princeton*. Pringle was a mousy type of man that had only attained his position as a captain because he happened to be the nephew of Lord Creed. "Ah, James, we have been waitin' for you. Please come in and have a seat." Roth took his seat behind the desk, leaned forward and clasped his hands knowing full well what was about to happen. He waited until all three were seated and had at least one sip of their drink before he started. "I have just returned from a meetin' with Lord Creed. I am to be placed in command of this fleet for the tradin' venture in the Far East."

"Why you?" Connery exploded. "This will only be your second trip there. I have been there and back five times. I am much better suited for command."

"It is true that I have only made one voyage to the spice islands, but mine was successful, you returned five times, poorer than when you left." Roth replied evenly. "Regardless, those are Creed's wishes and I will not dispute them."

"Of course you would not dispute them, they are all in your favor, but I will dispute them." Seth started to rise.

"You can dispute them if you wish, but in the meantime, you will stay seated and hear the rest of what I am goin' to say because I will not be sayin' them again."

"I will be damned if I will stay and be ordered around by a captain, junior in rank to myself." He rose from his seat, walked to the door, opening it he said, "I will say it again, I will get my satisfaction." Connery was staring right at Roth.

Roth, not moving a muscle, in a quiet even tone replied, "You will try."

Connery's eyes widened at this threat, but quickly narrowed. Without saying anything further, he turned and made his way to the main deck, leaving both doors open behind him. He could be heard yelling at workers and crewmembers to get out of his way as he pushed and shoved his way off the ship.

Roth stood and walked to the door, shutting it, he went on, "As I was sayin', Lord Creed has put me in command of this fleet for whatever reasons he has. I will be sailin' in four days' time, to be followed two days later by Connery. You, Pringle, will sail two days after that and Holmes, you will be bringin' up the rear."

"That is a strange arrangement, why aren't we all sailin' at the same time?" Holmes asked.

Not wanting to say what was really, on his mind because of the presence of Pringle, Roth replied, "He does not want to take the chance of losin' all four ships at the same time if we were all caught in the same storm."

"That is good of him to be so concerned with our welfare," Holmes said very sarcastically, seemingly unaware of the man sitting next to him, or simply not caring.

"I am to sail to the other side of the Cape and await the arrival of your ships. Then we will all sail together up the coast. We will stand a much better chance of success if we are together."

"It is good to know that Creed is concerned with our welfare." Holmes said once again.

"That is not everything. Creed has decided that Raynerd will accompany us aboard Connery's ship."

Holmes stood and began to pace the cabin. He made several circuits before he spoke, "That is not going to be good. The two of them are goin' to be nothin' but trouble."

A knock came to the door and Berkshire stuck his head in and said, "Excuse me sir, but there is a messenger on board sayin' that Captain Pringle is wanted back aboard his ship."

"Ah, that is what I have been waitin' for. If you gentlemen will excuse me, I must return to my ship." Pringle stood and began to don his coat and hat.

"Is there anythin' wrong that I may be able to help you with?" Roth inquired but was glad to see him leaving. Since he was leading the mission, he felt obligated to ask with hopes that he would not be required to help.

Pringle said, "No everythin' is all right. I have just been waitin' for a special shipment of furniture to arrive. The stuff that was put on my ship when she was first built was not what I had hoped for, so I am replacin' it."

"Very well then, I will see you again tomorrow. There are several things that we need to go over before I sail." Roth then motioned to Berkshire, "Mister Berkshire, would you please join us?"

The three men stood and watched as Pringle left the cabin, "He should not be a captain," Holmes stated, "he knows less about the sea then my cabin boy. His crew will be killed one of these days, he knows less about the sea than a common merchant does. Roth, I think that the three of them will spend most of this voyage conspirin' ways to take command from you," said Holmes, being a man not to mince words.

"Aye captain, I would agree with Captain Holmes. We would be better off with just the two ships on this trip." Berkshire stated nodding his head agreeably.

Roth stood and peered out the windows at the stern of the ship. He could see, because of the curve of the docks, all three of the other ships being prepared for the voyage. He could not help but admire them, their rakish lines were a thing of beauty. All four ships were almost identical, the only difference between them was the crews and Roth had the best crew of all. "There will not be any trouble. We will all have enough to do to keep us busy. The Far East is not an easy place to sail." Roth did not believe what he had just said and it was obvious that the other men did not either but they accepted it.

"Well, be that as it may, you can always count on me to watch your back. Now if you would also excuse me, I have several things that I must attend to also." Holmes grabbed his hat and coat and started to walk out the door.

"Come back when you can, I want to go over the methods that we must adopt to be able to trade profitably when we arrive at our destination."

"Aye Roth, I will." Holmes left the cabin with his head in turmoil. He was worried about his friend Roth. He knew that Raynerd and Connery were the kind of men that would stop at nothing to achieve their desires.

Roth was left alone with his first mate. He could not help but smile when he spoke, "You know of course, that you just ruined any chances of commandin' your own ship with this company. Connery has probably already been to see Creed."

"Aye captain, it was not a wise thing to do but it is what I did and I am prepared to stand by my actions.

"I do hope that there will be no further incidents until after this voyage has reached its conclusion."

"Cap'n, it is over as far as I am concerned."

"Fine, now I want you to clear out the cabin next to mine. We are going to be carryin' a passenger with us."

Berkshire looked at his captain in a puzzled way, not quite knowing if he should question him about what was just said but decided to do so anyway. "We will be carryin' a passenger sir? I thought this was to be a tradin' mission, not a pleasure cruise."

"I am bringin' along my daughter."

"You are what! How can you possibly think that she would be safe where we are goin'? This will be no voyage for a young girl. The dangers are just too great."

Roth turned to gaze out of the windows again, "Do you not think that I have thought about that? I really do not have much of a choice. If I do not take her, where would she go? What would she do? I assuredly cannot leave her in the cottage way out there on the fringes of the village by herself."

"But Cap'n, I beg you to reconsider."

"I have reconsidered and that is all the choice that I have. Now get a move on it, we only have three days to finish up what must be done before we sail."

"Aye, aye Cap'n," Berkshire said conceding the discussion.

Roth watched Edward leave to carry out his orders and thought to himself, 'there is a good man, one that he was proud to be able to call a friend.'

Well, it was time to go home to Kathryn and tell her the news. He could not wait to see the look on her face.

Upon entering the cottage, a pile of baggage standing by the doorway greeted Roth. Kathryn was nowhere in sight. "Kathryn," he called. "What on earth is all this?"

Kathryn came running down the stairs clutching another bag in her hand, "Oh father, you are finally back. I have been waiting all day for you to get here."

"There were several things that I needed to attend to while I was in town. Now, if you have time, would you be so kind as to tell me what all this is about?" Roth inquired.

Kathryn smiled at her father, stood erect and proudly said, "I knew that you would convince Lord Creed that I must accompany you and decided that I would gather a few things that I would need for the trip if we are to be gone for very long."

"This is just a few things?" Roth asked, looking over the mound of bags. "I don't think the *Galaunt* is large enough to carry all this, even if she were completely unloaded," he said with a grin.

"Oh father, I was very careful to only pack the things that I would need and not be able to do without. Now tell me, when are we going to move to the ship?"

"You are pretty sure of yourself, aren't you? Well, I guess there is no need to tell you that the decision was made to allow you to go. I must tell you that it is with great concern that I am allowin' you to go. It is not goin' to be an easy venture and it may prove to be very dangerous. My crew and I dare not think of what we could encounter if we do not get around the Cape before the winter storms. They are of a sort that you, havin' never been to sea, could not even imagine."

"But father!" Kathryn quickly and loudly interrupted, "We have had many storms right here. I can handle any storms we may encounter." Kathryn ran into Roth's arms and flung her arms around his shoulders, snuggling her head into his neck, "Father, we will never be apart again. I will take good care of you from now on."

Chapter 5
"Voyage"

The days were passing swiftly towards the day of departure. Roth had gotten Kathryn settled in her quarters and had shown her the galley, where she would be watched over and supervised by the ship's cook. The cook was a rotund gentle fellow with a quick and hearty laugh. The crew affectionately called him Pots. He was, by sailing ship standards, a very good cook or that was until Kathryn came aboard. Pots readily accepted Kathryn's suggestions of adding spices to the food to enhance the flavor, and sometimes just to give it flavor. The crew noticed a difference in the food. It was not long before they realized it was Kathryn making the difference and they were very free with the compliments.

She spent much of her free time above deck looking over the ship and getting to know the men. She found that they were more than willing to teach her about the ship and the skills required to sail her. This delighted her because she knew it would put her father more at ease. Soon she was laughing and engaging in the follies of being at sea even though there was lots of work to be done. Kathryn thought to herself that she had missed much time with her father while he was at sea and for now could see no reason why she had not been able to accompany him before. Maybe she would share these thoughts with her father later, but in the meantime, she was ecstatic to be here now.

Roth was glad to see that Kathryn was finding her place aboard ship but he still had that foreboding in his heart that he could just not seem to shake. The weather was starting to turn early this year in England and Roth hoped that it was not doing the same in the Southern Hemisphere. The success of this venture rested entirely upon the ships reaching and passing The Cape of Good Hope before the winter gales swept in from the south.

Creed had sent Raynerd every day to check on the progress of readying the ship for sailing. Roth had begun to hate the man and hate the company he worked with. It did not seem to him that Creed or Raynerd fully understood that preparations were being carried out as fast as humanly possible, but he was sure it was not fast enough to suit them. Raynerd had begun yesterday to make sure that Roth was aware that Connery had his ship ready and was just waiting for his time to sail. He told Raynerd at that time, if he thought Connery would do better at the head of the mission, then he would gladly step aside and let him lead. Raynerd ignored Roth's statement knowing Creed would not accept that. It was obvious to Roth by this time that he was in firm control of the mission, but it was also obvious to him that neither Creed nor Raynerd could allow it to show that they knew this also.

Raynerd had just left and Roth was standing at the stern railing looking across the river watching the sun settle ever lower in the western skies. Mister Berkshire ascended the stairs to the wheel deck and hurriedly made his way astern. Removing his hat and wiping the sweat from his brow he said, "Cap'n, the final load of supplies has come and the crew is gettin' it stored below decks. It looks like we can make way on the mornin' tide."

"This is very welcome news Mister Berkshire," Roth replied and then added sarcastically, "however, I will surely miss the daily visits from Raynerd."

"Aye that I will miss also, but a man has to make small sacrifices sometimes to be able to live a life at sea."

Roth broke out into a hearty laugh, here was another reason why Berkshire was so valuable aboard his ship. Berkshire easily recognized Roth's moods and usually had the right remedy for them, this time it was laughter.

It was several minutes before he could resume the conversation. "I will go and inform our employers of our readiness to sail. Have the men finish the loadin' and then release all but the necessary crewmembers for a last night on the town. They have worked very hard these past three days and deserve the leave, anyway, it will be a long time until their next one. When I return, I will relieve any that I can and will retain watch over the ship with my daughter."

"Aye, aye Cap'n," Berkshire replied and turned to make his way back to the main deck to supervise the loading of the cargo that had just arrived on board.

Roth left the railing and descended the stairs making his way to the gangplank when Kathryn, who was just coming up from the galley for some fresh air, stopped him. "Where are you going father?" she asked.

"We will be ready to sail with the tide in the mornin' and I was on my way to inform Lord Creed."

Kathryn, while wiping her hands on a towel that she carried while working in the galley, asked, "Would you like me to come along and keep you company?"

"What about your duties?"

"Oh, they can wait until I get back."

"Duties aboard a ship cannot wait," Roth said sternly. "Also, when I get back, we will be alone aboard ship while the crew is spendin' their last night ashore. Now young darlin', do you want to have to go back to work and finish your duties when we return or have them completed when I return?"

Somewhat disappointed by her father's logic, Kathryn replied, "I would rather spend the time with you of course. It will not take long and I will have a meal prepared for you when you return," she said with a devious little smile on her face. With that, Kathryn turned and made her way back below deck and the chores that awaited her.

Roth smiled after his daughter and suddenly realized that this was probably going to be their last time alone together for a very long time. He turned and walked down the gangplank towards town to meet with Creed.

The sky was beginning to turn a very bright shade of orange, turning the bluff and the river into, what Roth thought to be, a forest of trees, showing their finest autumn colors and a river of lava making its way to the sea. Light from lanterns and candles were beginning to appear in the shop windows and the homes of workers by the time that Roth made his way to the office of Creed.

There was still a light coming from the window of Creeds office and Roth knew that he would still be there. He made his way through an empty building to the second floor where he knocked loudly on Creed's door.

"Come in," a voice that sounded like Creed said from the other side. Roth opened the door and entered the room to be greeted by a standing Creed, who for the moment, anyway, appeared to be alone. "Ah my good Captain Roth, I hope it is with good news that you arrive so late. I have been waiting for you all afternoon wondering whether or not you were ever going to get your ship ready for sailing."

Roth shot a glance at Creed that caused the shorter man to open his eyes wide for a moment and take a precautionary step back. "M'lord, my men have been working around the clock to meet the impossible deadline you set for us and it was your men that were late with the deliveries of supplies that we needed to load before we could set sail." Roth could not stand to look at this man any longer and moved to devote his stare to the docks, and in particular, his ship that was lit up with lanterns from stem to stern.

"That may well be, but it is of no consequence," Creed replied in a rather offhanded manner. "What news have you brought for me? Are you finally ready to set sail?" Creed replied showing no remorse for his attitude towards Roth.

"Aye, m'lord, we will set sail on the mornin' tide and be out to sea by mid-mornin'." Roth said insolently.

Creed ignored the insolence and stated, "Fine, you can expect to see me again before you sail. I will be on the docks in the morning. I may have some last minute instructions"

"You need not bother m'lord. We will be sailin' with the tide shortly after the sun rises." Roth did not relish the idea of even one more meeting with this despicable little man. He would just as soon have this as their last time together.

"I am up before the first light. I will be on the docks," Creed replied as if knowing what Roth's thoughts were.

"As you wish m'lord, now if you will excuse me, I want to relieve the men watchin' the ship so they may have some time ashore before we sail." Roth did not wait for a dismissal. He merely turned and strode through the door and left the building. He could not have stayed there much longer, his hatred for that man was beginning to overcome his usually good self-restraint. It would not be a wise thing to tell Creed what he thought of him and his mission, not if he wanted to continue being the captain of the finest ship to set sail from an English port. Once he was on the open seas, he would not have to listen or take orders from him until he returned home and that was a long time from now. Anything could happen, maybe with a little luck, there would be new owners by the time he returned. After all, Creed was sending the majority of the ships from his small fleet on this mission and there would not be a lot of cargo coming in until they returned. Roth knew that the loss of these four ships would mean the ruin of Lord Jarvis Creed.

As Roth approached the ship, he could only make out two men onboard and they were both standing by the gangplank as if anxiously awaiting his return. As he neared the gangplank, he could make out Mister Berkshire and a member of the crew deep in conversation and failing to take notice of his arrival. Roth stepped on the gangplank and both men immediately turned to face him. "Ah Cap'n sir, I was beginnin' to get a bit concerned about you, seein' as it is night and all," Berkshire said with a gleam.

"Mister Berkshire when you must be concerned for my safety, day or night for that matter, is the day I shall retire from this life we lead. Now you and Charlie here head for the taverns and leave this duty to me and I will see if I can get through the night."

"Aye Cap'n, that is what we are about to do. Your relief will be here at midnight. Now sir, by your leave, we will depart." Both gave their captain a crisp salute and after receiving an equally crisp salute in return, mounted the gangplank and left for their night in the town.

Roth stood where he was for a few minutes as he watched them go. He knew his crew was not going to be at their best in the morning but he also knew that at their worst, they were still the best crew he could have under his command. His only worry was that they all make it back to the ship before she sailed in the morning. Catching the smell of something cooked, he turned and started to make his way to his cabin. Entering, he saw Kathryn standing alongside his desk, laying out dishes, evidently, she planned to join him for dinner. "I heard you come aboard and rather than greet you on the deck, I decided to get your evening meal ready for when you came to your cabin. I hope you do not mind me joining you, I thought that in the coming months, we might not get a lot of opportunities to dine together, because you will be so busy."

"I can see no reason as to why a daughter cannot have dinner with her father, especially when her father is the captain. Rest assured young darlin', there will be ample opportunities for us to dine together in the months to come." Roth moved over and gave his daughter a big bear hug. "Although I think that it will be the other way around, you will probably not have much time for me."

"Oh father, do not be silly, I am going to spend all of my time with you," she said proudly and with confidence. "Robert doesn't work me that hard and if I get right after my chores, it does not seem to take any time at all."

"We will see," was all that Roth replied before seating himself down to the meal before him. Kathryn must have gathered the remaining food items from personal stock at home. He marveled at what he saw, it must have taken Kathryn the better part of the day to prepare this, there was a whole roasted turkey, accompanied by boiled potatoes, corn on the cob and turkey gravy.

A fresh baked loaf of bread was also on the desk, Roth realized this was what he had smelled from the deck. It would be a long time before he would eat this good again. "Who is this Robert that you mentioned?"

"Oh father, you surprise me, do you not know your crew at all? Robert is the cook."

"So that is what his name is. I have never heard him called anythin' other than Pots."

"I refuse to call him that and the men are starting to call him by his proper name also and they are all starting to call me Katie. I think he never liked to be called Pots anyway."

"When did you find time to prepare this meal?"

"I did not do it all by myself. Robert helped me. I have never cooked a whole turkey before, so Robert showed me how to make stuffing and cook it. Most everything else, I did though. Robert is an excellent cook but he could stand to use more spice."

"It looks to me that you both are very good cooks." Roth did not say anything more after that because he was too busy enjoying the food. They both continued to enjoy their meal in silence.

When they had finished eating, Kathryn cleared his desk and returned the remains of the meal to the galley. "I will not be but a few minutes cleaning up this mess and then I will bring tea for us to enjoy topside if that would please you."

"That would please me very much. I will wait for you near the bow."

Roth made his way to the bow of the ship and found a long crate, covered with a thick tarp to sit on and look at the stars. The moon was very low in the sky and left a long white reflection on the surface of the river. It was not too cold out here in the open tonight, but still, Roth was thankful for the coat he was wearing. He leaned back against the starboard rail where he could keep an eye on the gangplank, not so much as from fear of theft, but rather to watch for his crew as they came aboard for the night, some of them may need some help getting to their hammocks. Roth pulled out his pipe and struck a match along the railing to light it. From the glare of the match, Roth could see where the shipwrights had made their repairs. A few days at sea with the sun beating down upon the new wood would fade it until it blended into the color of the rest of the original starboard railing. Only the practiced eye of someone familiar with the building of ships would then be able to distinguish it from the original.

Kathryn found her father in deep thought when she made her way to the bow of the ship. Taking a seat on the same crate, Kathryn handed her father his cup of tea. "I hope you like it this way, I did not feel like bringing everything out here." Kathryn said.

Roth looked at his daughter and smiled, "I am sure it will be to my liking young darlin'."

Kathryn leaned back against the railing and let her gaze rove around the rigging that she was beginning to know by sight and name. "Father, what is it that has been bothering you these past few days? You should be happy that all preparations are completed and we will be able to finally set sail on the tide."

"That is what is botherin' me, young darlin'. I am not at ease with this voyage," he replied, not taking his gaze from his daughter. "I have a feelin' that all will not go well and that makes me very concerned for your safety."

"Oh father, do not be worried about me. I am old enough to take care of myself, as I have proven, and the men will watch after me to make sure that I do nothing that could cause injury to the ship or me. I can swim, I have been on the ocean before and I have my charm to protect me. Anyway, what about Brian, he was with you on your last voyage and he came back unhurt."

"Brian has been a cabin boy for over two years now. He is quite aware of what a ship is all about and is more than capable of fending for himself when at sea."

"All right then, I will spend more time with Brian and have him teach me the ways of a sailing ship bound for the Far East and to fend for myself while at sea."

Roth could only roll his eyes up and say, "Now I have that to worry about you and my cabin boy roaming around my ship."

"Oh father, he is just a boy."

"And you are just a girl."

"I am not, I am a galleys mate," Kathryn said proudly.

Roth could not help but smile and said, "See that you keep it that way *galleys mate*. Now I think it would be wise for you to find your berth and get a proper night's sleep. Tomorrow will be a very long day and you will not find a lot of time for rest until we reach the Far East. I am goin' to remain here until my relief comes from ashore and then I will get some rest also."

Kathryn would not be that easily dismissed. She could not help but wonder why she had never been able to go to sea with him before and now would be as good a time as ever to discuss it with him. Roth noticed his daughter's hesitation to leave. "What are you thinkin' about so deeply? Are you not tired?"

"Yes father, I am a bit weary, but I have questions that only you can answer. Father, why was I never taken with before? It does not appear to me that this could be so dangerous for a younger person. Sometimes I cried with so much longing for you while you were gone. I had neither you nor my mother and many times I just felt so alone. Gramma Beth was very loving and very caring of me and I loved her dearly, but nothing could compare with the love that I felt for you. I never felt the love of my mother, which made you even more precious to me. Father, please do not ever leave me alone again. I do not think that I could stand the loneliness that I felt again."

Roth looked at his daughter and felt the warmth of love and guilt at the same time. It was like no other feeling he had ever felt before. It took a few moments for him to be able to speak. "My darlin', I know that it was a very difficult situation for you to be in. If there were anythin' that I could do to erase it, I would. You should know some things. While your mother was carrying you, she was excited about loving you. It was the happiest time of her short life. You are a symbol of the love we shared, being a part of both of us. Beth told me that your mother held you and kissed you on your cheek and expressed her love to you before she passed on. She had also made Beth promise that I would know, so that I could tell you someday when the time was right and you were old enough to understand. She said she would always be with you." Roth, trying very hard to hold back his emotions, took his daughters hand in his and said, "I never felt that I had left you completely alone. I knew she was there and you were bein' watched over."

Kathryn held her father's hand tightly and quietly sobbed, "Father, I think now that I was given my life by two of the most prefect parents a child could ever have hoped for. In addition, I am beginning to understand why it was that you were reluctant to take me along with you and possibly place me in harm's way. Most of my questions have been answered and I am so happy that you and I could share this time in our lives together now."

Roth, pulling himself together, patted her on her shoulder and said, "Now my young darlin', you are off to bed." He smiled and gave her a kiss on the forehead.

"All right father," Kathryn said as they broke from their hug, "I do hope that your relief can stand watch so you can also get some rest," she said. Kathryn reached for her father once again and said, "Don't worry father, everything will turn out all right, you will see." With that, she turned and made her way back to her cabin.

Roth watched her go and thought about how much she meant to him and how it would affect him if anything were to happen to her. He repressed those thoughts almost as soon as they entered his head.

That was no way to be thinking the night before he was to start a rather hazardous voyage. No, it was no way to be thinking at all.

Kathryn was awakened by the sounds of activity above her. It was not yet dawn and men were already moving about the decks preparing for departure. She hurriedly dressed and made her way to the galley to help Robert prepare the morning meal. Upon entering, she found Robert already at work.

"Ah Katie, you finally be risen' huh. Well, you get on outta here and go watch the sights on deck. I would be venturin' a guess that you have never seen a sailin' ship depart from onboard afore. Now you be gettin' on up there afore it is too late. I can handle the cookin' alone one more time I be thinkin' and you can return after we clear the port," Robert said as he gently pushed her out the door.

"Thank you Robert, you are right, I was hoping that I would be able to be on deck when we left. I will return as soon as we start to make way." Kathryn really needed no help to leave her duties, she was as excited as any fourteen-year-old would be, starting out on the biggest adventure of her short life.

When she got to the main deck, she saw that it was starting to get lighter in the East and men were already climbing the rigging and starting to unfurl the topmast sails. She turned towards the wheel deck and saw her father there, deep in conversation with Lord Creed and Raynerd. Her father did not look very happy and Creed was doing most of the talking. Kathryn hesitantly moved to her father's side. Roth was taken by surprise. He was not expecting her. He turned and gave her a hug and with a grin, he interjected, "My lord, if I may, I would like to introduce my daughter, Kathryn,"

"So, this is the young whelp that has caused all the trouble these last few days. Well see to it that you do not shirk your duties, there will be no free passengers on my ships." Creed, whose eyes were level with Kathryn is, turned to glare at the child and was surprised to see her glaring back at him with the same look of disdain and contempt he would expect to see from her father.

"You need not worry about my daughter, my lord, she knows her place and is familiar with her duties," Roth stated, barely able to keep his anger under control.

"Well see that she does and see that she does not interfere with your duties to my ship."

"Yes m'lord. Now if you would please depart the ship, I can get underway before we lose the tide."

"Yes captain, you are right, the sooner you leave, the sooner you will return." Creed said no more as he and Raynerd walked across the wheel deck and climbed down the stairs only to be confronted with the fact that the crew had already raised and stored the gangplank away. The only way off the ship was by a rope ladder hanging over the side. Three sailors were required to help Creed over the side and down to the dock. Creed shot Roth a look of pure hatred just before his head disappeared over the side. Roth looked down at his first mate and found him looking back and smiling. He was sure that Berkshire had planned it so that the gangplank would not be available for use and the two men would have to climb off the ship, much to their discomfort. Roth hated those two and did not care that Berkshire had done what he did, he only wished that he had thought of it first.

As soon as Roth saw the two men walking away from *his* ship, he called, "Mister Berkshire, rig up the towing rope and lower the longboat." Roth could wait no longer to get away from the one man he despised the most. "Make ready to cast off the bow line." Roth could see the men lowering the longboat into the water and the other sailors ready to operate it when it reached the water.

When the longboat was in the water and the men aboard, it was not long before they had rowed out far enough to completely take up the slack in the towline, "Cast off the bow line," Roth called out to his first mate. Men were already throwing off the heavy rope securing the bow of the *Galaunt* to the docks when Kathryn turned her sight from the longboat to watch his orders being carried out. The men in the longboat started to haul heavily on their oars, slowly pulling the great bow of the ship away from the dock. She was amazed at the awesome show of strength that allowed only eight men in a longboat to move such a large ship as the *Galaunt*. "Prepare to cast off the stern line and prepare to lower the topsails," she heard her father order. Kathryn watched as the men in the rigging slowly made their way out across the yardarms to take up the positions to unfurl the sails. When the ship had turned just enough to clear the dock Roth called out, "Cast off the stern line and lower the topsails." Kathryn felt the sudden forward movement of the ship, as it was finally free of its fetters securing it firmly to the dock and the wind caught in the sails. "Mister Berkshire, secure the tow line and retrieve the long boat so that we may make our way to the channel."

"Aye, aye Cap'n," Berkshire turned to the men standing alongside him and said, "You heard the Cap'n, haul in that line. You men," he called to the sailors, "standing along the port rail. Catch that longboat the first time or you will be swimmin' after it and haulin' it back to the ship and be quick about gettin' her on board."

Kathryn had not left her father's side since coming above deck and was now proudly standing alongside him at the fore rail of the wheel deck. She could hear the cries of the people standing on the docks calling out their best wishes for the voyage and occasionally above the din, she would hear a last farewell from a loved one. Kathryn remembered how many times over the years that she had been one of them, but now she was part of the crew leaving others behind and was anxiously wondering what it was going to be like to finally be on the open seas, sailing with her father.

Kathryn looked down on the deck and saw that the crew had retrieved the longboat and were carrying it across the deck to secure it tightly to a loading hatch mid ship.

"Mister Berkshire," he called out. "Release the jib and prepare to lower all sails." Kathryn heard Berkshire relaying his commands to the men on the bow and to the men in the rigging. Roth turned to see how far they had progressed from the dock and found that they were too far to be heard from the shore anymore. Passing the *Royale*, which was anchored, in the harbor, Kathryn saw Connery standing on the wheel deck of his ship and noticed that neither man acknowledged the other as the *Galaunt* made her way out into the channel of the river on her way to the sea. "Lower all sails," Roth called and turned to his daughter. "The show is over young darlin', it is time for you to get back to your duties."

"Oh father, can I just stay up here until we reach the ocean?" Kathryn inquired as she watched the men moving from one yard to the other, untying the cords that were securing the bundled canvas to the yards. She watched as all the great sails caught the wind and caused the ship to gather more speed as she plowed her way through the water.

Roth turned to look down at his daughter and said with a smile, "The ship is under way now and all hands are required to perform their assigned duties."

Knowing that her father was right, she scowled and sighed, "All right father." Kathryn left the wheel deck, but before going below deck to the galley, she turned and took a last long look at her father. It was this vision of him standing proudly, with a look of confidence, on the wheel deck, with his hands resting lightly upon the rail and his hair streaming out behind him in the wind, that Kathryn took with her as she went below to the galley.

Chapter 6
"Storm"

After several days at sea, Kathryn was beginning to find that her life was becoming routine. With the help of Brian, she had explored every nook and cranny of the great ship. Brian, she had found, knew quite a bit about sailing ships and it was not long before she earned his trust enough for him to tell her about himself. He was fourteen and been serving as a cabin boy since he was eight. His parents had died and Brian found himself in an orphanage run by a pair of old unmarried women, whom obviously did not like children. They would often hire out the orphans to the local townspeople to do the jobs around their homes that they deemed unworthy of themselves. They would tolerate nothing from their charges and dealt out punishment for the most minor of infractions. Brian hated it there and was often the focus of their contempt for the children. On one particular night, Brian was accused of stealing a broach from one of the old women. They whipped Brian for a very long time in front of the other children as was their fashion, but Brian would not confess to the theft. When the women saw that Brian could not take much more punishment, they locked him in a closet. Brian knew that after they had rested, they would resume the beatings until he confessed. He had not stolen the broach so he had nothing to confess too. During the night, he heard the distinct sound of the door being unlocked but it was not opened. Brian was very afraid and did not move for a long time. Finally, he gained enough courage to try the door to see what would happen. He was not really surprised to find it unlocked. He cautiously pushed it open until he had a clear view of the room beyond. There was no one there. Brian crept out of the closet, up the stairs, past the old women's room and quietly entered his own room that he shared with over a dozen other young boys like himself. Moving as quietly as he could, he made his way to the small area of the room to which he was assigned. He was just starting to gather his things when the old women burst into the room and one of them cried, "Ah ha, I knew that you would lead us to the broach."

Brian turned and yelled back at them, "I did not steal your broach!" Then as quickly as he could he grabbed the small bag that contained his meager possessions and ran to the other end of the room.

"You have no place to run boy, give us the broach and we will let you go to bed," cried the larger of the two women.

"I do not have the broach!" Brian retorted almost pleadingly.

"Just give it to us and we will forget about the whole thing," one said as they both started to advance across the room. Brian let them get within a few feet of him before turning, took up the pitcher on the table against the wall, and flung it as hard as he could at the nearer of the two. Seeing what was happening, she threw herself against the other woman and both went down in a heap. Brian seized this opportunity and ran down the aisle between the beds and out the door. He knew that the old women would not be able to catch him now if he could just keep on running. Therefore, that is what he did. He ran until the first light of morning started to show along the horizon. Tired, he sat down and leaned up against a big tree by the side of the road. He thought that he was probably safe and soon fell asleep.

When he awoke, he found himself lying in the back of a long wagon, covered with a warm blanket. There were two other small children in the back with him and he saw that there was a man and a woman riding on the seat in front. "He's awake, Mum!" the elder of the two children said.

Brian, squinting from the glare of the sun in his blackened eyes asked, in almost a whisper, "Where am I? Who are you?"

"Oh, thank goodness. For a while there, I thought maybe the beating you had received did more harm than I thought. You have been asleep for two days now. Can you tell me your name and what happened to you?" the woman said as she climbed into the back to examine him. Brian slowly began to tell her the story but was not sure of who she was yet. "It is just as I thought, did I not tell you George that this little boy was an orphan and those two crazy old bats up at that home had done this to him? Did I not tell you that?" Turning her attention back to Brian, she patted him on his forehead and brushing his hair back, continued, "There, there now, you just rest here in the wagon, we are not going to take you back there." Brian felt comfort in those words. "We are going to Liverpool. George here is a carpenter, and there will be good work for us there."

Brain traveled with the family for four days before they sighted the river and the town of Liverpool with its great docks and wharfs. George soon found work and moved his family, including Brian, into a small cottage near his place of work. Brian loved it there. He would spend his days down at the docks, looking at the great ships and watching as the men working there, toiled in their jobs of loading and unloading cargo. It was not long before a man approached him one day and asked him if he would like to sail on one of the ships someday. Brian told him yes because he could not think of anything he would rather do. The man asked him if he would like to become a cabin boy. Brain knew what cabin boys did and knowing that they went with the ship to sea replied with an ecstatic, "Yes!" The man was happy to see his excitement, then told him that there was a ship sailing in the morning and that the cabin boy had taken ill, so they were trying to find a boy that was willing to take his place. Brian told him he was willing, so the man told him to go home and if he got his parents' permission then he could join the ship. Brian told him that he was an orphan and had no parents. The man replied, "If that be the case, then go be gettin' your things and meet me at this ship and I will be bringin' you afore the Cap'n." Brain ran all the way to the cottage and while he was gathering his things, he told George and his wife what had happened. Times were hard right now and it was not easy to feed an extra mouth so they did not try to dissuade him. They expressed their concern about his desire to go to sea at such a tender age but told him that he would be missed and never forgotten and, in the end, even encouraged him to go safety. Brain thanked them for all they had done for him and ran out the door back to the docks where the man was waiting for him. He followed the man to a ship that was crowded with men doing final tasks to make ready for sail. They boarded the ship and the man introduced him to a tall rugged looking man with wavy black hair and the bluest eyes he had ever seen. "So, this is the boy you told me about? Well, he looks like he is fit enough for a cabin boy. Alright, I will take him to the Cap'n."

This new man led him astern of the ship and to a cabin where he knocked on the door. Brian heard someone behind the door bellow, "Enter." They both walked into the cabin and Brian saw a man sitting behind a desk. This man was not quite as large as the man that led him here. "Mister Roth, is this the new cabin boy that you have brought to me?" the man asked briskly.

"Cap'n, this is the new boy that was sent to replace Billy," Roth replied.

The captain stood and walked around the desk and looking down at Brian inquired in the same brisk tone, "So, you want to be a cabin boy huh? You know that it will not be easy." Brian was very nervous being around such big men, especially the big one with the blue eyes, and could do nothing but nod his head yes. "Very well then, Roth, I am making it your responsibility to take this young lad and teach him the duties he is expected to perform."

It was then that he was taken under her father's wing and taught everything that he knew now. When her father was promoted to Captain and given his own ship, Brian had begged to be taken along, Captain Roth agreed and Brian had been on this ship since.

Kathryn loved Brian's story and dreamed at night how it would have been if she had been the one chosen to be the cabin boy instead of Brian. She was alone now with her thoughts in her favorite place. Her favorite place was the bow. Here she could watch the dolphins, when they would suddenly appear, riding the wake of the ship and jumping in and out of the water making their peculiar sounds that she had began to imagine being directed at her. Sometimes one that she recognized by a long scar down its side, would rise out of the water on its tail and move backwards away from the ship chattering the whole time. It was as if it was inviting her to join them in their play. She wondered what it would be like to be able to swim as they did and what they were saying and if indeed, they were trying to talk to her.

The weather had remained calm for the most part. They had experienced a few rain showers and the wind had come up strongly on one occasion and tossed the ship around angrily, this had caused Kathryn to pay a visit to the railing. She had never been seasick, as one of the crew had told her about before and she hoped that it would not be like that for the entire voyage. Finally, over the days, the sickness passed and she gained her sea legs. This was not anything like she had experienced before sailing around the river and occasionally out to sea in her small craft that she had learned to sail. The *Galaunt* was a great ship of the sea. She rode across the water with her bow sending great sprays of mist over her decks into the faces of the crew as they worked on deck. The wind in her sails made the canvas pop as it changed intensity and the ropes were constantly singing with vibration from the tension.

Kathryn had not realized how far it was from England to the Cape and was beginning to wonder if they would ever get there. Her father had told her that they were halfway there when they had begun to round the great bulge of Africa. That had been several weeks ago. Yesterday she had overheard some of the crew saying that they would be in the southern waters of the Cape in just a few more days. She was getting excited to see that part of the ocean and knew that it was the most dangerous part of the voyage. She would be glad when it was over.

The closer they got to the Cape the colder it was becoming. Kathryn needed to don a jacket whenever she made her daily trek topside to enjoy the fresh salty air. The weather was also starting to change. The rain was coming more often and the wind was getting more intense. Clouds blocked the sun more often than not and she was beginning to miss the warmth that it had created. She could sense the foreboding in the crew as they neared the passage around the Cape. These men had been there before and knew that even in the summer this was not a place to be lax in their duties. They were always checking something to make sure that things were just right aboard ship and all lines and ropes were tight and secure, but now they were being extremely cautious.

It was on the bow that she stood when her father came up behind her and said, "Tomorrow we will be startin' to round the southern tip of Africa and the Cape of Good Hope. I will be glad when this part of the trip is behind us. It seems to me like the weather will indeed hold long enough for us to make the passage and then it will be smooth sailin' up the eastern shores of the continent to the islands of the Far East."

"I will be glad when this part of the trip is over also. The men are starting to get nervous about it and it is starting to make me a little worried too," she said with a concerned look as she turned towards, her father. "Father, do you foresee any problems?"

"If the weather does indeed hold, then it will be a simple task to make our way around the Cape into the safer waters of the Indian Ocean," he said reassuringly and took hold of her with the hopes of providing what warmth and assurance he could give to her.

The next day they changed their course to east by southeast and started their way around the Cape. As the days progressed and the weather held, they were beginning to think that they were going to have a safe passage after all. That night they went to bed thinking that the worst was over. The next morning, however, it was obvious that the weather was due for a change. The clouds ahead were becoming much darker and lower in the southern skies. Occasional flashes of lightning could also be seen as if they were sparking from inside the darkest of the clouds.

It was towards evening that Berkshire made his way to the wheel deck to speak to Captain Roth. "Have you takin' notice of the storm buildin' to the south of us? It looks also like there is another growin' in our path to the east."

"Aye, that I have Mister Berkshire. The one in front of us seems to be moving straight at us and could meet up with the other sometime tonight. With any luck, we will be able to sail through the one in front of us afore they can combine. That one out there to the south looks like it could be growin' into a major blow," Roth said.

"That is luck that I do not think that we will be a havin' sir. Those storms will be upon us afore the night passes and I do be thinkin' that ye are right in assumin' that we are in for a very stormy night! I think it would be wise to secure the ship for stormy weather before we set the sails for the night," Berkshire stated, knowing in his mind that his captain would also be entertaining the same thoughts.

"Aye Mister Berkshire, these are my thoughts also. Have the men make sure that everythin' is fastened down securely while there is light enough to see what they are doin'. Also see to the holds to make sure that there will no shifting of cargo and nothin' will come loose during the night," Roth returned. "One more thing if you will. Stop by the galley and ask Kathryn if she would join me after she has finished with her duties. I would like to have a few words with her before the storms are upon us." Roth added.

"I will be headin' in that direction to check below decks right after I get the men movin' with securin' things topside. I will be glad for an excuse to grab a mouthful of somethin' to chew on," he said with a grin. "I will gladly relay that message for you Cap'n. I can understand your worry for the young lass and it will be good for you and her to spend some time together."

Roth watched as his first mate descended the steps to the main deck where he began shouting orders to the men working there. His thoughts were indeed on the approaching storms and he knew that they would be assailing his ship in just a few short hours. He had been through many storms, but for some reason, this time he had more worries than he thought were justified. What was it that was gnawing at his heart? His was a good ship, manned by a very good crew that knew their business well. He could not quite place his finger on it, but he felt in his heart that something was going to happen that could change his life forever. He had felt those feelings of foreboding when he was talking to Creed about the voyage and then again that first night out. He could not help but wonder if he was being apprehensive and overly concerned because of the fact that his daughter was now aboard. He could only hope that this was the cause.

The *Galaunt* made very good time the remainder of the day. The winds were building and the crew kept the sails trimmed to get the very best possible speed out of their ship.

Just after nightfall, the eastern storm hit. With it came stronger winds and a heavy downpour of rain. Just as Roth had figured, it was nothing to cause great alarm. The swells had risen to about ten feet and Roth had ordered the crew to rig the ship for foul weather.

Kathryn had finished her chores for the night and decided to go topside to see what it was that her father wanted to talk to her about. She donned her heavy oilskin coat, made her way to the wheel deck, and found her father in conversation with Mister Berkshire. She liked the salty old first mate. He had first made her feel like a real member of the crew. She remembered the first day that she had come aboard. Her father had introduced her to Mister Berkshire. It was the first time that they had met in person but not the first time that she had seen him, for he had been at Beth's funeral, and her father had been telling her about him for many years now. She had always pictured him just as she was now seeing him and felt as if she had known him all of her life. She stood almost at attention as she watched him look her up and down for a few moments. Scratching his head, he said, "Looks a might bit on the scrawny side for a sailor, but I be thinkin' that after a few months at sea she will put on some muscle." He had said teasingly. "We might just as well get started. Grab that box and take it with you on your way to the galley, Pots has been hollerin' for it all day." It had taken her completely by surprise, she had thought that she would get a chance to look around the ship before she had to start work, so she ran over and picked up the box and moved off towards the bow. "Where do you think you are a goin with that box sailor? You plannin' to throw that box off the bow or are you just practicin' for when you go flyin' off? The galley is that way," he said pointing over his shoulder. Turning red as she heard the men on the deck start to laugh, she turned and started in the direction he was pointing. "Oh my, where is it that you be a findin' them Cap'n?" he said with a twinkle in his eye. "I guess I had better be a showin' this new hand where the galley is afore she gets herself lost and we all must spend the rest of the day findin' her. Follow me young lass!" She meekly followed with her head hung low trying to hide the embarrassment she was feeling now. The man that she thought she knew was a kind, good man that would not treat anyone the way he had just treated her. Her father had just stood there and not said a word in her defense. Maybe it had not been a good idea to want to follow her father after all. They made their way to the galley where a big heavy man took the box from her and shoved it under a shelf where it was obviously kept. Mister Berkshire introduced her to the man, it turned out that this was the cook. "Let me introduce you to your new helper Pots. Her name is Kathryn and from what I hear, she will soon be a teachin' you how to cook," he said with a broad smile.

Pots laughed and held out his hand and said, "Glad to make your acquaintance young matey. I could sure be usin' the help tryin' to keep this lot of misfits and pirates fed. Maybe with you on board they will be findin' someone new to complain to about the food," he said as he warmly shook her hand.

Mister Berkshire then added, "Take it easy on her and let her work into her duties slowly until she gets used to being on board." Kathryn remembered bursting out and saying in a very defiant tone, "I am very capable of being able to carry my own load if you don't mind." Both men had just stood there looking at each other until they could contain it no longer and broke down in a very hearty laughing spell. Finally, it was Berkshire that first was able to speak, "Aye matey, seein' as who you are, there is no doubt about that, but still, let's be takin' things lightly for a short while until you become a little more familiar with the ship and the men aboard her. There will be time enough to show your worth, and there be nothin' you be havin' to prove to me. You are goin' to make a fine sailor and if you be listenin' to me and ol' Pots here, you will be learnin' your duties in no time." She now saw the man that she had come to know and realized that this was just his way of making her feel like part of the crew. In fact, she had become fond of Berkshire and Pot's. A slight smile appeared upon her face as she recalled these memories.

Her father finished talking to Mister Berkshire, turned to her, and said, "We are in for some very rough weather tonight and I want you to stay in your cabin until it is over."

"But father, I have been in storms before, why can't I stay up here with you?"

"This is not going to be a storm that you would want to be up here in, trust me," he said over the growing howl of the wind.

"I will be alright and if it gets too bad, I will go to my cabin," she replied.

Roth turned squarely towards her, bent down to look directly into her face, and sternly said, "You will go to your cabin young lady and you will go to your cabin right now. I am going to have enough to worry about tonight without havin' to worry about you also. Now, without another word, I will see you in the mornin' after we pass through this storm."

Kathryn turned and started to run from the wheel deck to her cabin when her father caught her by the shoulder and turned her around to face him. "Kathryn, I am sorry for the way I just spoke to you but you must realize that I worry about you so much that sometimes I just get a little overprotective when it comes to you. The storm that we are goin' to have to sail into tonight is as bad a storm as I have ever seen and believe me, I have seen my share. What we are getting' hit with now is nothin' compared to what we will experience as soon as the storm that is movin' towards us from the south meets up with this storm here. I know that I overreacted before but you must trust me when I tell you that it will be better for you to stay in your cabin until it is over. So, please be my good girl and do what your father asks," her father pleaded, pulling her close to give her a warm hug.

Kathryn returned the hug thinking of how very lucky she was to have a father that loved her so completely. She spoke softly, "Alright father, I will do as you say." She moved away from him, descended the stairway leading from the wheel deck to the main deck, and turned to enter the hallway that led to her cabin. Her father had never spoken to her so harshly and it had frightened her. What had come over him? Was this storm really going to be as bad as he had said? First, she was frightened, not only by how her father had treated her, but also from what this night could possibly bring. She had come to accept that her father's actions had stemmed from his love and concern. She held this thought until she fell off to sleep.

Just before midnight, the two storms met. Conditions changed almost immediately, producing gale force winds and waves of over 25 feet. The helmsman had to fight very hard to keep the *Galaunt* sailing into the now swiftly changing winds. The wind and the waves wanted to move the ship in every direction and tossed it about, seemingly from wave crest to wave crest, as if it were no more than a mere feather being blown around by a small breeze. The clouds were pitch black and very low in the sky. The only time Roth could distinguish between the clouds and the sea was when lightning lit up the night sky or when a particularly large wave broke near them, sending out a phosphorus mist that temporarily outlined the waves' crest. The sea was an angry black boiling mass. Waves were constantly crashing against each other throwing up great amounts of mist making the very air that the sailors were breathing, thick and moist. The *Galaunt* was holding its own so far. Roth had long ago sent for another helmsman and the two together were able to maintain a somewhat steady course.

"I am wonderin' sir, if you think that other storm will ever get here? This night is turnin' out to be dull. I am thinkin' maybe I will be turnin' in for the night," Berkshire yelled facetiously almost directly into Roth's ear, to be heard above the howl of the winds.

"I am not agreein' with you there. I think maybe, we are in for a very long night," Roth answered smiling, knowing that this was how Berkshire hid his concerns. Just then, a rather large wave broke over their heads, soaking both of them to the skin.

"You may be right there Cap'n," Berkshire said laughing between coughs and shaking what water he could from his clothes, simply to be soaked again as another wave broke over the ship.

Roth yelled over the loud sounds of the storm and said, "I do not think I will be goin' to my cabin any time soon." Both men broke out into boisterous laughter.

The wave that had just soaked her father rolled the ship to starboard and tossed Kathryn from her bed. She found herself lying on the floor wondering where she was. After realizing she had been tossed from her bed, she became aware of the tossing about of the ship. She climbed back onto her bed and had to hold on to prevent herself from being tossed to the floor again. Her father had been right, this was indeed the worst storm that she had experienced and was quickly becoming fearful of the night and being alone.

It was not long before she could not stand it any longer and decided that she had to be with her father. She stood and finding that she still had her clothes and coat on and opened the door. Brian was just passing her cabin door at that moment and she saw that he had apparently just come in from the storm. He was dripping large amounts of water along the way and he looked to be soaked through. He turned and looked at her and asked, "Where is it that you be goin' Katie?"

"I am going up to the wheel deck to be with my father. I am afraid and tired of being alone," she said as she made her way for the door.

"Hold on there a minute," he said grabbing at her coat. "You don't want to be out there, it is very dangerous out there!"

She turned to him and pushed him away. "You were just out there and you are all right. I am going to find my father and you are not going to stop me!" she said, opening the door and running out.

She was immediately blasted in the face with an icy cold wind and thrown back against the still open door. Brian caught hold of her shoulder and steadied her against the wind. She shrugged herself away and moved towards the stairway holding tightly onto a safety line that had been rigged earlier in the day. As she neared the stairway, she could see from the numerous lightning flashes, the roiling seas in front of her. She was amazed at what she was seeing. She had never seen waves like these before. She was witnessing and feeling as the ship climbed up to the crest of a wave and then felt the ship teeter just as it tilted to make its way down to the bottom of the trough. She nearly lost hold of her grip on the safety line. Climbing the stairs to the wheel deck was a chore, even with the help of Brian, who had followed her into the night. The wind was threatening to blow her over the side and the waves were slamming into her at every step. When they finally managed to reach the wheel deck, they were noticed immediately by her father and Mister Berkshire who came rushing over to them, giving them the support they needed to get to the railing and hold on.

"What are you two doin' up here?" Roth demanded. "Kathryn, I thought I told you to stay in your cabin until mornin'! As for you, lad, I thought you had more sense than to expose my daughter to these kinds of danger. What is it you have to say for yourself?" He asked, bending down to be heard by both of them.

"It was not Brian's fault father. I was scared and afraid of being in my room alone and wanted to be with you. Brian tried to stop me but I was determined to be here so he just helped me," she replied.

"Well, you cannot stay here. It is too dangerous for you to be here. I will have Brian take you both down to your cabin and Brian will stay with you so that you do not have to be alone. You do as I say!" he declared sternly.

"Father, I don't want to be away from you! Please let me stay," she pleaded.

"I cannot do that Kathryn, please understand that I am only thinkin' of your welfare and demand that you do as I ask," he said. He turned to his cabin boy and said, "Brian, see to it that Kathryn is returned to her cabin and do not leave her until you are ordered otherwise."

"Yes sir," he said as he took Kathryn by the arm and led her across the railing to the stairway.

They had just reached the bottom of the stairway when a gigantic wave slammed into the ship broadside. The ship rolled precariously over onto her port side engulfing both of them underwater. As the ship righted, Kathryn found herself alone on deck. She anxiously looked around and saw Brian over the side, desperately clinging onto the railing, trying to keep from plunging into the churning waters below. Kathryn moved to the railing and reached out to grab for him but found him to be just beyond her reach. She stood and looked around and saw a rope coiled not far from where she was standing. She made a move for it just as another wave crashed into the side of the ship causing her to lose her footing and she was catapulted over the side. Kathryn cried out to her father as she was falling but her words were drowned out by the noise of the winds. She fell directly onto Brian, knocking his head against the side of the ship and both of them fell into the sea below.

When she returned to the surface, she saw that the ship had moved past her. She looked around and saw Brian not too far off to her left. Brian saw her at about that same time and started to swim towards her. Another massive wave passed between them and when it had cleared, Kathryn saw that Brian had been washed almost out of her sight. Kathryn tried calling out to him, but knew that it was no use, the storm was making far too much noise for her to be heard. Kathryn was quickly tiring and was having trouble staying afloat because of her water soaked clothing. She fought to keep her head above the water and during her struggle, she thought of the pendant that her father had given her. With one hand, she took hold of it and brought it to her face remembering the words her father had said about the legend behind it. She remembered how he had told her that this pendant would protect sailors from the sea. She grasped it tightly and found comfort in its feel as she slowly lost consciousness and slipped beneath the surface of the water.

When she regained consciousness, she realized that she was still alive, but well under the surface of the water. She kicked frantically to the surface and immediately started to look around for the ship and for her friend Brian. She could see no sign of the ship but she finally saw Brian about forty feet away from her struggling to keep himself above the surface of the heavy sea. Kathryn started to swim over to him just as he started to sink into the ocean. She dove after him and was surprised at how easy it seemed that she was able to get to him before he had a chance to sink very far. She grabbed a hold of his collar and hauled him back to the surface. He was unconscious but he was breathing and she was very glad about that. Kathryn spotted a large floating object and proceeded to drag Brian towards it. When she got to it, she found it to be a wooden hatch cover that had apparently been washed overboard from the *Galaunt* the same time that they were. She struggled but finally managed to place ab on the top of it. She clung desperately to the hatch cover, not having enough strength to pull herself up to join Brian and soon found herself falling asleep with fatigue.

She was rudely awakened with Brian kicking and trying to push her away from the hatch cover. She saw that it was morning and could not understand why Brian was kicking at her as he was. She yelled at him to stop and saw Brian open his eyes wide. "Get away from me you monster," he yelled. Brian was terrified at what he was seeing.

Kathryn did not know why he was reacting this way and asked him what was wrong. Brian moved back away from her and said, "What are you? What do you want? I have never before seen anything like you." Thrashing at her with his feet, he cried out, "Get away from me!" He crawled to the far side of the cover and curled into a fetal position trying to protect himself from her.

She made a grab for him and that is when she saw her hand. It was gray in color and she could see that her arm was gray also. She was somewhat terrified herself. As she looked behind her, she saw that she had a tail like a fish but not like any fish, she had seen before. Her tail was long and slender and its color was iridescent. It seemed to glow with a luminous rainbow of colors in the early morning sunlight. Actually, she thought it to be very pretty. It looked very muscular and she realized that this was why she had been able to swim so effortlessly. She turned back to Brian and understood now why he was acting so strangely towards her. She thought to herself, 'How am I going to make him know who I am if he will not listen to me?' It was then that she thought of the pendant. Reaching down she took hold of it and brought it out of the water. She stared at the pendant and realized that she had taken the form it represented. She remembered now what the legend said. It had said that no sailor would drown as long as this pendant protected the wearer. She was not a sailor, yet she had been transformed into that form which the pendant represented. She recalled her father telling her that the presence of this strange being was the protector of all men at sea. "Could that really be?' she questioned to herself. 'Am I now the protector?' Regaining her thoughts she turned back to Brain and found that he had lapsed back into a sleep, she brushed his hair back out of his face and felt comfort in the knowledge that he would all right.

Kathryn suddenly realized that she was no longer human and felt remorse in the knowledge that her father had lost his daughter, the only family that he had. She only wished that she could be there at his side. While thinking this, she realized that she too, would never be able to be with her father and she began to feel the same loss that she felt when her gramma died. The thought of never being able to be with her father again was almost overbearing and she was consumed with grief.

Kathryn suddenly let out a long sorrowful sound, a sound very similar to a moaning wail. For some odd reason she felt compelled to look at her pendant again. It was as though she was having an awakening. 'I am going to be able to be with my father at all times. I am no longer a frail daughter that he must constantly protect. I can protect him now, all the days of his life,' she thought. She wondered how she was going to be of help to him. Her heart filled with joy as she thought of the many ways, she may be able too, hoping that she could be there at the right time. 'I am now the Mermaid, the one my father spoke so fondly about. I am a creature of the sea now and cannot survive on land. It would be better for father to think that I was gone and had indeed drowned, rather than know that I was alive in this form. If he knew I was alive somewhere in the sea, I would always be on his mind and he would spend the rest of his life looking for me.' She did not want to see her father suffer any more than he had too so she made up her mind that she would not let her father know.

The sea was calm now and the sun shown itself brightly above the surface, sending a golden glow through the waters. It was then that she realized that she was no longer alone in the water. The light now allowed her to see a dolphin behind her. It seemed strange to see one so close to her. She had always enjoyed them from a distance. The dolphin started chattering to her excitedly and rose out of the water on its tail and she immediately knew that this dolphin was the one that had always seemed to invite her to play when she saw the long scar down its side. She spoke to the dolphin, but was not surprised, when it did not answer her back. She did notice, however. That it seemed to be very excited. It was swimming around her, and the hatch cover, very quickly and would sometimes dive deep into the water and come back up to leap clear of the water and arch gracefully over both her and the cover that held Brian. The dolphin would come right up to her and chatter in her face and then turn and speed off only to return when it realized it was not being followed. It eventually gave up and soon swam off disappearing in the distance. Kathryn wished that there had of been some way that she could have communicated with the dolphin because she was increasingly becoming concerned that Brian would not last long out here alone. He had swallowed a lot of seawater and was beginning to cough and choke in his sleep. It would not be long before he would need something to drink. She began to look around and saw a barrel floating not too far off and swam over to see what it held. When she found it, she saw that it was floating almost straight up in the water. It was still covered so she could not see inside. It did, however, look like one of the many water barrels that could be found here and there on the deck that contained fresh water for the working crew. Perhaps it had been washed overboard by the same wave that had washed both her and Brian over the side. Kathryn pushed the barrel over to the hatch cover and tied it to the side with a piece of rope she found dangling from the cover. She dove back into the sea to see if she could find something that he could use to drink. Much to her dismay, she realized the waters were much too deep to recover any object and would take quite some time to find anything. She did not want to leave him that long. On her way back to Brian, she encountered a large school of tuna, upon seeing her they scattered but she managed to catch one of them and decided to take it back to him. Upon her return, she found Brian starting to rouse so she put the tuna on the hatch cover and dove back into the sea before he saw her. She surfaced not a long distance from the cover and continued to watch Brain to ensure that he would remain safe until her father could return.

Brian regained consciousness from time to time, but upon finding that he was alone, he concluded that he must have dreamed that he had seen the monster. 'It had to be a dream,' he said to himself, 'how could he have seen a monster like that, especially a monster that had talked to him?' Puzzling as that was to him, he is now aware that there was a rather large fish on the cover with him. He thought again to himself that this fish must have been what he had seen in a somewhat distorted vision. He then noticed that off to the side of the cover there was a barrel tied to it with a rope. Now this was odd, he could not remember doing that. Very weary at this point, Brian thoughts turned to Kathryn, the ship and the fact that he was on the open sea far from anywhere alone. Where was Kathryn? Could it be that he had failed in his mission and lost her. Where is the ship? The sun was almost blinding him and this made it very difficult to see anything because of the glare on the water. He found himself stressed and fearful. Would he ever be found? This was his last thought as he again slipped off into a deep sleep unaware that he was being watched under the thoughtful protection of Kathryn who had never really left him, but simply had just moved out of his sight where she could still watch over him.

Kathryn had thought that tuna had looked rather good. She could not understand why she had not taken one for herself as she now was finding herself rather hungry. Just then another dolphin appeared. This one seemed to be rather laid back compared to the first one. It started making chattering sounds as if it were trying to talk to her. Sometimes she thought she even understood what it was saying, but she soon dismissed that idea. She hoped that the ship or any ship for that matter, would be along soon and Brian would be rescued. She was finding herself anxious to explore in this new form she had. She glanced again at the dolphin and reached out to touch it. She was surprised to find that its skin was very soft and smooth. She stroked the top of its head only to find that it seemed to enjoy her touch and made almost a musical sound. She had heard these sounds as she had sat and watched them play from her spot on the bow. Remembering how it had seemed to her that they frolicking in the wake of the ship. She then felt a sense of warmth and a smile crossed her face.

Her thoughts now returned to Brian and she hoped that Brian would become aware enough to think about eating the fish and drink the water. She wanted so much for him to be safe. After all, she had now assumed the role of protector.

Chapter 7
"Search"

The next morning dawned clear and bright, the storm having passed during the night. Roth and Berkshire were still on the wheel deck, having spent the entire night there. "Mister Berkshire, maybe you had better conduct a thorough search of the ship and inspect for any damage we may have sustained during the night," Roth said without taking his eyes off the horizon. "I can see that we are missing a forward hatch cover, I wonder what else washed overboard last night."

"Aye Cap'n, I was thinkin' the same things myself. I would hate to think that we lost anything important. I will get right on the inspection, and if I may be so bold, you should go below and get some rest? I am thinkin' that I and the crew can handle this ship for a while without you standin' watch," Berkshire said with a twinkle in his eye, knowing his captain would not leave his post until he was sure that everything had survived the storm of last night.

"I think that I will stay here for a while longer until you have completed your inspection. Then I will check on my daughter before turnin' in for a short rest," he replied.

"Aye, Cap'n," Berkshire gave a crisp salute and moved off towards the stairs.

Roth watched as his first mate walked across the main deck looking up into the rigging, evidently seeing nothing that caused him great concern. Occasionally he would stop on the deck and inspect something, giving it a pull or a push to see if it was still secure. Towards the bow, Roth noticed, Berkshire stopped and looked all around before calling out to two crewmembers standing nearby. "You two there, come over here and secure these water barrels. It looks like maybe we lost one or two of them last night. No sense in leavin' the rest loose to roll around all day". The two crewmembers rushed over to where Berkshire was indicating and began to roll the loose barrels back to their spot along the starboard rail. Berkshire then stopped at the forward hold and looked around to check if maybe the hatch cover was somewhere nearby. Since it was not, he began checking the hatchway itself for damage. Satisfied that it was all right, he descended through the open hatch to begin his inspection below decks.

It was about an hour later that Roth saw Berkshire hurriedly ascending the stairs to the wheel deck. Rushing over to Roth, he excitedly said, "Cap'n, I just stopped by the galley and Pot's told me that Kathryn did not show up for her post this mornin' and asked if maybe she was a little under the weather after the storm last night. I stopped by her room, found it empty, so I went to look for Brian, and he is nowhere to be found either. I did not see either of them durin' my inspection. I think that maybe you should order a full inspection of the ship by all members of the crew and find them."

Roth's eyes widened with this report and the worst of thoughts swiftly entered his mind. "Mister Berkshire, rouse all members of the crew and let us begin the search immediately," he said as he rushed towards the stairway. Roth's first stop was his daughter's cabin, and indeed, it was empty. Rushing back out onto the main deck he saw that the crew was already gathering and Berkshire was issuing orders as to who would look where. Knowing that Berkshire would efficiently handle the search, Roth made his way down to the galley to speak to Pots. Finding him he asked, "When was the last time you saw Kathryn?"

"It was right after she finished cleanin' up after last night's dinner. She said that she had to hurry because you wanted her to report to you," he said drying off his hands with a small towel. "I have not seen her since. I figured that the storm had made her sick, so I did not go to roust her out of bed. I saw no cause for alarm because she is never late without a very good reason for it," he added.

Roth then told him about last night and added that she was not in her room.

"I will join the men right away sir and help with the search of the ship", Pot's said laying the towel down and rushing out of the galley.

Roth knew that this man was now deeply concerned for Kathryn's welfare because during this voyage they had become very close. Roth then went to Brian's quarters and finding nobody there, returned topside to find Berkshire.

Roth found him talking to a group of sailors near the bow. "Mister Berkshire, have they been found yet?" he asked while not wanting to hear the reply.

"I am sorry to tell you that they have not. These men have searched everywhere that a body could fit and have found nothin'," he said. Reluctant to add what he must say next, he uttered soberly, "I am afraid that maybe they were washed overboard last night."

Roth's heart sank at hearing those words, for that is just what he had been thinking. "Order the ship about, we will return to the spot where we last saw them aboard and begin a search there," he said, choking back the fear of what might have happened to the two of them.

"It will be a mighty task to get back there sir. We were blown all over the ocean last night, but if it is possible to find them, this crew will do everythin' it can to do so!" he stated and immediately called out the orders to turn the ship about and return to the area of where they were last seen.

Later that morning, Roth inquired as to their position. "Cap'n sir," Berkshire said, "as near as I can tell, this is where we were last night. I have men in all the nests scanning for Kathryn and Brian, but they have seen nothin' yet."

"Very well Mister Berkshire, have the men keep a sharp lookout, they are out there somewhere and we have to find them soon," Roth said sadly.

The ship sailed around all that day and not a sign of them was found. Roth was getting very tired but could not leave his post on the wheel deck. He was starting to blame himself for the loss of his daughter and nothing could take that feeling away from him.

It was just after sunrise the next morning that one of the lookouts called down to the deck that he could see sails on the horizon. Roth gave the order to steer the ship towards the oncoming ship.

Upon nearing the ship, Roth recognized it as the *Royale* commanded by Captain Connery. It was midday before both ships were within hailing distance of each other.

Captain Connery and Raynerd were ferried in their longboat over to the *Galaunt.* Raynerd was the first to speak. "Why are you still here Roth? You should be miles from here," he said with a scowl.

"We were caught in the storm two nights ago and my daughter and cabin boy appear to have been washed overboard. We are conductin' a search for them", Roth answered impatiently.

Raynerd looked at Roth and firmly stated, "If you have not found them by now, then it is unlikely that you will find them at all. You have a mission to perform. The loss of two crewmembers is not as important as the mission is. I suggest that you turn your ship around and get on with it."

Roth stared back at Raynerd with a look that made the other man cringe back a step or two. Roth stepped up to his face and retorted, "*Your* mission is not nearly as important as the lives of two of my crew, even *if* one was not my daughter! I still think they are worthy of every effort to find them. They may both still be alive out here and they must be found!"

Captain Connery stepped between the two men and confronted Roth, "We have both lost men at sea before and we both know that finding them is a fool's errand. If you have not found them by now, you will probably not find them at all. If they did not drown, then the sharks surely got them."

Roth made a lunge at Connery but was stopped by Berkshire as the first mate grabbed him around the shoulders. "We all know that if it came to a choice between your crew and your wealth, the men would be found wantin'. You have no regard for anyone other than yourself. I am surprised that your crew has not mutinied long before now. How can you call yourself a captain? You are nothing more than a slave driver," Berkshire said with an air of disdain and complete contempt for the captain of the *Royale.*

"You will die for that statement," Connery screamed as he reached to draw his sword.

Roth was quicker though and drew his sword to protect his friend. Upon seeing this, Connery turned to face the larger man and said, "My quarrel is not with you, but rather this insubordinate whelp you call a first mate".

"When you are on my ship, you will deal with me first," Roth said glaring at the smaller man he was facing.

Raynerd put his hand on Connery's arm, pushing his sword down towards the deck.

"Now, now gentlemen, this is not the time to be fighting amongst ourselves. We all have a mission to perform and I think that is what we should be getting back to," Raynerd said glaring at Roth.

Roth could not believe what he was hearing and thought to himself, 'Can these two not see that it is my daughter out there?' He then angrily addressed Raynerd, "You can return to your mission if you chose, but I and my crew are going to stay here until my daughter and cabin boy can be found. I will not leave this area until I am certain of their fate. Now get off my ship!" He turned to Berkshire and said, "Escort these men back to their longboat and see to it they leave immediately."

Connery and Raynerd were astounded by the tone of the captain's voice. Connery shot a glance around them noting that several crewmembers were present. He felt it better to save his anger for another time and proceeded to take his leave. Raynerd, however, not knowing how close he was to being thrown overboard by Roth, stated "Have it your way then Roth, but in mind that this mission is what we are here for and if you do not complete it you will pay dearly. And believe me when I say dearly."

Roth, barely able to control his temper, looked at Raynerd with a glare of contempt. He replied quietly but strongly, "Then so be it. Now take your leave."

It was then that Berkshire broke the spell of the moment saying, "Now if you, kind gentlemen will follow me, we have a search to get back to. If you are not going to help, then return to you ship and let us get back to it."

Connery could not believe what he had just heard. "Why you insubordinate little whelp!" he yelled. "I have had all that I am going to take from you."

With that, Connery's hand quickly moved to draw his sword, but again, it was Roth that was the quicker. His sword seemed to appear in his hand, as he swiftly laid its edge, not so lightly, on Connery's hand before he was able to draw his sword. "I think that I must agree with my first mate, it is time for you two to be leavin' and let us get back to *our* mission," he said as he slid his blade lightly over the back of Connery's hand, leaving a thin red line of blood from the cut he had imposed.

Connery, upon seeing the blood on his hand, yelled, "You will pay for this. Both of you will pay," he said in a low threatening voice.

Raynerd grabbed the shoulders of Connery and said, "This is neither the time nor the place. These two will pay, but for now we need them." Turning to glower at Roth, he followed with, "You can stay here and continue with your foolish search, if you wish, but always remember who is really in charge of this mission. I will grant you this day and this day only to search. If you have not found what you are looking for by the end of daylight today, then you will abandon this foolish purpose of yours and make the repairs to your ship that are required. Then you will make great haste to catch up with us before we reach the Islands. Do I make myself perfectly clear?"

"The only thing that you have made clear is your total disregard for anyone, or anything for that matter, except for wealth. Now, if you would excuse us," Roth said, pointing his still drawn sword at the side of the ship where their longboat was tied, while he continued to look Raynerd right in the eye.

Breaking eye contact, Raynerd turned, moving towards their boat, and said over his shoulder, "We will go now but remember what I said. It would be a grievous mistake for you not to heed my words."

"Oh, fear not, we will see each other again," Roth said menacingly as he watched the two men climb over the side of the ship to their boat and continued to watch as their crew rowed them back to the *Royale.*

Returning his attention to his first mate and seeming to calm down, he said, "Well Mister Berkshire, I think that we had better set sail and find our missin' crew."

"Aye, aye Cap'n," Berkshire said, and then he ordered the crew to set sail.

It was then that a crewman came up to them, saluted and said, "I beg your pardon sirs, but there is something up on the bow that I think you should come and see."

Mister Berkshire asked, "What is it?"

The sailor, feeling a little uncomfortable, said, "It is a dolphin sir, and it is actin' very strangely. I am thinkin' that you should come and see for yourselves."

He did not have to point out the dolphin, Roth saw it as soon as he reached the bow. The dolphin was racing in from the port quarter and stopped just before crashing headlong into the ship. It then rose up on its tail and swam backwards away from the ship on the same line chattering all the time. When it got almost out of sight, they watched it dive back into the water and race towards the ship again, where it once again stopped, rose on its tail and swam away.

"That is mighty peculiar if ye do not mind me sayin'. How long do you reckon it has been doin that?" Berkshire asked the crewmember.

"I have been a watchin' it since about the time you two and the other two," at which point the crewman broke out in a wide grin, "were havin' that quiet little conversation over yonder. It is almost like it is tryin' to tell us somethin'."

"I think that I might agree," Roth stated. "I have heard tales over the years of dolphins savin' shipwrecked sailors."

"I have heard the same tales Cap'n," interjected Berkshire. "Maybe it is trying to tell us to follow it."

"Well, seein' as how you may be right and seein' as it seems to want us to go in about the same direction as we were goin', I suggest that we follow it", Roth said flatly.

Berkshire did not even wait for further instructions before he was shouting out orders to follow the dolphin. The dolphin seeing that the ship was following leaped in the air and started to swim off in a very straight line.

Upon seeing that his orders were being carried out, Berkshire looked back to the sea before them when he heard his captain say very quietly, "Oh please, let it be so." He remained quiet as he thought the very same thoughts.

The ship sailed on this course throughout that day, with the dolphin swimming unwaveringly on the same line. It had slowed early on when it saw that the ship could not keep up to its fast pace. The men in the lofts had been told to keep an alert eye on the seas before them. Captain Roth, by now, was convinced that the dolphin was indeed leading them to what he hoped would be his daughter and Brian.

It was then that he heard from above, a shout. A crewmember was yelling to those below that he could see a dolphin leaping from the water over something floating beneath it. As Roth scanned around the seas before him, it seemed as if everyone on deck was moving towards the bow of the ship to see for themselves.

As they neared the site, Roth could now clearly see the dolphin, its silvery sides glistening in the afternoon twilight as it trailed a torrent of water that sparkled orange from the setting sun behind it. He could make out that there was indeed something floating on the water. It appeared to be the missing hatch cover with something, or someone, he was hoping, laying on it. Yet it appeared that if it was someone, it was only one.

As they drew nearer, Roth ordered the sails hoisted, bringing the ship to a standstill in the water. They could all see by now that it was a hatch cover and there was someone laying on it but they could not see whom. "Lower the boat", Roth ordered in a rather loud and excited voice.

The boat had no more than touched the water when Roth, Berkshire and four of the crew, boarded it and started rowing the short distance to the floating hatch cover, with Roth rowing hardest of all. They stopped rowing within oar distance and used the oars to pull the cover towards them. Roth reached out and turned the body over, seeing that it was Brian. Brian's eyes opened slightly as he murmured, "Katie, you are back." That was all he got out before he lost consciousness again. When Roth heard that, he was sure that his daughter was alive and here somewhere. "Kathryn," he began to call. "Kathryn where are you?" All the men in the long boat began to look around and as they were looking, they were all calling out Kathryn's name.

Berkshire, after several minutes, hesitantly spoke the words that no one wanted to hear, "Cap'n, it appears that she is not here. We would have seen her by now if she were, sir. We need to be lookin' after Brian here."

Roth knew that he was right, although it was very hard to admit to himself that his daughter was indeed lost to him. "You are right," he sadly admitted. Roth reached out with both hands, took Brian under the shoulders, and brought him into the boat, laying him gently on the bottom. It was then that he saw the swelling and bruises on Brian's forehead. To Berkshire, who was at the other end of the boat, he said, "Tie a line onto the cover and we will tow it back to the ship. And be quick about it, we need to get this lad back onboard."

While Berkshire was tying the hatch, Roth noticed that there was a large fish on it and a water barrel tied alongside. He thought this to be strange and wondered how Brian had been able to acquire these items. It was odd and the fish appeared whole. Lost in this train of thought, he was surprised when he heard Berkshire calling to a sailor from the other end of the longboat, "Are you havin' problems there matey?" Berkshire looked to be feeling very impatient at this time. "Have you a need of help?" Roth asked in a perplexed tone.

"No Cap'n, I am fine and ready. I was just ponderin' as to where this fish came from and how this barrel came to be tied to the cover. I will explain my thoughts when we get back aboard ship."

When they got back to the ship, a sling was lowered to bring Brian onboard. The four crewmembers scrambled up the side while Berkshire and Roth remained in the boat examining the cover. "It would appear from the condition of the boy that he was probably unconscious the whole time he was out there," Berkshire said. Roth said nothing and Berkshire continued, "I wonder how that barrel got tied up, and that tuna, where do you think it come from?"

"It would appear that someone else has been here. It had to have been Kathryn," Roth said.

"You are probably right," Berkshire said. Then he yelled out towards the sea, "Kathryn", but heard nothing in return except the sounds of the waves slapping softly against the side of the ship. "I hate to say this Cap'n, but if she was around, we would have seen or heard somethin' by now."

"I know that you are right, but I hate to think that she could be out there hopin' that I will come and save her." With that, Roth lowered his head away from his longtime friend and caught the sobs just in time.

Berkshire could hear Roth fighting to hold back the tears, so he rose and climbed up the side of the ship leaving Roth to his grief.

It was a while before Roth could regain his composure and was able to return to the deck of his ship. When he did, he noticed that the crew avoided looking him in the eye and they were all moving around with their heads bowed down. He knew that they were feeling the same as he, so he did not find any reason to say anything at that time. He made his way to Brian's bunk, knowing that would be where they had taken him and found the area crowded with people. He said that maybe some of them should take Brian to Kathryn's cabin where he could receive better care. He watched as a few of them took hold of Brian and started off towards her cabin. He informed the others that they could probably find something else to do for a while and this caused the remaining crew to withdraw, just leaving Pot's, Berkshire and himself. He asked Pot's and Berkshire to join him in Kathryn's cabin with Brian.

"He has a nasty bump on his head that would explain him not being conscious and he was a mumblin' somethin' a while back. It was somethin' about Kathryn. Sounded like you came back Kathryn or somethin' like that," Pot's said.

"That is what it sounded like to me also Cap'n," Berkshire added.

Roth gently reached down and touched the boy's shoulder and softly said, "Brian can you hear me. It is the captain. Brian, can you hear me," He repeated.

"It is no use," Berkshire said, "We have been tryin to get him to talk to us since he did before but have had no success."

"OK, I am goin' to go to my cabin for a bit and think about what we should do next. Come and get me if anythin' happens or if he wakes up," Roth said as he stood to leave.

"I am of a thought that he will be alright soon sir, nothing appears to be broken and he looks as if he nearly drowned out there, but I am sure it is a bit of sleep and warmth that is all he be needin' now. He will be as good as new by mornin', you wait and see," Pot's said as Roth walked out of the cabin. He added to Berkshire, "There is a man that has lost his whole world."

Roth, however, did not go to his cabin. Instead, he made his way to the wheel deck where he could watch as his crew brought the cover and long boat onboard. He watched as the men secured the boat back into its cradle amidships and began an inspection of the cover. Not finding any apparent damage they picked it up and moved it back to the hatch from which it came. Roth noticed one of the crew moved back to where the cover had been laying and stooped to get a closer look at something on the deck. He picked up what appeared to be a piece of rope and upon standing up again he shook his head, dropped the rope and walked over to the cabin area where he disappeared through the door. Roth moved over to the stern railing and gazed out upon the reflection of the setting sun across the vast empty seas before him. He thought he heard a splash and looked down at the water below him and thought he caught a glimpse of something swimming under the ship. He hurried to the port side, but did not see anything emerge from that side so he rushed back to the starboard side hoping to see something there. Seeing nothing on this side either, he began to wonder if maybe he had imagined it. No, he could still see it in his mind. He could still see the iridescence of it just before it slid under the ship and he still had the feeling of calm and peace he had felt when he first saw it. What could it have been, he wondered to himself and decided that he had better not mention it for a while.

Curiosity got the best of him and he made his way to the spot where the crewman had found what appeared to be a piece of rope. Nearing the spot he saw the rope. Picking it up, he saw instantly what the crewman had seen, it was a granny knot. Any sailor worth his salt would not make a knot like that, they would tie a square knot.

He was disturbed from his thoughts by a crewmember that came up behind him. "Sorry to be a botherin' you Cap'n, but Mister Berkshire sent me to fetch you along to the boy's cabin. He is awake, sir."

"Thank you," Roth said. Pocketing the rope, he made his way to the hallway leading to Kathryn's cabin. Upon entering the cabin, Roth noticed a piece of rope hanging over the back of a chair.

"He has been askin bout Kathryn sir," Berkshire said as Roth moved over to the side of Brian's cot. "He keeps sayin' that she was with him the whole time. He said that it was she that tied the barrel to the cover."

"Is that true Brian? We have looked all over and can find no trace of her anywhere," Roth asked gently as he sat himself down on the cot alongside of the boy. It was then that he again looked at the piece of rope. He could see that it was tied very poorly, not a knot that he would expect to see tied by Brian.

Brian tried to sit up, but Roth placed his hand on his shoulder and gently held him down, "Sir, I seem to remember seeing her off n' on as I drifted."

Roth interrupted him and said, "Brian you have had a terrible experience. Why don't you start from the beginnin' and tell us how you happened to be in the water."

Brian, noticeably more relaxed, started to tell them what he remembered. He told them what had happened after the two had left the wheel deck. He started with the first big wave that knocked him over the side and how Kathryn had been trying to reach for him. She had tried but could not quite reach him when the second wave hit. He told them that this wave pushed Kathryn over the side where she landed on top of him and knocked his grip from the ship away, plunging them both into the icy water below. He could not remember what happened after that until he woke to find himself on the cover. The only thing he left out was his dream of seeing Kathryn. He tried not to remember that because he still could not believe what he had seen. He ended his tale with his awakening here in his cabin.

Roth leaned back against the wall and thought for a spell before he said, "When we first got to you, you said 'You have come back, Kathryn.' Do you remember saying that?"

"No sir, I do not remember being rescued from the cover," he replied.

Berkshire asked, "When was the last time you saw Kathryn?"

"It was just after we went in the water. I saw her swimming a short distance from me and I tried to swim towards her. A big wave crashed down on us and drove me deep into the water. I swallowed a lot of seawater and I almost lost my senses. When I got back to the surface, I found myself alone and Kathryn was nowhere around. The last wave must have washed us apart," Brian answered.

Roth then asked, "When you were afloat, do you remember tyin' that barrel to the cover?"

"What barrel?" Brian questioned.

"When we found you, there was a water barrel tied alongside the cover that held fresh water. You said earlier Kathryn that tied the barrel to the cover. If you did not tie it, how do you suppose it got there?" asked Roth.

Brian looked a little startled at that and all three men noticed. Berkshire asked, "Is there something that you are not telling us, Brian?"

"It was just a dream, it had to be a dream," the boy uttered.

"What was just a dream? Maybe you had better tell us of this dream," Roth said.

Brian hesitated before he began, trying to get the thoughts clear before he told these men what he had thought he dreamed. "I dreamed I awoke in the water after the wave drove me under, I could not stay afloat any longer and started to sink. Suddenly a hand grabbed mine and pulled me back to the surface. I did not see whose hand it was for as soon as I broke the surface I must have passed out. When I again awoke, I found myself on top of a hatch cover. I tried to sit up but found I was unable to do so. I only succeeded in rolling over. When I rolled over, I saw something in the water hanging onto the side of the cover. I suddenly realized that it was not human and tried to get away. When I moved it started to talk to me and sounded like Kathryn. As my eyes cleared, I saw that it was a human, but then again, it was not, for it was the color of the sea. I looked closer and I could almost believe that it was Kathryn. I felt like I must have been dreaming. I thought of this being a monster while it was talking to me and trying to fight it off. I must have passed out again because the next thing that I can remember is finding a barrel tied to the cover and a fish lying next to me. "I know it had to be a dream but it all seemed to be so real."

Berkshire reached over and took hold of the rope and asked, "Do you remember tyin' the barrel off with this rope?"

"No sir, where did that come from?" asked Brian in a very troubled voice.

"It was on the cover with you when we found you," Berkshire said.

"I believe Kathryn tied the barrel to the cover, but I am not sure what was real or what I dreamt." Brian was becoming anxious by this time.

"Calm down son, we believe that you are tellin' us the truth as you remember it," Roth said to Brian reassuringly. "Now you had better get some more rest, you have had a very bad night and day, but first I would like you to do something for me if you would." Pulling the piece of rope, he took from the main deck from his pocket. As he handed it to Brian, he said, "Would you please tie a square knot for me." As

Brian took the rope and quickly tied the knot, he handed it back to Roth. Looking at the rope for just a moment he then addressed Mister Berkshire, "I would like to see you on the wheel deck when you are through here."

"Aye Cap'n," he said as Roth left the room. "Pot's, make sure that there is someone keepin' an eye on him until he is up and around and make sure that he gets some food in him." Berkshire turned and left to meet the captain on the wheel deck, barely hearing Pot's reply, "Aye, aye sir."

When Berkshire climbed to the wheel deck, he found Roth pacing from one side of the deck to the other. "You wanted to see me Cap'n?"

Roth stopped pacing, looked at his friend and said, "Yes, I did. I wanted to know what you think about the story Brian just told us."

Berkshire moved to the stern rail, leaning his back against it to gather his thoughts before replying. "Well, as near as I can tell, Kathryn must have been with him at least part of the time. From the condition Brian was in when we found him, I find it very unlikely that he could have retrieved that barrel and secured it to the cover."

Roth came and stood by Berkshire, pulled the rope from his pocket and handed it to Berkshire and asked, "What do you make of that."

Berkshire took the rope and pulled a matching piece of rope from his pocket before saying, "You are thinking the same thing as I was and after seeing Brian tie a perfect square knot, I am sure that he did not secure that barrel to the hatch."

"In my mind it could have only been Kathryn that tied it. She could never tie a proper square knot and also how do you explain that fish? I can see no way for anyone to catch it unless it was already dead and floating on the surface."

"I was thinkin' that has to be the case. The storm must have killed a bunch of them and left them all floating on the surface." Berkshire responded. "I do not want to say this Cap'n, but that could possibly explain what happened to Kathryn."

"How is that?" Roth inquired, knowing the answer but dreading to hear it.

Berkshire hesitated a long time before answering. Finally, he said, "If it was a large kill, it would have attracted sharks. Cap'n, I hate to be the one to tell you this, but I am afraid that Kathryn may have been taken by a shark."

Roth felt as though he could collapse upon hearing this. He had been thinking the same thoughts, but upon hearing them expressed by another person, forced him to believe it as a definite possibility. "I am of the same thoughts, but I want to believe that she is out there somewhere, I can almost feel it."

Berkshire said, "Cap'n, I know it is a very hard thing to except but you must face the facts. If, indeed, she was there with Brian, then where is she now? She had no other place to go. She would not have tried to find the ship and would have died from the icy water tryin' to swim to shore."

"I know that, but I cannot give up hope," Roth said in an impatient tone.

"Sir, as a friend, I am tellin' you that you must accept it. There is no other explanation," Berkshire replied, ignoring Roth's reply.

"Thank you Mister Berkshire. I should like to be left alone for a while if you please," Roth stated flatly.

Berkshire wished there was something else he could say, but said instead, "Aye, aye Cap'n. I will be below decks if you need me further." With that, Berkshire left Roth alone on the wheel deck.

Roth leaned heavily on the stern rail and began to sob. "Kathryn, oh my sweet Kathryn, I am so sorry. I should not have let you return to your cabin alone. I should have taken you there myself. I should never have accepted this mission. If it were not for the greed of Creed and Raynerd, we would be sittin' in peace before the fire in our cottage. Why did they have to force me into comin'? They knew that I did not want to. If they had waited until spring, this would not have happened. Kathryn, somehow, I feel that you can hear me. Rest assured Creed is going to pay for what has happened. I will never forgive them. They will regret that they ever heard the name Roth." He was very angry by this time and turned to find Berkshire but he was nowhere in sight.

Roth did not know it, but Kathryn was hiding in the shadows of the stern and heard every word that her father had said. What could she do? How could she let him know that everything was all right? A tear fell from her eye as she slowly slipped beneath the surface. Kathryn decided to follow the *Galaunt* to see to her father's safety. She would somehow find a way for him to know that she was still with him.

Chapter 8
"Revenge"

Roth made his way below deck and was immediately assailed by the stench of unwashed bodies and the stagnant water of the bilge. He knew that he most likely did not smell any different, but that was life aboard a sailing ship. As he passed through the crew area, he saw that the crew tried to keep their place as livable as possible. On most ships, this area would usually be strewn with old clothes and other assorted items associated with men living together in small tight quarters. There were a few men asleep in the hammocks that were tied between the supports for the upper deck. He left them to whatever dreams they had and moved forward. When he came to the galley, he saw that Pot's was busily doing his never ending duties, the endless cleaning and the continuous preparations getting ready for the next meal. His job was probably the most tedious of any duty aboard ship, with men coming and going all the time, ending or starting their shifts. He had to prepare several meals a day and now he had to do it alone.

Again, his thoughts turned to Kathryn. He could see her moving around in here, helping with the cooking and cleaning. He had never heard her complain once during the entire time she had worked down here. It must have been very hard on her. She was used to an open space where the air would circulate more freely. He wondered how she had been able to stand not even being able to take a bath.

A sailor coming up from the hold area interrupted him from those thoughts. "Cap'n sir, Mister Berkshire sent me to fetch you. There is some damage in the forward hold that he thinks you had better see."

"Thank you, Tom," he replied in return. He moved to the steps that Tom had just come up and descended to the cargo area, making his way through the stacks of cargo his ship carried, to the forward hold.

He saw Berkshire and the cargo master, Smitty, inspecting a section of the holds overhead.

"You sent for me Mister Berkshire?" he asked.

Berkshire and Smitty both turned towards him when they heard his voice. "Aye Cap'n, Smitty here was showin' me some damage to the supports here. Those timbers came loose during the storm and knocked against the hull. We are takin' on water sir, not enough to cause alarm, I have the men on the pumps and they have been able to stay well ahead of it. I am thinkin', though, that we had best be puttin' in somewhere and get to fixin' it proper like."

Roth moved over to where they were pointing and immediately saw the cracks in the hull. Berkshire was right about the amount of water seeping in, but another storm, even a small one, could make those cracks a lot worse. "I agree with you Mister Berkshire, have the crew shore this up as well as possible and then we will make our way to Mozambique. There are friendly ports there that I am sure will welcome us and be happy to accept our trade. This will also give the crew a chance to get some needed shore leave. I know that I would welcome a chance to get off this ship for a while."

"Aye Cap'n," Berkshire replied knowing that his friend could use some down time for himself without the constant demand of the daily routine of running the ship.

Roth returned the way he had come previously and made his way back to the wheel deck where he started giving orders to turn the ship Nor' westerly. As the ship turned, he walked over to the stern rail and gave the sea behind one last look, still not being able to give up the thought that Kathryn was out there somewhere. Quietly whispering a last goodbye, he reluctantly turned back to his duties.

As the sails lowered and caught the wind, Roth could feel his ship gather speed and, again, come alive. He knew, however, that what he had once felt during these moments would never be felt in quite the same way again.

Roth spent most of the time, during the run to Mozambique, in his cabin. Berkshire was becoming concerned for his captain. Roth seldom stayed in his cabin any longer than necessary.

It was in his cabin that Roth heard a pounding on the door. He opened the door to a very excited young crewman who started uttering words faster than Roth could understand. "Whoa there laddie, slow down a bit and start over,"

"Sir, we have spotted land off the port beam. We need you topside. Sir, are we really going to be able to go on shore?" he asked excitedly. "This would be my first step on foreign land!"

"Aye laddie, if all goes the way it should then I see no reason why it should not, we will all get a break on shore. Now get on back to your duties and tell Mister Berkshire that I will be along presently." He turned back to his cabin and looked at his desk where he had been previously working on his log. He thought to himself how excited Kathryn would have been about the prospect of setting foot on another land. He smiled as he thought of her when she was that excited. She would talk as fast as this young crewman had and he would have to slow her down the same way. He lingered for a moment on that notion and the smile turned to a grimace and his eyes began to moisten. Shaking his head, he had to stop those thoughts and get his mind back on the task of getting his ship to land. He hastened now to the wheel deck and saw for himself that there was, indeed, land off to their port side. Mister Berkshire was at his post alongside the helmsman.

"Glad to be seein' you Cap'n. It will not be long afore we reach a port, sir. We should be alongside a dock afore nightfall."

"Very good," Roth replied. Roth left the wheel deck and made his way to the bow. He remembered how this was where Kathryn liked to come and he saw that the crate, where she would sit as she looked out over the sea, was still there. He moved over to it and remembered how she looked as she sat there with her hair streaming out behind her in the breeze with the ever-present smile on her face. He moved his gaze from the crate to the water and saw, at once, dolphins swimming in the wake alongside his ship. Roth watched them for a while, deep in thought and somehow found them comforting, not realizing why. Before long, he made his way back to the wheel deck.

Upon his return, he walked up to Mister Berkshire and asked, "Is there anythin' that I need to know?"

Berkshire quickly responded, "Aye Cap'n, the leak in the forward hull has widened a little from the constant movement of the hull, though still not a worry. I will be glad when we make port and can fix it proper."

"What do you figure will be our time in port?" he asked.

"It will not take long at all to make the necessary repairs and the crew could use a little time ashore sir," was Berkshire's response.

"Good, I want to be back at sea as soon as possible," was Roth's reply.

"Do you mind me askin' about the hurry Sir? The crew could use a rest and we could use a few supplies," Berkshire inquired.

"Yes, there is a reason for the haste, but that will have to wait until we are ready to sail again," Roth said flatly as he turned his gaze towards the sea and land before him.

Berkshire knew that was all Roth was going to say and turned his attention back to the running of the ship.

It was turning into night, with the sun, a huge orange ball, setting to their right, when they caught sight of the port. It was not a large port. It was actually nothing but a long wharf jutting out into a deep protected lagoon. A long narrow reef protected the lagoon, keeping the rough seas out and making for calm waters within. There was a narrow slot in the reef and it was to this opening they were sailing. As the *Galaunt* made its way through the opening the crew could see on both sides, a multitude of different colors belonging to a vast variety of undersea life and the many different colors of fish that lived in them. Passing through the opening, the bottom dropped off again and the ship made its way to the wharf ahead.

It did not take long to tie up to the dock and Berkshire immediately started doling out the orders to the crew responsible for the repair of the ship and the others to the task procuring and restocking of supplies. Berkshire felt that if he added an incentive to the crew to work faster then they would be able to go ashore sooner.

"Mister Berkshire, when you have finished here, I would like to see you in my cabin," Roth said.

"Aye, aye Cap'n," was Berkshires response as Roth left the wheel deck and went to his cabin.

In his cabin, Roth could hear the sounds of repairs to his ship and knew that his supervision was not required. His crew knew what to do and anyway, he had important things to think over and do.

Roth was looking over a chart he had spread out on his desk, when a knock came to his door. Knowing it was Berkshire, he said, "Enter."

Berkshire entered, closing the door behind him. "You wanted to see me sir?"

Roth gestured towards a chair in front of his desk and watched as his first mate sat down. "Edward," he began, noticing that by calling him by his first name, made Berkshire sit a little more comfortable. "I have been doing a lot of thinking as of late. I cannot get past the feeling that all that has happened is the fault of Creed. If his greed had not been so overwhelmin', this voyage would never have taken place and we would all be home where we belong and my Kathryn would still be with me."

Berkshire interrupted, "Sir, we all feel the loss of Kathryn."

Roth raised his hand to stop him from talking, "Please let me finish." Roth paused for a few moments before continuing. "I know that it was my decision to bring Kathryn along, but I really had no choice. You did not know that he threatened to end my life at sea if I did not make this voyage. Did you?"

Before Berkshire could respond, Roth again raised his hand. "The sea is the only life that I know. Givin' it up would have been the most difficult thing that I would ever have to do in life, but if I could have foreseen what was going to happen, I would have done so without a second thought." He then stood and started to pace his cabin. He was lost in his own thoughts a long time before he continued. "Alas, I could not and I lost Kathryn. Creed forced this upon me and therefore I feel that I must make him pay for my loss. It is my intention to ruin him as he has ruined me."

Berkshire, confounded by his friend's words, implored, "What is it that you are plannin' to do? What is it you can possibly do?"

Roth continued his pacing, back and forth across his cabin and it was a long time before he replied. "I aim to take this ship and destroy as many of his ships as I can before I am captured or killed." With that,

Roth stopped his pacing and gazed out the window overlooking the dock.

"What about the crew? Have you thought about them?" Berkshire asked. "What about me, do you think that you are the only one that feels a loss?"

Roth looked right into his friend's eyes and loudly stated, "I *will* take this man down! I will find a few different men willin' to go with me and leave you and the crew here! You will be safe here until you can find passage back to England."

Berkshire stood, walked over to his friend and placed a hand on his shoulder. They both stood there like that watching the activities on the dock for a long time before Berkshire said, "Roth that is a long and hard road that you are purprosin', one that will probably end up with you, and all that follow, hangin' from the gallows. I think that you had better think it over long and hard before you take up that path."

Roth turned and faced Berkshire. "What is it that you think I have been doing since the day I lost Kathryn? Do you think that this is somethin' that just popped into my head? Think about it you say, I have done nothing *but* think about it."

Looking deep into Roth's eyes, Berkshire asked, "Is there nothin' that I can say to dissuade you from this course of action?"

"No! I have made up my mind and it is what I am going to do," Roth replied coldly.

"Then you leave me no choice. You have been my friend for many years now, and I cannot let you go alone. I will accompany you through whatever happens," Berkshire said.

"I cannot let you do that. As you say, you have been my friend and I could not let anythin' happen to you. You are probably right about endin' up on the gallows," Roth tersely replied.

Berkshire chuckled and said, "I remember once tellin' you that I would follow you to Hades and back. Well, I guess the gallows would be just another stop on the way."

A smile crossed Roth's face as he placed both his hands on Berkshires shoulders and said to him. "Now it is you that had better think things over. I am not goin' to say anythin' more about this until the ship is repaired and ready to set sail."

"You do as you see fit, but my mind is made up. Where you go, I go," Berkshire responded.

Roth continued to stare into the eyes of his friend, finally he said, "You are a good man Edward, you are more of a friend than any man could hope for. Think hard on what you decide. I would hate to see anythin' happen to you." Moving away from Berkshire, Roth returned to his desk and began to look over the map spread across his desk.

Berkshire walked over to the desk and looked down at the map. He could see that Roth had drawn lines upon it representing the course they had sailed. He saw that Roth had circled the area where they had lost Kathryn. He also saw that there were lines on it showing the courses of the *Royale, Princeton* and the *Noble*. There were also lines upon it from their port in Mozambique, ending with a large X, marking his estimated intercept point of first, the *Royale*, the *Princeton* and then on to the *Noble*.

"Well, Nathan, I think maybe you had better fill me in on your plans," Berkshire said.

Roth looked up at him, seeing there was probably not anything he could do to dissuade Berkshire, started telling him what he was planning to do. They both remained in his cabin going over the plans well into the night, while unheard and unseen, the repairs and loading of supplies went on.

Two days later, the ship was ready to set sail. Berkshire was with Roth in his cabin, where they were deciding on how best to approach the crew.

"I have been quietly going about askin', each of the crew, how they felt about the loss of Kathryn. The crew agrees that it is somethin' that should not have happened. I think that if you were to ask them, they would all be more than willin' to go along with us," Berkshire said.

Roth thought this over before saying, "They are a good crew, but I could not ask them to follow me at a time like this."

Berkshire said, "I think that that is somethin' for them to decide. I have the crew assembled outside waitin' for you."

Pausing for a short time Roth somberly spoke, "Very well then, let us go and see for ourselves how they decide." Roth walked out of the cabin and they both made their way to the wheel deck, where Roth turned to his men. "Men," he began, "I have decided that this ship and I are not goin' to complete the mission that we were assigned. I totally blame Creed and his insatiable glut for profits, for the loss of Kathryn. I demand satisfaction for that loss. I have decided that the only way for me to gain restitution is to hurt Creed in the only place that will matter to him, his purse. Therefore, it is my decision that I am goin' to take this ship, and destroy every ship Creed owns, startin' with the *Royale*. I am goin' to leave it up to you men to decide whether you want to follow me. If you decide not to follow, I will leave you here. You will be safe here until you can secure passage back to England." Roth stopped here for a moment, pondering what to say next. "I am ready to sail on the tide, your time to decide has come. The tide comes in one hour, those of you who wish to stay, can stay. Those who wish to leave will have time to gather your stuff and go ashore. You will go with my blessin's and thankfulness for bein' all that I could ask for in a crew." Bowing his head Roth turned to leave the wheeled deck, but did not move very far, when he noticed that none of the men where moving. "Ponder your decisions wisely men. It is not a mere trifle I ask you to embark upon." With that, Roth left the wheel deck and without a backward glance, made his to his cabin.

Roth had not quite made it back to his desk when he heard say his name. Turning, he saw Berkshire standing in the doorway.

"Cap'n, I think the men have made their choice. Maybe you had better come back above deck." Berkshire stood aside as Roth stepped through the doorway and made his way outside. he immediately saw that not a single man had moved. Climbing to the wheel deck, he turned and said, "Well, I see that you have all decided stay." He smiled to himself and again reflected on the character of his crew. "If that is the case, Mister Berkshire, would you detail the men to their duties and prepare the ship to sail." At this point Roth felt humbled. He had indeed been blessed with a noble crew.

He stayed on the wheel deck and listened to Berkshire as he issued the orders to get the ship ready. How many times had they pursued a new mission doing just that? This time he watched as the men to their stations to pursue a vendetta. Once again, he felt great pride in the men that comprised his crew, he only hoped that he was not leading them to their demise.

The hour passed quickly and when the time came for the ship to set sail, the men were ready. Berkshire ordered the men to lower the topsails and untie the ship from the dock. The topsails caught the wind, and the ship slowly started to move away from the dock.

The ship was gaining speed as it made its way to the opening in the reef. As it cleared the reef, Berkshire ordered all sails lowered, and the ship was soon gliding across the water.

Roth ordered his helmsman to steer a course along the coast, keeping it in sight. He did not want to sail past the *Royale* in the unlikely event that the other ship had anchored, for some reason or another, in some remote cove or river mouth.

It was very dangerous to sail this close to the shore for two reasons. First, there were the hidden reefs and rocks that were difficult enough to see during the day, let alone at night, but the ship remained at full sail. Roth also knew that a Dutch or Portuguese warship could be lying at anchor in some of those same inlets, ready to catch the winds as they poured off the continent, waiting for any unwary ship to sail by. However, those same winds would help the *Galaunt* achieve a speed far greater than the weaker winds out at sea would move the *Royale*. Roth was betting on the fact that he could gain enough time to get ahead of the *Royale*.

Roth could smell the land that lay off his port rail. It had the smell of hot, humid soil. He could also detect the smell of ripe fruit. They were less than 1000 meters from the shore and Roth could easily make out the features that comprised the coast of Africa. He wondered what it was like inland in that jungle. The jungle, he knew, contained a variety of life. He could see great flocks of water birds flying, riding the hot tropical winds that were flowing from the hot steaming jungle, out to the cooler sea. Occasionally he would hear the scream of some wild beast as it prowled the shoreline in its endless search for a meal. As they passed the rockier shorelines, Roth could hear, as well as see, the waves crashing against them, forcing great clouds of mist into the air. Sometimes a rainbow would appear in them as they slowly descended back into the sea.

The *Galaunt* made very good time catching these land borne winds. After only three days of sailing past a seemingly unending stretch of unblemished beaches, Roth gave the order to change course due East.

It was just after noon the next day, when a lookout first spotted sails dead ahead. It was not long after that he could tell that the ship was, indeed, the *Royale*. He gave the order to fire off one cannon to alert the other ship of their presence. Through his telescope, He could see the other ship loosening its sails to allow the *Galaunt* to catch up. The ship was going to catch up all right! He ordered his gun crews to ready themselves for a volley at the *Royale's* masts as they sailed past the slowing ship. Roth watched as they quickly closed the distance. Roth told the remaining crew to man their stations and make it look like they were preparing to bring the ship alongside the *Royale* so as not to arouse any suspicions as to what their intentions really were. Roth ordered his helmsman to keep the *Galaunt* to the port side of the *Royale* so that the other ship would not see the gun ports on their port side were opened and ready for action. At what seemed like the last moment, Roth ordered the ship hard to starboard and the port side brought to bear upon the unaware ship slightly ahead of them. Roth saw both Connery and Raynerd as they simultaneously realized what was happening. Roth saw Connery turn to issue some order to his crew, but that order never reached fulfillment. As the *Galaunt* passed along the starboard beam of her sister ship, Roth gave the order to fire. Eight guns fired almost as one and Roth watched as the iron cannonballs found their targets. All three masts of the *Royale* seemed to explode in a shower of splinters. All the masts were struck below the lowest yardarm and the remaining masts and rigging fell onto the deck below or into the sea.

It was over in just a few seconds and the *Galaunt* made her way past the now helpless *Royale*. Roth let the ship sail a short distance before he ordered it to turn and bring the starboard guns to bear upon the bow.

"Withdraw your guns and surrender or on this pass we will blow you out of the water," Roth yelled as they neared the *Royale*. He could see that the other crew were still preparing to fight so he ordered that two guns fire at the *Royale's* waterline as they passed. The first shot hit the bow about three feet above the waterline, but the second struck her at the waterline and seawater immediately began to flow into the now doomed ship. The *Galaunt* made a turn to port and soon had its starboard guns bearing again on the *Royale*. Roth yelled, "You have had all the chances you are going to get, Connery. Now lay down your weapons and withdraw your guns." This time Roth saw an immediate response to his command and ordered his ship alongside the *Royale*.

As the *Galaunt* was coming up alongside, Roth noticed that Mister Berkshire had already ordered several men to take up arms. The men were keeping the *Royale's* crew covered so that they would have no time to pick up their weapons and fight back. After they had tied the other ship to theirs, they began pouring over the rails to secure the men and weapons of the defeated crew.

Roth made his way down to the starboard rail where he found Berkshire directing his crew. "Well Mister Berkshire, it seems that there is no turning back now. Shall we proceed on and pay our respects to our commander?"

Berkshire chuckled and said with a wave of his hand, "After you Cap'n."

Both men then jumped over the rails and landed lightly on their feet on the deck of the *Royale*. Roth started to make his way to the wheel deck. Berkshire shortly hesitated, while he gazed around the deck, to assure himself that all was well and his men had everything under control before turning to catch up with his captain.

Connery, followed closely by Raynerd, came charging down the steps and hurried to confront Roth. Connery was yelling, "This is treason, mutiny and piracy." Waving his arms around to point out the destruction, he continued, "Look at what you have done to my ship, she cannot sail in this condition. In addition, from the looks of it you have hulled her. I will see you hung for this!" He quickly made a reach for his sword. Connery had failed to notice, however, that during his tirade, Berkshire had moved over to his left side and had already drawn his sword and at this moment was bringing that sword up. Berkshires first swipe caught Connery along the outside of his right hand and his second, opened a deep gash on his left shoulder. Forgetting the sword and his wounded hand, Connery brought his right hand up to cover the much more severely wounded left shoulder and stared in astonishment at his assailant. Gathering himself back together, to Berkshire, he turned and said snarling, "You are going to pay for this." Turning back to Roth he said, "I am going to see that both of you are hung for these crimes and this traitorous act."

"I would be thinkin' 'bout whether or not I was going to see tomorrow, if I were you," Berkshire stated.

That opened Connery's eyes in surprise, but Raynerd was first to speak. "You surely cannot be thinking about adding murder to your growing list of crimes?"

"I have no plans on murdering anyone," Roth said. "In fact, I had planned on makin' you my guests, aboard my ship. Mister Berkshire would you and your men please escort the crew and these two aboard our ship?"

"Aye, aye Cap'n," Berkshire barked an order to his men to escort the *Royale's* crew to the bow of the *Galaunt*. Turning back to Connery and Raynerd, he said with a smirk and gestured towards the *Galaunt*, "If you would be so kind."

Connery and Raynerd both glared at Berkshire, as if ready to protest, but realizing their dilemma, moved towards the *Galaunt*.

Roth watched them go before turning to look over the damage that he had caused. Roth's heart sank as he saw what he had done to this once proud and noble ship of the sea, but he also knew that what he had done was something that had to be done. He also knew that the job was not yet finished. Looking around, his eyes came upon a lantern hanging on the side of the door leading to the aft cabins. Finding that it was full, he poured its contents of coal oil out upon the deck. He then removed his belt pistol, bent down and fired off its charge. This ignited the coal oil from the lantern. Standing back up, he watched for a few seconds to assure himself that the flame would take. Satisfied, he returned to his ship.

The *Galaunt* moved off a short distance from the *Royale*, everybody on board was watching the ship as it slowly burned down to the water line and started to smolder. Roth found where Berkshire was holding Connery and Raynerd and walked over to them.

"You must be the devil," Connery hissed. "You will indeed hang if it is the last thing that I do."

Roth, already feeling angry over the death of the *Royale*, had heard all he was going to hear from Connery. "Enough! I have heard all that I care to listen to from your mouth, Connery. Berkshire, put these men in chains and secure them below, I do not want to hear another word from either of them. Have that arm looked at, I would not want our distinguished guest to suffer unduly." With that, he turned away and made his way to the bow.

As he approached the bow, he could see the crew from the *Royale* seemed to be a little ill at ease wondering what was to be their fate. He was determined to put their fears to rest. "Men, I am not going to stand here and try to justify to you why I did what I have done. I have my reasons and those reasons do not include you. I am here to tell you I do not intend to harm any of you anymore than I already have. I am not sure what I am goin' to do with you, but you will receive no further harm if you do not cause any trouble." Roth paused here for a few seconds to let what he had just said sink in. "I am not even goin' to have you bound, unless there is reason too. But, let me warn you of this, if anyone causes any trouble, then you all will suffer." He paused again here. "Do you all understand?" He was pleased to see that all of the twenty or so men were nodding in agreement. "Good, then we will see that you will have plenty to eat and what little freedom I can allow you under the circumstances as long as you cause no problems for my men or ship. That will be all then we are finished here. Mister Berkshire, will you please follow me to my cabin?"

Upon entering the cabin, he gestured to Berkshire to take a seat. "Well, as I said before, there is no turning back now. We have succeeded in destroyin' one." Roth walked over to the window where he could still see the smoke from the burning hulk, that earlier had been the proud vessel *Royale,* as it started to slowly sink into the sea. He thought to himself that could have just as easily been his own ship burning out there on the open seas. If Connery had had any idea of what was about to transpire, he could have done as much damage to the *Galaunt.* He felt satisfied with what he had planned and the outcome. Turning back to Edward he said, "The *Princeton* cannot be far behind. Pringle is a much better tactician than Connery and knows how to get the most from his ship. We had better get ready for him. We will use the same tactics on him as we did with the *Royale* and take him by surprise, but I do not want to inflict as much damage on her as we did the *Royale.* I think that I will allow Pringle to keep his ship and return home. We can also put the crew, except for Connery and Raynerd, on his ship and give them a chance to see their home and families again. As for Connery and Raynerd, I have thought about putting them in a longboat and letting them take there own chances and this thought has been weighin' heavily on my mind. I do not consider myself a ruthless man, so therefore I have decided that after we have taken the *Princeton*, I will put them ashore and leave them to fend for themselves."

"Cap'n, do you think it wise to try and take the *Princeton* with the crew of the *Royale* on board? Pringle will undoubtedly see them before we are close enough to use our guns."

"We will leave them where they are. Pringle will think that the *Royale* must have come into some sort of catastrophe and we were lucky enough to have been able to save them. It may very well work to our advantage to have them seen. Pringle will assuredly assume that we are comin' to him for assistance. That will allow us to move in closer and our gunners will have the opportunity to be more accurate with their shots. Again, I want to reiterate to you that I want the *Princeton* left in sailing condition. Pringle and his crew have done nothing to warrant harm. I plan to ruin Creed, not kill the people that must work for him. It is in his ships that his fortune lies, so it is his ships, which I will destroy. Give the orders to come about and we will begin our search for the *Princeton*."

"Aye, aye Cap'n," was all that Berkshire replied. He rose from his seat and with a nonchalant salute, he left the cabin leaving his captain in deep thought.

Berkshire walked out onto the main deck, into the bright sunlight, wondering in his own mind what would become of all this. He knew that what they were about to do was wrong, but after all, Roth was his captain, not to mention the best and possibly the only friend that he had ever had. He made up his mind right there and then that no matter where this path led, he would stand by his friend to the end. Looking around, he could see that many of the men were probably having similar thoughts of their own. Most of the crew was huddled in small groups obviously talking about what had just taken place and what was going to happen next. Berkshire decided that the best way to get those thoughts out of the crew's mind was to give them something to do. He gave the orders to come about and watched as the crew scrambled to carry out their assignments. Berkshire knew that the crew was loyal and would follow their Captain regardless of where he led them.

In his cabin, Roth heard Berkshire issue the orders to come about and could already feel his ship making its turn to go in search of the *Princeton*. He walked over to the cabinet containing his maps and selected one. He moved to his desk and unrolled it. A map showed the entire route that they had traveled. He began to plot upon it the distances that he assumed the *Princeton* had been able to sail each day and came to a point where he thought they should be by now. Calling for the cabin boy, he gave him orders to find Berkshire and tell him return to his cabin when he was able.

It was not long before he heard the expected knock on the door. "Enter." He was not surprised to see his first mate but was surprised to see him followed by Pot's and the Chief Helmsman.

"Cap'n, I anticipated this summons and have brought along the Helmsman. Pots here has some concerns over our supplies, so I thought that I would bring him along as well," Berkshire stated after seeing the look of wonder on his captain's face.

"Sir, with all these new bodies on board that will have to be fed, I am afraid that our stores will not last but a few short days. I am not mindful of the extra work that will need to be done, but I be askin' your leave to recruit the *Royale's* cook to be givin' me a hand if you would not be mindin'," Pot's said.

"No Pot's, I have no objection at all to you recruitin' whomever you think that you need to keep up with the extra work. I apologize for not thinkin' of taking the extra supplies from the *Royale*, but we will have to make do with what we have until we can take on more stores. I am sure that I do not have to tell you that no one on this ship will go hungry and that no one will get preference over anyone else, includin' myself. Is that understood?"

"Aye Cap'n, it is understood. Now if you will excuse me, I have some feedin' that needs to be attended to." Pots then saluted and left the cabin.

"Cap'n, we will need to know where we are goin' and set the proper course," the helmsman stated. The helmsman was a big man with almost no hair on the top of his head. What hair he did have, he wore long, hanging about his shoulders. His face was deeply tanned and wrinkled from the many years he had stood his post at the wheel. Roth could see him standing there with the wind blowing in his face and his hair standing out behind him like a flag blowing in the wind.

"Yes, Mister Miller, step over to my desk and I will show you where I think we are goin'." All three walked over to the desk where Roth still had his map spread out and Roth proceeded to inform both men what he had in mind. Having completed his briefing he dismissed the men and returned to his thoughts of what was going to happen next. It was not long before he decided to go up on the wheel deck for some air. He was standing by the stern rail looking out over the sea when he heard a sound that was being carried along with the wind. He had heard this sound once before and still wondered what it could be.

It only took a few days before they got to the area where Roth thought to encounter the *Princeton*. He was standing on the wheel deck and noticed the dolphins that always accompanied them. It seemed to him that there were more every day and he could not help but wonder if they knew of some impending disaster that he or the crew were unaware of. He, as well as several others of the crew, even thought they saw one that was not like the others, but they never got a clear enough view of it to be sure. He pondered over this for a minute and decided to take leave to his cabin. Tomorrow will be another challenging day. As he left the wheel deck, he heard that sound again that reminded him of a mournful wail carried on the winds.

The next day came and everyone heard the lookout shout, "Sails on the horizon!" Roth rushed to the wheel deck, taking out his telescope, he began to scan the horizon. It was not long before he too, could make out the sails that the lookout had seen. He gave the order to the crew to hoist all sails and make haste to intercept the distant ship.

The *Galaunt* glided across the ocean surface as if it knew what lay ahead. The winds were good and the sails were full. The distance closed in a short time and the crew, having already been briefed, got ready for the attack they were about to make.

Roth decided that the best way to cripple the *Princeton*, without causing too much damage, was to take out the sternmast and the mainmast on the first pass, leaving only the foremast. This would allow the ship to still make headway. Roth had chosen his best gunners to man the cannons that would be used for the attack.

As the two ships approached each other, Roth could see that the *Princeton* was lowering its sails to come to a stop. This is just what Roth had hoped they would do. He could also see Pringle standing on the wheel deck giving orders. He wondered what his fellow Captain was thinking and what he would be thinking in just a few moments.

The *Galaunt* was still moving very rapidly as it came alongside the *Princeton*. Roth saw the look of wonder change to surprise as his gunners opened fire. The shots were true to their mark and he saw the two masts topple over the side of the ship and plunge into the water, hanging there held by the rigging attached to the ship. Roth ordered his ship to come about and assume a position broadside to the stern of the *Princeton*, with all guns to bear, so as not to put his ship in danger of retaliation.

When his ship was in position, Roth moved to the port railing making his way through the crew of the *Royale*. He could see the looks of puzzlement on the faces of some and the looks of admiration on the faces of others.

"Surrender your ship or be blown out of the water," Roth called out to the other ship.

Pringle pushed his way through the men that had gathered at the stern rail and bellowed, "What are you doing? Why did you fire on my ship?"

Once again, Roth called out, "Surrender your ship or you will be blown out of the water!"

"Have you lost your mind? How dare you order me to surrender my ship?"

"For the last time, surrender your ship or you will be fired upon." Roth restated.

Pringle noticeably slumped and spoke. "Of course I will surrender, but pray tell me why you are doing this."

"All of your questions will be answered in due time. Stand down and prepare to be boarded," Roth commanded.

Roth gave the orders to bring the *Galaunt* alongside the *Princeton*. After the ship was alongside, Roth was the first to cross over to the *Princeton* and made his way to the wheel deck where he encountered an extremely irate Pringle. Pringle glared at Roth with a look of dismay, "Now would you like to tell me just what it is you are doing? You are acting no better than a common pirate."

"You may call me what you like. I have but one desire at this time and that is to ruin Creed and the only way for me to do that is to take away his means of power and source of wealth. I mean no harm to you or your crew, but I aim to destroy Creed's fleet. In this, I feel that I have no choice. The reasons will be known to you soon enough."

Pringle raised his voice to Roth, "Now listen to me you young ……"

"No, you listen to me," Roth interrupted in a calm but deliberate voice. "You are goin' to do exactly as I say or you will also feel my wrath. I will not be deterred from my mission. Whether you understand or not is of little consequence to me. You will know soon enough the reasons behind my actions. You may even come to understand, but for now, I will tell you what you are going to do. I am going to transfer the crew of the *Royale* to your vessel and you are going to follow me in my search for the *Noble*."

"And if I don't?"

"Then I will sink your ship! I have already destroyed the *Royale* and have Connery and Raynerd in chains below. As you can see, I have taken the crew of the *Royale* aboard. I cannot accommodate your crew aboard the *Galaunt* so therefore I am willin' to spare your ship. I can, however, put you with Connery and have your First Mate assume command to save the crew if he will follow my commands. Otherwise, I will not hesitate to destroy the *Princeton* and all on board, if I am forced to do so," Roth replied coldly and evenly as he stared Pringle in the eye. With that remark, Roth suddenly realized what was happening and felt his adrenaline level decrease. His voice dropped to a calm tone and he continued by saying, "I am, however, hopin' that you will not force me to take those extreme actions. This of course will be your choice. What will it be?"

"Do I have a choice man? I think not! You leave me no choice but to go along with what you say, but make no mistake, I will not abide by or ever condone what you are doing," Pringle answered harshly.

"That is your prerogative but you are makin' a wise decision to follow my commands." Roth felt a sense of relief knowing that now he would not have to enforce his threat. "You will inform your crew that we will tolerate no interference and that they are to follow my commands to the letter. I am not a killer of men and your crew are safe as long as they do as they are told. When you are aware of why this is taking place, I am sure you will understand, at least that is my hope."

Roth turned to Berkshire and told him to remove all weapons from the *Princeton* and to spike all but two of the cannon before moving the crew of the *Royale* onto the *Princeton*. Pringle begrudgingly gave the orders to his men to cooperate with the officers and crew of the *Galaunt* and give them no further cause for reprisal. Knowing that the danger was over, Roth left the wheel deck of the *Princeton* and returned to his own ship leaving Berkshire to carry out his orders.

Returning to his cabin, Roth suddenly became overcome by his actions. He knew that what Pringle had said was true, but his thoughts turned to Kathryn and his resolve did not lessen. He managed to take two of Creed's best ships and swore that before it was over, he would take them all. This still would not bring his beloved Kathryn back but it would allow him to feel some sense of revenge, a feeling he had never experienced before.

It was not long before Berkshire returned to inform Roth that all preparations had been made and they were ready to set sail. "Pringle has been told where to rendezvous with us and he also knows what will happen if he fails to show up on time."

"Then set sail Edward and let us get on with the hunt for the *Noble*."

Kathryn was floating a long distance from the *Galaunt*, so as not to be seen by anyone aboard either ship. She had seen all that had transpired and once again, was greatly saddened by what her father was doing, knowing in her heart, that it was all because of her. She did not know, at this point, what to do. She was still very afraid of letting her father know what had really happened to her for fear that his reactions would be similar to Brian's and she would be rejected. Each time she observed the ship she wanted to go nearer to try to see her father. When she knew she could not do this is when she would start to sing the same mournful song, sometimes in tears, a song that she had learned from her grandmother Beth, many years ago. Beth had told her she would always sing this song to Kathryn's mother when she was sad. It had become a source of solace to her. One day she would know what to do, she just had to wait and see what would happen until that day arrived. She knew there were certain things that she could do to protect him but she also knew that she could not do them now.

Aboard the *Galaunt*, Roth turned and looked out towards the horizon when he suddenly heard the sound that he had been hearing almost every day since he had lost Kathryn. It still gave him an impression of great sadness and at the same time, gave him a feeling of warmth that he could not explain nor understand.

Chapter 9
"Resolution"

Kathryn was swimming effortlessly behind the stern of the ship, staying just beyond the ring of light from the watch lanterns, sneaking a glimpse of her father as he stood alone by the stern rail. She knew what was running through his mind. With the events of the last several days, she knew that her father was acting completely out of character but what could she do? He was not a violent man but rather a kind, gentle person and she knew, in her heart, that what he was doing had to be the result of her being lost at sea. Again, she found herself struggling with the idea of showing herself to him but could not find the courage to do so.

She had been by the ship since the change had come over her and had desperately wanted to let him know she was there, but she had remained hidden from all eyes because she was ashamed to be seen. Recalling the look on Brian's face when he awoke and saw her in her present state haunted her and it was not the reaction that she wanted to see on her father's face. Tears streamed from her eyes while thinking her father would never see her as she was but now only see her as the hideous creature that she had become. She might not ever see that loving look in her father's eyes again and it tormented her constantly. Looking back on the time of her insistence to go with him to sea, Kathryn could now only feel remorse. Had she not been so insistent, this may not be happening now. She longed for his jocular laughter and loving hugs, and the sparkle of delight she felt at those times. Her mind wandered to remembrances that were more familiar. If only somehow, this was just a nightmare, she would awaken and find the world as happy as it once was.

It had been several days now and Kathryn had found herself slowly becoming accustomed to this new environment. While exploring her new body she found herself to be a different color, her skin was a gray color more like the color of the dolphins that she found herself constantly surrounded by. Her hair was now a very dark shade of brown, almost black, but still with a hint of red, and had noticeably thickened, flowing out behind her as she moved through the water. Her hands had grown a fine web, like gossamer, between the fingers and she was slowly gaining muscle in her arms. The biggest change was that she now had the tail of a fish. Not like that of an ordinary fish either, but more like the tail of a whale only much more delicate, more like the tail of a dolphin. The lower half of her body was a beautiful iridescent color that changed with the light of the sun in the day and the moon in the night. It curvaceously tapered from the hips down, ending at the tail that lay parallel to her sides. She thought that this was what gave her the ability to fly through the water with very little effort. She had not seen her face yet. She was sure that she must look hideous, therefore she resolved that no one would ever see her, especially her father for fear he would not recognize her.

Her hearing had also become much keener. She could swim under the hull of the ship and hear almost everything that was being said and because of her familiarity with the activities of the crew aboard the ship, what was being done. This is how she knew what her father was doing and why he was doing it. It distressed her greatly to know that she was causing her father to turn completely against his nature. He looked so lonely standing there by himself. She wished that she could share a loving hug with him. That reassuring kind of hug that only a daughter can give her father. They had often shared these hugs on the occasions when he had left and then returned from the sea. They had left her with a feeling of warmth in the knowledge of the love that he felt towards her and she felt towards him. She so wanted to make him feel that way now. She would sing softly the songs that she thought her father would recognize, but even those came out as a dim melody that was also carried away.

Since she had begun to adapt to her environment, she had learned rather quickly from the dolphins where to get the nourishment she needed for sustenance. Kathryn quickly realized that she could out swim any other fish in the sea and this made it very easy to catch the food the dolphins led her to feed on and to avoid any of the dangerous predators that she might come upon. Sharks were very common in these waters and she had already experienced many encounters with them. She found that she could easily flee from them with her speed and agility, but the dolphins were her protectors in these situations. They would know when such a threat was near and would close in on her and their young to form a protective barrier from the shark. If the shark wandered close, they would ram it in its gills with their snouts until it turned away. As with the dolphins, she found that she could not breathe underwater but with one breath she could stay underwater for extremely long periods, so she would tend to stay near the surface so that she could rise and get the air when the need arose. In addition, she found that the dolphins were a very happy group and liked to play. It was to her delight when she found that they were accepting her as one of their own. It was fun racing with them and riding the ships wake. She would even sometimes find herself laughing as she did before.

She was deep in thought when she noticed the intensified activity on board the ship. She drew nearer to the hull to see if she could hear anything to give her a clue as to why the hurried manner of the ship's crew. She could only hear the shuffle of many feet aboard the vessel but no one seemed to be talking. She swam deeper in the water until she was well ahead of the *Galaunt* and surfaced to see what she could see. With only her head above the surface of the water, she looked all around until she spotted what appeared to be lights not far from her position. She knew instantly what all the excitement was about, but she had no idea what to do about it. Diving back underwater, she let herself drift until she was back under the hull where she resumed keeping pace with the ship wondering how she could communicate with her father.

Meanwhile aboard the ship, Mister Berkshire had already given the order of no talking. When the lookout had first reported lights, Roth and Berkshire had a quiet meeting in his cabin. It was decided if this was indeed the *Noble*, it then might be best to approach her in the dark and capture her at first light. With this plan decided, Berkshire gathered the men on the gun deck and briefed them as to what the captain saw as a way to take the *Noble* with the least amount of injuries to both crews or damage to either ship. Each sailor received their orders and immediately went about their assigned tasks. Therefore, that was what the crew was doing when Kathryn tried to hear what was going on. They were silently going about their business quietly and in the dark. She thought she might swim ahead to see what they may be preparing for.

Sailing a ship under full sail at night is a hard and dangerous thing to do but sailing without light makes it nearly impossible. The helmsman, however, was doing a remarkable job of keeping the wind in the sails. He knew that the hard part was yet to come. He would have to bring the ship around in a turn that would send them in the opposite direction. That would require sail tending and that could be very dangerous in the dark. For now, however, his only concern was to keep wind in her sails until told to maneuver.

The other men aboard the *Galaunt,* which were not on duty, were getting what rest they could, but sleep would not come easily on this night. They knew that tomorrow could well be a busy day. For some, it could very well be their last day if things do not go as planned. They had completed their assigned tasks and having been briefed well before sunrise as to what the captain had planned and with daylight only a few hours away, they were starting to get anxious. The element of surprise was the essential component to the plan.

Roth was in his cabin alone but rest would not come to him. He had gone over the plan so many times in his head and every time he did so, he found something else to worry over or something else that could go wrong. He finally decided to go up on deck and see how his plan was progressing.

Upon reaching the wheel deck, he was greeted by Mister Berkshire who gave him a nod of recognition and welcome to the deck. Berkshire started to move from his spot of command when Roth lightly grabbed his shoulder, nodded a no and signaled him to stay put. Roth wanted to walk the main deck and observe his men to see if there was any reason to change his plan. It looked to him as if all preparations for the morning were well underway. There were several barrels scattered around the deck and some canvas hanging from the lower yards that gave the ship a look of disrepair and abandonment from being in a storm. They would also provide the crew with concealment when the *Noble* came to investigate, or at least that is what Roth hoped would happen. He turned to look off in the distance for the lights of the *Noble* and gauged that they were probably close enough and returned to the wheel deck and signaled Berkshire to start the turn. Berkshire gave a couple of short, almost inaudible, whistles. Roth could feel the ship begin to list slightly to port as the helmsman started to bring the ship around. He could also hear a faint rustle from the sails as adjustments were made so that the *Galaunt* would not lose the wind.

It seemed like a very long time before Roth felt the ship begin to pull out of the turn and resume straight sailing. He knew the helmsman had measured the turn by watching the lights of the other ship until it reached a position just to the starboard side of the stern post. So far, everything seemed to be working out to his satisfaction. He had to be well ahead of the *Noble* before daylight for his plan to succeed, but not out of sight. His plan relied on the lookout, aboard the *Noble,* being able to see them and come to their rescue or what their crew believed would be a rescue.

Roth's idea was very simple. He planned on the *Noble* mistaking the *Galaunt* for a derelict, forcing them to come in close enough to investigate. His crew was told to wait until the crew of the *Noble* prepared to board. At that time, his men would move out from their places of concealment and take aim at the sailors on the *Noble* but not fire. On the same signal, the gun ports would be dropped, to expose the cannon aimed directly at the waterline of the *Noble*. Roth was relying that his friend, Captain Holmes, would be intelligent enough to realize the hopelessness of his situation, and would choose not to fight an obviously losing battle. Still, he made it clear to his crew, that if the *Noble* chose to make a fight of it, then it was up to them to end it quickly with a minimum amount of injury and damage, but if the ship had to be sunk, then so be it. He hoped that this would not happen.

The *Galaunt* sailed along in this manner until the first rays of morning began to appear gently on the horizon. Roth nodded towards Berkshire and Berkshire gave the signal to the awaiting men to move aloft and prepare to furl the sails. Roth watched as his crew moved silently to their stations. He saw them start to lower some of the canvas, but not all. Some he had loosen to the extent that they would just flutter harmlessly in the wind adding to the effect of an abandoned vessel.

When this tasked was complete the men came down from the rigging, except the men assigned to man the crow's nest to keep a watch on what the *Noble* did. When they reached the deck, some took up positions amongst the scattered barrels and hanging canvas, while the rest went to the cannon to ready them for the possibility of battle.

With the *Galaunt* drifting aimlessly on the surface of the ocean, Roth and the rest of the men on the wheel deck took up their places of hiding and waited for the sun to rise. They all hoped that the *Noble* would spot them before too long.

Sure enough, it was not long after the sun finally started its rise that a quiet whistle could be discerned from the direction of the crow's nest. This was the signal that the *Noble* had taken the bait and changed direction towards the *Galaunt*. Roth could see in that direction from a small opening he had left in the railing. Before long, he could see the tops of the *Noble's* sails gleaming in the sun as it made its way towards the *Galaunt*.

In what, to Roth, seemed like an eternity, the *Noble* finally came close enough that he could start to make out men in the bow of the ship. He could see that they were looking through their scopes surveying his ship, looking for life. Roth hoped desperately that they would not see any of his men hiding on deck.

The ship was now close enough that Roth could see Captain Holmes on the bow giving orders to his men. Roth's tension was starting to ease as he could see that nothing appeared out of the ordinary on board the *Noble*. He could see now that his little rouse was working. Soon it would be up to Holmes how the events of the day would play out. Roth felt secure in the knowledge that his crew was prepared for either option and would act accordingly.

He watched the *Noble* make a slow turn to come alongside the *Galaunt* and was very near when Roth heard a shout from the approaching ship.

Roth heard, "Ahoy *Galaunt!*" Again, he heard, "Ahoy *Galaunt*, is there anyone aboard?"

The *Noble* was now so close that Roth heard Holmes give the order to stand by with the grappling hooks. This was the signal Roth and the crew aboard the *Galaunt* was waiting for. It would not be long now before they would move.

As the first grappling hook cleared the railing and the ropes were being tightened to take hold, Roth heard the gun ports flip open. As he rose from his hiding place, out of the corner of his eye, he watched his crew as they jumped out from their places of concealment. He could also see, with great satisfaction, them taking steady aim with their muskets at the stunned men aboard the *Noble*.

Captain Holmes was standing by the bow rail on the port side, looking down at the open gun ports and the cannon aimed at his waterline. Shaking his head slightly and with a stunned look upon his face, he slowly raised his head and stared incredulously across the short distance to the starboard side of the *Galaunt*. He was staring directly into the eyes of a man he thought was his friend.

Not allowing any time for Holmes to speak, Roth, in a calm but forceful voice said, "As you can see, I have you at somewhat of a disadvantage. It is now up to you to decide what will happen in the next few minutes. Have no doubt in your mind that I will indeed give the order to fire!"

For what seemed, to all the men facing each other that morning, like an eternity, Holmes answered hotly. "You are right about the disadvantage and I have no doubt that you are prepared to have those cannons fire. I have no idea why you are doing this, frankly I am surprised that you would, and I would very much like to know why you are threatening my men and my ship."

"If you do not force my hand, I mean no harm to your men, your ship or you. If you would allow me to explain, I think we can come to an understanding and we can end this now. Will you listen to my explanation?" Roth returned.

Roth watched as Holmes looked from him, back down to the cannon, then up to the men with muskets before Holmes spoke, still angry, "Your ship or mine!"

The tension that had built up on Roth's shoulders suddenly vanished as he realized that Holmes was doing exactly as he had hoped he would. "I would prefer mine. I am sure that you understand that." Roth answered calmly.

"Fine," Holmes answered disgustedly and continued to look around. Holmes was much calmer, but still angry. He took a few deep breaths before he spoke again. "First, I would like to ask that you have your men lower their muskets. We would not want any accidents to happen, now would we?" Holmes asked rather sarcastically.

Roth ignoring Holmes's attitude at this point, turned and gave Berkshire a nod. Berkshire immediately gave a short whistle and the gun crews, except of course the gunners, started to come up on deck, each bearing a musket. When the additional men were in position, Roth gave his men a signal to lower their weapons. Everyone on board both vessels visibly relaxed. Turning back towards Holmes, Roth said evenly, "Please tell your men to remain where they are until our talk is over."

Roth watched and listened as Holmes shouted the order to his men. When Holmes had finished and turned his attention back to Roth and Roth said, "Now it would be my pleasure if you and your first mate would join me aboard the *Galaunt*."

"With your permission, I will have my men secure our position." Holmes said.

"Permission granted," Roth replied.

Roth made his way to the lower deck and watched as men from both vessels brought the two ships closer and securely rafted them together. When this task was accomplished, the men from the *Noble* set their gangplank across to the *Galaunt* forming the final link between them. Shortly thereafter, Captain Holmes and his first mate walked across the gangplank to the deck of the *Galaunt* where Roth and Mister Berkshire met them.

Captain Roth was the first to speak, "I would like to introduce my first mate, Mister Berkshire." Mister Berkshire did not extend his hand for obvious reasons.

"And this, gentlemen, is my first mate, Mister Gilliard," replied Captain Holmes.

"We will have our talk in my cabin," Roth stated in a matter of fact tone.

"Lead the way. I am very curious to know your explanation of the outrageous actions you have taken this morning." Holmes extended his right arm towards where he knew Roth's cabin to be and watched, with a great amount of curiosity, as Roth turned his back on the others and moved calmly towards his cabin.

Opening the door to his cabin, Roth stepped inside and when Holmes, followed by Gilliard, entered, he motioned them to take the seats in front of his desk. Mister Berkshire, bringing up the rear, took up a position behind and to the right of the two guests, coincidentally, near a brace of pistols lying on the counter. This position afforded him the advantage if anything happened. A position also noted by both Holmes and Gilliard. Roth moved around the desk and motioned to everyone to sit before taking his own seat.

"Before we begin, may I offer you a glass of port, or maybe there is something else, maybe a little stronger, that you might desire?" Roth asked.

"I will accept the port, though I am not usually in the habit of drinking with a pirate," Holmes said as he turned to his first mate that nodded acceptance also.

"Mister Berkshire," Roth said, ignoring the insult, and continued with what he hoped would be a sign of trust and honor amongst gentlemen, "Will you please go and find Brian? Have him bring four glasses and a pitcher of our finest port to my cabin."

Without a pause or a word, Mister Berkshire left the cabin in search of the cabin boy.

"While we wait, I will begin my explanation." Roth went on to tell them the story of what had happened, bringing them to this point. He told them of his hesitation in taking this voyage and of the threat of never going to sea again if he did not make this voyage. How this had forced him to bring his daughter along because there had been no time for him to make other arrangements for somewhere to live until he returned. He told them of encountering the storm that had claimed the life of his daughter Kathryn. He told them of his attacks upon the *Royale* and the chaining of Connery and Raynerd in the hold below. He told them of his attack on the *Princeton*, why he had not sunk her and where it was now. Then he told them of his plan for revenge against the man that was responsible for it all, Creed. He then went on and told them the loss of Kathryn would never have happened and she would be alive now if it had not been for Creed's insistence and threats. He paused for a few moments as he felt the emotion of anger and the pain of her loss sweeping over him again. He stifled his thoughts and then continued to tell them they were just part of his revenge and the ruin of Creed.

Berkshire had returned during the story and had brought with him Brian the cabin boy bearing a platter with four mugs and a pitcher of port. While Roth was narrating his story, Berkshire handed out the glasses and poured the wine. He shooed Brian out the door of the cabin and resumed his position by the brace of pistols, which again was noted by the others in the cabin.

"So, there you have it." Roth stated. He watched, quietly, as both Holmes and Galliard sat shaking their heads and mulling over in their minds the story they had just heard. Both Holmes and Gilliard were shocked and troubled by his story, but still not appeased at the fact that they had been taken by force.

After a brief pause Roth continued, "I am not asking you for your cooperation or any help in doing what I feel I must do. What I am asking is that you do not hinder me in any way as I do what I must do."

"Have you gone completely mad?" Holmes said as he rose to his feet. Berkshire's hand started towards the pistols but was stopped by a glance from Roth. Holmes saw this and returned to his seat before continuing, "How can you possibly justify what you have done, and are apparently about to do, with the death of your daughter?"

"You have not lost a child so I would not expect you to know how that feels. I would not have lost mine if it were not for Creed and Raynerd's greed, so therefore I am going to take everything away from them so that they can see what greed can ultimately cost." Roth was determined not to lose control over his temper but talking about what had happened to Kathryn was making him quickly lose his patience.

"What of my men and my ship? What do you have planned for them in your great scheme of things? You surely do not plan on taking and using my ship?" Holmes asked with obvious signs of disgust.

"Your men and ship will be unharmed. I am going to transfer the men and provisions from the Princeton onto your ship and you will be set free to return home." Adding to that, he stated steadily and pointedly, "You will, however, return directly home, empty of all cargo and trade goods, except for the crews of the *Royale* and *Princeton*."

"What of the *Princeton*?" Holmes asked.

Flatly, with no hesitation, Roth replied, "That ship is forfeit."

Knowingly Holmes nodded his head. After a short while, Holmes looked Roth squarely in the eyes and said, "I do not, by any means, condone what you have done. Further, I am completely against what you are convinced you must do. However, for the sake of my men and ship, I will not interfere as I wish no harm to come to them or the others."

Roth paused, wanting to reach over and shake the hand of his friend but knowing within his heart that it would be refused, simply said. "Thank you, I can understand your thoughts."

A long moment of silence was broken when Holmes asked, "When do you expect the *Princeton* to arrive?"

"I expect her to be at our position sometime in the early evening," Roth said and added, "If she has not arrived by nightfall, then we will have to find her. She is in no condition to sail far on the open seas and would have to make landfall in order to do repairs. I can intercept her before this happens and Pringle knows this, so I am sure that he will be making his way to our position. It is the shorter sail and he is in desperate need of help if he is to save his ship and crew."

"This accident to your daughter has really made you into a cold ruthless man." Holmes noted. Wondering aloud he asked, "Where is the man that I have come to admire and accept in friendship?"

"I am still the same man that you have always known. Only now, I cannot afford friends if I am to complete the task that I have set out for myself to do." Roth said, turning away as if not being able to look at his old friend any longer.

"Very well, if that is the way it is going to be, then what is it that you have in mind that we do while we await the arrival of the *Princeton*?" Holmes asked.

"If I have your word," Roth said turning back towards Holmes and seeing him nod in agreement, "then you will stay aboard my ship, as my guest." Roth could not help but smile at this and was relieved to see Captain Holmes smile as well. "Mister Gilliard will return to the *Noble* to inform your men of the agreement and the decisions reached by you and me. He will also tell them that they are free to go about their business as usual but they are to make no overt acts towards my men or ship or we will fire our cannon and sink her."

"I am in agreement. Mister Gilliard, please return to the ship and follow those instructions." Holmes said as he gestured towards the door and indicated it was time for him to leave and inform the crew.

After Gilliard, followed by Berkshire, had left and the door was reclosed, Holmes turned back to Roth and asked, "Is there no way that I can convince you to stop this madness here and now, before matters get any worse?"

Roth looked him in the eye, pausing, shook his head no. He then stood and walked around the desk to the door. Stopping there, he turned back to Holmes and said, "Make yourself at home. With any luck, the wait will not be very long and you will be on your way home." Roth opened the door and stepped into the hatchway closing the door behind him.

Holmes watched as the door closed and then stood and walked over to where Berkshire had set the jug of wine and poured himself another mug. He chuckled to himself as he looked down upon the brace of pistols and saw that neither of them was loaded. He thought to himself how well Roth knew him. Knowing that it might be a while before he would be released, he made his way to the chair behind the desk.

Looking over the charts spread across the desk, Holmes could readily see that it was no accident that Roth was where he was this morning. The area was circled, attached to the circle was a line, bearing north, attached to another circle and with another line, bearing further north, to another circle. Holmes correctly surmised that the other circles represented the attacks on the *Princeton* and *Royale*. Holmes now knew beyond any doubt that Roth had definitely thought this through and it was not a spur of the moment act. With a sigh, he sat down on the chair and made himself comfortable while he waited.

Roth made his way out to the main deck and looked around to find Berkshire. After a moment, he saw him aboard the *Noble*, talking with Gilliard. Roth did notice with surprise that after Berkshire and Gilliard saw him come out to the deck, they faced each other and said some words, then nodded and shook hands before Berkshire walked away. Roth moved up to the wheel deck to await Berkshire. When he arrived, Roth asked him, "What was that all about?"

Berkshire answered, "Well Cap'n, it appears as if not everyone is against what you are doin'." With that said, both men watched as the crew of the *Noble* prepared to offload the trade items that they had on board into the sea to make room for the additional weight of extra provisions and the crews of the other two ships.

The *Galaunt* and the *Noble* must have sailed further than Roth had thought. The wait turned out to be of short duration and not as long as was anticipated. It was just shortly after noon when the lookouts, above, excitedly cried out that the *Princeton* was coming into view. Roth, standing on the wheel deck, turned in that direction to see if he could see the oncoming ship but it was still over the horizon from his view. It felt good to know that they were that close and he started to develop a sense of urgency to proceed with his plan.

Roth returned to his cabin to get Captain Holmes. When Roth came out onto the main deck, he looked north once again and saw that indeed the *Princeton* was now in view. He stood there for a moment, then turned to Holmes and together they quietly made their way to the wheel deck to watch as the *Princeton* made her way towards them. Holmes noticed, without comment, that the *Noble* was riding rather high in the water. Then he realized that during the time he was in the cabin, his cargo must have been offloaded to make extra room. Turning and looking back behind the *Galaunt*, he saw that this was true. His cargo was floating on water in a line as far back as he could see.

As the *Princeton* approached, Holmes could make out some of the damage Roth had inflicted upon her. He could see that she was missing two masts and the third showed damage to where it could barely mount any sail at all. He also noticed that she was listing, rather severely, to the port side. As it got nearer, he could see further damage to her gunwales and deck. He could only imagine that the men aboard her would not look much better. He released a sigh of sadness as he looked out at his sister ship, but at the same time, he was thankful his ship had not sustained such damage.

Thinking his ship might sink, Pringle brought the *Princeton* around to secure it off on the starboard side of the *Galaunt*. With the *Galaunt* in the middle, Roth's men had good command over both ships.

"We are here, now what?" Pringle angrily called over to Roth as his men tied off the *Princeton*.

Roth paused before replying. "As soon as your ship is secured, your men, with the help of my men, will offload your provisions, and what personal items you need, onto the *Noble* where it will be stored below by her crew. When that is completed you and your crew, along with the crew of the *Royale* are free to sail home aboard the *Noble*."

Pringle acknowledged with a nod and then started to issue the orders for his crew to begin the task of preparing his ship for offloading. While in the process, Pringle could not help himself from feeling a deep sense of loss for his ship. She had served him well and she had been his life as well as the crews, from the first day she had set sail. He felt he was losing his entire existence. "If only I would have known that a captain of our own company of ships would do this blasphemous act! I may have been able to save her! How do I face Creed?" His thoughts angered him but he had to follow orders to avoid further humiliation.

When the offloading was started and things were going smoothly, Pringle made his way to the wheel deck of the *Galaunt* where he found Roth and Holmes in a heated discussion. When he approached his fellow captains, they stopped their argument and turned to greet him.

"You made very good time getting here," Roth said sounding almost cheerful.

Pringle considered him for a moment before saying, "It is a miracle that we got here at all! That shot you put into us at the water line is letting a lot of water into our holds. We had every man aboard on a bucket brigade, bailing her out. That along with the bilge pumps barely kept us afloat. For the life of me, I still cannot figure out why you did it. Maybe now you will tell me!"

"That matter is of little importance at this time. Holmes will fill you in on your way home." Roth muttered absently.

Pringle exploded at that, "The matter may not be important to you, but it is very important to me! Roth, you are going to be hung for what you have done. Can you not see that?"

"I have no intention of letting myself or this ship be captured before I do what I must do." Roth replied with a cold anger.

"You mean to say that you are not finished yet? Are you mad?" Pringle screamed.

"Mad or not, I and my crew are now committed to what we are doing." Roth retorted.

Holmes chimed in, "I beg you to reconsider. Throw yourself on the mercy of the court. They will surely see it as you do."

"ENOUGH," roared Roth, "I have heard all I am going to hear about this. Do you honestly believe that the men you see below you are foolish enough to believe that they would only get a reprimand? No, we fully realize what awaits us at the end of this journey. We all loved Kathryn and we all agreed that Creed must pay. Now leave this subject and be thankful that you are going to be freed." Roth turned away and watched the progress of the offloading.

Holmes and Pringle could do nothing more than stare in disbelief at what they were seeing and what they had just heard. Eventually, they too turned to watch the men go about the business of getting things moved from one ship to the other.

With all four crews working together, the provisions and other needed supplies were quickly transferred to the *Noble* and now the men were starting to make their way aboard the *Noble*.

The *Noble* was fully loaded except for the two captains, when Roth said flatly, "It is time for you to leave. You have a long way to go."

As the two started to depart, Pringle turned to ask, "What about Connery and Raynerd?"

Without any pause or thought, Roth answered in a tone that said without doubt that he would not entertain any further discussion on the matter, "They will be staying here."

With a shrug, Pringle moved off towards the gangplank connecting the two ships. After he was across the crew of the *Noble* retrieved the gangplank, but not having room to store it, they simply cast it overboard. Roth's men, upon command, cut the remaining lines securing the *Noble* to the *Galaunt*.

The two ships slowly floated apart and when the ships were a safe distance from each other, Holmes gave the order to make sail. Roth stood where he was on the wheel deck and watched as the *Noble* sailed towards the south, steadily increasing her distance away from the *Galaunt*.

After the *Noble* had sailed over the horizon, Roth ordered the crew to cut loose the *Princeton*. The crew hurriedly went about their task, but felt a strong sense of sadness, knowing what would happen when they were through. It is not easy to watch a ship go down, especially a ship like your own.

Roth lingered in place long enough to witness the final resting of a fine ship. When it was over, he gave the order to set their course southwest and told the lookouts to pay careful watch for any land. He once had overheard that there were many islands found in that direction and an island would make a good dropping off point for the two prisoners he held below decks. As he turned to leave the wheel deck for his cabin, he paused to listen to the various commands that were necessary to carry out his orders.

Upon entering his cabin, he made his way to his chair behind the desk, sitting down the thought hit him. What now he thought, what are we going to do now?

He was snatched from those thoughts by a persistent knocking at his door. "Enter" he bellowed.

The door slowly opened, Mister Berkshire leaned in and took in the scene. He realized that Roth had taken a short nap. He asked, "Cap'n, are you ok? I have been knockin' for quite a while here."

Roth, while wiping his eyes, said, "I must have dozed off. I was sitting here thinking about our future."

With a sly smile, Berkshire said, "That was kind of what the crew was thinkin' about also."

"I know what we have to do first. We have to deliver the two that are below to the shores of some island." Roth said. "Then we will decide what to do next."

Berkshire suggested, "Possibly we can give the crew some shore time to relax as well as ourselves. It has been stressful on everyone."

Roth nodded in agreement and replied with a grin, "Why not start resting now Edward? I know that I would like to get some sleep and I am sure that the crew and you would like to get some also. Issue orders for the crew to stand down. We will just let her drift until morning."

"Aye, aye Cap'n," Berkshire said with a brisk salute and a broad smile.

The next morning, fully rested, Roth and Berkshire gave the orders to set sail and for the next day and a half, the *Galaunt* made her course southwest. When dawn broke the second day, they were in sight of an island. Noon found them sailing along the shoreline of the tiny island, looking for a place where they could safely land the long boat. It was not long before they found such a place and the *Galaunt* anchored as close to the shore as was safe. Roth called upon Berkshire to join him on the wheel deck. When Berkshire arrived, Roth told him to have the men go ashore and explore the island to make sure that it could sustain life. If it turned out that it was habitable, this would give his crew a chance to possibly replenish their supplies and enjoy some shore time. He gave permission to send a barrel of grog along with them.

As Berkshire was giving the crew their orders, Roth heard a chorus of jovial cheering and laughter from the men assembled on the main deck. Undoubtedly, they just learned of the barrel of grog. He smiled to himself feeling thankful that he had such a trustworthy, hardworking and loyal crew. They deserve this and he found himself thinking that maybe they might find fresh water to bathe in and laughing to himself, he thought we all could use that. Even though the stench was well earned, a crew at sea is not a good smell.

After a few days exploring the island and gathering much needed fruit and fresh water, Roth decided that it was time to leave the area. The only thing left to do was dispose of the prisoners.

Roth ordered the longboat put over the side and told Berkshire to get the prisoners.

When Berkshire returned with the prisoners in tow, Roth was surprised to see how terrible they looked. The smell was even worse. Roth could see that Connery still boiled with defiance, but he sensed defeat in the demeanor of Raynerd. Without saying a word to either of them, he ordered Berkshire to place them in the long boat. This done Roth climbed down the ladder into the boat and ordered it ashore. No one uttered a word as the crewmembers rowed the boat. When it hit the beach and was pulled ashore, the prisoners, still chained, received help, which was begrudgingly accepted by Connery, getting out of the boat. Crewmembers then began to unload the few supplies that they were going to leave behind for the two captives.

Roth asked Berkshire to remove the chains and set the prisoners free. "This is a good island, capable of sustaining life for a long time if you know what to do. Consider yourselves lucky because you are getting a better chance then you gave to me and my daughter." Roth said.

Connery spit in Roth's direction and growled, "I vow that I will survive this to see your death. Never rest a day without knowing that I am out there watching and waiting for the day that you will die before my eyes."

Roth stared back at Connery and wanted to make a reply but realized that it would make no difference. He had won and Connery knew it. He looked towards Raynerd and asked him if he had anything to say, but Raynerd just continued to stare at his feet. It was obvious that here stood a defeated man. Those weeks in the hold had taken a major toll on Mister Raynerd.

Pointing to his right, along the beach, he told Connery that the crew had found several fruit bearing trees and one even said that he thought he saw some sort of wildlife darting back into the forest from the beach. Connery did not even look in any other direction except straight at Roth with a hateful glare in his eyes.

Shaking his head, he ordered his crew back into the longboat and pushed off into the water before boarding himself. Connery broke his silence to alternate between yelling curses, oaths of vengeance and obscenities toward the rapidly moving boat. Roth could see that Connery continued to shout long after they had passed the point of hearing him.

Reaching the ship, Roth and Berkshire climbed back aboard. Shortly thereafter, the crew had the longboat out of the water and was busily stowing it away. Roth then asked Berkshire if he would gather the men in front of the wheel deck. Berkshire nodded in compliance.

Roth stood alone on the wheel deck as the twenty or so men gathered below him. He could see a few new faces standing amongst the crew, including Gilliard. He nodded his head to each newcomer, welcoming them aboard the *Galaunt*. From the wheel deck, he could see the beach where he had left the two men. Only one was visible, probably Raynerd, for he did not appear to have moved from where they left him. Connery was nowhere in sight.

After seeing that everyone was present, he started to talk. "Well, we have achieved our primary goal. Now it is time to think about the future. We cannot sail for home. Even if we were to arrive before the *Noble*, we would be arrested when she did return."

Roth paused here to gather his thoughts and listened to the mumbles from the crew. He did not discern any disapproval. Continuing he said, "We have all sailed on the few other ships belonging to Creed and we all know the trade routes that these ships use. In order to destroy Creed, we need to destroy his base of capital. That is his ships. Every ship that we destroy digs into his capital and pushes him further towards debt. It is my plan to hunt and destroy as many of his ships as we can find and plunder any cargo that they may be carrying. Most of his trading is conducted with the colonies in America. I say that we ply those waters seeking any ship flying the Crimson C." Roth paused while the crew gave him a shout of approval. Continuing over the shouts, Roth found himself almost yelling, "Any and all cargo we capture coming from England, we can turn around and sell for ourselves in America, and any cargo captured from ships leaving America, we can trade for supplies from the settlers of the southern islands." After listening to one more shout of approval Roth looked down at his first mate and gave the order to make haste south towards the Cape.

Chapter 10
"Capture"

Roth stood alone on the bow of the *Galaunt*. He was standing, looking at the place that Kathryn had liked to sit, on that old crate, where she would watch the dolphins that always seemed to be accompanying the ship. Never a day would go by that Roth would not visit this place. He could still see Kathryn sitting there, leaning over the rail to get a better view of the dolphins as they rode, so easily, the wake coming from the bow as the ship sliced through the water. With her long hair streaming out behind her, flowing smoothly in the wind and the ever-present smile that adorned her face. It was difficult to believe it had been two years ago today that the storm had struck the *Galaunt* and took his daughter away.

Roth was thinking about all the things that had happened over the past two years and the things that had brought him to this place. It had been a hard time for him and his crew. They had captured and sank over a dozen ships, all owned by Creed, and many of his crew had once sailed on those ships and the injured or dead had once been their friends. Roth, however, would go out of his way to prevent injury to anyone, but sometimes, that could not be avoided, especially lately. In the beginning, he could use the same tricks he used on the *Noble* and the *Princeton* and after the crews of those vessels would be loaded onboard the *Galaunt* and he would then transport them to either the Americas or back to England, which ever was nearest. Word of his doings quickly spread to both continents. After that, he found that some ships would put up a fight, a fight that was usually short lived due to the superiority of the *Galaunt*. Others would try to flee, when they saw that there was not much chance of them out running the *Galaunt*, they would just lower their sails and give up, knowing that this way the crew would survive.

Lately, however, Roth learned that he was having a profound effect on Creed from the captured Captains and their crew. He had also been told that Creed had gone deep into debt. Creed was also hoping that Roth would be stopped before much longer and he could once again start to make a profit. To help his goal along, Creed had gotten the government to agree that the captains of his ships, by not putting up a fight to save his ship, would be responsible for the loss and if he could not pay, would be put in prison. This agreement would ensure forcing them to fight regardless of their position.

This last battle had been the worst of them all. The *Marion* had been a good ship with a good crew. Her captain had shown that he had an exceptional knowledge of how to protect himself and put up a very good fight. The *Galaunt* had been sorely damaged, including the loss of her main mast. Roth had finally been able to get into a position where they could hull the other ship and that is what they did. The *Marion,* struck several times below the water line, quickly began to take on water. Roth had his men brought the *Galaunt* about and raced in to rescue anyone in the water. Roth could still see the men jumping off the rapidly sinking ship. He and his crew were only able to pick up a little over half of the other crew before the ship sank. When all was done, the remaining crewmen, the captain included, went down along with her. Roth always felt a great sadness whenever there was life lost, so he held the *Galaunt* in the area for most of the day in hopes additional crew might survived. As it was, only fourteen of twenty-three crew survived.

The damaged *Galaunt* sailed to the Islands of West India, so named by Christopher Columbus who thought that he had reached the East Indies by sailing west. During the voyage, one of the survivors, the Second Mate, was brought to the attention of Roth by Mister Berkshire. From this man Roth learned that Creed was at the bottom of his barrel. He was banking all he had left on one last voyage. The Second Mate of the *Marion* told him that the *Royal Troon* left England ten days after they did. These two ships were to sail to a remote harbor, near an American colony, where a cargo of highly desirable items would be loaded onboard and brought back to England. This could possibly bring a considerable profit to Creed. Roth questioned him further to learn the location of the harbor and what type of cargo was waiting there. The man could only tell him what cargo had been loaded onto the *Marion* but he had no idea what was to be loaded onto the *Troon*. Satisfied that he had learned all that this sailor knew, the man was returned to the others and the *Galaunt* continued towards the safe harbor.

After the battle, it took two days for the crew to ready the *Galaunt* to be able to sail and an additional two days to reach their destination. Arrangements were made for the quick repair of the ship and a restocking of much needed supplies. The time for repair would take about fifteen days. This would give his men plenty of time to rest on the beaches and be ready for another hunt, possibly their last. It also meant that the *Royal Troon* would have reached its destination and would have ample time to load her cargo and begin her long voyage home, a place that if Roth has his way, they would never reach.

The repairs were moving along nicely and they would be completed on schedule. Roth and Berkshire were alone in Roth's cabin pouring over the charts of where they had come upon the *Marion*. They were trying to decipher, from the routes taken by both ships to reach the America's, where the *Royal Troon* would be positioned now if they had reached their destination and completed their loading. The *Troon* could be no more than two days away from harbor and on her way home. A course was plotted that would put the *Galaunt* ahead of the *Troon* where they could lay in wait.

After Mister Berkshire left the cabin leaving Roth alone with his thoughts, he laid back on his bunk feeling somewhat anxious now that he was getting that much closer to reaching his vendetta against Creed. Although he knew in his heart that nothing could bring his darling Kathryn back. She would know that he did all he could to destroy the man responsible for the loss of her life. He lay in a dreamlike state visualizing her beautiful smile and the playful things she did smiling to himself before falling into a deep sleep.

The morning after the completion of the repairs found the *Galaunt* moving out of the harbor towards the open sea. When the ship had cleared harbor, Roth ordered the crew to hoist the sails of the main mast only. Roth needed to inspect the repairs before he started across the ocean. As he was inspecting the starboard side of the ship, in his mind, he could still see the terrible gash that the broken mast had left there. The mast had been hit twice below the main deck and when it gave, that was where it separated. As it fell, it sliced through the main deck like butter. Fortunately, for the *Galaunt*, the mast, hit about half way up, tore through the gunwales on its way to the gun deck, the increased resistance afforded by the side of the ship caused the top half to break off and the rest stopped its destruction at the gun ports. The *Galaunt* was still not out of danger, however, the massive weight of the mast and all its rigging had rolled the ship to nearly a thirty-degree list. Much further and water would begin to enter the ship through the slice and it would not take long for her to be pulled under to the bottom. Roth could still see the frantic rushing of the crew to cut the rigging loose and winch the lower portion of the mast through the slice and away from the ship before the *Marion*, also grievously damaged, could mount a counter assault. As the mast finally slipped through the gash, taking with it single cannon and another four feet of hull, the *Galaunt* immediately rolled back over and regained her balance. This afforded Roth the chance that was needed to resume the battle and eventually win the day.

Satisfied with the repairs, Roth started to return to the wheel deck. On his way there, Berkshire, who had been inspecting the decks below, intercepted him. Berkshire informed him that the repairs were good. Returning to the wheel deck, he gave the order to raise the remaining sail and start their hunt. He watched as the crew in the rigging untied the canvas, letting it fall, and heard the pop that they always made when they caught the wind and billowed. The *Galaunt* was in her element now, under full sail and racing across the waves similar to a skater on ice. It would take eleven days of hard sailing like this to reach the point where Roth and Berkshire had determined they would be ahead of the *Royal Troon*.

Dawn on the ninth day of that race found Roth at the bow. He would start each day here where he could see the sunrise and assure himself that leading the ship were the dolphins. He still found it strange that the dolphins were always there, even when they were in harbor. The dolphins could be seen in the ocean just beyond the harbor mouth. Other strange sightings were spoken of but no one really believed what was being said. Some were haunted by it but did not feel free to say anything about what they thought they saw.

Roth returned to the wheel deck where he found Sandy, the Second Mate, in command of the deck. Relieving him, he took a moment to check the compass to verify the heading before he took up his position where he could watch all that was happening on the main deck. It was not long before Mister Berkshire joined him. Berkshire informed him that his inspections of the repairs were still finding nothing of concern. Then he mentioned that he had stopped to eat before he came up on deck. He went on to suggest that the captain should join the crew that was coming on duty for breakfast while he took over the watch. Roth did feel hungry so he took Berkshire up on his offer and headed below to the galley. Roth found most of the men already seated at the table. Pots was ladling out the morning meal as Roth took his seat at the head of the table. The men were mostly quiet as Pots served up the breakfast. When he had finished, it was Mister Willis, the Chief Gunnery Officer, better known to the crew as "Gunny", that was the first man to speak. "Cap'n sir, I was wonderin' if we could have a little talk while we eat."

Roth looked a little surprised at that request and answered, "Of course we can Gunny, what do you have on your mind?"

"Well sir, me self and some of the other officers and crew have been talkin' about how nice it was on the islands and how there is plenty of space for a man to settle and maybe even prosper. We know that if we get the *Troon* then Creed will be ruined and there will no more need for us to go on with what we are doin'. So here it is sir, we would like to know what the future holds for us." Gunny asked.

Roth thought this over for a short while before he spoke, "I have given that some thought also. You are right about the islands of course. They would be the ideal place to settle. Furthermore, it would be more than what we had set out for ourselves to do concerning Creed, if we stayed on the path we are on now." Roth paused for a time before he spoke again. "If what we have heard is indeed true, then I myself would like to stop. We are not pirates, we were never meant to be. We have accumulated a sizeable sum of money over the last two years. I see no reason why we could not become honest traders once again. There is a great need for trade in the Americas and I can see a profitable future. Let me discuss this with Mister Berkshire and we will see what happens.

For now, though, we must concentrate on the job before us. The *Royal Troon* is a well-armed ship, as we all know. Her sister ship, the *Marion*, was almost the end of us. We must remain alert at all times if we are to be successful in this hunt."

"Thank you sir, the moral of the crew will heighten on word of this. Do not you be worryin', we will be ready! This may be our last fight, so we will not let you down." Gunny replied boldly.

Roth could not help but be proud of this crew. They had always been there when he needed them and they were vowing to do so again. "Thank you. That is all a Captain can hope for."

Roth returned to the wheel deck to find Sandy in command of the deck once again and Berkshire nowhere nearby. "Sandy, where is Mister Berkshire?"

His voice filled with concern, Sandy replied. "He was called below to take a look at the hull in the forward hold sir, apparently the side of the ship took a greater blow than we thought and some of the hull planks are working loose. He asked me to inform you of the situation and that he requests that you join him as soon as possible."

"Thank you Sandy. Stay where you are, I will be below decks." Roth turned and left the wheel deck making his way to the forward hold.

Berkshire spoke as soon as he saw Roth. "There you are. I was just about to send someone looking for you. As you can see, we are taking on water. Nothing to worry about yet, the bilge pumps are able to stay well ahead of it, but if we do not take some strain off these planks, it is only a question of time before the planks give way. We need to slow the ship down and give these planks time to reseat themselves before we venture into a possible battle with the *Troon*."

Looking at what Berkshire pointed out to him, he could readily see where the planking had worked loose. "Exactly, I agree with you. When you have finished here, find me on the wheel deck. We will go to my cabin and plot what the loss of time will do to our scheduled plan of reaching the point where we expect to intercept the *Troon*." Roth felt a pang of anticipation as he always did, when he knew he was one step closer to taking Creed down.

"Aye Cap'n," Berkshire replied.

Roth took one more look at the leak before returning to the wheel deck. He had not liked what he had seen. If they got into a running sea battle with the *Troon*, the stresses that would be put on the hull would be tremendous, possibly allowing those planks to spring out of place. If that happened, the *Galaunt* would sink like a stone. Assured that he had a great crew and well built ship, he found himself feeling a bit more positive.

Reaching the wheel deck, Roth asked Sandy to give the order to ease off on the sails. He listened and watched as his orders were being carried out. By letting off on the sails, the ship would be allowed to slow and thus relieve a lot of the pressure on the hull. The *Galaunt* slowed noticeably and he suddenly wondered if indeed they would make it to the *Troon* on time.

Before long Berkshire returned to the deck and reported that the planking had been reinforced as well as they could without major repairs and the leak had been slowed considerably. Roth thanked him and turning to Sandy he said, "We will be in my cabin. You are in command."

"Aye, aye Captain," Sandy said as he saluted and turned back to his position near the forward railing watching the goings on of the ship and crew.

After getting a reading on their speed by throwing a float off the bow and timing it to the stern, Roth could accurately gauge their speed. They then went to his cabin to plot how long it would now take before they would start their hunt. Roth had planned to be well ahead of the *Troon* when they made the turn that would put them on the opposite track of her. They determined that they would have to make a minor course adjustment due to the lack of speed. The important thing was that they would now have less time before they met with the *Troon*. In fact, that time might be as early as tomorrow morning.

Berkshire went back out on deck to inform the rest of the crew of the change of events. There were still many things that needed to be taken care of before the *Galaunt* could effectively fight. Berkshire handed out the various tasks and returned to the captain's cabin. He found Roth where he had left him, still looking over the charts to make sure that there had been no mistakes and they were on the right course. Joining him they both reworked the calculations far into the afternoon.

Evening found Roth and Berkshire standing near the main mast. They had just finished conducting a tour of the ship to verify in their own minds that the ship was as ready as it could be for the fight they hoped would be coming in the morning but at the same time, dreaded it had to come at all. Everything had been stowed away where it belonged and the decks were clear of any obstructions that could hamper quick movement around the main deck. The guns were clear of everything not needed to fire cannon. Stacks of shot and powder could be found next to the remaining fifteen of her cannons. During the brief conversation they had with Gunny, they learned that all the gun crews were resting in their hammocks, but still ready to act at a moment's notice. Roth agreed that they had better get their rest now because there would be no rest tomorrow.

The topic of discussion was crew. The ship carried a crew of thirty-eight, each capable of manning a cannon. It took two sailors to fire each cannon. All fifteen guns were loaded, but not yet primed, and ready for battle. Only one line of cannon would be required at a time, counting Gunny that would require fourteen to sixteen sailors. That left twenty-two men including, Roth, Mister Berkshire, the second mate Sandy, Pots and Brian the cabin boy. Roth would command the overall battle and issue orders for maneuvering and firing of the cannons, while Mister Berkshire would be in charge of the crew, making sure those orders were carried out in a timely fashion. Sandy would be the acting Helmsman. Pots would be caring for the injured and wounded. Brian would be on the gun deck, supplying bandages, if needed, water and pickle juice. The air on the gun deck, during battle, became foul in a hurry and water was needed to wash out the eyes. The pickle juice would be needed to rid the crew of the terrible headaches the powder used in the guns, caused. Leaving eighteen able bodied seamen to man the main deck and be responsible to keep the ship moving. Roth thought, they would need at least nine to man the rigging and work the sails. He felt confident that he had what he needed going into battle.

Seeing that everything looked ready and there was nothing left to do, Roth told Berkshire that he was retiring to his cabin and wanted to be awakened two hours before sunrise. He made one more tour of the ship before he left to try to get some rest.

He entered his cabin and went to his cot. He knew that he would get no sleep tonight. In his mind, he contemplated, as he had so many times before, how the battle would go. Still, he could not shake the feeling he had, that everything in his life was going to change tomorrow. He had no idea what that could be, but nevertheless the feelings were there.

Roth was still awake when the knock came to alert him that it was two hours before dawn. He acknowledged that he was awake by opening the door to his cabin while the messenger was still in the hallway. He thanked him and made his way to the wheel deck. He was met by Mister Berkshire and Sandy, who was already at the helm. He nodded to both men and turned his stare to the faint glimmer of light barely discernable on the eastern horizon.

About an hour before sunrise, they heard a sound. Berkshire was the first to identify it as cannon fire. In a few more minutes, there was no doubt about what they were hearing. There was no mistaking the sound of cannon fire as it rolled along the surface of the ocean. Just over the horizon, they began to see faint flashes and knew that a sea battle was just to the north. Roth ordered the ship turned in the direction of they believed was the battle.

Before the sun cleared the horizon, they still heard cannon fire in the distance. When it did rise, they got a look at two ships engaged in what sounded and looked like a fierce fight. They could see, through their scopes, that the larger of the two participants was stalled on the water and showed massive damage to her masts and sails. It was also listing to such an angle that it appeared as if the ends of the lower yardarms might be in the water. The smaller of the two, obviously an old Spanish galleon by design, looked like it had just finished a raking pass and was starting a turn to make another on the hull of the listing vessel. As they neared closer to the battle, they could identify that the larger of the two ships could be the *Troon*. It was obvious to both men that the smaller Spanish ship must have ambushed the *Troon* in the night. The *Troon* was much larger, better armed, and should have been able to handle the smaller ship with ease.

Mister Berkshire nudged Roth's arm and pointed in the direction of the *Troon*. At first Roth could see nothing, and then he picked out a longboat as it made its way, precariously, through the tangled mass of what was left of the rigging of the once proud ship. When the longboat worked itself clear of the wreckage, Roth could see three sailors feverishly begin to row away from the sinking ship. Through his scope, he could see five, maybe six, people in the longboat. The three sailors rowing, another at the tiller and what appeared to be someone, holding an injured man or possibly a child, in the bow. It looked as though they had tried to time their escape when the Spanish were on the other side of the ship. Neither, obviously, was aware of the *Galaunt* rapidly approaching from the south. Neither Roth nor Berkshire could see anybody on either vessel looking in their direction, although the longboat was pointed right at them. The Spanish must have caught a glimpse of the longboat at the last moment because they were turning away from the ship, as if to pursue the longboat. It turned out that Roth's guess was right, the Spanish ship continued its turn to make its way around the stern of the stricken *Troon*. A few more minutes and the *Galaunt* would be close enough to save the people on board the longboat. As the Spanish ship rounded the stern of the *Troon*, it sighted the *Galaunt* speeding in their direction. Quickly it turned away to the northwest and raised all sails as if it thought it could outrun the *Galaunt*. Roth gave a mock show of a chase until he was certain that the Spanish had departed, not to return. Roth then gave the order to return to the *Troon*.

Returning to the area of the fight, they could find only debris in the water. Floating amongst that debris were bodies of the men that had fought and died aboard the *Royal Troon*. Roth could see that the longboat had not ventured further than it had, when the *Galaunt* passed it in chase of the Spaniards. Roth ordered his men to launch their own longboat and retrieve the dead sailors for a proper burial at sea. After the longboat was in the water and performing its grizzly task, Roth ordered the *Galaunt* to be moved to the other longboat drifting away to the east.

As the *Galaunt* approached the boat, he could see that it was a young man in fine dress at the tiller. The young man could not be any older than Roth had been when he first put to sea. He also saw that the young man and the three sailors were aiming muskets at the *Galaunt*. Roth had to admire the bravery or maybe just audacity of the men aboard the small boat. Four muskets would not be enough to save them from the ship drifting towards them. Roth ordered the ship to stop well out of range of the musket and called out, "Ahoy the longboat, put down your muskets, we wish you no harm. Put down your weapons and we will bring you aboard." Roth saw that the people aboard the boat had a quick discussion. The young man seemed not to want to give up that easily, but he was deferring to the man in the front of the boat who appeared, now, to be holding a young child. Maybe the man in the front was the captain or at least a superior officer. Roth gave the order to move ahead slowly after he saw them lower their weapons. The *Galaunt* was brought alongside the longboat and lines were thrown down to it so it could be brought closer. Ladders were lowered over the side as Roth made his way to the deck above the small boat. He saw to his surprise that the man in the bow was not a man at all, but a woman who looked to be ten years Roth's senior. She was cradling an injured child in her lap. The young man and the other men, who turned out to be Royal Marines, helped the woman up the ladder first. Roth sensed an air of authority with this one and he already knew she was in charge. He also noted how the marines were behaving towards her. The injured child needed to be carried up the ladder by two of the marines. As they neared the top of the ladder, Roth and Berkshire reached over the side and with Roth taking the shoulders and Berkshire the legs, they brought the child onto the ships deck. Someone had laid his jacket on the deck to use as a pillow and Roth, realizing now that the child was a young boy, settled his head on it. As they laid him down, the rag covering his head slid off to reveal a wide gash and the glint of bone, just below the hairline. Roth called for Pots, the closest person on board to resemble a doctor, and told him to take him to the galley and patch him up as best he could. Pots told the nearest sailor to get a door from one of the cabins and bring it here immediately. The sailor did not even seem to be gone before he returned with the door. Motioning to another sailor to take his feet, the first to take his shoulders, the three of them gently lifted him and carefully placed him on the door. With another motion, he had them lift the door and follow him.

While this was taking place, the three marines and the young man climbed the ladders and were onboard. When the young man first stepped on board, he immediately turned towards the woman to make sure that she was ok and then watched as the others took the boy away.

After a moment, he turned and faced Roth and inquired, "Permission to come aboard sir?"

Roth spun around and found it hard not to laugh at the serious look on the face of this prim young man, but controlling himself, he said, "Permission granted." Stepping forward he offered his hand and said, "I am Captain Roth and this is the *Galaunt.*"

Looking at but refusing the hand, the young man said very arrogantly, "I know who you are. I know that you are a scoundrel and a rogue and should be tried and hung for your crimes at sea! I demand the immediate surrender of yourself and this ship. Furthermore, I demand passage to England for the woman, her son, myself and my men."

Ignoring the insult and nearly bursting out in laughter from what he equated as a Chihuahua barking a challenge to a Great Dane. Roth said with a low tone of authority, as he leaned into the young man's face. "Well young lad. I do not know if you have noticed, but you are unarmed and on my ship. I don't see as you are in any position to make any demands of me or, for that matter, my ship. I just saved your lives for the love of might!"

The blood quickly drained from the young man's face as he realized the mistake he had just made, but he still tried to show an air of defiance. He was about to say something else, when the woman stepped forward and with a waving motion of her hand, silenced him. "You will have to forgive my nephew, he is young, new to the ways of the world and as you can see, very inexperienced in the art of diplomacy," she said as she glanced in the direction of the young man while shaking her head. Roth could not fail to notice the look of pain followed by anger that flared across his face. She went on to say, "It is indeed very important that we get to England at the very earliest that we can."

"If you do, as you say, know who I am, then you also know that I would not be welcomed in England." Roth said laughing.

She did not hesitate and said, "I am well aware of the welcome you would receive in England. I am also aware that you have made several visits to Ireland where you have left men that crewed vessels you have destroyed."

She paused here as if to gather her thoughts before going on. Before she could say anything else, Roth held up his hand and said, "This is not something that needs to be discussed at this time. First and foremost, I and my crew have a duty that must be seen too." He looked at Berkshire and gave the order to return to their longboat. Berkshire acknowledged with a nod and moved off to give instructions to the helmsmen.

Roth started to make his way towards the wheel deck when he turned back towards the woman and the lad. He was thinking that it might be a nice gesture to ask them to join him. He put on his big toothy grin and in his civil voice, said graciously, "It would be my pleasure if you would join me on the wheel deck." Nodding, she accepted, whereby Roth removed his hat and with a courteous bow, he ushered them towards the stairs chuckling to himself.

Roth put them both out of his mind for a while as he tended to the task before him. The ship reached the longboat and nine bodies were brought aboard. Roth watched as the crew prepared each for a burial at sea. They had had to do that several times over the course of the years. A line of nine planks were arranged on the port side and each body was laid on a plank.

Roth left the wheel deck and took his place by the planks. Removing his hat, a signal for all to remove theirs, he said, "Lord Father we commend the souls of these brave men to your care, and to the deep, we commend their bodies." With that, each plank, in turn was raised and the body it held slid silently into the sea.

The woman remained on the wheel deck and took all of this in. She was very confused. She had heard that Roth was a cruel man with raffish manners. What she was witnessing, however, was quite the opposite. The obvious concern he had shown over her son was not expected and she had watched as her nephew had insulted him and had tried to provoke him to no avail and now this solemn ceremony for those dead men that should not have meant anything to him. He did not know them, but still, he afforded them a service and remanded their souls to our Lord. What kind of a man was this Captain Roth, she wondered? She broke from her reverie to see Roth coming her way. He stopped to talk to a man who in turn talked to another man that immediately rushed off, and then they both started towards the wheel deck.

Roth walked straight up to the woman removed his hat and said, "Perhaps we can start over?"

"Perhaps we should." She said politely.

"Then allow me. I am Captain Nathan Roth and this is my first mate, Mister Berkshire." Berkshire and the woman nodded to one another.

"My name is Elizabeth and this flighty young man is my nephew, Charles," she said with a smile. Roth turned towards the young man and offered his hand again but received a scowl in return. Elizabeth continued, "The lad that you have below decks is my son Rupert."

Choosing again to ignore the obvious insult from the young man, Roth did not see that behind him Berkshire had taken notice and looked like he did not intend to forget it. "I have made arrangements for you to dine, in my cabin. Afterwards, if you would like, we will discuss the request you have asked of me." At this time, he shot a look at the young man who remained aloof and detached. His arrogance and rudeness reflected disdain. Roth wondered why.

"I am looking forward, with eagerness, to having that discussion," Elizabeth returned, feeling much more comfortable in Roth's presence.

"Fine, shall we?" he said with a gesture towards the stairs. When Elizabeth started to move, he said to Berkshire, "Mister Berkshire, would you please see to Charles and then see that he gets squared away?"

"Oh yes Cap'n, I will see that he gets squared away." Berkshire said in a very malicious tone.

"I must protes…" The young man started to say, but was cut off by Elizabeth who simply stated, "Go with the man, Charles, and I bid thee, do not be a problem." Without another look, she turned and descended the stairs. Roth gave Berkshire a cautionary stare before he too turned and descended the stairs. "When Pots is finished with the child, take the young lad to Kathryn's cabin. We might as well start getting some use out of it." Berkshire nodded.

She waited for him at the bottom of the stairs and he led the way to his cabin. He opened the door and motioned for her to enter. She was presented with a table laid out fit for royalty. It seemed as if everything on the table was made of silver, including the lit candelabra. "You set a very fine table." She said looking over her shoulder.

Roth replied slyly, "One acquires things here and there."

"Yes, I suppose one does." Elizabeth said with a knowing smile.

Roth helped her to her seat at the near end of the table and moved around to his seat at the other end. They had no sooner sat down, than Pots entered with a pot of steaming soup that he began to ladle into the soup bowls. As one course was finished, Pots brought in until they could eat no more.

After Roth finished his last bite, he leaned back and threw his napkin onto his plate, then said, "It is a good thing that I do not always eat like that, I would look like Pots." They both laughed.

Two seamen came in and cleaned off the table. After they finished Pots reappeared. Roth looked at Elizabeth and asked, "Would you like a glass of wine before you retire?"

"I would like maybe just a touch of sherry, if you have it?" she said with a guilty smile.

Pots nodded his head and left the cabin. Neither spoke as they awaited his return. Both were in their own thoughts. Pots, not gone long, knocked on the door before entering. In a fine crystal glass, he handed Elizabeth her sherry and to Roth, he handed a glass of cognac.

"Please tell me how you happened to be on board that ship." Roth inquired.

"It is quite simple, I needed passage. An officer of the Royal Marines delivered a message that I was needed at home immediately. We heard that you were in the area and had taken the *Marion* after a long running battle that some said may have damaged your ship beyond repair. So after discussion, with the officer in charge of the contingent that delivered the message, it was decided that I would seek passage on the *Royal Troon*, as it was the first available ship., We thought we only had you to worry about and we were sure that we could get to England before you found us. We were wrong as it turned out," she stated.

Roth thought about this for a moment before asking, "What made you think that I would come after that *Troon*?"

She eyed him for a second then replied. "It is well known that you are seeking revenge against Lord Creed. It has been said that you believe he is responsible for the loss of someone close to you and the *Troon* was his last ship." She knew instantly that she had made a mistake.

Roth's eyes had narrowed and his face began to flush as he looked at her. He did not speak because he knew that he would regret anything he said now. He turned his head and looked out the windows until he could compose himself. Finally, he turned and said, "His last ship, you say?"

Elizabeth, thankful that he had not lost his temper, replied, "Yes, the poor man has suffered tremendous losses at your hand. I was told that if this ship did not make it, he would be ruined and possibly thrown in prison for his debts.

With that, Roth forgot everything else that was said and replied, "You are right, we were hunting you. I had heard the same thing about Creed. The *Marion,* indeed, gravely damaged the *Galaunt,* but we were able to make it to port for repairs. We would have engaged you this morning. We were beaten to the punch, however, by the Spanish." Pausing, as if a thought had suddenly entered his head, Roth went on. "Maybe you can explain to me why the Spanish, who were very out classed, risked their lives to attack the *Troon.* They do not usually go out of their way to attack large armed vessels."

"They were waiting for us as the sun started to rise. They were alongside before anyone realized it and opened fire." She went on to describe the events of the morning. When she was done telling of the attack, she went on to say, "A bookshelf had fallen from the wall and caught Rupert on the forehead, knocking him unconscious. The door to our cabin was above me and I could not get him and myself up to it. That was when Charles showed up. If it had not been for Charles and the marines, Rupert and I would be on the bottom with the rest. The marines informed me their commanding officer had been killed along with the rest of the contingent. He also said that they had not seen any others alive. We made it to the longboat and the marines were able to wrestle it onto the water. You know the rest of the story," she said, ending her narration.

Roth quietly listened until she had finished. After a polite pause, he said, "You had quite the morning it seems. Now, I think it is time that you got some rest and we will continue this discussion in the morning. I ask that you stay here and use my cabin as if it were your own, now if you will excuse me I will take my leave."

"Wait." She cried. "What about taking us to England?"

"As I said, we will continue this discussion in the morning," Roth replied softly but firmly. As he opened the door, he turned back to her and said, "As soon as I leave here, I will go and check on your son. If there is anything that you need to know, I will come back and tell you. If I do not return, you will know that everything is fine." With that, he quietly closed the door behind him.

Elizabeth watched him leave. She was more confused now than before. She knew that he was a pirate, but there was something, something she could not put her finger on, that told her that this man was more than just a pirate, much more. Still, she decided that she would not yet reveal who she really was. She was becoming very tired, so she lay down on the cot, thinking about the events of the day and especially this evening and was soon fast asleep.

Roth made his way to the wheel deck, where standing next to the helmsman, he found Berkshire and Sandy. When he approached, he inquired as to the young man. Berkshire told him that he had straightened him out and added, "Pots wanted to thank you for the additional help."

Roth smiled at that. He went on to say, "Well Mr. Berkshire, what do you think of our guests?"

"I am not rightly sure what to think. I got to talking with the three marines and they told me that their original contingent consisted of twenty men, led by a full colonel. I asked them if they were there to protect the ship and they said no. It seemed to me that they realized they should not be talking about what they were doing here and became silent," Berkshire explained.

"She told me that they had delivered a message. With what you told me and what she said, it seems strange to me that someone would send a colonel, let alone twenty Royal Marines to deliver a message. And to send them all the way from England adds more to the mystery." Roth mused.

Berkshire asked, "Did she tell you what was in the message that was so important?"

"No, she just said that she was needed at home. Also, I would like to know why an old Spanish Galleon, which was out manned and out gunned, would attempt a ship such as the *Troon*. Things just do not add up," Roth said.

"They surely do not, that is for sure! I think that there is more to this lady than meets the eye," Berkshire agreed.

Roth was silent for quite some time before he spoke again. "I don't know why she wants us to take her to England, but I think for now we will make our course due east."

"Are you sure that is a good idea?" Berkshire inquired. "Maybe we should find out more before we commit ourselves. This might be a trick to lure us closer to England."

"We have plenty of time to learn more. If we are not happy with what we learn, then we can always turn around and head back to the islands. There is more here that I want to know about. So, for now, east it is." Roth said in a commanding tone.

Berkshire knew there was no more room for discussion. "Aye, aye Cap'n," Berkshire said as he repeated the commands to the helmsman and to Sandy, who had the night watch.

Roth stood for a moment longer then went below to find a place to rest for a while. He needed time to think about the events of the day and try to understand the meaning of this strange woman that they had brought on board the *Galaunt*.

Morning found Roth in his normal spot. He was, as he never tired of doing, watching the dolphins and thinking of his daughter. He was pulled from his thoughts by the sound of footsteps coming his way. He turned and saw Elizabeth coming towards him. Her dress was very dirty and torn in several places but that did not detract from the manner in which she carried herself. She was moving across the deck as if she owned it and had every right in the world to be there. The men were even bowing out of her way. Who is this woman? Roth thought to himself.

"Good morning captain. Am I disturbing you?" she asked, as she kept moving forward. "Mornings are the time of day that I like the best. Things are still quiet and the air always seems sweeter." She paused seeming to be enjoying the view. Turning to Roth, she said. "Captain, please tell me about this Kathryn."

Startled, Roth turned his head before asking. "What do you know of Kathryn?"

"Nothing, I heard the name mentioned yesterday when you assigned Rupert her cabin and I could not help but notice the reaction you had when I said that about someone close to you," she answered. Watching him stare out over the ocean for a very long time made her think that he was not going to tell her.

Suddenly in a low sad voice he said, "She was my daughter. She is indeed that someone." Roth again poised himself in position and resumed watching the dolphins with his thoughts carrying him far away.

Elizabeth thought that she had seen a tear in his eye before he turned away. She knew now that she had struck a very emotional response and regretted that her curiosity had made her do it. She had to find out about Kathryn. Without another word, she left Roth to his reverie and made her way below decks to find the galley. It was not really the galley she was looking for, it was Pots. She saw someone scrubbing out a deep pot in the corner and asked him where she might find Pots. She was surprised to see Charles pull his head from the pot and give her a scowl.

From behind her she heard, "Back to the pot young sire, you know what Mister Berkshire said would happen if you did not do what you are told." Then turning towards Elizabeth, he smiled and said, "How may I help you ma'am? Would you like some food?"

Elizabeth was surprised to see that how fast Charles had gone back to cleaning the pot. Trying very hard to keep herself from laughing, she replied, "No thank you, I'm not very hungry. What I am really after is some information."

"And what information might that be, ma'am?" Pots inquired.

"I would like to know about Kathryn."

Pots thought about it for a minute before starting to tell her about a girl that was once aboard this ship and how, in a terrible storm, she was lost at sea. Over an hour later, Elizabeth now understood why Roth was reluctant to talk about Kathryn and why he had chosen the quest that he was pursuing. This directed her thoughts to Rupert and she felt the need to go to him and hold him close. She found him to be much better and that gave her comfort. She lulled him to sleep as she lay down along side of him. Deep in thought, she could not possibly fathom what she would do if she lost a child, especially an only child. The pain would be excruciating. A man handles pain with anger. Yes, now she could completely identify with this poor man. How could someone not see the reasoning behind this vengeance?

Later that evening, Elizabeth found Roth on the wheel deck and asked if he would like to join her, in *her* cabin, for dinner.

The mention of *her* cabin brought a smile to his face. "Yes, I would be honored," he said bowing good-naturedly. He followed her down the stairs and into the passageway towards his cabin. Reaching the door, he again held it open for her and then helped her to her seat. As he was moving around the table, he saw that there was a different arrangement than before. Now there were four places set out. He had no more than realized what that meant, when there was a knock at the door. Roth and Elizabeth, at the same time, both said, "Enter." They looked at each other and laughed.

Roth saw young Charles hold the door open as the young lad, Rupert stepped through the hatchway. Elizabeth rose and hugged her son. "Rupert, I would like to introduce you to, Captain Roth, as I told you earlier, this is the man that saved us yesterday."

Rupert turned to Roth and hesitantly extended his hand as he said, "I am very grateful for what you have done and are still doing for my mother, uncle and myself."

"The pleasure, as it is turning out, is all mine. If there is anything that you require, please do not hesitate to tell me or one of my men." Roth said shaking his hand gingerly.

"I hope that you do not mind that I invited Charles," Elizabeth replied. "After all the kitchen really is no place for him."

Before Roth could reply, Charles stepped through the door and snapped to attention giving Roth a crisp salute, he said. "Captain, I am at your service, sir."

Roth returned the salute thinking to himself that he needed to ask Berkshire what he had said to this young man. With Elizabeth smiling beside him, Roth again extended his hand and said, "You are most welcome Charles." This time his hand was not refused. Then turning towards the table, he said, "shall we?"

As Roth was helping Elizabeth into her seat again, he saw the stitches in Rupert's forehead and commented, "It is good to see you up and around. How are you feeling?"

Rupert relaxed into his chair and said, "I am alright. It was just a bump on the head. After talking with your man, Pots, I feel rather foolish about how I came on board."

Roth smiled and said, "We were more concerned about the gash on your forehead. We had no way of knowing how you were hurt and if anything further may have been broken. There is no need for you to feel foolish. Just be thankful that Pots was taking all precautions in mind. We are all happy to see you have recovered so well. Pots told me that the wound will heal nicely."

Small talk dominated the rest of the meal. Roth did notice, however, that every time the conversation lead to something that might give him a clue as to who these people were, Elizabeth would change the subject. In addition, he could not fail to notice that whenever Charles would ask a question of him or answer a question, he always ended with sir. Roth still wondered what Berkshire had said that had made such a quick turnaround in his attitude.

After the meal ended and the crew had cleared the table, Elizabeth suggested to Charles that he take Rupert out on deck and show him the ship. Charles readily agreed. He had had enough of this captain and watching his aunt dote on him. It was beneath her station and he could not understand why they could not just come out and tell this captain who they were.

When they had left and the door was once again closed, Elizabeth turned to Roth and, smiling, asked, "Where would you like to begin our discussion tonight?"

Roth thought about that a few moments and finally said, "Well, I guess we could start off by you telling me who you are and why a squad of Royal Marines was escorting you home." Roth saw Elizabeth's eyes widen at his inquiry regarding the marines. She thought to herself, 'surely that would raise a question in anyone's mind'.

However, she only hesitated a moment before answering, "Who we are, as I have told you before is unimportant. We are just a simple country family. As to the marines, they were merely taking the only vessel home that was available, not escorting me."

Roth was not sure that he believed her, but decided to set that aside as he asked, "Then maybe you can tell me why it is so important that you get to England."

"After what you have done for us, you deserve to know the truth." She paused here. "Charles is the only surviving son of his father. He lost an older brother a few years back. Last year, my brother asked me if I would accompany Charles to the Americas to look after his interests there. I accepted, taking Rupert with me, we sailed to America and came to live in Jamestown. The message that I received, told me of the trouble that my brother was having and his need for us to return to England." Looking at Roth, trying to gauge his reaction to her story, she went to say. "I am hoping that you will understand my need to return to my brother's side and also to understand why I am pleading with you to take us there. I, however, find myself in a quandary." Taking a sip of wine, she continued, "I do not see you as a scoundrel, traitor or pirate. I find myself sympathizing with your quest. I truly understand your reasoning. I do not want to put you in a position to be captured or for that matter, imprisoned. What I cannot question is that my journey back to England is of utmost importance. I wonder, perhaps, if you could find another route to take us home without risking yourself or this ship."

Roth silently mulled over things that she had said and how he may be able to accommodate her and not overly risking himself or the crew. Rising, he excused himself from the table and proceeded to his desk where he sat down and began to shuffle through the charts lying there. When he had satisfied himself that he had the ones he wanted, he laid them out and started to study them. After what seemed like at least an hour, Roth looked up from his charts, and looking at Elizabeth, said, "Alright, I will take you there, on one condition. You tell me who you really are."

Elizabeth, immediately replied with some regret, "I am sorry. I cannot tell you any more than what I have already told you."

Roth listened to what she said and knew nothing more would help to learn who she really was and why it is so important for her to keep it secretive. Roth said, "I believe I may have found an alternate route. Now if you will excuse me, I have to give those orders to the night watch. I bid you good night." He stood and left the cabin, leaving Elizabeth feeling she may have angered him.

Roth reached the wheel deck and walked to the stern to find Berkshire staring at the phosphorus wake that was running out from behind the ship. "I have decided to take them to England. We can land them in Ireland and then be on our way back to the islands and retirement."

Berkshire, never diverting his gaze, implored, "What did she say to convince you?"

Roth simply said in return, "Let's just say that she appealed to my fatherly side and leave it at that."

"Aye, aye, Cap'n," Berkshire said taking a deep breath. He knew there was no room for further discussion, which left him a bit apprehensive.

Over the course of the next several days as the *Galaunt* made its way across the Atlantic towards the islands of Ireland, Charles became much more attached to Roth. He would follow him everywhere and Roth showed an enormous amount of patience in allowing Charles to do so. Had it been known, however, Roth rather enjoyed having him around. The young man was very eager to learn and Roth enjoyed teaching him. Elizabeth was happy to see this, for she too had developed a high respect for Captain Roth, and had expressed as much to Charles.

They were expecting to sight land the following morning and as the sun started to peek above the horizon in the eastern sky, Roth heard the lookout cry, "Land ho."

It was hard for Roth standing on the wheel deck to discern land because the sun was shining in his face, but he was sure they were headed in the right direction. Roth knew of a small cove located on the western shore of Ireland where he planned to leave Elizabeth and the others. It was only a short distance to where they would be able to get help and seek shelter for the night.

The *Galaunt* was nearing the site of the hidden cove as the sun was beginning to move into the western skies. Roth had to get into the cove, unload the longboat, get the passengers on shore, and then get back out before dark or he would have to spend the night anchored in the cove, something he did not relish doing. Roth could see other ships in the distance, but did not worry about them because this part of the ocean often contained many ships.

As they neared the entrance of the cove, Roth ordered the *Galaunt* in. The cove was big enough to accommodate a ship the size of the *Galaunt* with room to turn around. He, however, had the ship anchored in the middle, knowing the wind would turn them and ordered the longboat into the water. His men made good time putting the boat in the water. Elizabeth, Charles, Rupert and the three marines were already near the rail waiting for the ladders to be put over the side.

Roth walked over to the group and Elizabeth said as she offered her hand, "It has been a pleasure getting to know you and your ship. Maybe one of these days I will be able to repay you for your generosity."

"The pleasure was all mine, I can assure you. To have you and your family on board has been a treat for me and my crew. Rupert brought back many memories of when Kathryn was on board and that had been good for the moral of the crew. I doubt that we will ever meet again, but I will not forget the time we have had." Roth said as he gently gripped her hand.

Charles came over to where they were standing and spoke. "Captain, this has been an experience that I will never forget. Some day in some way I will repay you for what you have done for us." With that he offered his hand and Roth accepted.

Roth helped Elizabeth over the side, two of the marines, who were already aboard, helped her into the longboat. Charles thanked Roth one more time before he climbed over the rail and descended the ladder into the boat.

Roth watched as the ropes securing the longboat to the ship were cast off and the boat started to drift away from the *Galaunt*. When it was a safe distance away, the marines lowered their oars into the water and started to move the boat towards the shore.

Roth stared at the boat as it rapidly made its way to the shore. He was thinking to himself that he still did not know whom those people were, but he had developed a great respect for Elizabeth and he was sure that the feeling was mutual. He roused himself from his thoughts and went back to the wheel deck. Once there he gave the order to raise anchor and make way to the cove entrance.

As they neared the entrance, Roth ordered an all stop and sails raised. Berkshire came up on to the wheel deck to see why they stopped. Roth merely pointed out to sea and Berkshire, with the aid of his telescope could plainly see a British Man of War sailing north, about three miles out to sea. "We will sit here and let her pass. I doubt that she has seen us." Roth said.

Roth could see that she was a 2nd rate ship of the line. He could clearly make out the three decks of nine guns making twenty-seven. The *Galaunt* is no match for that, her only chance would be to run, and still that would require everything the *Galaunt* could put out.

As Roth watched the ship sail by, Berkshire tapped his arm and pointed a little further south. Here was another 2nd rate ship of the line and Roth did not need his telescope to know this. This ship was less than a mile from their position and there was no doubt that they had seen them. The Man of War was starting into a turn to come and investigate. Roth could not afford to let them close enough to see who they were, so he shouted out the order to lower all sails and bring them tight. The *Galaunt* nearly leaped out of the water when the wind caught her many sails, seemingly at once, and she started to move towards the entrance.

As the *Galaunt* cleared the entrance and entered the open sea, Roth could see the Man of War picked up significant speed also. However, the *Galaunt* was increasing her lead. Roth saw the other ship change its course to try to intercept the fleeing vessel. Darkness would be upon them within the next hour and Roth could turn the *Galaunt* behind the ship to the west and become lost in the darkness.

They felt a slight vibration and Berkshire hurriedly left him on the wheel deck and made his way below decks. Berkshire came back to the wheel deck and said, "Cap'n the planks have sprung, we are taking on a lot of water."

Roth turned around and surveyed the coastline. Finding a suitable spot, he told the helmsman to steer towards that short stretch of sandy beach he had picked out. Turning back to Berkshire, he told him that after the ship was rigged for this course, he was to gather all the crew together at the bow. Berkshire knew what Roth had in mind and did not need to ask what they were to do after the ship was beached.

Berkshire did as he was ordered and when he had all the men on the bow, he briefed them as to what they were going to do after the ship grounded. After the briefing and he was sure the men understood, he returned briskly back to the wheel deck.

Roth had relieved the helmsman and was steering the ship on a straight course to the beach. The *Galaunt* had slowed significantly and the Man of War behind them was quickly gaining on her. Roth could see that all of her gun ports were open. The ship was preparing to fire on the *Galaunt* as soon as she came within range.

Roth was calculating the distance to the shore and he was sure that the *Galaunt* would make the beach before the Man of War could open fire. He was thankful that the men would have time to escape into the night. He told Berkshire that he did not want to see his ship reduced to a pile of tinder so he had decided to surrender the ship over to the British. Berkshire tried to talk him out of staying on board, but Roth told him that it was less likely for the British to hunt them in the night if they had him in custody. This would give them time to get away. Berkshire knew this was the right thing to do, so without any more argument, he gave his captain a salute before making his way back to the bow. Roth watched him a moment then turned his attention back to the task at hand.

Roth had to bring the ship onto the beach at a perpendicular angle to the shoreline to prevent it from rolling over. The bow was already becoming very heavy with the water coming in and the ship was becoming very sluggish. 'Just two hundred more yards is all I need,' Roth thought to himself. Am I going to make it? Roth wondered if the *Galaunt* would bottom out before they reached the shore. It was not long after that thought that Roth felt the ship hit bottom. They were still at least a hundred yards from the shore, too far for the crew to escape. As if the Galaunt heard his thoughts, she broke free from whatever she had hit and actually seemed to gain speed for the final charge up the beach.

The *Galaunt* hit the beach and with a strange swooshing sound, she slid up the beach until her bowsprit was nearly touching the forest surrounding the beach.

Roth was thankful that she stayed upright. He went to the stern post and from the flag box, he removed a large white flag that he proceeded to attach to the stern post. He walked over to the port side and could see that the men were off the ship and making their way to the forest. As the last man was to enter the forest, he stopped and threw one last salute Roth's way before continuing into the forest. Drawing a heavy breath, Roth thought to himself, nothing left to do now until the Man of War arrived. He took one last look around his beloved ship and then found a place by the stern rail, sat, and awaited his fate.

Roth noted that the dolphins were swimming a short distance away. They were darting back and forth in the water directly behind the stern as if to fend off any attacker. No, that cannot be, they are probably just feeding on the fish that gathered around the stirred up bottom. He thought about how the dolphins had always been with the ship. Never once could he remember them not being there.

It was not long before the great Man of War sailed into range to open fire, Roth stood and raised his hands in the air. The ship of the line came to a stop about two hundred yards offshore with its starboard complement of cannon brought to bear on the helpless *Galaunt*.

Roth saw the ship lower two boats in the water and watched as the sailors aboard those boats started rowing towards him. As they made their way towards him, the other Man of War arrived and took up station with its port guns aimed in the direction of the *Galaunt*. Roth watched as the boats approached and could see an officer in the bow of the lead boat, standing erect and looking straight at him. When the boats came within hailing distance, the officer yelled out. "Are you the *Galaunt* and are you indeed surrendering?"

"Yes," Roth yelled back with some reluctance.

Whereas the officer returned, "Do I have the pleasure of addressing Captain Roth?"

"You do." Roth replied.

As soon as he said that, he saw the sailors in the second boat put down their oars and take up muskets that they pointed at Roth.

The office asked, "Where is your crew?"

"They are gone." Roth answered.

The officer finally said, "Stay where you are, keep your hands in view, we are coming aboard."

Roth stayed where he was but sat down while he waited, he did not think they would shoot him yet. The wait was not long before he saw men climbing up and over the bow and moving in his direction. The officer, who turned out to be a naval captain, was the first to mount the wheel deck. He walked straight over to where Roth was standing and stood looking at him. As his men formed on the wheel deck, he turned to a sailor and simply said, "Put this man in chains and take him to the Admiral."

The sailor did as ordered and Roth was chained and forcibly removed from the *Galaunt* and shortly found himself in the boat being rowed out to the first ship to arrive. When they reached the ship, he was again forcibly hauled onto the main deck where he was met by an Admiral. The Admiral was an old man that had obviously spent his entire lifetime at sea. He was dressed in a neat uniform that left no mistake that he was the man in charge. He looked Roth up and down and even walked around him looking him over. He completed this inspection before he said anything. Finally, he spoke. "So, this is the great Captain Roth? I have to say that I am a bit disappointed. I would have expected the man that raised so much mayhem on the ocean to have at least put up a small fight so that we would have had the pleasure of being able to destroy your ship as well as your crew. Obviously, all the rumors were just that, rumors. Take this man from my sight and throw him into the brig."

Chapter 11
"Punishment"

Only a few days had passed when Roth felt the ship slow. He knew, from experience, that they had been sailing on a river since early yesterday, and this slowing must mean that they were near their destination. Before long, he heard the sounds that told him that the ship was being tied alongside a dock. Not long after that, four sailors appeared, with two of them carrying muskets. One of the unarmed sailors unlocked his cell and the other stepped in to pull Roth to his feet. Both sailors then dragged him out of the cell and started him towards the stairs leading to the decks above. His legs were stiff, but the sailors would just drag him along if he slowed. Before long, they reached the main deck and Roth was greeted with bright sunlight. His eyes were not accustomed to the brightness, so he closed them and immediately tripped over something on the deck and fell to his knees. He heard laughter and someone say, "The great Captain Roth, finally brought to his knees!" Someone else yelled, "Maybe we should just hang him here ourselves!" From another he heard, "Hanging would be too good for him, let's just throw him over the side!"

Roth's eyes were starting to adjust to the light, when he heard from behind him, "There will be no hanging today. This man is to be brought before a panel and properly tried before he is hung." This brought forth another round of laughter. The same man commanded, "Get him on his feet and off this ship!" Roth was still on his knees when someone pushed him with their foot and sent him sprawling face down on the wooden deck. Someone else then grabbed him by his hair and hauled him back to his feet. Roth turned and glared at the man that had shoved him. The man pulled himself away from Roth just before other mates dragged him to the gangplank.

From the top of the gangplank, he could see that they had brought him to London. Below him, he saw an open cart surrounded by several mounted soldiers and surrounding them was a throng of people. When this crowd saw him, they started to shout out insults. He heard people wish him dead more times than he would care to remember. When the sailors reached the wagon, they threw him into an opening in the back. When Roth landed, he was greeted by the rank stench of old stable straw and a smell that told him this wagon had recently hauled pigs. He climbed to his feet to try to escape the smell. As soon as he got to his feet, the crowd started throwing rotten vegetables at him, sometimes even a small stone. Some poked him with sticks, and they all shouted their hatred towards him. The escort simply moved away and did nothing to stop the abuse that was being showered upon him. It got so bad that even the driver had to climb down from his seat. He moved to the front of the oxen pulling the wagon and started to lead the team off the wharf to the roadway beyond, where the escort of mounted soldiers awaited. The slow plodding pace of the oxen afforded ample time for the crowd to exhaust all of their ammunition. Eventually the crowd thinned and the driver was able to regain his seat. He then followed the south side of the river until they came to Borough High Street.

Roth could see the old London Bridge as they passed it. He now knew where they were taking him. They took him to a large brick structure known as the King's Bench Prison situated in the center of Southward.

After reaching the prison, Roth was dragged from the wagon and led into one of the buildings. Inside the building, there was a staircase, leading to the prison and dungeons below. After a long climb down the stairs, they finally reached the cellblocks. It consisted of a long corridor with cells on both sides. At the end of the corridor was another set of stairs leading to the dungeon and the torture chambers. Here they were met by a brute of a man who stood at least a foot taller than Roth and was twice as wide. Saying nothing, he grabbed Roth by the wrist chains and threw him against the wall. Roth hit the wall hard and was able to open his eyes just in time to see the jailer's boot smash him in the head. This blow almost rendered him unconscious, but unfortunately, it was just almost. Roth could not see as he was dragged to his feet. He heard one of the original guards tell the jailer to hold him up like that and proceeded to pummel his body. With his arms pinned behind him by the jailer, Roth had no choice but to take the punishment. In agonizing pain from the beating he was receiving, Roth was starting to succumb to the point where the pain was starting to become numb.

He did not know how long this went on but eventually he was aware of being dragged about halfway down the corridor where whoever had him by the chains, stopped. Roth was then roughly pushed into an already occupied cell, where he heard the door being closed and bolted behind him. Roth lay on the floor disoriented and could barely move. It was a while before he could raise his head and take in his surroundings. He saw that the cell was about 10 x 10 with no other visible openings that he could see, other than the door. The wooden door had a covered slot about two thirds of the way up and another down by the floor. Roth figured this was how they would push in food, if they bothered to feed him at all. His mouth felt dry and he could not help but hope they would give him water soon. He noticed the cell had stone cots on either sidewall and it was in one of these cots that he saw another man.

As his eyes became more accustomed to the dim light, he could see that the man was sitting cross-legged on the cot looking straight at him. It was obvious that he had been here for quite some time, his gray hair was long and matted and his beard touched his chest every time he took a breath. Both men stared at each other not saying a word. Roth, finally having to give into the beating he had just received, lowered his head and fell fast asleep.

Roth awoke engulfed in pain. It seemed that he hurt from head to toe. One eye was swollen shut and his mouth felt like it had encountered a wall. Raising his hand to his head, he felt a moist rag resting on his forehead. Opening the one good eye he had left, he realized that he was no longer on the floor, but lying on his back on one of the stone cots. Rolling onto his side, he could barely make out the man on the other cot. That man must have put him on the cot while he was passed out. He tried in vain to sit up but could not find the strength. The other man rose from his cot, taking Roth by the shoulders, laid him back down while he said, "You are in no condition to get up. You just lay there and rest." Roth did as he was told and soon again was fast asleep.

He awoke to the sounds of someone rustling around the room. He did not hurt quite as bad now and tried again to sit up. This time he succeeded. One eye was still swollen shut but he could open the other. When he did, he saw the man kneeling down by the door. He watched the man rise and turn back to him. The old man said, "So you have decided to return to the living have you? I thought there for a while that you were not goin' to make it. You took a terrible beatin' and you can be sure that you are lucky to be alive. The guards have been in here a couple of times to check on you. I think they started to worry about whether or not you were going to make it. They told me to do what I could for you and brought me clean water and some rags to clean you up. Lord knows I tried, but from the looks of you, it does not look like I did any good at all. Just then, they heard the jingle of keys and the heavy door swung open and the giant of a man strode through.

He walked up to Roth and roughly grabbed his chin and bent his head back. "You have done well Quincy. You keep on workin' on him. The king wants him to be healthy. It seems he has some special treat in store for this one." He said as he let go of Roth's chin and went back out the door, locking it behind him.

Roth gave him plenty of time to move down the corridor before he said, "King? Why do you suppose he would want to see me? I know why I am here but I would not think it would be at the pleasure of the king" he wondered aloud.

Later, he was rudely aroused from his sleep. He awoke to find someone poking him in the arm with some sort of pointed object. He quickly sat up, grabbed the object, which turned out to be an ornate walking stick, and then turned it to his attacker. He was immediately subdued by two others in the room, one being the giant tormentor. "See we told you that he has been fightin' us the whole time he has been here." He heard one of the guards say. He quickly realized that resistance would just get him hurt more and relaxed in their grip. The guards relaxed also, but did not completely release him. He heard, "May I have my cane back?"

Roth could not see who was talking but opened his hand and felt the cane taken from him. With that the guards let him go, but did not leave his side. He looked up at the other man in the cell and was surprised to see a very short man standing there. He was dressed in very expensive fineries and wore a white powdered wig. He held his walking stick in front of him and looked as if he was leaning on it with both hands. There was a faint smirk on his face and he stood just slightly higher than eye level as he stared at Roth. They stared at each other for some time before the man spoke. "I am Reginald Tollier the 3rd, Esquire. I am a Barrister and have been assigned to represent you before the upcoming King's Bench, where you will be tried for the crimes of murdering King James family."

"Murder, when was it that I was supposed to have *murdered* the King's family?" Roth surprisingly inquired.

The Barrister proceeded to explain rather impatiently, "When King James became ill, he sent a message to his sister, Elizabeth, informing her of this and requested that she return home as soon as possible. According to a source, privy to the doings of the Spanish Court, we have been informed that a Spanish captain reported that he was witness to the sinking of the ship carrying the royal family. He claimed that it was you, who attacked the ship, so viciously, that there would be no hope for any survivors. The captain had gone on to say that it was miracle that he was able to escape and report this crime. You gave chase but were unable to match his superior seamanship. How say you?" He went on to ask.

"What was the name of the ship that the royal family was sailing on?" Roth calmly asked.

"No one has informed me as to the name of the ship, but I am sure that all will be answered tomorrow when you appear before the panel." The Barrister answered.

"Tomorrow, isn't that a little soon?" Roth inquired.

The little man shook his head and replied. "When the king heard that you had been captured, he issued the order to have you drawn and quartered, but was advised against that by a very close advisor. The advisor told him that it would be better for the monarchy if he put you on trial, thus showing the people that he was a fair and honest king." He continued, "You had better think about anything you would like to say tomorrow, though I don't think it would do any good, but you might as well have your say." He turned and walked out into the corridor, followed by the guards.

Not realizing that he was speaking aloud, Roth said. "How could I have been so stupid? It was right there in front of me the whole time."

"Of course you were stupid! You were stupid to become a pirate in the first place." The old man remarked.

"That is not what I mean." He said and thinking to himself, Elizabeth. Of course, it had to be. The King's sister was Elizabeth and she had a son named Rupert. "There has been a mistake. The King's family is not dead."

"What do you mean they are not dead? You heard the man, there was a witness." The old man quipped.

"No, they are not dead. They are in Ireland where I left them." Roth answered.

"Ireland?" The old man inquired.

"How long have I been here?" Roth hurriedly asked the old man.

"Counting today, it has been nine days, all tolled." He answered.

Roth considered that. "Nine days. They should have been able to arrange for transportation by now and should be well on their way home."

"What is this craziness you are telling? Are you trying to tell me that the King's family is not dead and they are just in Ireland? You are making no sense!" The old man exclaimed.

"Yes, that is exactly what I am saying! I don't know why I didn't put it together all that time we were aboard ship." Roth went on to tell the old man the story, ending with putting Elizabeth ashore in Ireland. The old man was amazed by what he had just heard.

The guards came for Roth early the next morning. Roth had no idea what time it was, there was no light in the prison. He was taken up the stairs and dragged outside to an awaiting cart. He thought that it looked just like the one that had brought him here. There was one thing that was the same about this cart, it was open and as they passed through the gates of the prison, the crowds were there to greet him. He began to be pelted by anything that the crowd could lay their hands on, but this time the escort stayed where they were and soon the pelting stopped, but the crowds remained lining the street. Roth was driven west along Borough Road, being constantly bombarded with curses from the crowd, until they came to the Thames River. There they boarded a ferry and crossed the river. Once on the opposite shore they turned north and continued on their way until they came to Westminster Hall. This was the seat of government and this was where the parliament met and this building housed the King's Bench.

The Court of the King's Bench grew out of the King's Court, or Curia Regis. At first, it was not specifically a court of law but the center of Royal power and national administration, consisting at first of the King himself together with his advisors, courtiers and administrators.

At some unknown stage, a court independent of the King's personal presence grew out of the Curia Regis, consisting of a number of Royal judges who would hear cases themselves. It, however, is recorded that, in 1178, Henry II ordered that five judges of his household should remain in Curia Regis, referring only difficult cases to him.

Roth was taken to the rear of the building, hauled from the cart, and ushered him towards the door. Inside the door, there was a short hallway with cells on either side. Several of the cells were occupied, but an empty one was found and he was locked away. The cells were nothing more than open cages and he could see the other occupants staring at him. When the guards left, they started to yell at him. They hated him as much as the crowds on the streets and their threats were the same. Occasionally, some guards would come and take one of the prisoners and leave through a door at the end of the hallway.

Finally, it was Roth's turn. The guards opened the cell, and Roth, learning from the past, stood and walked to the cell door and did not offer any resistance at all. The guards still grabbed him by both arms and pulled him from the cell. In this manner, they led him to the door, opened it and pushed him through. Behind the door was a stairway, leading up, Roth started to climb the steps when a guard tripped him and he went sprawling onto the steps where he was again, grabbed by the two guards and partially dragged up the steps before he could regain his footing. After a short climb, the stairs turned to the left and led to a brightly lit room above. The guards pushed him up these last steps onto a landing with two chairs and five steps leading to the prisoner's box where he would stand during the duration of the proceedings. As he climbed the steps, he could see the panel of five judges to his left with the clerks of the court arranged in front of them. To the right of him was the table used by the barristers and behind that was the public gallery, and today it was full to standing room only. In front of him, there was a raised platform with one chair in the middle and three rows of benches flanking the chair. The chair was occupied by a man that was staring straight at him. The stare contained a hatred that was so intense it could almost be felt. Roth had never seen him before but he knew that this had to be King James. It was rare for the king to attend, but this was a special occasion. Roth barely noticed when the proceedings started. From the look he was receiving, he was sure that the outcome had already been decided. He just wondered what form of execution was going to be used. Before he knew it the judges were preparing to announce sentence, but first one asked Roth, "Is there anything you would like to say before you are sentenced?" Roth, never removing his gaze from the king simply said, "Your family is not dead. The Spanish have lied to you. They were the ones that attacked the *Royal Troon*. I was able to scare them off with the *Galaunt* and rescue your son, your sister, her son and three royal marines. We then brought them to the shores of Ireland and set them ashore. At that time, they were all fine and happy to be safe and on their way home."

A loud murmur arose from the gallery and a judge held up his hand for silence. The king spoke next, "If, as you say, they are indeed alive, why is it that no word of their whereabouts has been received by this court?"

"I cannot explain that sire, but I do know that they were alive and well when I saw them last." he answered.

"I think you are lying. Why would the Spanish attack a British ship? You on the other hand had every reason to do so. You committed this heinous crime against the realm and me and now you will pay for it. If it was up to me, I would see you put to death now." Looking at the judges, the king gave a signal to continue.

The center judged nodded and said, "Nathan Roth, you are hereby found to be guilty of the charge of murdering the royal family and are hereby sentenced to death. You will be brought before the executioner on Tower Hill, tomorrow at noon, where you will then be beheaded." The gallery gave a loud cheer, and as word of the sentence reached the people outside, a loud cheer arose from them.

Roth was grabbed from behind, dragged from the prisoner's box and pushed down the stairs. He regained his footing where the stairs turned, but with the guards pushing him, he did not remain standing and rolled down the stairs to the bottom. Reaching him and dragging him back to his feet, they propelled him through another door at the bottom that opened onto a courtyard. In this enclosed courtyard was a wagon, different from the one he arrived in, this one was enclosed. Roughly throwing Roth into the back of the wagon, one guard commented that it would not do to have him receive any injuries that might prevent the festivities planned for tomorrow. The door was slammed shut and bolted. The wagon began to move and Roth wondered where he was going now. He still could not stop wondering why Elizabeth and the two lads had not yet made their way home.

When the wagon stopped and the doors opened, Roth found that they had taken him to the Tower of London. The Tower of London was situated on the Thames River, just outside the city of London. The tower had been originally built by William of Normandy and had been used as a prison for those that had committed crimes against the country. Tower Hill was a small rise, separating the Tower from the city of London. Roth was taken to the Raven Tower and there placed in a small cell on the fifth level of the tower. The cell had a barred window that looked out over Tower Hill where Roth could see the scaffold and its block from this window.

As the sun began its descent in the western sky, Roth was watching the smoke from the many chimneys of London. The door to his cell was suddenly opened and his barrister walked in accompanied by four rather large Royal Guardsmen. He said, "I have been sent to tell you that there is someone that would have conversation with you. It seems that you have friends in very high places. I have transportation waiting. Will you come of your own accord?"

Roth looked from the barrister to the guards and simply said, "It would appear that I do not have much of a choice."

"You have no choice," the barrister flatly stated.

Roth was escorted out of the cell and down the stairs to the open courtyard. There, awaiting them was an enclosed carriage and four more guards wearing uniforms that he did not recognize. he was led to the carriage and the barrister opened the door and motioned him to get in. When he entered the coach, he saw that it was occupied. Sitting in the back was a man wearing a hooded cloak. The hood was pulled low over his forehead, making it difficult to make out any features. He motioned to the seat on the opposite side of the coach and Roth sat down. He then gave the command to move and the carriage departed through the riverside gates and left behind the Tower of London.

"My name is George Villers, Duke of Buckingham and advisor to the king." The Duke said as he pulled the hood from his head. "It seems that the realm owes you a bit of gratitude. Shortly after the trial, word was received that a ship bearing the king's family had arrived at the docks. When the King's sister heard what had taken place, she told the king the truth of what really took place out there on the ocean. She gave a strong argument for your case, persuading the king to rescind your death sentence, and even went so far as to recommend a pardon. Unfortunately, you affected the lives of many more than just Creed and a full pardon was impossible. Those crimes alone would be enough to have you hung." The Duke paused here and stared at the heavily curtained window. Roth pulled the curtain aside a bit hoping to get a glimpse of where they were going. The Duke immediately pulled the curtain back in place and said, "There is a reason why they were closed. It is imperative to your security that no one knows who is riding in this coach. It will be told that you took your own life during the night, in the case that someone else may continue to search for you with vengeance." Roth shook his head acknowledging in agreement of understanding, though in his thoughts he chuckled to himself that indeed he had made untold numbers of enemies during the course of his revenge.

Before long, they came to the London Bridge. Roth figured that they were headed back to King's Bench Prison, but found he was wrong when they turned and began to follow the river. It was here that the Duke began again. "Giving that you had saved the lives of the kings family, it was decided that you would be exiled. It has been arranged for you to be transported to our penal colony in Botany Bay where you will be a freeman. However, if you ever try to leave the colony and return to England, the sentence of death will be carried out."

Roth knew they had arrived at the docks without being able to see them by the smells and the clacking of the horse's hooves on the cobblestone by the wharfs. Presently the carriage came to a stop and the Duke said, "Outside, you will find a ship that has been contracted to carry you on your way." Roth stood and opened the door to leave the carriage, when the Duke spoke again. "Remember, do not try to return for you will, indeed, be put to death without mercy." Roth turned and looked at him, then stepped out into the night. He turned and watched as the carriage moved down the long line of wharfs until it disappeared into the night. Turning back towards the wharf, he saw before him a 4th rate Ship of the Line. These were ships that had over thirty-eight guns, but less than fifty-four. They were essentially a one-deck frigate, developed to do a multitude of tasks. Such as, reconnoitering ahead of the main fleet and delivering dispatches to and from the fleet leadership to convoy duty and even privateering, during their early days of service. Roth also saw three burly sailors waiting at the bottom of the gangplank. Walking towards them, he saw that one carried chains for both the hands and the feet. As he neared them, two rushed out and grabbed him, pinning his arms to his sides. The third quickly placed him in chains. With this accomplished, the two that held him released their grip and sent him sprawling, towards the gangplank. Picking him up, they proceeded to drag him up the gangplank, not giving him chance to regain his footing. Reaching the top, they hurled him onto the deck face down.

Before he could roll over or sit up, he felt the point of a saber on the side of his neck. "Well Roth, it has been a long time, how have you been doing since we were last together?" He heard as he felt the point of the saber move from his neck to the underside of his chin where a slight pressure brought him to his feet. He found himself looking at two points of hatred, the eyes of a man that he never thought he would ever see again. The man he was facing was Captain Seth Connery. "Surprised to see me, Roth? Surprised to find that I survived your banishment on that pathetic little island? Well survive I did," Connery said with a sneering grin. Never releasing the pressure from the tip of the saber, Connery went on. "Raynerd didn't last a month before I fed him to the sharks, but I was able to live on that island for better than a year before a vessel came by that I was able to signal. From there, I made it back here. Finding that my services were no longer needed, no little thanks to you, by Creed, I signed on with the navy and received command of the *HMS Hampshire*, the vessel on which you stand. I thought that I would just kill you if I ever saw you again, I still think that I should, but a Fleet Admiral ordered me to transport you to Botany Bay. I don't know how you managed to evade the gallows, but you are in my charge now, and I vowed that I would see you dead and that is a vow that I intend to keep." He lowered his blade and ordered his men to drag him down to the brig. The same two that had brought him onboard, again grabbed him and drug him below decks to a cell that was as far forward as you could get to in the cargo area. It was reached by working through a maze of stacked cargo to the point where the curvature of the ships bow began its steep rise. Here the forward end of the hull was barred off from the rest of the deck and it was here that they intended to keep Roth.

Before they threw him into the cell, however, they searched him. Finding a knife, the sailor in charge used it to cut away Roth's coat so they would not have to remove his chains. After satisfying themselves that he did not carry any more weapons, they grabbed him by his arms and threw him into the awaiting cell.

Connery must have only been waiting for the arrival of Roth for it was only a short time before he felt the ship begin to move. The passage down the river was a smooth trip and he was well aware when the ship reach open water. Being in the extreme bow as he was, the up and down movement of the ship as it crested waves and dove down troughs, tossed Roth around the small cell. He felt ill from the constant movement and tried as best that he could to anchor himself. He finally found a spot where he could find some comfort and soon drifted off to sleep.

Upon awakening, he did not know how long it had been since they threw him into this hellish place. It seemed like a very long time ago that he was brought down here. In the blackness, he could not ascertain whether it was night or day. He could feel the emptiness of his stomach and his mouth was very dry. If only someone were available for him to make an inquiry, he would ask for some water and maybe something to eat, but it soon became obvious that he was not going to see much of anything or anyone for that matter.

It became apparent that he was not well received on this ship. More times than not, the sailors he did see, during the long voyage, would ignore him completely or hurl insults at him. Even the seamen that brought him food would sometimes just dump it into his cell.

They had not removed the chains he was put into, and his wrists and ankles were beginning to bleed. This brought the rats from their places of hiding and made it impossible for Roth to get any rest. If he fell asleep he would be awaken by a rat chewing on a bloody area. After a couple of days of this, he tore off his vest, tearing it into strips, he used it, along with some of his drinking water, he had finally been given, to clean the wounds. He then used other strips to stuff between the cuffs and his raw skin in hopes that this would stem the bleeding and the rats would leave him alone. With some thought while fending the rats off in the blackness of the hold, he began to assume that when the seaman brought him his food that it must be daylight and the rats were scared off. He also learned that he could rest during the day when the rats were in hiding and be rested when the night came and they came out of hiding.

Before long, the rats did not bother him as much. Only when he had his food thrown at him and he had to compete with them for the meager amount of food that there was, that he even noticed them anymore.

After what seemed like an eternity, it came as a surprise when two sailors came down to the brig and released him from his cell. They proceeded to push him up the ladder to the main deck. The glare of the light was very hard on his eyes and almost blinded him. It took several seconds before he became able to see.

Looking out over the ocean, he saw that they were nearing a small island. The majority of the island was well covered with trees and had a long sandy beach on the island side of a cove that was protected by jagged rocks. It looked to him as though one end of the island consisted of a high jagged peak... It was to this island that Roth could see that they were sailing.

The sailors pushed him along the deck until they came to where Connery was standing, near the starboard rail. Connery turned from gazing at the nearing island as the three men approached.

"How do you like the island I have selected to be your future home?" Connery said with a smirk. Connery saw that Roth looked a little surprised when he said this, so he went on. "Don't tell me that you really thought that you were going to be delivered to the colony." Chuckling as he said it. "I gave a lot of thought to leaving you on a barren atoll, but I think that it would be better if I repaid the kindness and concern you showed for me in a like manner. As you can see, the island will probably sustain life."

Roth watched as the ship made its approach to the island towards the peaked end. About two hundred yards from the point where the rocks that protected the cove began, Connery ordered the ship stopped. He walked over to the rail where the gangplank would ordinarily be affixed and stood by an opening, beckoning Roth to join him. Usually while the ship is at sea, there would be a piece of railing fastened here. However, at this time, Connery had evidently ordered it removed. He turned to Roth and said with a sweeping wave of the hand, "Behold, your new home." A sailor walked up to the pair and handed Connery something that Roth could not see. Connery dismissed the sailor and turned back to Roth saying, "I would not want it said that I left you stranded without anything to help you survive as you were kind enough to do for me," He said with smugness as he handed a small pewter mug to Roth. Roth recognized it as one of the mugs that he had packed with the supplies that he had left for Connery and Raynerd. "Also," Connery said, "here is something to keep you going until you find resources on the island." He handed Roth a piece of stale bread and laughed. "Oh, I almost forgot, here is something else that you might find of use." Connery was smiling very broadly as he showed Roth what it was that the sailor had brought to him. It was two heavy metal keys. Roth knew instantly that they had to be the keys to his shackles and manacles. Roth could hear the crew, standing behind him, laughing.

Connery started to twirl the key ring around his finger and steadily watched Roth's eyes. When he saw that they were following the keys, he let the ring loose and it sailed over the rail and dropped into the sea with a splash. Connery simply said, "Oops."

Before he realized what was happening, he was being pushed towards the opening in the rail, by some sailors behind him. As he neared the edge, Connery grabbed hold of him, forcibly spun Roth around to face him and said with a smile, "I *told* you that I would see you die!" Laughing at having the satisfaction of saying that, he gave

Roth a final push that sent him out the opening and into the clear blue water below.

Roth was able to get a breath before he hit the water. The chains immediately started to drag him to the bottom, about forty-five feet below him. He struggled desperately to swim back to the surface but the chains impeded him enough that he knew he would not make it.

Connery leaned over the rail and watched as Roth struggled, but the drift of the ship soon put Roth under the ship and out of sight. Connery ordered the crew to get the ship underway and moved to the stern of the ship to see if he could get one last glimpse of Roth before they moved out of the area. He no sooner reached the stern rail and leaned over, when he saw Roth still struggling as he neared the bottom. The ship was starting to pick up speed and it was not long before Connery lost sight of the man he had just condemned to death. He was about to turn away and resume his duties, when he thought he saw a flash of something shiny in the water. He strained his eyes but he did not see it again. It must have been a glint of sunlight, he thought to himself, as he turned and left the rail.

Roth had always been able to hold his breath for a long time, but he knew that he was not going to make it to the surface, so he relaxed and slowly settled to the sandy bottom below. As he hit the bottom, he realized that he still held the mug and what was left of the bread. He saw that he had attracted a number of small fish that were feeding on the bread as it broke away from the main piece. He opened his hand, released the remains of the bread, and brought the mug up to where he could see it and thought about the last time he had seen it. As he began to lose consciousness, his thoughts turned to Kathryn and the last thing he saw before he lost consciousness was Kathryn's face before his.

Chapter 12
"The Island"

Roth was dreaming about Kathryn when he became aware of a feeling of warmth on his face. He slowly opened his eyes and was blinded by the brightness of the sun that was straight above him. From its position, he knew that it had to be around noontime. He slowly raised himself to a sitting position, looked out across a sparkling blue expanse of water and realized that he must be on the beach of the small island that he had seen from the ship. Abruptly the recollection of how he had left the ship came back to him like a nightmare. The visions in his mind were of him struggling to reach the surface, but with being weighed down by the chains, he had been unable to rise from the bottom. Then he remembered the sudden feeling of calm just before losing consciousness as his thoughts had shifted to Kathryn. He looked at his wrists and saw that they were still clasped in the heavy iron manacles that he had worn for the entire voyage. He also saw that his feet were still chained. How did he make it to shore, he wondered?

Suddenly realizing his plight, he scanned the horizon looking for the *Hampshire*. Unable to sight the ship, or any other ship for that matter, he was satisfied, for the moment at least, he was safe from the clutches of Connery. He was sure that by this time Connery had sailed on, sure in his mind that Roth had drowned. Relaxing, he turned and took stock of his surroundings.

He was indeed on a beach, but his feet were still being lapped by the relentless motion of the waves as they made their way up the beach to where he was sitting. He could tell by the motion of the water that the tide was just starting to go out. He realized that he was sitting at the line of high tide and had probably been in the water until just a few minutes ago because his clothes were still wet. Had he been washed ashore by some unknown force of nature? He could think of no reason why he was still alive. Then the thought hit him, maybe I am not alive and this is heaven. No, this could not be because he suddenly realized that his wrists and ankles were very sore from the chaffing of the iron that he wore. No, he thought, in heaven he would feel no pain and would probably not still be chained.

Looking to his left, he found that he was only a very short distance from the base of the peak where it met the beach. Looking up, he could see that the peak rose almost vertically from his seat to the crest that was maybe no more than fifty feet, maybe slightly higher, above the surface of the water. He followed the cliff back to where its gradual decline met the thinly spaced palms that were scattered on the beach behind him. He could see that beyond the palms was a lush thicker growth of green vegetation.

Turning to his right, he followed the line of the surf to the point where the sand met a low-lying outcropping of stone. This outcropping projected itself into the water for several yards where it gradually sloped into the water and pointed towards several rocks that were in line that were just starting to show as the water lowered. He had seen these rocks from the ship, protecting the cove. Where the sand met stone, it was probably as high as he was tall, the vegetation was denser beyond this outcrop and there were fewer palms.

Looking along the line of rocks, he could see that they were curving in a gentle arc and if they continued, they would gradually meet the base of the peak. Nevertheless, as it was, they still allowed for somewhat of a break that kept the waters of the cove calmer than the ocean around it.

Following this imaginary line back to the peak, his gaze landed upon a small ledge about a foot higher than the high water mark. Sitting on this ledge, in an upright position, was the pewter mug that he had held when he went overboard.

He stood and, still being chained, slowly hobbled over to the ledge and grasped the mug with both hands. He brought it up to his face for a closer look to assure himself that it was, indeed, the same mug. Satisfied that it was the same mug, he suddenly realized that the only explanation for this was that he was not alone. There had to be someone else on the island.

Turning back to the trees he shouted, "Hello." Getting no response, he shouted again, "Hello, come out where I can see you." Still, he got no response. He started to walk towards the trees when he noticed that there were no tracks in the sand. He turned and looked back at the way he had come and saw that his tracks were plainly visible. Looking at the hill before him, it was obvious that only a mountain goat would be able to traverse the rock and it would have a difficult time. He knew then that whoever had saved him had done so by water. He could still see nothing on the water that would hide someone unless a boat had gone around the edge of the peak where he could not see.

He now hurried, as fast as he was able, up the beach to where the vegetation started and slowly made his way around the rocks to where the peak sloped down. Seeing that it would not be too hard of a climb, Roth started to make his way up the slope. The slope was covered with small bushes that kept catching at the chains, but eventually Roth made his way to the top.

At the top was a lone tree of a type that Roth was unfamiliar with, but it bore some kind of fruit. Forgetting the tree for the moment, Roth looked down from the peak at his surroundings. To the east was the shear drop off that he could see from the beach. Scanning northward, he saw that there was another island or rather a small atoll, about three hundred yards from the north side of the island and was separated by a channel that was running from east to west. There was no vegetation on the atoll and it looked very inhospitable. The vegetation on the island ran to within a few feet of the channel. From where he stood, he could see the entire island and knew instantly that there was no place that someone could hide a boat of any size. He looked back towards the cove and could now see clearly the line of rocks that protected the cove. Under any other circumstances, Roth would consider this view very spectacular. He could see for miles out to sea and marveled to see the way the waves were marching towards his small speck of land. He could actually see the bottom of the cove from where he stood. It looked very smooth and sandy.

Roth, exhausted, sat down with his back against the tree and stared out over the western side of the island. He figured that this part of the island was maybe, four hundred yards at its longest point and two hundred yards wide at its widest. Except for the peak and the outcropping of stone, the island was entirely covered with small bushes and here and there fruit trees of the sort the Roth was now sitting under only much taller and wider. The palms were mostly grouped near the edge of the beach, but he could see others, here and there along the channel and a few amongst the bushes. Spying a piece of fruit that had fallen from the tree, Roth picked it up and examined it closely. It was three to four inches long, ovoid in shape and had a smooth, waxy sort of skin. Splitting it in half, Roth was surprised to find that its pulp was like a peach. He had heard of a fruit that grew in the south called a mango and wondered if that was what this fruit was. It had a little bit more fiber and was not as juicy, but it was very much like a peach. In the center, he found a single, elongated seed. The pulp smelled sweet so Roth decided to try it. To his surprise, it was sweet, not as sweet as a peach, but very good. Eating the rest of the fruit, Roth looked around for some more.

After eating his fill of fruit, Roth knew that he had a source of food, but he would need water if he were to survive. He knew that there had to be water somewhere because fruit trees would not grow in salty water. Therefore, he made his way down the hill in search of fresh water. He figured that his best bet to find water was around the hill, so he started to work his way around the rocks towards the north side of the hill. Failing to find what he was looking for, he started back towards the beach.

He was just about there when he saw a cave in the hill. The cave was in a recess in the side of the hill that faced towards the trees, which accounted for how he had missed it when he first walked by it. The opening was not very big, about three feet high and two feet across. He could feel a slight breeze as the air was being drawn into the opening, so he knew that somewhere on the other side of the hill there was another opening. The opening made a slight turn just inside the cave mouth so Roth could not see very far. He would need light before he could explore the cave further.

Before Roth did any exploring of the cave, he decided to see what there was to see on the other end of the island. Walking through the palm trees, he saw several nuts that had fallen from them. Here was another source of nourishment. He also found some nuts that had fallen quite some time ago and had split open revealing the broken inner nut.

They were all rotten, but Roth saw the fiber stuff between the husk and the nut, he knew that with just a little heat he could get a fire started. He immediately set out in search of the other materials he would need.

Around the nearest tree he found everything he needed to make fire. All about him were fallen branches and other pieces of wood. He noticed that there was an abundant amount of driftwood piled against the rocky outcropping. He knew that he would have plenty of firewood if he could get a fire started. Gathering his materials, he made his way back to the mouth of the cave.

The first thing that he did was make a small mound of very dry twigs that was hollow in the center. Next, he tore a thin strip of cloth from his shirt. He twisted the cloth tightly and attached each end to a long piece of branch making a bow. Looking around, he found a small piece of broken rock that was pointed on one end. With this rock, he carved a small tapered hole in a piece of bark that was about the same width as a thicker branch he had found, but slightly wider. He was careful only to leave a small hole through the other side. He then took some coconut fiber and grinding it together, he made a very fine nest of dusty fiber. He found a flat rock the size of his palm that was indented on one side. Using his carving rock, he made a point on one end of the short branch. He then made a rolling loop in the bowstring and inserted the pointed stick through it. Placing the pointed end in the tapered hole in the bark, he took the flat rock and held it to the other end. By moving the bow quickly back and forth, he could make the branch spin very rapidly and before long, he had created enough heat to make the edges of the small hole, glow as cinders. He picked the bark up and holding it against the fibers, started to blow into the hole forcing the heat onto the fibers and before long the fibers began to smoke and suddenly turned to flame. This he placed in the hollow of the twigs and by blowing on the fibers, he eventually got the twigs to ignite and watched as they all began to burn. He added a few more small twigs to his pile and gradually added more wood until he had good fire burning. Pleased with himself, he immediately set out on his next task, that being to make a torch that would give him the light to investigate the cave.

This proved to be an easy task. When he was building his fire, he had thrown the remainder of the coconut husk in the fire. He saw that it burned very slowly but put out a constant flame. He found a straight piece of branch and using it as a handle, he poked it through the husk and he had a torch. As soon as he neared the mouth of the cave, he saw that the smoke from his torch was being drawn into the cave. He surmised that the other opening was higher than this one and opened on the cooler air above the water, thus pulling the warmer air from the land it made for a natural draft.

He entered the cave and made his way around the bend. Just beyond the bend, the roof of the cave became higher until he was able to walk upright. The floor of the cave was sandy and somewhat firm and inclined upwards as it went along. He had only walked about twenty feet when he came to a cavern. It was not very large, about fifteen by twenty feet and had a flat floor and a ceiling the he could not quite make out with this light. He saw that there were natural ledges all around the perimeter of the cavern. There was another opening on the far wall and Roth thought he could hear the sound of dripping water coming from that direction. He quickly crossed the floor of the cavern and went into the other passageway. He had not gone very far when he came upon what he was looking for, water. He found a small pool about a foot deep and four feet in width. He cautiously knelt down and tasted the water. It was sweet and pure. Taking a large drink, he moved back to the larger cavern and made his way back out into the fading sunlight. Now he had everything he would need to survive, food, water and fire. He set out to find as much firewood as he could carry and moved it into the larger cavern where he made another fire in the corner where the draft was the best. He would need to keep this fire burning all the time. He made another trip outside where he gathered a bunch of mangos that he would have before he slept. He also gathered a large armful of palm fronds that had fallen and carried them into his new home where he spread them on a long narrow ledge that he would use as a bed. Finally, he retrieved the pewter mug where he had dropped it and took it into the cave. He then returned outside and set about to explore his island.

He was just returning to the beach as the sun was beginning to set. He moved part of his original fire from the mouth of the cave to the beach where he hoped it might signal a passing ship during the night. He built up the fire until he was sure that it would burn well into the night and made his last trip of the day into the cave.

When he awoke the next morning and had a good drink from the spring in the inner chamber, he made his way out from the cave and walked out onto the beach. He was looking out across the water of the cove when he noticed that on the ledge, where he had found the mug, was a fish of medium size. He walked over to the ledge but had to wade out into the water a short distance to get to the fish. The fish was obviously fresh and could not have been on the ledge for any length of time because it was still alive. He wondered how it got there. The ledge would not be under water when the tide came in for it was too high. Was it possible that it could have flipped up here and not been able to get back down? Roth grabbed the fish and was about to make his way back up the beach when he noticed that there was something else lying on the ledge. It was a set of keys. He knew immediately that they would unlock the manacles that held his wrists and ankles. Finding the right key, he removed the clasps and rubbed his torn and bleeding wrists and ankles. This was the first time that he had been free of them for many weeks now and it was good to have them off. He was about to fling them as far out into the water as he could when he realized that they might come in handy for something. He set them on the ledge and washed his wounds in the salty water of the cove before he once again took up the fish and made his way back up the beach to the spot where he had, the night before, made the fire.

When he reached the fire, Roth saw that some of the larger logs that he had placed on the fire were still hot. Finding one of the smaller logs that had an unburned end that he could grasp, he took it to a shady spot under the palms where he dug a shallow hole and placed it there. He gathered an armful of twigs and branches and placed them on top. It was only a few minutes until he was able to coax them into a good blaze. Roth found the piece of stone that he had used yesterday to sharpen the branch and took it and the fish back down to the water where he proceeded to clean it and prepare it for cooking.

Moving back to the fire, Roth put the fish down on a flat rock nearby and went in search of materials to make a spit. It did not take long to find the pieces he needed.

He returned to the fire and placed the forked pieces of branch on each side of the fire and took a longer straight piece that he had found and threaded the fish on it. He took the fish, placed it over the fire, and leaned up against a nearby palm to watch it cook.

His first thoughts were about the keys. How did they end up on the ledge? He knew that they should still be lying on the bottom of the ocean where they had been thrown overboard. It did not seem possible that they could have washed up on the ledge. The only explanation was that someone placed them there. Roth knew, from climbing the hill and his explorations yesterday, that there was no one else on this island and from the looks of things, there had never been anyone either. Still, they were on the ledge.

He was still thinking about them when he saw that his fish was done cooking. He pulled it off the stick and stripped off the skin from one side of the fish and began to eat large chunks of the cooked flesh.

He had picked the fish clean on one side when he had gotten his fill. He took the other half of the fish and stripped the skin from it and placed it on a flat rock out in the sun to dry it so that he could eat it later in the day.

He spent the rest of the day fixing up his cave and cooking area. He gathered more palm fronds and stored more mangoes in the inner chamber for emergency purposes. Using the added palm fronds, he placed them on his bed to make it a bit softer and more comfortable. Outside, in the cooking area, or kitchen as he began to call it, he constructed a small table out of a somewhat flat piece of driftwood that he thought would be suitable for preparing any fish that he might catch in the future.

Late afternoon, he decided to stop his work for the day and finish eating the fish from that morning. He went into his cave and got a mug full of water and took it out to the kitchen and then retrieved the fish from the rock where it had been drying all day. He settled down against the palm and began to enjoy his evening meal.

His thoughts soon turned to the keys once again. He was deep into this thought when he finished his meal. Roth came out of his daze and saw that the sun was beginning to sink behind the horizon and he knew it would be dark soon.

Before turning in for the night, he walked down the beach to the large pile of wood he had prepared and added some to his signal fire until he had a large blaze. Returning to the kitchen, he stoked the fire. He then lit his torch, took up his mug and started to make his way back to the cave. As he was entering the cave, he stopped. He could hear a sound. He had heard that sound before many times while at sea. It was coming from out in the cove. Slowly he made his way down the beach towards the water listening to the soothing melodic sound that still reminded him of the sea whispering. As he neared the edge of the water, from the glow of his large fire, he could just make out the line of rocks that enclosed the cove. With his eyes, he followed the line of rocks to the bigger rock at the end that marked the opening to the cove. He thought it was there that the sound was coming from. He strained his eyes peering into the darkness, thinking there was something on the rock, a silhouette of some sort. He closed his eyes for a second, but when he reopened them, the silhouette was still there. He called out, "Ahoy out there," and with a splash the sound stopped and it was gone. What had it been? He continued to stare out into the darkness for some time, but whatever had been on the rock did not return and he was beginning to wonder if he had seen anything at all. After a while, he gave up and returned to his cave.

It was very dark in the cave. Only a faint hint of fire was to be seen in the far corner. He added more wood to the coals and before long, the fire had the cavern lit nicely. He made his way into the side chamber, got himself a drink from the pool. Roth looked at his pewter mug and knew that he would have to get something to carry water in if he was going to spend most of his time outside. He went back to the main cavern and ate a mango before settling in for the night. He drifted off to sleep thinking about what it could have been that he saw on the rock.

When he awoke and left the cave the next morning, the first place he looked was out to the big rock, but it was still underwater. He shook his head and knew that he had imagined the whole thing. As he was turning away, he noticed the ledge. There, as before, it held a fish. He waded into the water and made his way out to the ledge. A fish was not all that was there. The ledge also held a rusty knife about eight inches long. Roth took hold of the knife and could see that it probably had not been wet for very long because there was not that much rust on it and it was still sharp. Roth grabbed the fish and made his way back to the beach.

He found his scraping rock and used it on the knife to clean away the rust and found that it came off very easily. Cleaning the knife, he kept looking out towards the big rock, thinking that maybe he had seen something after all. How else could this knife have gotten there, if not placed there by someone? There *had* to be someone else on the island. Today he would set out to find them.

The knife came in very handy cleaning the fish and Roth made quick work of it and in no time at all, the fish was on the spit, cooking.

After he had finished eating half of the fish, he placed the rest in the sun to dry. With this done, Roth set out to gathering wood for his three fires and hopefully find things to improve on his living quarters.

When he had finished his tour around the island, he decided that he would take another hike up the peak and look around to see if he could find where his mysterious night visitor was hiding. It did not take him as long to reach the top of the peak now that he was shed of the chains and soon he was looking down and could clearly see everything that this island held. He studied every facet of the island that he could see from his vantage point and could not find any evidence that another person could be hiding. Glancing down towards the water of the cove, he could now see the big rock above the waterline. The rock was smooth and rounded from the continuous wash of the waves that it received and Roth could see nothing that might resemble the figure that he perceived he saw there last night. There had to be an explanation for the knife and the keys, but Roth failed to discern what it could be.

By the time that Roth returned to the beach, the sun was nearing the horizon and he knew it was time to add more wood to his signal fire. As he was dragging the larger pieces of driftwood across to the fire, he noticed a box like object floating in the water a few yards off the beach. It was almost totally submerged and this was why he had not noticed it sooner. He waded out to retrieve it. It turned out to be a chest. It was not very heavy so he carried it up onto the beach. Upon closer examination, he could see that it was watertight. He opened it and was surprised to see that it held many smaller bottles labeled as spices. He closed the chest and decided that he would check it out more closely when he got back to his "kitchen". He then returned to the business of fueling his fire. This did not take very long and soon he was on his way back to his cooking area.

He set the chest down next to his cooking fire. The sun was setting so he added a few more pieces of wood to the fire to make it burn brighter. He once again opened the chest and began to look through the various bottles and jars it contained. There were spices of all kinds and most importantly, near the bottom, he found a small bag of salt. This was pleasing because he knew that he would need salt if he were going to survive very long. In addition, a small bag contained some needles and an assortment of threads of different measures of thickness. In the bottom of the chest, he found two sets of flatware and under that, he found a cleaver, just what he needed to crack the hard thick husks that held the coconut meat. This was obviously a cook's chest. He thought to himself that this chest could well be a residual of some ships tragic end. Sighing, he lamented his own ship and crew and for the first time, since his capture, he felt very much alone. Memories of how the *Galaunt* fell returned him to the reality of how he found himself here. "If only I could have left Kathryn ashore, none of this would have taken place," Roth found himself thinking. His eyes watered up thinking about his dear sweet daughter, she had been so young and so full of life. Soon he was finding himself angry or maybe even angrier at Creed than he had been when he first lost Kathryn.

Arousing himself from his musing, he rose and walked to the nearest palm tree, found a recently dropped coconut and brought it back to the fire. The cleaver made short work of removing the husk and revealing the nut inside. He took the nut and shook it near his ear and could hear the swishing sound of the milk inside. With his knife, he made two holes in the top of the nut and raised it to his mouth and slowly sucked the liquid from the inside, savoring every drop. Then he took the cleaver and with a strong stroke, cut the nut in two. With the knife, he cut out a large chunk of meat from the inside and sat back to enjoy it by the side of the fire. He now had another source of nourishment.

As he sat by the fire relishing the taste of the coconut, he peered past the glow of the signal fire out towards the rock. Nothing was there that he could see. Again, he thought that he had imagined it the night before. His gaze moved towards the ledge. It is still a mystery, which he

was determined to solve. Before long, he found himself beginning to tire, so he banked the cooking fire and moved into the cave.

The next morning when he emerged from the cave, his first look went to the ledge. He was not surprised when his gaze fell upon another fish lying there. He waded over to it and as he turned away, he saw a large piece of canvas half-floating in the surf and half lying on the beach. While wading over to it, he could see that it was a piece of sail. He grabbed it by one edge and dragged it further onto the beach. Leaving it there, he walked up to his cooking fire and placed a few smaller pieces of wood on it. Upon returning to the canvas, he noticed some strange marks in the sand. Looking closer he could see that something large had been pulled along the sand leaving a shallow trough. It was then that he noticed the handprints along both sides of the trough. They looked as though they had aided with dragging the canvas up the beach, but then dragged an object back down to the water. He knelt down by one of them and saw that they were much smaller than his, perhaps belonging to a young man or a woman. He studied them for quite some time and concluded that whoever had made them was dragging something along. He could tell that wherever the hands had touched the sand, there was a rise in the trough, indicating that the weight of the object was being lifted as it was being moved back towards the water. Here was another mystery. Who or what would have made these marks and not walked on the sand. Who was on this island with him? He looked out towards the sea and suddenly it came to him that there must be another cave on the seaside of the hill. Without hesitation, he waded out to the where the water met the rock and began to pull himself along the rock out towards the opening of the cove. It did not take him long to reach the point where the cove met the sea. He continued to pull himself along the base of the peak as he entered the ocean. The waves immediately began to beat against him and threatened to tear him from the rocks and wash him out to sea. He held on tightly to the rock and struggled to pull himself along.

He was getting very tired as he finally rounded the end of the peak and started to make his way back towards the island on the backside. It was quite some time before he was at the channel that separated his island from the atoll. He pulled himself up on the sand of the atoll and laid there resting from the ordeal. He had not found anywhere that someone could have been hiding and realized that he had wasted his time. After resting for some time, he pulled himself to his feet. As he was turning to go back to his island, he looked down and saw, to his surprise, that the marks he had left in the sand were similar to the ones by the piece of canvas. Now he thought he knew how the marks had been made, he just had to figure out who made them.

When he got back to the beach, everything was how he had left it. He went down and finished dragging the large piece of canvas up on the sand and spread it out so that it could dry. It was indeed a large piece, measuring maybe thirty feet by twenty feet. It had to have come from a sail at one time or another. It was stained the way you would expect it to look after a long time at sea. By the time he finished with the sail, he was getting very hungry and retrieved the fish from the ledge. He took it to water and prepared it for cooking.

It was late afternoon before Roth finally threaded the fish on the stick to cook. Today the fish would receive some salt and other spices, so Roth, being very hungry, was looking forward to his first meal of the day. He ate the whole fish this time because there was no sense in saving part of it because it was already getting dark. He sat around for a while to let the food settle and think about the days activities before he set out to gather the firewood for the beach signal fire.

After starting the fire on the beach, he went back to the cooking fire, took the cleaver to a coconut, and cut the husk away to get to the nut inside. He bored two holes in the top of the nut and sucked the insides dry. After he had broken open the nut to retrieve the meat within, he sat back and surveyed the cove. His thoughts were on the ledge and how the fish were brought there every day. Maybe, if he stayed up and watched, he would catch whoever it was that was leaving the fish. With that decision being made, he decided that he would conceal himself in the bushes behind his kitchen and keep a watch through the night.

Roth knew it was very late or very early in the morning when he thought he saw some movement in the water around the ledge. Holding very still, he waited until he saw, from the glow of the signal fire, a figure rise up from the water. He could make out a few features and saw that the person in the water had very long red hair. The person had their back to him so he could not see their face. However, he could see that they held a fish in their hands. Roth stood and stepped out from his place of hiding and shouted, "Hello there." The person turned suddenly and seeing Roth, dropped the fish and vanished beneath the water and was gone with a flash of iridescence. Roth could not believe what he had seen, or even imagine what he had seen. The person was a young woman, she had very long red hair and her skin seemed to be a pale shade of grey. He had not seen her for very long so he could not make out the features of her face but somehow she had seemed familiar. How could she have been familiar? He was hundreds of miles from his home and doubted that there would be someone else from England marooned on this island as he was. He stood there for quite some time thinking about what he had seen when he finally decided that whomever it had been, was not going to return. He walked over to the cave entrance and turned one last time to glance out over the cove, hoping that he had not scared them off for good. Feeling a sense of loss, he entered the cave and made his way to his cavern.

The next morning when he awoke and emerged from the cave, he was very relieved to see that whoever had been there last night had indeed returned and had brought another fish. He was happy to see that he had not scared them off. After he had witnessed what he had seen the night before just confirmed to him that he was not alone on this island.

He wondered again, who it could have been. He was almost positive that it had been a young woman for she had long red hair. Where could she be coming from? He had searched the island and had found nothing, not one clue of anyone living on his island. Roth mused over the events of yesterday and began thinking about the canvas and the marks in the sand. He now wondered if the girl he had seen had made them. It appeared to look like the marks had originated from the sea.

He went about the business of building up his cooking fire and cleaning the fish. With these tasks completed and the fish hanging over the fire on the spit, Roth settled back against his tree and continued to think about the previous night. He wondered why she had not stayed and let him know who she was. She must be afraid of him for some reason. Why if she were, would she bring him food every day? This made no sense. She had obviously been on the island before him and surely, she must be lonely for company. It suddenly came to him that the sounds he had been hearing at night, sounded the same as he, Berkshire and the rest of the crew had heard from the *Galaunt.*

He got up, walked down to the beach, and called out, "I know you are out there somewhere. Come out and show yourself. I will not hurt you." Getting no response, he called out again, "Please come out of hiding. I only want to know who you are and thank you for the fish." Still there was no response. He stood there for a while and seeing nothing or hearing anything, he decided to return to his cooking fire and have his breakfast.

After he had finished his breakfast, Roth spent the rest of the day fashioning various items from the canvas sheet. He now had some bags that he could use to carry water. In his cave, he used a large piece of the canvas to cover the palm fronds that were his bed. He filled the water bags from the spring in the inner cave and carried these outside. This would save him from the need to go into the cave every time he got thirsty. He also used a large piece to cover his kitchen area to protect it from any rain that might fall, something that had not happened since he had been on the island.

Satisfied that he had accomplished what he considered a good day's work, he stored the remainder of the canvas in his cave. He returned to the dried fish that he had set out that morning and again settled back against a tree to enjoy his afternoon meal. As he sat there chewing the dried fish, his thoughts went back to the night before and he slowly drifted off to sleep.

When he awoke, he saw that the sun was beginning to set. He got up and stretched, he looked out over the waters of the cove and with a shock saw someone sitting on the rock looking back at him. Even from this distance, he could tell he had seen the same person before. He slowly lowered his arms, afraid that any sudden movement might scare her away again. He decided that he would try to wave to her and see what would happen. Tentatively he raised his arm and waved at her, he was very surprised when the young lady waved back. He slowly started to walk down the beach and when he came to his signal fire, he stopped. He wondered if he acted as though he was not going to force the issue, she would stay where she was. Roth went about the business of lighting the fire with his back towards the girl. After he had the fire going brightly, he again turned towards the rock, to his sadness, he saw that the girl was gone. He scanned the other rocks in the cove but she was nowhere to be found. Well now, he thought, this was a beginning. He decided that he would not stay up this evening hoping to catch her leaving the fish. Rather he would just go into the cave and see what would happen the next day.

He awoke the next morning with a feeling of excitement, looking forward to what the events of the day might bring. When he emerged from the cave, his first glance went to the ledge, and to his joy, there was a fish lying there as well as a coil of rope. It was then that, from the corner of his eye, he saw the girl sitting on the rock. He turned and waved and was glad to see her wave back. He called out, "Thank you for the fish. Would you like to come and eat some of it with me?" He saw her head lower as if in sadness and watched her slide into the water again.

The next day it was the same thing. He would wave and she would wave back, but she would not speak or let him get any closer. Thus, this is how it went for days that turned into weeks.

During all this time, Roth continued to find various items that made his life on the island more bearable. He now had lanterns and whale oil to fill them with, more clothes and sometimes a few items of furniture that he used in his cave and kitchen. He was sure that the girl on the rock was responsible for all of this. He did not know where she was getting them or even where her place of hiding was, but he was grateful and wished there was some way for him to let her know how grateful he was. Over the weeks and months, he came to realize this girl made the sounds he heard in the early evenings. She would sit out on the rock and sing well into the night.

He awoke early one morning and left the cave. When he looked over towards the ledge, he was surprised to see the girl was just placing the fish there. He did not know what to do, but he decided that enough was enough. He was going to end the game that she had been playing all these weeks. He said, "I hope that you will talk to me. By now you should know that I mean you no harm and am extremely grateful for everything that you have done for me. Please do not leave." She turned quickly upon the sound of his voice but did not hurry away as she had always done in the past. Roth made a move towards her to see what she would do. He was surprised when she did not sink beneath the water and disappear as usual. The sun had not yet risen, so he could not make out her features, but it was getting brighter. He continued to make his way towards the ledge and as he entered the water, she started to back away. Roth had already made his mind up that if it was possible, he was going to make contact. He continued to wade out into the water and she continued to back up. The sun was just beginning to peek above the horizon when he had waded out far enough that just his head was above the water. She was still a ways away when he realized why he had thought that he had recognized her so many weeks ago. "Kathryn?" he whispered. "Kathryn is that you?" Roth saw the look of surprise that came upon her face just before she slipped beneath the surface of the water. Roth felt an ache in his heart as he watched her disappear. He cried out, "Kathryn, please don't go." He saw her surface again a few yards out from where she had gone under, so again he tried to talk to her. "Kathryn, if that is you move closer so that I can see you." Roth thought her face took on a look of sadness as she slowly slipped beneath the water and vanished from sight.

Roth stood in the water for a very long time until he concluded that she was not going to return. Could it really have been Kathryn? How was it possible that she even knew where he was, let alone be here herself? Feeling emotionally lost and with a pain in his heart, he found his way back to the beach and collapsed onto the sand, feeling heartbroken. He began to relive the storm in which she had drowned and became overwhelmed by the grief of losing her. Roth sobbed as though he had never done so before. He had failed in his attempt to meet or talk with her and he needed her to answer all of these questions. She *had* been lost in the storm so long ago and had surely drowned, yet he felt in his heart that this was Kathryn. With that thought, he turned and started back to the water. His whole world stopped when he got to the ledge, he was consumed with the feelings that she must return. He needed her to be Kathryn. When he found himself looking at the fish, he became very confused. It was there. How had it gotten there if not placed there by someone? He had to admit to himself that there was indeed someone else here with him, but he also came to realize that he must have mistaken the identity with someone that he so dearly loved and would have liked to see. With this thought, he grabbed the fish, waded out of the water, and crossed the beach as he made his way to his kitchen.

Roth was not very hungry but he still prepared the fish and placed it on the spit. He climbed into a hammock, something he had fashioned from some spare canvas and rope, to think and watch it while it cooked. First of all, the person that he had seen had long and flowing red hair. This was the same as Kathryn, so maybe this was why he thought it could have been her. Secondly, the person that he had seen had light gray skin, Kathryn's skin had been rosy. This thought raised another question in his mind. What race of people had gray skin? Could it be that a race of people lived in the area that had gray skin? This thought alone was enough to convince him he had not seen Kathryn.

He had his breakfast and went about doing his chores for the day, all the time thinking about who it had been and how he was going to make further contact with her.

As Roth was finishing lighting the signal fire on the beach, he happened to glance out towards the rock in the cove. Sitting on the rock was the girl staring back at him. He said, "Hello" and waved. He watched her until the sun set beyond the horizon and then turned to walk to his kitchen area. When he neared the kitchen, he stopped and listened. He could hear that sound, a melodic sound that seemed to carry on the breeze. Turning the rock, he suddenly realized it was the girl making this sound. He thought that was impossible, the first time he had heard the song was aboard the *Galaunt*. This girl could not possibly have been the source, for the *Galaunt* had been far out to sea when he had first heard it. He stood and listened, enraptured, to the soft flowing song. It was the same whispering sound that he and Berkshire had listened to while standing on the wheel deck of the *Galaunt*. He knew that he had to make contact with the girl, this was the only way he could solve the mystery.

The next morning, he awoke early and as he emerged from his cave, the first place he looked at was the ledge. The fish was there, but the girl was nowhere in sight. He looked out towards the rock, but she was not there either. With sadness and a touch of loneliness, he retrieved the fish and went about his daily chores, all the while looking out to the rock hoping to see the girl.

This was how it went for the next several days. Roth would awaken early and hurry out to see if he could find the girl, but always it was the same, she would be nowhere in sight, the fish was always there, but the girl was not. Every night he would stay up as long as he could and listen for her song, but he would always find himself going into the cave hoping that tomorrow she would reappear.

Roth had all but given up hope of seeing her again when he was surprised one morning as he emerged from his cave and there she was. She was in the water near the ledge and Roth got the impression that she was waiting for him. He stood near the entrance of his cave for a few moments and watched as she came nearer to the beach. He started to walk down the beach and was happy to see that she did not retreat as she had done previously. He kept walking until he reached the waters edge where he stopped. She still did not move. The sun was up, it was a bright morning, and she was close enough now that he could see the features of her light gray face. There was no more doubt in his mind now. It *was* Kathryn. He stood there for quite some time taking in the vibrant look of health that shone on Kathryn's face. Was he still in the cave asleep? Was this a dream? No, he was awake, he could feel the heat of the sun on his body and the waves lapping upon his feet.

He entered the water and quickly waded over to where she was. "Kathryn, how can this be? I thought I lost you during the storm." He moved closer until he was face to face with her. "Oh Kathryn, I have missed you so much." He reached out and took hold of her shoulders and with no resistance, she came into his arms. He held her very tightly and began to sob.

They stayed in this position for quite some time until Roth felt Kathryn start to pull away. Kathryn moved back slightly but did not release her hold on his hands. She started to speak but found it somewhat difficult to get out the words. It had been so long since she had used her voice to communicate. Seeing her father filled with a mixture of joy and tears did not make it any easier. It was going through her mind how she would explain to him why it had been so long before she decided to reveal herself. She managed to choke out the words with some emotion of her own to tell him "Yes Father, it is I." Roth, excited at hearing the sound of his beloved daughter's voice, filled with a mountain of emotions. He had so much to say and so much to learn he did not know where to start. After a moment of silence as they stared at one another, he asked her how this all happened. How can you be here? Kathryn did not reply, she simply reached down and took hold of the charm that hung on her neck and brought it above the surface of the water. Roth looked at the charm and immediately recalled its meaning. He knew the story behind it, but he had never really believed it. As he was musing over the charm, Kathryn could see the expression of question in his eyes and realized that it was time for her to reveal the truth.

"Father, I am not still the daughter that you once knew, there have been many changes that have come over me. These changes are the reason that I have not come forward sooner. When I first fell overboard, I found myself swimming through the water with little effort and at first, I did not know why. It was dark and I could not see my body in the water, but I did know that my legs felt very different. I came to the surface and the first thing that I saw was Billy floating nearby. I also saw the hatch cover that had knocked us off the ship. I swam over to Billy, dragged him to the hatch cover, and managed to get him up on it. He was unconscious but still breathing. I stayed with him, clinging to the cover, until the storm ended and the sun came up. This was when I first noticed my hands. They were, as well as my arms, a glossy shade of gray. It was about this time that Billy awoke and looked at me with horror in his eyes. I told him that it was just me, Kathryn, but he shrank away from me, covered his eyes and called me a monster. It was then that I swam away from the cover and hid from his view. As I was swimming under the water, I got my first glimpse of my legs. They were not legs anymore, but a long tapered tail with fins at the end like dolphin." She took her father's hand and gently pulled him across the cove to the rock where she often sat. She helped her father climb onto the rock and then pulled herself up beside him. She did not take her eyes off him and did not miss the look of surprise when he got his first look at her body and was happy when the look of surprise did not turn into a look of horror.

Roth watched as Kathryn pulled herself, with little effort, onto the rock. He could not believe what he was seeing. Her head and shoulders were, other than the gray color of her skin, still that of Kathryn, or rather a slightly more mature Kathryn, but that is where it ended. From just below her navel, iridescent scales similar to a fish, started and extended down to where they ended at a long horizontal fin similar to a whale's. Roth looked back to her face where he saw a sad look of apprehension on her face. He reached over, took her once again in his arms, and hugged her as tightly as he had done before.

Roth held her for a while longer before releasing her. He leaned back where he could get a better look at his daughter. He looked at her from the top of her head to the tip of her tail, then reached over, and gently held the charm around her neck. "You are a mermaid," He exclaimed with amazement.

"Yes, it would appear so. The charm obviously worked." She said with an air of great conscientiousness. They both seemed rather amused at that, while smiling at each other.

After a moment of silence, Kathryn stated, "Father, I must leave you for a time, I cannot stay in this sun for very long because it dries out my skin and I have been out of the water for longer than I should be. I will not be very far away and will come back to talk some more this evening. Let me help you back to shore then I will come back this evening and we will talk some more." With that said she slipped back into the water and waited for her father to jump in and then took his hand and pulled him quickly towards the shore.

"I will be looking forward to this evening," he said in a rather excited voice.

With a beaming smile Kathryn replied, "Thank you Father for your understanding and acceptance. I love you and have missed you so much also." She swam back to the middle of the cove and disappeared beneath the surface of the water.

Roth sat on the shore and watched the spot where she had disappeared and was very surprised when he saw her, flanked by two dolphins, leaping high out of the water in a prefect arc and reenter the water with a splash. The trio repeated their performance one more time and with another splash, they were gone.

Roth went through his daily chores thinking about the morning and his reunion with his daughter. He could hardly wait until the evening came. Finally, when the sun was low in the western horizon, he lit his signal fire and made his way to the other end of the beach where the rocks made their way into the water and climbed the nearest rock. Making his way to the end of the rock where it sloped down into the water of the cove, he sat down on a wide flat spot and waited for Kathryn to appear.

He had not waited long before he saw her swimming from the ocean into the cove. He called out to her, got her attention, and watched as she gracefully swam over to where he waited. Kathryn hopped onto the rock and they stayed there well into the night telling each other the stories that had brought them to this point of time until Roth could not stay awake any longer. They hugged and bid each other goodnight and promised that they would meet again in the morning.

The next morning Kathryn was waiting for him by the ledge. Roth waded out to greet her. After hugging his daughter, he reached for the fish and asked her, "Would you like to join me eating this after I get it cooked?"

"It has been so long since I have eaten anything that has been cooked, I doubt that my system would tolerate it any longer. You go ahead and fix it for yourself and I will meet you on the rock later," she replied.

As agreed earlier, they met on the rock and talked, once again, well into the night. This turned into the routine that both enjoyed.

Roth was happy once again and knew now that he would not be alone on the island anymore.

Chapter 13
"William"

Roth tried to spend as much time with Kathryn as was possible. It was only limited to the amount of time she could stay out of the water and Roth needing rest or food. At those times when he did need food, he would watch her as she played with the dolphins in the water of the cove. Roth chuckled to himself thinking that she had found a source of companionship and really enjoyed it. It lightened his thoughts knowing she was not alone and unhappy. She had explained to him that they were her constant companions. She thought that they stayed with her to offer protection but she told him that she was not afraid for her life in the ocean. There was beauty in the seas that were beyond comprehension. She so wished that she could share this with her father rather than just try to describe it to him. She boastfully exclaimed that she could swim faster than any other creature in the sea. However, sometimes when she was doing something else, the dolphins would keep a vigilant watch over her. So, this was how their days and the nights passed.

One morning when he awoke and emerged from his cave, he saw there was no fish on the ledge. He made his way down the beach, looked out over the cove and past the opening to the ocean, and could not see her or any of the dolphins. This was not the first time that this had happened, but it still worried him none the less. He would have to fend for himself today if he wanted to have anything to eat. He said to himself that she was probably out gathering, something that she loved to do, and would return later in the day or maybe not until the next morning. He had other things to eat so he would not miss eating but he would still miss her.

He went about his chores for the day, but always kept a watchful eye on the cove and the waters near the entrance. He did not even see a dolphin all day. After lighting his signal fire, he went to the rock and waited well into the night for her to come. It was with a heavy heart that he went into his cave that night. He attempted to sleep but he could not help but think about why she was not there. It was then that he remembered that she had reassured him that there was nothing to worry about because she could handle herself quite well in the water.

The next morning he hurried out to the beach, but was again disappointed when did not see her or a fish on the ledge. Where could she be, she had been there everyday since he had been on the island, with the exception of gathering days and even then she was usually back no later than the next morning.

The days passed and there was no sight of her. It had been four days now since he had last seen Kathryn. He was beginning to think that maybe she was gone for good. He was having a difficult time even getting himself to do the things that he had done every day since his arrival on the island. He was not eating well and was having a very hard time even getting out of the hammock. Nevertheless, he always kept constant lookout for her in the cove. Just two days ago, there had been a couple of dolphins swimming in the cove. He had watched them all day hoping they were telling him that Kathryn was with them, but he soon came to believe that they were also looking for her in the places that she was known to have been. Something bad must have happened and Roth knew that there was no way that he could ever know.

It was on the fifth day, when he emerged from his cave, that he was greatly relieved when he saw Kathryn sitting on the beach. He also saw that she was not alone. Lying there a short distance away from the water's edge, was a body. Roth rushed down to the water and throwing himself to his knees beside her, he took her into his arms and held her tightly. "Oh Kathryn, I have been so worried about you. Where have you been?" he asked with the sound of relief in his voice.

"The dolphins found me in the night and from their excitement, I knew that something was wrong and I had to go with them. I followed them for two days and they led me to this young man," she replied as she pointed towards the body. "I found him clinging to a large piece of planking and barely alive. I could not swim fast dragging him and that plank along, so it took me longer to get back here than I had hoped," she replied. "Can you help him father?" She was obviously very concerned.

Roth released his daughter and turned to look at the young man next to her. He could see that he had been in the water for a long time. His skin was baked and peeling from the sun. He could also discern that he was still alive, but just barely. He was not sure that there was a lot that he could do for him. He turned back to Kathryn and said, "I will take him and settle him in the hammock and see what I can do."

Roth had weakened, but he still had enough strength to pick the young man up and carry him up the beach. After he settled him in the hammock, he grabbed one of his water bags and slowly poured a small quantity of water into the lad's mouth. The lad stirred when he felt the water enter his mouth and began to cough. "Easy there youngster, don't drink too much to fast." He then poured some water on a rag and began to wipe the young man's face. He saw the lad open his eyes and try to say something. He took the water bag, brought it close to the young man's mouth, and began to let a little more water run into his mouth. The lad coughed again and reached for the bag. Roth let him have it and watched as he started to gulp the water from the bag. Roth pulled the bag away and said, "Slow down, you are going to make yourself sick."

After a few more drinks of water, the lad fell back and went to sleep. Roth made sure that he was all right and then made his way back down to the edge of the water where he saw that Kathryn was waiting a few feet away in the water.

"Is he going to be all right father?" she asked.

"I think that he will be fine. He is asleep now. He looks like he has been adrift for some time. But I think that he will be all right after he gets a little bit of rest and eats some food," he answered back.

"I will go and catch a fish and be right back," she said. She pushed herself back into the water and disappeared from sight.

She had only been gone for seemed like just a few seconds when she reappeared holding a fish in both hands. "That was quick," Roth said.

"There are plenty of fish in the cove and they are easy to catch," she answered back with a smile. Roth took the fish, smiled and returned to his kitchen and started cooking.

He was just taking the fish off the fire when he heard the lad speak hoarsely, "May I have some more water please?" Roth, with a warning to drink slowly, handed him a water bag. "Who are you and where am I?" he haltingly asked.

"My name is Roth and you are on an island that I have been marooned on for quite some time," he answered back.

"I have heard that name before, but it was always associated with a bloodthirsty pirate. You sir, are surely not him, are you?"

Roth thought for a few seconds before answering, "Yes, I am probably the man that you have heard about. I suppose there are many stories out there about me, but bloodthirsty? I don't think that I could ever truly be called that, for if a life could be spared, it was spared."

The young lad spoke quickly, "It has been said that you were responsible for many ships being sunk and you were captured and sentenced to the penal colony of Botany Bay. How did you end up here?"

"I was indeed sentenced to spend the rest of my life in colony, but as you can see, I did not make it there. It is a long story as to how I became marooned on this island." At this point Roth began telling the lad the story.

The young man listened intently and was totally enthralled by the tale he was hearing and was unwilling to interrupt.

When Roth finished the story, he asked, "How did I get here?"

"You were found adrift by my daughter and she brought you here to me," Roth replied.

"Your daughter?" he inquired. "I do seem to remember someone talking to me. That must have been her but I thought I was dreaming."

"Can you tell me who you are and can you remember what happened to you and how you ended up in the water?" Roth asked.

"My name is William, William Cameron, and I am, or was, an able seaman aboard His Majesty's Ship, *Wanderer*. We were sailing to Australia with a load of supplies for the prison colony at Botany Bay when we struck something in the water that tore out the bottom of our ship. The *Wanderer* went down very quickly and I was able to swim clear and grab onto a piece of her shattered hull. The next morning I found myself alone. There was very little debris in the water and no one else was around. I surmised that she had gone down with all hands except for me. From that point on all I can say is that I was adrift with no water for I do not how many days. The next thing that I remember, or I that I remember, is someone talking to me. Then I awoke and you were over me giving me water," he stated.

"Then you have been without water for at least five days. You are very lucky indeed. If Kathryn had not found you, you would not be here to tell me this story."

The young man said, "That is twice that you have mentioned your daughter. Where is she? I would like to thank her proper."

"Be patient, you will get to meet her in due course," Roth said. "You must be hungry. Try and see if you can eat something." Roth handed him a plate with a small portion of fish on it.

The young lad took it and with a thank you, he proceeded to eat. Roth saw that it was not easy because his lips were very raw and cracked. However, he was able to get what was on the plate eaten. "Would you like some more?"

"Yes please. That is very good and it seems like forever since I have eaten anything!"

"Kathryn caught it in the cove," Roth boasted. "She provides fish and many other items for me. She delights in surprising me with not only fish but also other items you can see you can see by just looking around," he said as he pointed to the many things around them. "She seems to know exactly what I need to survive here and she lightens my heart," he added with a smile.

William ate another portion of fish without further conversation and quickly fell asleep, obviously exhausted by his plight and full stomach.

Cleaning up and putting the remainder of the fish out on the rocks to dry, he then made his way back down to the water where he saw that Kathryn had returned.

"Well?" she asked.

"He is a strong young man and I think that after a few days of food and rest, he will be just fine," he said with a small smile as he noticed the look of concern on her face.

"That is so good to hear, I was afraid that I would not make it back in time for him to survive. He was very far away." Turning her back to him, she swam out into the middle of the cove where she dove under the water and disappeared, then playfully made a flip in the water and waved at him. Roth laughed at the sight of her showing off. He was glad to see that she still had her sense of humor.

He spent the rest of day idly catching up on things that he had let go these past few days. He checked in on the young man occasionally and always found him to be asleep. Roth knew that he needed rest to speed along his recovery so he did not bother him.

After he had lit the signal fire and checked in on the young man and he found him to be still sleeping. Assuring himself that all was well, He made his way to the rock where he would meet Kathryn for their nightly talks. She was there waiting for him and the first thing that she asked impatiently was, "How is he doing?"

Chuckling to himself he answered, "He is doing just fine. He is still sleeping and I hope that he sleeps through the night. He will probably be up and around by morning,"

She then started to ask all sorts of questions concerning everything that the young man said and what he could remember. Roth, still laughing inside, told her all that he had said and reassured her that he did not remember her as his savior. He could not help but notice the relief that came over her face as he said that last part. "You are not going to be able to hide from him. You know that don't you?"

"I know, but I think that you had better break it to him first. I still remember the look of horror that came over Brian's face when he first saw me and I don't think I could take that again," she said sadly.

"There, there my young Darlin', there is nothing to worry about. You are still very pretty and I am sure that after the initial shock of seeing that mermaids really do exist, he will become a very good friend."

"Father, you have to say things like that because I am your daughter. You would find beauty in me no matter what," she said with a coy smile. Kathryn had not displayed that playful nature in a long time, Roth thought to himself. He did not want to spoil that now.

He thought about this for a short time and finally said, "Kathryn, you know that I would not lie to you. You have changed for sure, but the beauty that you always had is still with you. You have not changed in anything other than shape and that is not a bad thing either. You are still the same person that you have always been. I think that you will be surprised, when you finally decide to meet William. Always remember,

I haven't had much time to talk with him, so we don't know what kind of a person he is yet."

"You are right, Father. It may turn out that I don't want to meet with *him* at all," she answered with a giggle. Upon hearing that, Roth laughed out loud. "Oh, how I love you young Darlin'!"

"Tomorrow, we will know," he said with a smile. "For now, I am going to check on him one more time and then I am going to get some sleep. It has been a long day and we both need some rest. Good night young Darlin', I will see you in the mornin." He gave her a hug and a kiss on her cheek, climbed down from the rock and started across the beach to his cave in better spirits than he had felt in a long time.

When he neared his kitchen area, he saw that William was now sitting up in the hammock watching him move across the beach. William said, "Was that your daughter you were speaking with?"

Roth stopped and answered, "Why yes it was. Could you hear us?"

"Just a few words here and there," William answered. "Is there something wrong with her? Why doesn't she come here with you?" he queried. He then added, "She has a lovely voice and it reminds me of the voice that I imagined I heard while I was adrift."

Roth thought about these questions and wondered if he should just come out and tell the young man the truth. He decided, as he had told Kathryn, tomorrow would be the right time. "You may not remember, but I told you earlier that it was Kathryn, my daughter, who rescued you and brought you here. There is nothing wrong with her, she may be a little different from you and I, but she is young and healthy and still, in my eyes at least, as beautiful as the day she was born. Tomorrow when you have rested a little more, we will talk and I will tell you all about Kathryn and if she is willing, you will meet her. Now you lie back down and I will see you in the morning." With that, Roth turned, took his lantern, and entered the cave for the night.

William laid there for some time thinking about what the old man had said. She may be a little different. What could he have meant by that? What was with all the mystery? Why didn't his daughter live here with him? William decided that he would go and see for himself but as he tried to stand, he found that he was still too weak to venture from the hammock. He lay back down and realized that the old man was right, tomorrow would be time enough. As he laid there trying to go back to sleep, he heard a soft singing sound coming from across the cove. He sat back up and looked out across the water and from the light of the fire, he could see someone sitting on a big rock out in the water. They were much too far for him to make out any features, but it was definitely where the sound was coming from. Could that be the old man's daughter, he wondered? If so, her voice was pleasing and he knew that he would have to meet the person that could sound so fascinating. He sat there and listened well into the night until the singing stopped and the person disappeared from the rock.

William woke early, feeling very thirsty and hungry. He found that he was feeling much better than yesterday, so he decided that he would see if he could get up and move around. Getting to his feet, he looked around and saw a bag hanging from a palm tree near where the hammock was tied. Going to it and finding that it contained water, he untied the top and took a long drink from the contents. Satisfying his thirst, he looked around again until he spotted what he thought was dried fish on a rock not far from where he stood. As he was slowly walking to where the fish was, he heard a noise coming from the water. He turned in time to see a person, or rather what looked like a person, emerge from the water and place a flopping fish on a small ledge. He stood there as the person turned in his direction and made eye contact, it was a girl. As soon as the girl saw him looking at her, she sank beneath the water's surface and was gone. William rubbed his eyes and thought to himself, 'did I really see that or am I still delirious?' No, he was sure that he had seen something and walked down to the edge of the water. The fish was there and still flopping around just as he had seen it, but where was the girl? He looked out over the water to see if she had surfaced somewhere else but saw nothing. Where did she go? Could this be the daughter, Kathryn, that the old man had talked about? He could remember that she had long red hair, but from there he was sure that his mind had been playing tricks on him for he thought that he had seen that she had gray glossy skin. He was sure that he had imagined it all, but the fish, it was there.

"Ah, I see that you are feeling better this morning."

Startled from his musings, William turned and saw the old man standing by the base of the cliff. Where had he come from?

Roth, seeing the confusion and look of shock on the young man's face said, "Are you alright? You look like you have seen a ghost."

"Where did you come from? I didn't hear you walk up," William managed to ask.

"Come here and I will show you," Roth replied.

With a little effort, William made his way to where the old man was standing. When he reached the spot, he could now see an opening in the side of the cliff that was previously hidden from his view.

"This is where I sleep. Not far from this opening is a cavern that I have made into a bedroom. It is also where the fresh water comes from. I will show it to you later after we have had the breakfast that I see Kathryn has delivered to us."

"So, I wasn't seeing things," William said. "I wasn't sure that what I saw was real or something that my mind made up."

"You saw her then?" he inquired, pausing as he waited for a reply. When he received no reply, he went on to say, "No you weren't imagining it. She is real. But as I told you last night, she is a little different from you and me." Roth decided that he would come right out with it. "She is a mermaid."

William could not believe what he had just heard. Last night this old man had seemed very normal to him, but now he sounded like he was completely off his rocker. He must have been on this island for a very long time to make up a story like that. He figured that he better find out a little more to see what he was up against and whether or not he was in danger. "Surely you have gone mad," he ventured ahead to say. "There is no such thing as a mermaid. That is just a story that the old sailors tell to try to impress those that are not familiar with the sea. You have obviously been on this island so long that you are making up friends to keep you company."

"So, it is mad that you think I am?" Roth said with a chuckle. With a grin, he went on, "Well you saw her. You tell me what you saw and then we will talk about my madness."

William, taken aback by the old man's bluntness, thought back on what he had imagined that he had seen. The girl had risen from the water and she did have gray skin. She had gone underwater and from what he could see, had not resurfaced. No, he thought to himself, there is no such thing as a mermaid. He could not even believe that he was even considering such a foolish notion, even in his own mind. "Ok, let's just assume that what you are saying is true. How is it that you could possibly have a daughter that is a mermaid?"

For a time, Roth went about the business of preparing breakfast and did not acknowledge the question. After he had the fish over the fire and cooking, he finally said, "It is a tale that will not be short in the telling. But I guess that since you are now a part of it, you should probably know the whole truth." Roth began telling the story of everything that had happened over the last few years. He tried not to leave anything out and spent a long time explaining why it was that he had done what he had done, the deeds that had earned him his reputation.

William turned out to be an avid listener, seldom interrupting with a question and was quite engrossed with what he was hearing. They spent the rest of the morning with William asking more questions and Roth, patiently answering. It was early afternoon, with the sun high in the sky, when they both fell silent. William lay back in the hammock and was soon asleep. He knew that the young man was still very weak and needed more rest, so he took no offense from it and went about the daily activities.

It was just after he started when he noticed that Kathryn was sitting on their rock. He strode over to where she waited and climbed the rock to join her. "Well Kathryn, I told him the whole story from start to finish."

"What did he say?" she asked.

"He did not say anything other than ask me a lot of questions to help him understand different parts of the story. As far as to whether or not he believed everything, I do not know because he fell asleep shortly after I finished," he answered.

"Asleep, how could he have fallen asleep? Does he not care about anything?" she quipped.

"I am sure that he cares more than you realize. Remember young darlin', he needs rest and food. I am sure that he listened and will need time to digest everything that he heard. I will bring him here tonight and let you make your own judgment as to how much he cares," Roth countered.

"Do you think that is wise? What if he doesn't like me?" she asked.

"Then it will be his loss if he doesn't like you. You know that you two are going to have to meet eventually. He may be here on the island for a very long time, but I do not intend to give you up just because he cannot accept you as you are. He will just have to get used to it," Roth said flatly.

"You are right of course. I was not thinking. I am tired of hiding and I am *not* going to do it anymore," she stated.

"Now that is what I wanted to hear. Now run along and do whatever it is that you do during the day and let me get done with my chores so that we will have more time for us to visit this evening," he said. They hugged and he kissed her cheek and Kathryn lowered herself back into the water and swam away. Roth watched her leave and wondered to himself what this evening was going to bring. It could prove to be quite interesting.

William woke up late in the afternoon and Roth offered him water and some dried fish, which he took willingly. He was feeling much better and wanted to get a little exercise, so Roth had him help with the gathering of wood for the signal fire. Roth noticed that William was very quiet while they worked and knew that he was thinking about the conversation they had earlier. After they had the beach fire going, Roth said, "Well I think that it is about time for you to meet Kathryn." He looked at William for a second and then turned and started, with William trailing behind, to make his way down the beach to the rock where he hoped that Kathryn waited.

He was disappointed when he saw that Kathryn was not there. "Well, where is this mermaid that you think you see?" William asked in a somewhat haughty tone.

"I am here." William turned to the sound of the voice and was shocked to see the most exquisite creature that he had only imagined that he had seen earlier, floating in the water just a few feet from where he stood. He knew now that it had not been a dream, for there in front of him was the most beautiful young woman that he could ever remember seeing. Then it dawned on him that she had gray skin and from his view, he could see that, under the water, there was an iridescent color where her lower body should be.

"William, allow me introduce you to my daughter, Kathryn," Roth said. William was too bewildered to utter a word. He had never, in his wildest thoughts, believed that he would ever see what he was seeing before him. Here was the reality of all the stories that he had ever heard and again he was not sure if he could really believe what he was witnessing. He turned towards Roth and saw that he was intently looking at him and then again looked back towards the creature that was in front of him. Finally, he spoke, "It is true, everything that you told me is true."

"Yes, as you can see with your own eyes, she is real," Roth replied with great veracity. "Sometimes I fail to understand the naiveté' of youth!" he added.

Still looking at Kathryn and seeing her look back at him with the bluest eyes that he had ever seen, he said, "My name is William Cameron and I would like to say that it is my greatest pleasure to meet you. I would also like, from the bottom of my heart, to thank you for finding me and bringing me to this island, saving my life."

"I am Kathryn Roth and you are very welcome. However, I must tell you that it was not me that found you." Turning and pointing out into the cove where William now noticed a pair of dolphins swimming nearby. "It was they that found you and in turn brought me to you."

"Then I am also very beholding to them," William said as he bowed deeply towards the swimming dolphins.

"Your father has told me much about you and I must admit that I found it very hard to believe and I was beginning to think that he had gone completely mad. But now seeing you, I find that everything he said was vastly understated."

Kathryn, taken aback by what William had just said, was not sure what to say. Finally, she spoke, "You don't find me hideous looking?"

"On the contrary, I think that you are the most beautiful person that I have ever laid my eyes on," he answered.

They talked to each other for quite some time with William asking question after question. Eventually Kathryn joined them on the rock. Roth could see that William was very intrigued by Kathryn and she even allowed him to feel the scales on her. Soon it became apparent that William was getting very tired and was having a hard time staying awake. Kathryn finally suggested that Roth take him back and put him to bed before he fell off the rock and she had to save him again. They said their goodnights and Roth hugged and kissed her. She then slipped off the rock and disappeared in an instant.

While returning to the hammock, where he slept, William said, "I feel as if I woke up in a fairy tale. I must be the luckiest person alive. Not only was I saved from sure death, but I have also met a dream come true."

The next day when Roth emerged from the cave, he first noticed that the hammock was empty and William was nowhere in sight. He looked at the ledge and saw that it held a fish. When his gaze roamed over to the rock where they had talked last night, he saw Kathryn and William together engaged in conversation. Roth decided to leave the young people alone and waded out to get the fish and fix breakfast.

As the fish was nearing the point of being ready to eat, Roth looked up and saw that William was almost back to the fire. He could see that William had a look of deep thought on his face and began to wonder what the two of them had been talking about. As William drew nearer, Roth asked, "Is everything alright?"

"Oh yes! We were just talking about getting me back to health," he replied and went on to say, "Kathryn has asked me to go for a swim later this afternoon and I was just wondering if I will be able to keep up with her. I am not sure if I am in good enough shape to go very far and I would not want to disappoint her with my weakness."

"If I were you, I would not worry about that in the least. Kathryn is a very intelligent girl and she nursed her grandmother for a long time when she became ill. I am sure that she will not let you strain yourself more than you can handle," he stated.

Together they sat in silence and enjoyed their breakfast. When they had finished, they both went together and worked on the chores of the day. After they had finished, William lay down on the hammock and rested for a while.

When William awoke, he saw that Roth and Kathryn were down by the ledge talking and he went down to join them. They both looked in his direction as he made his way to them. He saw that they stopped talking when he got near and somehow knew that they had been talking about him. Kathryn spoke first when he got nearby. "William, father tells me that you are worried about being able to keep up with me in the water." Kathryn looked at William and stated, "Trust me when I say this, even on a good day you would not be able to keep up with me if I choose not to let you," she said with a smile on her face. "There is nothing to worry about, I will not let you do more than you are capable of handling until you regain your full strength or is it that you are faint of heart?" she teased.

"Oh, a challenge," William retorted, while wading further into the water. Taking her hand, he allowed her to lead him further out into the water until he could no longer touch the bottom. Roth sat on the shore and watched them swimming together in the cove. It was so good to see the youngsters frolicking so happily. It was not long, however, before he saw Kathryn leading him back toward the shore. It was apparent that William had tired from his gleeful activity. Roth waded a short distance into the water and helped William to the shore and then to the hammock where he immediately fell asleep.

Kathryn was waiting for him, with another fish, when he returned to the water's edge. "Is he alright?" she asked.

"Do not worry, he is fine. He is still much weaker than he thought and just needs more rest. Next time you take him swimming, remember that he is still very weak and it will take some time before he is completely healthy. I don't think that it will take very long before he fully recovers. He has something to look forward to, something he seems to enjoy more than either of us may have thought he would. Let me take the fish and get it ready for when he wakes up and then we will meet you at the rock," he stated. Seeing a look of concern on Kathryn's face, he continued, "You did *not* do anything wrong. I am sure that he wanted to impress you and just over did it. He will be fine when he awakens." He saw Kathryn sigh and visibly relax with a smile.

Roth had the fish ready and was waiting when William woke up from his nap. "I guess that I am not as ready as I thought I was. I think that Kathryn had to save me again." William stated with a smile.

Roth laughed and said, "Yes, I think that might be true." They sat in silence as they ate the hot fish.

After they had finished and cleaned up after the meal, it soon became apparent to Roth that William was anxious to go back to the rock and meet with Kathryn again.

When they finally made it to the rock, Roth was not surprised to find that Kathryn was already there waiting for them. She was quite anxious to find out for herself that William was, indeed, all right and the little swim that afternoon had done him no harm. They all talked for some time and Kathryn finally started to relax, confidant that William was going to be all right. Eventually the talk turned towards the charm that Kathryn wore. It seemed like William had many questions and wondered if it could really be possible that the charm was responsible for the changes that had come over Kathryn. He even had Roth retell the story about the old sailor that he had gotten it from.

Every day after that, Kathryn took William for a swim and every day William got stronger and soon his health and strength returned. It was not very long after that, that he, with the aid of the dolphins and Kathryn, was able to spend a great deal of the day, out in the water and swim long distances around and away from the island. Roth could see that he was losing his daughter to this young lad. At first, this saddened him, but after a time, he came to realize that it was probably for the best. Now she finally had someone that she could spend her time with besides an old man and the dolphins.

This is how the time passed for the next several weeks. Swimming all day with Kathryn and spend the evenings gathered together on the rocks talking about various things, but the talks always seemed to end up being about the charm.

There soon came a day that William asked Roth if he would mind if he became Kathryn's mate. Roth was stunned, how could they possibly become mates? He reminded William that he was human and Kathryn was anything but. William told him that after much thought, he was willing to ignore that fact if Kathryn was willing also. He knew that William and Kathryn were becoming very fond of one another, but somehow, he knew, Kathryn would end up being hurt and this was not something that he could allow to happen and he told the young man that he would not allow it.

Roth watched as the young man sadly walked to the water where his daughter waited and watched as they slowly swam out of the cove together and into the open water of the ocean.

He was still thinking about their conversation of the morning when William returned and watched him closely as they sat in silence and ate their afternoon meal.

That evening, Roth reluctantly accompanied William to the rock where Kathryn waited. The conversation was general in nature and Roth knew that Kathryn had no idea about the conversation that the two men had had that morning. They talked for a while when suddenly William changed the subject, once again, to the charm. He asked Kathryn if it would be possible for him to hold it and examine it closely. Kathryn was hesitant at first because she had never taken it off her neck since her father had first given it to her. Finally, after a little persuasion from William, she pulled it over her head and handed it to him. William did not hesitate and put it around his neck and then standing, he dove headfirst into the water. Kathryn immediately followed.

As William hit the water, he was disappointed that nothing seemed to have happened. He surfaced and found that Kathryn was right there in front of him. "William, what are you trying to do?" she yelled at him. He did not know what she meant by that because it was obvious to him that he had tried to do and it was just as obvious that it had not worked for he did not feel any different.

"Kathryn, I just wanted to be with you forever and I was hoping that if I had the charm, maybe, just maybe, the same thing would happen to me. Forgive me, but I just had to try, I could think of nothing else," he replied in his defense.

She did not say anything for a few seconds but finally said, "William, you have no idea what you are trying to do. I want to be with you also, but this is not the way. You cannot possibly be sure that this is what you want."

"Of course I am sure, over the past few weeks I have come to know that I am deeply in love with you and I would do anything to have you love me back," he said sadly.

"William, I love you too, but you do not have to do this. We will find another way for us to be together," she said softly. "You are trying to make a choice that you will never be able to change."

"Just my act of leaping into the water with the charm should have shown you that I am serious. Why else do you think that I would have done that?" he answered.

Kathryn looked at him for several minutes before she simply said, "Then somehow, together, we will find a way."

Hearing the reassuring tone from her voice, he smiled. He looked back at Kathryn and saw that she too was smiling. He reached for the charm, pulled it over his head and with both hands, placed it back where it belonged, around her neck. He then took her by the shoulders and pulled her close to him. He did what he had wanted to do for a long time, he kissed her fully and passionately, a kiss, Kathryn returned freely without reluctance.

After a few minutes, they both reluctantly released one another and slowly swam back to the rock where Roth was waiting impatiently for them.

Upon their return, Roth looked at William and said, "When we talked this morning, I had no idea what you had in mind. If I had, I would have told you that it was impossible for you to become like Kathryn. It was a very foolish thing that you did, but it *did* show me that you are serious when it comes to my daughter. This is not the answer but I am sure that if we put some thought into it, we can come up with an answer that will work."

Chapter 14
"Galaunt"

It seemed to Roth that he was spending more and more time alone on the island. William had been spending some of his daylight hours helping him with the daily chores, but Kathryn was spending more and more time with William in the cove. Roth felt guilty over the fact that he was feeling a bit jealous about this. He chuckled to himself when he realized what he was thinking and quickly shrugged it off.

One morning, he found himself sitting on the beach happily watching the two youngsters laughing and playing together in the cove. There were also several dolphins in the cove and they were joining in on the fun. They had found something that resembled a ball that floated and they were tossing it all around. The dolphins would bat it with their snouts and then all of them would go chasing after it with poor William always bringing up the rear. Kathryn did not seem to mind at all, she now had, at least in her own mind, a mate. It was beautiful to see them all leap out of the water together in unison over William and fall splashing down together and then leaping out of the water once again. They never seemed to tire of this game and continued to do it all day long.

This was one of those rare days when Kathryn and William stayed close by and spending their time playing and swimming alone in the cove. Usually they were gone all day, but they would still spend every evening on the rock talking with Roth. William had started to ride on Kathryn's back, holding onto her shoulders, enabling him to go where she went and he seemed very excited about the fact that he could explore and spend much more time with Kathryn. As far as Kathryn was concerned, Roth could see a new glow about her and he was sure in his heart that she was as happy as she had ever been.

The evenings spent on the rock were full of the tales of the new things that William had been learning and experiencing. He was not at all hesitant to tell Roth that he was happier now than he had ever been as a sailor.

Roth spent his days getting back into the routine of doing his chores and now, thanks to Kathryn and William, reading. Only a few days before and not long after William's newfound freedom, Roth awoke one morning to find that they had found a medium sized crate and brought it to him. When he opened it, to his surprise he found that it contained many books of all sorts. There were several books written about people that he was familiar with and of course, there were books on history. It was the history books that he enjoyed the most. One in particular that he enjoyed was one written about the Roman Empire. He was amazed at what they were able to accomplish in such a short period of time and how far and wide the Empire had expanded its authority. Other works that he liked reading were the plays written by a fellow Englishman by the name of Shakespeare. He had always enjoyed going to his plays when he was home and now, he had most of his works in book form. Another book that he liked to read and found himself rereading, was a tale about another seafarer by the name of Ulysses. He did not believe any of the tales attributed to him but it was still good reading.

So, this now became the routine of the days that Roth spent on the island.

It was on one of those lazy days, late in the afternoon with him lying in the hammock when he was, abruptly, brought out of his reverie by the sounds of yelling coming from the cove. He looked in the direction of the sound and saw an obviously excited Kathryn as she, with William riding on her back, quickly swam across the cove. He hurried down to the water to see what had her so excited.

"Father, father," she stammered. "There is a ship out there. It is just beyond the horizon and I think that it is flying a British flag," she excitedly exclaimed.

Roth immediately asked in a calm voice, "What direction is it moving?"

"It is north of here just over the horizon, I do not think that they can see the island from where they are. They are sailing, on a southeasterly heading and are not quite directly north of the island yet. I am afraid that they will not come close enough to see the island. Do you think that they could see a signal and it can attract their attention before they get too far away?" she asked.

"Yes Kathryn, if I can make enough smoke, they just might see it and come to investigate its source." Roth turned and made his way to the signal fire where he began to place the wood he had available there on the ashes and coals and hurried back to the palms that lined the beach and began to gather as many fronds as he could carry and drag along behind him. With this load he ran down to his signal fire and hurriedly placed them on top of the pile of wood he had already built there. He got the fire burning and hurried back to the palms where he gathered another armful. By the time that he returned to the signal fire, it had taken hold and with the wetness of the palm fronds, he saw that they were beginning to smoke heavily. The more fronds that he placed on the fire, the more smoke he was able to generate. Fortunately, there was not a lot of wind, so the smoke was rising nearly straight into the air. Roth was happy to see that it was rising to a height much higher than the peak and he knew that it could be seen from a great distance if anyone was looking in that direction.

Satisfied that he had enough smoke, he returned to the edge of the water. He was not surprise when he saw that Kathryn and William were no longer anywhere in sight. He assumed, correctly as it turned out later, that she had swam back out into the ocean with William to watch where the ship was sailing.

The sun was beginning to set and Roth had seen no sign of the youngsters or the ship on the horizon. He had given up hope of anyone seeing the thick smoke and quit adding fronds to the blaze. He was in the process of adding more wood to the signal fire when he heard Kathryn's excited voice calling him from the rocks.

He hurried over to where she waited and had not quite gotten there when she said happily, "They turned and are heading straight towards the island." William suggested that they swim back out and trail them to make sure that they were, indeed, still heading for the island.

Roth watched as they disappeared into the growing darkness. It was only a few minutes before Kathryn and William returned with the news that the ship must have seen the signal fire and sailed close to the island where it had dropped anchor for the night. Roth figured that the captain of the ship would not want to risk running into any submerged rocks that could possibly be surrounding an island that he was unfamiliar with. So, without a doubt, he would want to wait until morning when he could see clearly before making the approach to the island and investigate the source of the fire that they were now able to see from where they lay at anchor.

The conversation that night naturally centered on the ship and what it was doing here and what this could possibly mean to them. Kathryn interjected it was possible that this ship may be looking for the wreckage of Williams ship on the possibility there might have been survivors or maybe they could even be looking for Roth. He, however, was hesitant to think that this would be the case and assumed that this ship just happened to be in the area and had seen the smoke and simply came to investigate. Kathryn was not sure and she was obviously worried for her father. William tended to agree with him, he could not imagine why anyone would not believe him to be dead and send a ship on a very costly mission to look for him or anyone else aboard that doomed for that matter. Besides that, how would they know where to look? Someone would have to know that Connery had defied a King's order and had not delivered Roth to the prison colony at Botany Bay as so ordered. This act of defiance, alone, would potentially cost Connery his life. They discussed all aspects of why the ship was here but, in the end, they had to admit that they did not know and would just have to wait until morning to see what it was going to do. Kathryn and William made another trip out to sea to make sure that the ship was still where they had last seen it. They returned a short time later to inform Roth that it was still there and they had seen a man looking through a telescope at their fire. Reluctantly, Roth decided that he and William should get to bed early to make sure that they were up before the sun rose. In this way they could greet anyone on the beach if a shore party did arrive as he expected it would.

The next morning, before the sun had risen above the horizon, Roth was out on the beach near the water where Kathryn and William, who had obviously awakened earlier than he, were floating in the water. As the sun rose and began its ascent in the morning sky, he was able to start seeing things clearly, he could see the ship as it lay at anchor off the island. It was still a long way off but there was something familiar about this ship, but Roth could not think of what it was. It was not long after that he saw the ship haul in its anchor, set its top sails for maneuverability, and make its way a little closer to the island where it stopped and dropped its anchor once again. Roth could now make out the lines of the ship and immediately knew why it had seemed familiar to him. It looked just like the *Galaunt,* but Roth knew that it was not possible, when he had last seen her, she had been grounded deeply on a beach in Ireland. This ship had to be the *Noble.* Roth had allowed the *Noble* to safely sail away home and in his heart he knew that this had to be her. He felt a lump rise in his throat as he thought back upon the things he had done that led him to be marooned on this island.

As Roth was contemplating the name of this ship, he saw the crew of the vessel lower a longboat. Watching the crew rowing their way from the ship into the mouth of the cove and finding its way to shore, Roth began to get anxious. Kathryn and William had long since disappeared from sight leaving Roth standing on the beach alone as he watched the longboat ground itself on the beach. Then men jumped into the water and pulled it up on the sand to keep it from floating away.

Roth could not believe his eyes when he thought that he recognized the first man to set foot on his island. He looked like, what Roth perceived to be, a slightly older Edward Berkshire, his old first mate and best friend in life as well as his friend aboard the *Galaunt,* but that could not be, why would he be here? Both men stood staring at each other for some time before the man, with a big smile, finally broke the moment and strode up the beach to where Roth stood.

"Cap'n, you surely are a welcome sight for these sore eyes. We had just about given up any hope of the likelihood of finding you alive," Berkshire said.

"Edward?" Roth asked with great exuberance. "Are my eyes beginning to fail me? Can this possibly be you? How is it that you are here?"

"Nathan, your eyes are not failing you, it really is me," he laughed. "To answer your other question, we are here because we have been lookin' for you," he replied.

"Looking for me? Why on earth would you be looking for me?" Roth asked with amazement.

Berkshire started to laugh when he saw the look of total bewilderment on his friends face. After a moment he was finally able to answer, "When we heard a story that there just might be a possibility that you could still be alive and stranded on some remote island somewhere in this area, we came lookin'."

"But the last time I saw you we were on that beach in Ireland where we beached the *Galaunt*," Roth said and then asked once again. "How is it that you are here now and how did you get your hands on the *Noble*?"

"Well now, that is a long story and will take some time in the tellin'. First, however, I think that you should know that the ship sittin' out there at anchor, is not the *Noble*," he paused for a moment, "though, I can fully understand why you may think so, it is not. It is the *Galaunt*," Berkshire answered with obvious pleasure when he saw the look that came over Roth's face.

Roth's gaze went from Berkshire to the ship anchored out in the ocean. He could see it now and his heart skipped a beat as he came to recognize her. After a few minutes, he said, "When I saw her last, she was beached two-thirds of her length and in the hands of the British, how did you get her here?"

"Well, Cap'n, that, as I just said, is a very long tale to be sure, one that I will be happy to tell in its entirety. First, however, I would like you to get on board so that we can set sail and get you away from this forsaken island."

I have a better idea," Roth said. "Why don't you send your men back to the ship and we will take breakfast here together? There is something that I think I must tell you before I can consider leaving,"

Curious as to why Roth did not want to leave immediately, Berkshire looked at him for a few moments, then turned, and walked back down the beach to where the other men waited. After a brief conversation with them, the men pushed the longboat back into the water and headed back to the ship.

Berkshire stood silently and watched as the longboat safely cleared the rocks before returning to Roth's side where he again stood watching the longboat.

It was Berkshire that finally broke the silence, "Ok Cap'n, what is it that you would like to tell me?"

Roth thought for a second and said, "I think that I would like to hear your tale first, but let's eat while you are telling me how you come to be here." Roth looked over to the ledge and saw that it was empty. "Well now, we may have a problem, it seems that this mornin's breakfast has not been delivered."

Bewildered, Berkshire followed Roth's gaze to the side of the cliff but could not ascertain anything out of the ordinary. Finally, perplexed by what Roth had said, he asked, "Delivered? You have your breakfast delivered?"

"That is part of what I have to tell, but first let's go up to the fire and see what else I have to eat and then we will tell each other our tales," Roth suggested.

They turned and started to walk up the beach when they heard a splashing sound behind them. They turned just in time to see something slip back into the water and vanish from sight. Berkshire was surprised to see where there had been nothing before, was now a fish flopping on a small ledge that he had not noticed. Roth laughed and said, "Ah, breakfast."

Berkshire just stood there saying nothing as he watched Roth wade out into the water and retrieve the fish. When he returned to where they had been standing, Berkshire turned to Roth and stammered, "Where the blazes did that come from? How did that fish get there and what the heck was that thing I saw?"

Roth laughed loudly and after he was able to get himself back under control said, "I am sure she would not like to be called a thing." Roth could see the look of total confusion of his friend's face and continued to chuckle.

"She?" was all the Berkshire could get out.

Roth, still laughing, took his friends arm and led him up the beach to the cooking fire.

"As you have seen, I have quite a tale to tell also. But first, let us get this fish on the fire and then I will listen to how it is that you are here," Roth said lightheartedly.

When they reached the fire, Berkshire could scarcely believe his eyes, he saw a table surrounded by four sturdy chairs and neatly stacked on one end was what looked like china plates and silver flatware. Berkshire sat down on one of the chairs and continued to look around. He saw his friend, Roth had created himself the closest environment possible to make himself comfortable. He could see that Roth also utilized whatever he could find to make several shelves that held all sorts of items that included cast iron pots and pans, there was even a shelf that contained many jars and bottles that looked like they were full of spices and herbs. There was even a large piece of canvas covering the area.

Berkshire sat, in confused silence, at the table and watched Roth as he carefully prepared the fish. After just a few minutes of work, Roth finally got it on a cast iron grill that was placed above a bed of glowing coals.

Roth stepped over to the table and asked Berkshire if he would care for some wine before breakfast. Berkshire, still having trouble believing what he was seeing and hearing, said quizzically, "Wine? Are you going to tell me that you have wine?"

"Of course I have wine, what would life be if one did not have wine. I even think that I might have a little ale left over if you prefer that," Roth answered.

Berkshire, puzzled, said, "Well if I have a choice, make it wine." He watched as Roth picked up a lantern and entered a small opening in the side of the cliff disappearing from view. It was only a short time before he returned and set a large heavy pewter flagon and three ornately designed pewter mugs on the table.

"Would you please do the honors and pour the wine Edward, while I put this salt pork on the fire so that it can warm while the fish is cooking?" Roth asked him with a grin. Roth was enjoying the confused look on Berkshires face and knew that eventually he would start asking questions. It was just a matter of when.

Berkshire, still bewildered, took hold of the flagon of wine and was surprised to find that it was cool to the touch. He poured the wine and slowly took a drink, to his surprise, it was cold and possibly the finest port wine that he had ever tasted. What was goin' on here, he wondered to himself? Cold wine, salt pork and fresh fish, this was, indeed, a tale that he was more than anxious to hear.

Berkshire watched as Roth busied himself around the cook fire and was dumbfounded as he watched him add some herbs and lightly spiced the fish as it cooked, reminding him of a chef he had once watched prepare a meal.

It was not long before the fish was ready and the salt pork warm. Roth brought it to the table on a finely engraved silver serving tray. Setting it down he nonchalantly said, "You had better dig in while it is still hot, it is better hot."

Berkshire, with his mouth agape, took one look at the serving tray and being unable to contain himself anymore, asked, "Cap'n, I cannot take it any longer. You have got to tell me how all of this came about and where did all this stuff come from?"

"I am sorry, old friend, but that will have to wait until this evening. I promise that I will make everything clear to you then. The fish is getting cold, eat up," Roth stated in a way that told Berkshire that he was not going to learn anything more at this time so he did as he was told and preceded to eat.

They finished the meal in silence and then took the eating utensils and plates down to the edge of the water where they proceeded to clean them. After that chore was done and the items were put away, Roth finally said, "Now Edward, if you do not mind, I think I would very much like to hear you tell me your tale."

Edward started his tale by telling Roth how he and the crew had hid out in the woods not far from where the *Galaunt* was beached. "We watched as the crews from the British ships looted and took anything of value from the ship and anything that could be used aboard their vessels before they finally left. We were very glad that they did not lay off the coast and reduce her to kindling. I guess they thought that she was too far up the beach to be refloated. After a while, when we felt it was safe, we came out of hiding and began to inspect the *Galaunt* to see if there was any way that she could be salvaged. She was a very long way up the beach, but to our amazement, we found that there was only a slight amount of damage to her hull. Lucky for us that you found the only sandy beach for miles to run her aground. It was then that we decided that if we could get her back into the water, she could be repaired.

"We spent the next couple of weeks digging long deep trenches on both sides of her and as far under the hull as we dared. When we let the water into the trenches, we were astonished to see that she floated freely in the water. We then pulled her, with the aid of the longboat, back out into deeper water. We made what repairs, to her hull that we could while we were digging the trenches and were very happy when we saw that the *Galaunt* remained afloat and seemed not to be taking on much water. We then sailed her, as best we could with all the damage to her masts, to a remote Scottish port with repair facilities that I had heard about many years before. Villagers, that were not at all fond of the British, operated it. There we were able to make all necessary repairs to make the *Galaunt* seaworthy once again.

"It was while we were in the Scottish port that we had received word that you had been put on trial, found guilty of all charges and sentenced by the King, himself, to be put to death. We had many talks about the possibility of making a rescue of you, but these talks came to naught. Shortly after hearing the first report, we received word that the king had commuted your sentence to life imprisonment. We heard that the reason for this change was that the King had since learned that we had not been responsible for his family's death, but actually had saved their lives from the hands of the Spanish. We also learned that the King, in his gratitude, had granted all members of our crew pardons for our part in the rescue and safe return of the Heir Apparent Charles, Elizabeth and her son.

"After nearly a year of intense work, including that time spent refloating her, the ship was finally ready to set sail. The remainder of the original crew and me, acting as captain, decided that it was time for us to return home and find out for ourselves if what we had heard was true. When we arrived home, we found out that everything was true, we had indeed been pardoned. We also found out that because of the magnitude of your crimes against others, you were sent to the prison colony at Botany Bay to serve out a life sentence. In addition, we learned, with no great sadness, on my part, to be sure, Creed had lost all his remaining assets due to poor investments and could not repay any of his loans and debts and had been sentenced to debtor's prison.

The irony of the story was that he had been shipped off to the prison in Botany Bay where, as far as anyone knows, he still is. Therefore, it came to be that seeing as the *Galaunt* had no rightful owner, she became ours by right of salvage.

Having long since finished off the wine, Berkshire paused for a moment and asked, "Did I hear you correctly earlier say that you might have some ale left over. This is a long story and I am beginnin' to work up a mighty thirst?"

"Indeed, you did my friend. Let me go and rinse out this flagon and I will see what I can round up." Roth grabbed the flagon from the table and picked up the lantern from its place of rest and once again disappeared into the side of the cliff. It was only a few minutes until he returned. He took Berkshires mug and poured some ale until foam began to run over the side. He then poured himself a mug full.

Berkshire took a small tentative sip from the foamy mug and to his complete surprise, it was neither flat nor stale and found it rather refreshing to the taste. "This is very good. You have a lot to explain, my good man," Berkshire said as he stared at his mug. He then added, "An *awful* lot to explain."

Roth laughed and said, "All in good time my friend. Be patient and soon I will make everything clear. Now, if you do not mind I would like to hear the rest of your story."

Berkshire took another drink of the delicious ale, and then continued. "With all the principles in the case now accounted for, I decided to try and petition for an audience with the King on your behalf. After several unsuccessful attempts, I decided to try and petition for an audience with someone more familiar with the happenin's at sea, the Kings sister, Elizabeth, and plead your case to her. We finally got an audience and I was able to tell her the story as to why you took the actions that you did and was able to convince Elizabeth to see the king on your behalf. She must have given a very persuasive argument for she was able to obtain a full pardon for all crimes against you. The real surprise came when Elizabeth sent a messenger to summons me and announced that she would finance the mission to retrieve you from imprisonment in Australia with only one stipulation. The stipulation, as it turned out, was a mere favor to the crown. It was that I would accept a cargo of supplies bound for Botany Bay and transport the cargo at no charge for shipment. This I accepted readily because I would do anything necessary to gain your release from that forsaken prison.

"So, after only a few weeks in port, the *Galaunt* was loaded and finally ready for the trip south. We made good time on the voyage and soon arrived at our destination. Upon arrival, we were told that you had not been delivered to prison and that you had died in route and was buried at sea. I found this hard to believe so I inquired further to find out the name of the ship and her captain. When I learned that it was Connery, I became very suspicious and investigated further. It was then that I learned that shortly after departure from Australia, the Hampshire was lost at sea with only a few survivors, Connery, fortunately, was not among them. I could learn no more other than the survivors who had been taken to England. I was able to get a load of cargo on consignment and we sailed for home. On our return to England, I was able to find one of the survivors and he told me the true story of your torture at the hands of Connery. He could not tell us exactly where you had been marooned, or even if you were alive because he told us that Connery had thrown you overboard in heavy shackles. With our profits, we procured another load of cargo bound for Australia and within the month we were again bound for Botany Bay.

"We tried to sail, as best we could without any maps, the same route as the Hampshire would have sailed, but were unable to find any islands that resembled the one that we were lookin' for. This is our fifth trip south and more than likely the last we would make because we were losin' faith in what the survivor had told us. We were even beginnin' to lose hope that we would ever find you alive and if it had not been for the smoke we saw, we would have sailed right past this island not even knowin' it was here," Berkshire said. After a pause, he went on to ask, "How did you know to set that fire just as we were passing by?"

Roth thought for a moment before replying, "I was told that you were there."

"You were told that we were there? Who could have told you?" he asked. "We were well beyond the horizon, we could not see the island, and how did you see us?" Berkshire queried.

"That will all be explained this evening. Now I think it might be a good idea to signal your men and let them know that you will be spending the night on the island with me," Roth answered.

"You are bein' very mysterious and I am very curious as to what is goin' on here, so I will do as you say." Berkshire stood and walked down to the edge of the water, took his pistol from his belt and fired a single shot into the air. It was not long before part of the crew reached the island in the longboat. Berkshire met them on the beach and after a short conversation, they pushed the boat back into the water and started their short trip back to the *Galaunt*. Berkshire strode back up the beach to where Roth had remained seated at the table and said, "Alright old friend, it seems as to where I am your captive audience for now. I am anxiously waiting to hear the story of what has transpired here since your exile on this forsaken island."

The sun was still well up in the afternoon sky and it would still be a few hours before it sank below the horizon. "It will not be much longer, but for now you will still have to be patient. In the meantime, I will attempt to enlighten you to some of the story of how it came to be that I ended up here." Roth went on to tell Berkshire about the voyage with Connery that was supposed to end at Botany Bay. As he spoke of the decision that Connery had come to by throwing him overboard in shackles, he noticed the sun was beginning to set. Roth looked at Berkshire and said, "She will be here soon. Help me get the fire going and then it will be time for you to meet her and hear the rest of the story." He was also anxious to see Berkshire's reaction when he learned of the whole story.

"There you go with the she again. Who is this person that you keep talkin' about?" Berkshire inquired.

Roth did not say anything for some time and then said, "Come and I will show you."

Together they walked along the beach to the rock where Roth and Kathryn had spent so many hours together talking. As they climbed the rock Roth spoke first. "Here is where I think all your questions will be answered."

"Kathryn," Roth called loudly out across the water, "come here and show yourself, there is someone that I think would very much like to meet you."

Almost immediately as if she had been waiting for them to appear, Kathryn answered, "Hello Mister Berkshire. It is good to see you again. It has been a long time."

Startled by the sound of a female voice, Edward turned in every direction before he realized that the voice had come from the water. Looking down, he could see a young girl and a young lad floating in the water of the cove and not very far from the rock where he stood, but still far enough that Berkshire could not make out any details of them as they floated before him.

Seeing the look of total astonishment on Edward's face, Roth went on to add, "Also, I would like to introduce you to William Cameron. William is a young man that Kathryn found adrift from a shipwreck, barely alive, and brought him here in the hopes that I could nurse him back to health."

Berkshire, overwhelmed, just stood there staring down at the couple floating in the water. His gaze went back and forth from the young lad to the young girl several times before it finally settled on the young girl. He thought to himself that this young girl certainly looked like she resembled Kathryn, but how could this be he knew that she had been lost at sea several years ago. He continued to look at her for several more minutes before he finally found his voice again and asked, "Is that really you Kathryn?"

"Yes, Mister Berkshire, it is really me," she said as she swam closer to the rock. "However, as you can now undoubtedly see, I have changed somewhat from the last time you saw me aboard ship," she said with a playful giggle.

As she drew closer, Berkshire now could plainly see that it was indeed Kathryn. She had her long red hair and he could not mistake that smile, but even with only the light of the signal fire, he could see that she had light gray skin. Baffled, he turned to Roth and mystified he asked, "How did this happen? She was washed overboard that night with Brian during the storm off the cape. I was there the next mornin' when we found Brian alone on that hatch cover. I also remember the days we spent lookin' for her."

"Do you also remember the story that Brian told us about the sea monster that we passed off as him just being delirious?" Roth asked.

Berkshire recalled the memory, turning to Kathryn, said, "Was that you that Brian saw that night?"

With a look of sadness coming over her face, Kathryn replied, "Yes, it was."

"Before we go any further, jump up here and join us and let Edward get a good look at you," Roth said.

Roth moved over and gave Kathryn enough room for her to sit between him and Edward. William climbed up the rocks and took a seat on the other side of Edward, poised as if he would act quickly if the stranger made any move to harm his beloved Kathryn.

Kathryn saw this posture and said, "Relax William, there is nothing to worry about. Mister Berkshire and I are good friends and he would never do anything to harm me or you and if you give him a chance, he will be your friend too." She was very happy when she saw William relax.

Berkshire could not take his eyes off Kathryn, especially her tail. It was so long and sleek and the iridescent colors were constantly changing in the fire light. He could tell that it must be very powerful and could probably propel her through the water very fast. He also noticed that her face was no longer that of a young girl, but of a very beautiful mature young woman.

"I can honestly say that the wait you put me through today was well worth it. But now I think that it is time for you to tell me how this all came about," Berkshire said.

Roth went on to relate the story of the old fisherman that he had come upon and the charm that he had bought as a present for Kathryn. All the while that Roth was telling the tale, he could see a look of awe come over Berkshire's face as he was beginning to understand what had taken place.

After hearing all Roth had to say, Berkshire said more to himself than anybody else, "So it seems that it was true, we were not seein' things after all."

Roth asked, "What was true? Of what do you speak, what did you see?"

Berkshire paused for a bit of time before replying, "There were instances after Kathryn was lost, that some of the crew and I thought we saw somethin' in the water that we could not explain. Some thought it had to be a mermaid, but most others thought that was impossible and it had to be some sort of fish that we had never encountered before. We did not mention it to you however, because we did not want you to think that we were going crazy."

"I, myself, saw unusual things in the water on several occasions, but I always wrote them off as being a strange fish or perhaps a small whale," Roth stated. "I guess we may have all thought we were at sea too long," He joked.

The conversation continued along these lines well into the night with Berkshire asking question after question and Roth, Kathryn and William, answering as best they could. It was early in the morning when Berkshire finally ran out of questions and seemed satisfied that he understood the whole story.

"I must admit to you, my friend, that if I had heard this story and had not witnessed you and Kathryn being here, I would never have thought it to be possible. I cannot comprehend this happening to anyone. Trust me when I say it will not happen to you again. I shall see to it that you are returned to your rightful status and once again in command of your own ship," Berkshire said in an almost commanding voice. "I will be at your service, Cap'n, just like the days of old."

Roth gazed at Edward as he listened in wonder of what his friend felt and how strongly he had reacted, but was puzzled as to how he would accomplish this feat. He replied to Edward in a very sincere tone, "My friend let us sleep now and we will discuss your plans at length when we awaken with a fresh rest. I admire your willingness to help me return, but at this point, it has become increasingly painful for me to have relived this entire saga and I can see that it has vexed your emotions as well." At this point Kathryn and William were just watching and listening to two old friends getting caught up. Kathryn was so grateful that her father had such a devout friend. "You go rest and I shall return tomorrow morning," She interjected in their conversation. Roth and Berkshire gestured in acknowledgement and proceeded off, followed by William, to go get some sleep. As they walked away, they heard a splash of water. Roth thought, yes, this has been a good night and knew that he would sleep well.

It was mid-morning when Roth awakened feeling fully refreshed and finally emerged from his cave. The first thing that he saw was Berkshire and William bending over the cooking fire where he saw a fish laid out across the grill. He walked over to Edward and said, "I see that you have found our breakfast."

"Yes," he replied with a gleam in his eye, "it was delivered about an hour ago. Now I see why you look so fit. Kathryn has been takin' very good care of you."

"She, it seems, has never been very far away from me. I owe my very life to her."

"Changin' the subject," Berkshire said and went on to ask, "Did you give our little conversation about your command any additional thought last night?"

Roth pondered his reply for a few moments and finally said, "Yes, I did. I did not, however, reach any conclusions. I think that I would like to at least accompany you to Australia and take a little more time before I make any final decisions. I would also like to see how the rest of the crew feels about your offer."

Edward did not hesitate in saying, "You need not concern yourself with that. During our quest of searching for you, the crew and I have discussed on more than one occasion, the possibility that if we were to find you alive, we would like you to be the Captain of the *Galaunt* just as it was in the past."

"I am very grateful to hear that. I need to talk this over with Kathryn before I can make any decisions. I am not sure if I will be able to leave her," Roth said.

"Well then, let's eat this fish before it gets any colder and then we will go and see what she has to say about this whole matter," Berkshire stated.

The three of them carried on a light conversation while they enjoyed their breakfast, talking mostly about adventures they had shared during their earlier voyages, mainly revolving around the America's. Roth made the comment on how much he had enjoyed his time while in the new colonies and how beautiful the country had been. He even made the statement that when the time came to give up the sea, America might be the place he would wish to settle.

After they finished eating and got everything cleaned up, they made their way across the beach to the rock to see if they could rouse Kathryn. When they had climbed to the top of the rock, Roth called out Kathryn's name several times, they only had to wait a few minutes before she appeared.

"Kathryn, there is something that I need to discuss with you," Roth said. "Edward has offered me command of the *Galaunt* and I am thinking about taking him up on his offer, but I need to know how you feel about it before I make a decision."

She did not hesitate with her answer and said, "Father, that is wonderful. You have never been happy doing anything other than sailing from place to place. This is your chance to get off this island and back to what you love."

"Yes, that is one side of it, but I am not getting any younger and also I am not sure that I am willing to give you up now that I have you back," he said.

"Oh father, you are being silly," she laughed, "you will not be giving me up. As long as you are on the water or even near it, I will be close bye. I have never left you since my change. What makes you think that I will leave you now?"

"Well, I just worry about you. Will you be all right if we leave this place?" he asked.

Kathryn laughed at that with a smile and said, "Of course I will be all right. If you remember correctly, I have followed you more than halfway around the world and have not even come close to harm and I am not alone now, William is here, so I have a constant companion to share my experiences with. Father, you need to be with people, doing what you love to do and that is sailing."

Roth listened to his daughter very thoughtfully and when she had finished, hesitated only moments before replying, "All right then if you think that it is for the best then it is settled, I will take Edward up on his offer." Turning to his friend, he said, "It looks as though you have recruited yourself a captain."

Proudly Berkshire said, "Aye, aye Cap'n. Let me contact the crew, and then we will make preparations to set sail and continue our voyage to Australia on the mornin' tide." Berkshire climbed down from the rock, walked across the beach and again fired off a single shot signaling the crew to come ashore again.

Roth returned his attention to Kathryn. "Well young darlin', it seems that this will be our last day on this island. In a way, I think that I am going to miss it."

Kathryn replied, "Yes, I think that I will miss it too father, but there are going to be so many new adventures out there and I am looking forward to experiencing them. We have had some very special times here, they will be memories I will cherish forever. We had never had the good fortune to engage ourselves as we have here. I was very young and your work kept you away." She paused wistfully, before she continued. "But for now, I think I had better hide before the crew arrives. I will meet you here again this evening." Kathryn turned and disappeared with just a mere ripple, beneath the surface of the water.

Roth and William climbed down from the rock and strode across the beach to joined Berkshire watching as the crew rowed the longboat to where they stood.

When they arrived, Berkshire met them and informed them of Roth's decision. Roth could see a look of satisfaction appear on their faces and knew that the decision was accepted. Berkshire then sent them back to the ship to retrieve some packing crates for the few valuables Roth had on the island.

After their return, Roth, Berkshire, William and the crew spent the remainder of the day packing and moving things to store aboard the *Galaunt*. With this task completed, Berkshire told the crew that he and the captain would be spending one last night on the island and for them to come back at dawn to pick them up.

Roth, William and Berkshire stood on the beach and watched as the crew rowed the longboat back to the *Galaunt*. Then they went about the business of building up the signal fire. With the fire burning brightly, they made their way to the rock where they found Kathryn waiting.

There was not that much conversation that night. It was a sad time and everything that had to be said was either said last night or during their conversation this morning. Roth did, however, hold his daughter tightly throughout the night. Roth was very reluctant to release her because he did not know when he would get another chance to do so, but eventually he had to because the hour had become very late and they all had a busy day ahead of them tomorrow.

Chapter 15
"Australia"

Roth rose early the next morning and once again he found Berkshire and William hard at work cooking over the fire. "Ah Cap'n, it is good to see that you have finally decided to wake up and join the living. I am hopin' that you awoke with an appetite. Kathryn brought this fish a while ago and it is almost ready," Berkshire said.

Roth was indeed hungry and was glad to see that his friends had food ready. "I do indeed have an empty stomach and that fish might just be what it will take to fill it."

"I am sorry to say that we packed all the eatin' utensils yesterday, so we are goin' to have to just pick the meat off the bone," Berkshire said apologetically.

Roth laughed and said, "That will be more than fine with me, it will not the first time that I have had to do just that since I have been marooned on this island."

Berkshire smiled knowingly at that. They did not talk much after that and just went about enjoying the meal. Roth did, however, comment on the fact that Berkshire was a good cook and said that he wished that he would have been on the island with him to do the cooking because he did not really enjoy cooking.

Berkshire laughed at that and jokingly said, "Tween, you, me and that palm over there, I am glad that I was not here with you. I am thinkin' I am not cut out for life marooned on a desert island with a cantankerous old man like you."

The sun was still below the horizon but it was starting to get light. By the time it was light enough to see the *Galaunt,* they saw that the longboat had already been launched and was steadily making its way to the island. Roth, William and Berkshire were all standing at the water's edge when the boat finally made landfall. Roth was moved when he saw the occupants stand and give him a crisp salute. Roth, with a tear in his eye, crisply returned that salute and then waded out to the boat. As he neared the boat and was ready to climb aboard, he saw a hand reach out to help him. He looked up and saw Smitty, his helmsman, was the owner of that hand. Smitty said, "Welcome Cap'n sir, it is good to have you back." It was a simple welcome, but Roth had to fight very hard not to let the emotions that he felt at that moment rise to the surface and he quietly replied, "Thank you Smitty, it is very good to be back."

It turned out that all the men in the longboat were men that he had known and sailed with for many, many years. Men that had been with him all during his campaign against Creed and men that he knew he could trust with his life.

As they approached the ship, Roth was surprised that he could not see anyone aboard. This was unusual because he would have thought that at least someone would be watching for their arrival. The longboat reached the side of the *Galaunt* near a rope ladder that had been left hanging over the side. Roth was the first to climb the ladder and when he reached the top and peered over the rail, he was surprised to see the entire crew that had been left aboard, lined up in two rows. He climbed over the rail and as he set foot on the deck, another sailor, whom he also recognized, shouted, "Cap'n on board." All the members of the crew that formed the two lines immediately snapped to attention and brought their right hands up in a crisp salute. Roth was now overwhelmed with emotion and could not stop the tears that formed in his eyes. He stood there as if riveted to the deck for a few moments before he was finally able to get his emotions back in check. Berkshire and William by this time had also climbed aboard and stood at attention next to their Captain.

"At ease men," Roth finally said and then he proceeded down the row. He greeted and shook the hand of every man there. Berkshire then asked the new men to step forward and introduced them as those that had signed on since his capture. Roth acknowledged and thanked them for joining the crew and the welcome he had just received.

After the brief ceremony was concluded and the longboat was brought back aboard and safely secured, Roth, William and Berkshire strode across the deck and climbed the stairway to the wheel deck. Roth leaned against the forward rail with both hands admiring the ship for a few moments before he turned and looked at Berkshire. "Well, I guess it is time to weigh anchor and get underway for Australia. Make it so First Mate."

Roth turned back and set his gaze on the men as Berkshire gave the orders. He watched as the men turned the heavy turnstile that brought the anchor up from the bottom and other men as they clamored up into the rigging to drop the sails. Before long the great ship began to move as the sails caught the morning winds. Roth gave one last nostalgic look back out across the water to the island that had been his home for so long and in silence said a last good-bye knowing, happily, he would never see it again. He also looked for Kathryn. He did not see her but in his heart, he knew she was close by.

The remainder of the trip south turned out to be very uneventful. They had not encountered any storms and with these waters being controlled by the British, they had not seen any enemy ships. By the time they reached the waters around Australia, Roth had begun to settle back into his role of captain, but during the entire trip, he had not been able to shake the feeling that something was just not the same. It was not a feeling of foreboding that much, he was sure of. He had not seen Kathryn during the voyage and this did not help, he also knew that was not the cause either. Something was just not the same and no matter how much thought he put into the subject, he just could not put his finger on it. Oh well, he thought to himself, it must just be the fact that he was back at sea from his long absence. He hoped that eventually this feeling would leave and he would return to normal.

Roth was on the wheel deck with Berkshire as the *Galaunt* rounded the point and started to make its way into Botany Bay. Roth had never been to Australia, as Berkshire had, so he decided not to say anything and let Berkshire give any necessary orders. He listened as Berkshire shouted to take in the sail and slowly brought the *Galaunt* alongside the long empty wharf. Here they would dock the ship for the long tiring process of unloading their cargo. Roth glanced over the port that they sailed into. It was nothing compared to what he had thought it would be. It had a wharf and long warehouses just like all the ports he had ever sailed into, he could even see smaller buildings behind them that he assumed were businesses. He looked all around the bay and nowhere could he see anything that even remotely resembled a prison. He figured that it must be built further inland. Another thing that he noticed was that the large houses near the port and those built on the small hills overlooking the port, were surrounded with high crenellated walls, but the structures were to nicely built to be a prison. He turned to Berkshire and asked, "Where is the prison?"

"You are lookin' at it," Berkshire said as he waved his arm from one end of the bay to the other. "The walls you see are not meant to keep prisoners in but rather to keep them out. This whole island is a prison. The places that have walls around them are the housing areas for the troops that serve as guards and the administration personnel that run the prison."

"Are you saying that the prisoners sentenced to be here are not locked up?" Roth asked.

"Oh, there are some cells where those that have committed more heinous crimes are locked up, but the majority of criminals here have only committed petty crimes and are not a threat to anyone. There are prisoners here from all lifestyles and once they are brought here, they are free to live out their lives as they see fit. Those that had skills, learned in England, are free to practice those skills here, in fact most of them have. All the businesses that you will find here are prisoner operated. Actually, Botany Bay is little more than a jumping off place for most prisoners. There are settlements all up and down the coast that comprises the majority of the population of Australia and prisoners started the majority of those. They even have a few farms or stations as they are called here, some of them very large, further inland." Berkshire explained.

"What is it to prevent the prisoners from carrying on with their criminal ways?" Roth inquired.

Berkshire answered, "Crime is not tolerated here, not at all. All crimes are considered a capital offense punishable by death, even petty theft could result in bein' hung and all executions are public and everyone is required to attend, that makes for a great deterrent to crime. Everyone here is required to work, there are no free hand outs. Everyone here makes a wage, it is not very much, but it is enough for them to survive on. The government owns everything, all the stores, shops and even the farms. The pay scale is unique, if you run a farm then you earn slightly more than the man that works its fields. All the profits that come from any of the businesses are taken and put into a fund by the government and used to pay for anything that cannot be grown or manufactured here on the island and needs to be shipped in. That is where we come in. Makes for a good system in my opinion, no one is that much better than anyone else."

Roth was quite impressed with the arrangement and thought it would be a good system anywhere. He then asked, "What prevents them from trying to escape?"

Berkshire laughed and replied, "Escape to where? This is an island and the nearest land is hundreds of miles away across shark infested water. Ocean going vessels are only allowed to dock here at this harbor and the British have Warships that regularly patrol up and down the coastline. Inland is full of all sorts of hazards like snakes and crocodiles that make it almost impossible to survive for long very far from civilization. You will even find that if you want to leave the ship after we dock, you will be issued papers stating who you are and without them you will not be allowed back aboard ship. Also there had better be someone on board that recognizes you in the case that someone might try and steal your papers and make an attempt to sneak aboard."

Roth pondered this for a while as he watched his crew prepare for docking. As the ship was nearing its mooring point, Roth began to notice the people that were on the wharf. They were dressed for the most part in what he would call peasant clothes, ragged shirts and pants with sandals on their feet. Here and there, he also saw armed soldiers, about twenty to twenty-five, who were on constant watch. The peasant types secured the ship to the long wharf. After the ship was securely tied to the wharf, the deck crew of the *Galaunt* lowered the gangplank over the side. No sooner than it had been secured into place, Roth saw two very well dressed gentlemen, one large and portly and the other short and thin that he had not noticed before, start walking up the gangplank. He wondered where they had appeared from. Mister Berkshire met them at the top of the gangplank. After a short conversation, Berkshire beckoned Roth to join them. Roth made his way down from the wheel deck and strode over to where the three men were standing.

When Roth reached the three men, Berkshire spoke first, "Cap'n, let me introduce to you Mister Ethan Paxmire, he is the warden and chief administrator of the prison and Mister Carey Nailer, his assistant and day to day administer."

Roth bowed politely and shook both of their hands before saying, "I am Captain Roth, the commander of the *Galaunt* and it is my pleasure to meet you both. Welcome aboard our ship."

Mister Nailer scratched his head for a moment before finally saying, "Roth you say? That name sounds familiar. You are not by any chance the notorious Captain Roth?"

"I am not so sure about the notorious part, but yes, I suppose that I am that Roth?" he answered guardedly.

"I thought that name sounded familiar. You were supposed to be delivered to our fair community many years ago for a life sentence if my memory serves me correctly and it usually does. We were told that you had died and were buried at sea. Now it seems that you are here and can now start your sentence," the little man said.

He turned and called for the guards that had stationed themselves at the bottom of the gangplank to come and take Roth into custody when Berkshire spoke. "Hold on there a moment little fella, you cannot arrest this man."

"And why, pray tell, can I not have him arrested? He has been duly tried in a court of law and sentenced to spend the rest of his miserable life here on this island?" Nailer said very belligerently as he puffed out his chest.

The four guards had raced up the gangplank and were now in positioned around Roth with their guns leveled on him. No sooner had they assumed their position when they suddenly found themselves surrounded by twenty or more members of the ship's crew bearing all sorts of weapons acting more than ready to use them, if commanded, on the four soldiers. From somewhere below on the dock, they heard the blowing of a bugle and suddenly soldiers, dressed in the red of the British military, began pouring onto the wharf. It was only moments before the crew to the *Galaunt* found themselves hugely outnumbered.

Paxmire threw up his hands and turning to the soldiers on the wharf, said, "Stand down, there will be no acts of violence here today." With that said, all the soldiers lowered their weapons but it was obvious that they would still bring them into use if the need arose. "As you can see," he swept his arm around, "you are vastly outnumbered. I would suggest that you surrender this man to us before you find all of yourselves suffering his same fate."

Berkshire looked at his men and told them to also lower their weapons and when they did, he said, "This man has a King's pardon clearing him of all charges and commuting his sentence."

"Bah, why would the King pardon him for all the crimes that he has committed? I demand to see this so called pardon immediately," Nailer said.

Berkshire turned and walked across the deck and disappeared into the cabin area. A few moments later he reappeared carrying a rolled scroll tied with a red ribbon. Nailer made a grab for the document, but Berkshire shot him a glance that would have killed the dead and Nailer winced and backed away. Berkshire then handed the scroll to Paxmire who nodded a thank you. He then untied the document and unrolled it and read the contents paying particular interest in the seal that was at the bottom. After a few minutes, he rolled the document back up and retied the ribbon around it and handed it to Roth. "It seems that you are right. Though it is beyond me as to why the King would pardon such a man as you but pardon you, he has. You have to forgive my assistant. He takes his job very seriously and sometimes he can be very overzealous in carrying out his duties." He then turned to Roth and with a deep bow, said, "You have my deepest apologies and hope that you will forgive us for this misunderstanding and enjoy all the hospitalities that we can offer you during your stay with us." He offered Roth his hand, which, without as much as a hesitation, was accepted. "Now Mister Nailer, release these troops immediately and let these men get back to their duties, they have much needed cargo that must be unloaded." Turning back to Roth he said, "It would be my great honor if I could have the pleasure of you and your officers joining me for dinner at my quarters this evening."

Roth, still a little dazed, replied, "Thank you very much. It would be an honor to dine with you and your family."

Paxmire, followed by a humbled Mister Nailer, turned and made their way down the gangplank and across the wharf where they disappeared from sight behind one of the warehouses.

Roth turned to Berkshire and saw that he was already looking at him and at the same time both men began to laugh. "Well now, that was not quite the greeting that I was expecting.

"Nor I," answered Berkshire. "Now if you will excuse me, I will see to the unloadin' of our cargo." Berkshire turned and began issuing orders to the men that were still standing nearby.

"Mister Berkshire, I think that I am going to take a stroll around this fair village and see where I was once destined to spend the rest of my life. You have command. I should not be very long because it does not look like there is that much to see."

"Aye, aye Cap'n, but is careful, there are dangerous types out there," Berkshire laughed.

Roth retorted with, "I will be on my guard every minute." As Roth climbed down the gangplank, he was met by a uniformed guard that informed him that he would not be allowed to carry any firearms off the ship onto the island and that he would have to leave his pistol with him. Roth understood why this was and without hesitation handed his belt pistol to the guard. He was about to remove his sword and knife when the guard told him that he could keep those for his own protection. The guard then handed him a slip of paper, which upon close inspection, identified him as a visitor to the island. Roth chuckled and walked away across the wharf in the same direction as Paxmire and Nailer had taken.

As he rounded the corner of the warehouse, he was surprised to see a long cobbled road before him. There were several people walking along the street and because of the way they were dressed, he assumed that they were prisoners. There were even a few horses tied to posts here and there. As he started his walk down the street, the first building that he came upon was a single story structure with a sign in front of it that read Administration. Roth thought to himself that this must be where Paxmire and Nailer worked.

It was a short distance before he came upon another building that he thought must be a general store because there were items stacked and lined across the front. Roth decided to enter and look around. A stout old man greeted him at the door and inquired if there was anything that he could help him with. Roth thanked him but declined, stating that he was just looking. The first thing that he noticed was that everything he could see looked as if it had been imported from the finest shops that

England had to offer. He asked the old man about this and was surprised when he told him that everything that he saw was manufactured right here on the island. Roth thought that there were, indeed, many fine and skilled craftsmen held on this island.

The next building that he entered was a cobbler's shop. The first thing that caught Roth's eye was the many rows of shoes and boots that lined one entire wall of the shop. He looked down at his old worn boots and decided that maybe it was time to treat himself to a new pair, for it had been many years since he had had anything but this old pair of boots on his feet. As he was looking for a pair that he liked, a short plump elderly lady suddenly appeared at his side and said, "You will not find what you are looking for out here."

Shocked by the sudden appearance, Roth turned to the woman and politely asked, "How do you know what I am looking for and for that matter, if I am looking for anything at all?"

She let her gaze fall to his feet and with twinkle in her eyes said, "That is quite obvious is it not."

Roth laughed and said, "They are in pretty bad shape and you are right, I am thinking of maybe purchasing a new pair if the right ones can be found. You said that I will not find what I am looking for out here. Where do you suggest I look?"

"The shoes and boots that are on display out here are for the people that live around here and are not of the quality that a gentleman like yourself would want to own. My husband is the cobbler here, it just so happens that he is just finished a pair of boots ordered by one of the officers of the guard, and I would be willing to bet that they are just your size. Let me go check with him and I will be right back. Feel free to look around at our other wares and see if there might be something else that you like." She glanced at his belt and said, "It looks as if you could also use a new belt."

Roth walked to the other side of the shop where he saw belts of all types hanging on hooks and pegs fastened to the wall. One in particular caught his eye. It was hanging, by itself, from a peg in the wall at the end of the long line of other belts. As he got nearer, he could see that it was finely tooled along the entire length. On closer inspection he realized that someone had put a lot of time in the tooling. It was the finest belt that he had ever seen. It was adorned with a large square shiny brass buckle that only enhanced the beauty and quality of the belt.

"Now that is a fine choice you have made there sir. I spent many hours on that belt and consider it my best work."

Startled once again by the woman, Roth turned and saw that this time she was not alone. Standing by her side was a very tall man with thinning hair and spectacles. He had a broad smile on his face and he was holding a pair of knee length boots in one hand.

There was something familiar about this man but Roth could not place him. Still looking at him, Roth politely said to the woman, "You are a fine craftsman or craftswoman if you prefer. This is a wonderful belt and if it is for sale, I would be proud to call it my own."

The woman smiled broadly and said, "Then maybe you might also be interested in these." She went behind the counter and withdrew from a shelf, a sheathed dagger. She pulled the dagger from its sheath and handed it to Roth. It had a finely carved bone handle with an engraved hilt. The blade, itself, was also engraved with sailing scenes. When he took the sheath from her hand, he saw that it was a perfect match to the belt. She reached under the counter once again and produced a small leather pouch that was also tooled to match the belt. Looking at all the pieces together, Roth was astounded and said, "Madam you are beyond any doubt, a great artist."

Looking once again at the man, he said, "Let me take a look at those boots and see how well they fit." The cobbler handed him the boots and Roth saw that they were well made with thick substantial leather yet very supple to the touch. Finding a chair, Roth sat down and pulled off one of his old worn boots and replaced it with the new one. To his amazement, it fit perfectly. He pulled off his other boot and inserted his foot into the new boot and stood up and walked around a bit before he said, "These fit like a glove and will need no breaking in. I will take everything that you have shown me, what is the cost?"

The cobbler looked at his wife and Roth saw her nod slightly before he spoke, "There is no charge for these items, Captain Roth. We present them to you with our heartfelt gratitude for partial payment of a debt to you that we will never be able to repay."

Startled and very surprised that this man knew his name. Roth asked, "How is it that you know my name? Have we ever met and what is this debt that you speak of?"

The cobbler answer, "It is little wonder that you do not recognize me, but on the day that you saved the King's son, sister and her son from sure death at the hands of the Spaniards, there were two others on that small boat dressed as Royal Marines. I was one of those men and you saved me. So, as you see, I owe you, my life."

Roth remembered that day but still did not recognize the man before him. Roth asked, "How did you end up here?"

The cobbler replied, "I am not a prisoner here, my wife, Ruth, is the prisoner. When I finally made it back to London, I was told that she had been caught stealing a loaf of bread and sentenced to spend her time here on this island. I sold everything that I could and booked passage here so that I could be with her. Her sentence is almost up and if we can raise enough money for fare, we will be allowed to leave and return to our home in England."

Roth reached into his pocket and withdrew five large gold coins and as he started to hand them to the cobbler he said, "You *will* take these and I will suffer no arguments over it. Put them away and when the time comes and Ruth is released you will have money to get you home and even some left over for a new start."

Roth could see the look of immense gratitude on both their faces as he handed the cobbler the coins. The cobbler took them reluctantly and handed them to his wife and shook Roth's hand, vigorously, as they both thanked him.

It took Roth quite a long time before he was able to leave the cobblers shop, but when he found himself back out on the street, he was not sure as to what he wanted to do next. As he was about to cross the street to visit the tailor's shop, he heard the cobbler yell, "Captain Roth, beware behind you." Instinctively Roth reached for his sword and withdrew it as he was turning. The warning had come none too soon, for as he turned, he saw a man brandishing a three pronged pitchfork aimed straight for his heart. He was barely able to parry the blow and as he did, he heard the man scream, "I will kill you, if it is the last thing I do on this earth, I will see you dead." The man attempted again driving the pitchfork into Roth, but this time he was ready and caught the thrust between the tines and forced the pitchfork aside and with his left hand smashed the man in the jaw, knocking him to the ground. Roth did not hesitate and brought the point of his sword to rest upon the downed man's throat. It was now that he recognized his attacker.

"Creed!" Roth hissed between clenched teeth, "Can you give me one good reason why I should not drive this blade through your neck and finish what I have wanted to do for years."

Before an obviously terrified Creed could utter a sound Roth heard someone say, "Drop that sword old man or we will shoot you dead where you stand." Roth looked up and found that British soldiers surrounded him with their muskets aimed directly at his head. It was a young officer, Roth noticed, that was giving the orders. He had no choice but to oblige, so he tossed the sword away, near the young officers' feet, where there would be no chance of Creed using it. "Now if you will accompany us, we will go see the administrator and he will decide what to do with you."

Roth, still angry, turned and glared directly at the officer and defiantly said, "I can see no reason as to where I should accompany you anywhere."

Taken aback by the glare he was receiving from Roth, the young officer, mostly as a show for his men, rose to his full height, and stuck out his chest. In the sternest voice he could muster, answered, "Attempted murder is a crime and I think that is all the reason I need to arrest you and bring you before the administrator."

The cobbler came to Roth's rescue. "Sir, I believe that you are making a grave mistake here. This man has done nothing more than defend himself. That man on the ground came up behind him and tried in vain to stab Captain Roth in the back with that pitchfork lying over there. If I had not seen it in time and shouted to warn him, he would have succeeded."

Other people that had witnessed the attack started to say the same thing, backing up the cobbler.

The officer then said, "Well maybe I have made a mistake or maybe I have not. It will be up to the administrator to decide who is in the right here."

Roth, tired of this young officer's stupidity, calmly walked over and picked up his sword. Still holding his sword and standing not more than an arm's length away, looked the officer straight in the face and calmly said, "Run along then and make your report to the administrator." Roth turned away, sheathed his sword and started to make his way to the tailor's shop, where he had been previously going before Creed appeared. He had not gone more than a step when he said over his shoulder, "Oh, one other thing, do not forget to take that scum with you, I do not relish having to finish your job for you."

"Now you just wait a minute sir, I am not done with you," the young officer stammered.

"I am done with you, however," Roth said and smiling inward to himself for still being able to handle a situation like that after all these years, continued across the street, climbed the steps leading to the tailor's shop, opened the door and entered.

Later that evening found Roth and Berkshire standing on the deck of the *Galaunt*. Roth was dressed in his newly purchased clothes and armed with only his new dagger, having decided to leave his belt gun and sword behind. He was talking with Berkshire, who was also dressed in his finest, but had a sword at his side when they saw two British soldiers, start to ascend the gangplank. As they neared the top, the soldier in the front said, "Permission to come aboard sir."

It was Berkshire that responded, "Permission granted, what can we do for you?"

The same soldier answered, "We have been sent by the Administrator Paxmire, to escort you to his home."

Roth chuckled and said, "Well then, I guess we had better not keep the administrator waiting, after you gentlemen." Roth and Berkshire followed the two soldiers down the gangplank.

It turned out that it was quite a walk and then a short climb to the house where Paxmire lived. He lived in one of the larger houses on the small hill that Roth had seen when the *Galaunt* had sailed into the harbor. Another man met them at the gate and led them to the front door. There, another man that took them into the house and then led them to what Roth perceived was the parlor. There were other men, including Nailer, in the room, that for the most part, were all dressed in military uniforms. One of them, Roth recognized was the young officer he had the encounter with earlier. As soon as Paxmire saw them he came over and said, "Ah, Captain Roth, it is good to see you again." He shook Roth's hand vigorously.

"Mister Paxmire, please allow me to introduce my First Mate, Edward Berkshire."

"Edward and I have met before on his other trips down here but let me say it is good to see you again and as always you are welcome in my home." He also shook Berkshires hand.

He took Roth by the arm and led him further into the room and up to a gray haired officer, obviously of high rank. "Captain Roth, let me introduce you to General Sir Thomas Willingham, he is the commander of all the troops and naval assets stationed in Australia."

"It is a pleasure to meet you General," Roth said with a smile as he extended his hand.

Roth was surprised by what came next. "I am well aware of whom this scoundrel is and I must say it is certainly not a pleasure to meet you." Turning to Paxmire he said, "Ethan, I cannot believe that you would allow this murderous pirate into your house and show him welcome. If it was up to me, I would have him hung before the night is out, if for nothing else then for what he did today."

Roth withdrew his hand and started to step towards the General but was refrained from doing so by a light touch on his arm from Paxmire. The administrator said, "General you are right when you say that this is my house and in my house, it is I and I alone, that makes the decisions on who is to be allowed to enter. This man has received a King's pardon for the crimes that he is alleged to have committed and that alone, at least in my mind, atones for any previous actions that he may have taken. I, for one, do not think that it is my place to presume that I know more than the King and if he thinks this man is worthy of a pardon, then I will willingly agree with that decision and make Captain Roth an honored guest in my house. As far as what took place today, I have read the reports and I believe that the captain did nothing wrong."

"Well, I do not presume to know all the circumstances behind the Kings decisions but I do know the facts about this scum and I will not make him a friend and I will surely not dine with him," the General stated with much malice in his voice.

"That is your choice General, but I will tell you this, Captain Roth is welcome in my house and if he chooses to stay then he will dine in my house tonight." Paxmire stated flatly. "The choice is yours captain, what will it be?"

"Mister Paxmire, I am truly sorry to ruin what promised to be an enjoyable evening. Mayhap it would be better if I just left and let you continue on with the dinner as you had planned," Roth stated calmly never taking his eyes off the General.

Paxmire then said, "Nonsense, you are as welcome in my home as any other invited guest and if you wish to stay and enjoy this exquisite meal that I have had prepared then you can stay."

"Hmmph," grunted Willingham. "As I stated earlier, I will not remain in the same house with this man."

"Suit yourself," was all that Paxmire said.

Upon hearing this, an obviously stunned Willingham stared at Paxmire for a few moments before he said, "Then I will bid you farewell." Willingham turned and barked a crisp order to his men and without a backward glance, retrieved his hat and coat and led his men out the door into the night air. As they were leaving, the young officer that Roth had humiliated in front of the townspeople shot him a murderous glance. Roth thought to himself that he would have to avoid any further contact with him because he knew that it would only lead to violence, something he would prefer to prevent if it was at all possible.

After the door closed behind them, Paxmire once again turned to Roth and said as if nothing has happened, "Now would you like to accompany me into the dining room?"

Roth was amazed at the calmness that Paxmire showed throughout what could have been a very dangerous situation.

Roth and Berkshire followed Paxmire and Nailer into the dining room where they were greeted by a sight that almost overwhelmed them both. Neither had ever been in a dining room that showed so much opulence. Several places were set on the long dining table with crystal goblets and what looked like very fine china and the flatware was of the finest silver. There were several silver candelabras set along the middle of the table and there were three candle lit crystal chandeliers hanging from the ceiling.

Paxmire took his position at the head of the table and Nailer sat on the side to his right. Roth took the seat on the left hand side of the table with Berkshire claiming a seat next to him.

There was little conversation during the dinner that was served by several servants in many courses. Roth thoroughly enjoyed the meal that proved to be much better than most food that he had ever eaten and it was surely better than what he had been eating lately. It was obvious that Paxmire held a place of great importance here.

After dessert was finished, Paxmire suggested that they return to the parlor for a glass of wine and maybe a cigar.

When they were seated in the plush overstuffed chairs that adorned the parlor, a servant brought in crystal wine glasses and another brought in the wine and proceeded to fill each glass. Another brought in a box that held some very fine looking cigars which he offered to each man. All but Nailer accepted. As each took a cigar from the box the servant offered a clipper and then lit the cigars for them.

Before Roth had a chance to sample the wine, Paxmire said, "The wine you are about to sample is made right here on the island. We have been very fortunate to be able to locate some areas where grapes thrive. The same is true of the cigars. We imported several plants from the America's and found that they do quite well in the coastal areas east of here."

Roth swirled the wine in the glass as he admired the color and took a small sip which he rolled around in his mouth. He found it to be very delectable. He said, "I must say that this is very good. You are indeed fortunate."

They sat there for a while and enjoyed the wine and smoke for a few minutes before Paxmire once again spoke. "I could not help but notice that the pardon you received was issued not that long ago. It has been over ten years since you were supposed to be sent here. Would I be too forward to ask what you have been doing all that time or where you have been? I know you have not been with Mister Berkshire or I would have known that."

Roth paused, for a few seconds, before he started to tell the tale of his being marooned and how Berkshire had found him just before arriving here.

Paxmire pondered this for a few moments before he said, "You are very lucky to have a friend that would go that far out of his way to look for you, even when the chances were you had drowned and were long dead."

There was silence in the room for several minutes before Paxmire spoke once again. "I would like to take this opportunity to apologize for the unfortunate incident that you were involved in this morning."

Roth replied, "Think nothing of it. I have been in situations similar to that several times in my life and have come through them all without much harm."

"Still I am ashamed that it happened while you were a visitor on my island and would like to take this time to ask you if there is anything that I could do to make it up to you, anything at all," Paxmire said apologetically.

Roth thought about this offer for a minute before he said, "Actually there are two things that you could do for me if it would not be too much to ask."

"You need only to ask and if they are within my power to grant then I will be more than happy to oblige," Paxmire answered.

"Ok then, first I would like to ask what will happen to the man that attacked me this morning," Roth asked.

"He will be brought before a board and charged with attempted murder and more than likely he will be put to death. Why are you concerned?" Paxmire asked.

"Well, it is a long story and one that I should probably not go into, but if you would do me the favor of sparing his life and instead condemning him to a life of hard labor. That would more than satisfy me," Roth answered.

"That must be some story that you are not telling and I will honor you by not asking more," Paxmire said. He turned to Nailer and said, "Carey would you please take care of that. I am sure that you can find some sort of job for that man that is befitting of his crime."

Nailer simply nodded and said, "It will be done."

At that, Paxmire noticed that Roth's and Berkshire's, as well as his own, glasses were empty and with a signal a waiter entered the room and began to pour more wine.

After the waiter servant had left them alone once again, Paxmire looked over to Roth and said, "I believe you said that there were a couple of things that I may be able to do for you. Might I ask what the second may be?"

Roth did not hesitate as he began. "Are you familiar with the wife of the cobbler?" Roth asked.

"Ah yes, Ruth I believe her name to be. She does rather fine work. I have several pieces of leather that she has made for me. Does this second favor concern her?" he asked.

"Yes, it does," Roth said. "I believe that her sentence is almost completed and I was wondering if it might be possible for me to purchase her early release. The cobbler did me a great favor today and I would like to repay it if it is possible that I can."

"I am afraid that I cannot answer that at this time but rest assured that I will have Carey look into it first thing in the morning," he said as he looked towards Nailer who replied with a nod of agreement.

The rest of the evening was spent with Paxmire telling Roth about the history of Australia and how it had become the prison that it was. This was something that Roth found to be very interesting and it saddened him when Paxmire said that maybe they should call it an evening for he would have liked to hear more.

The four men walked together to the front door and Paxmire said, "Thank you for coming Captain Roth, I hope that you enjoyed my hospitality as much as I enjoyed your company and hope that we can do it again sometime in the future."

"It has been my great pleasure and I have enjoyed this evening immensely. It has been a very long time since I have been able to sit and enjoy good food and great company," Roth replied.

"I believe that the pleasure has been all mine. I found your tale to be very interesting and would someday like to hear the rest of it for I somehow had the feeling that there is more to tell. But enough of that, we both have a very busy day ahead of us tomorrow so I will say good night. I have arranged for you to be escorted back to your ship by some of my military guards if you do not mind. It can be dangerous for someone that is not familiar with the island to wander around alone at night, for this is a prison after all," Paxmire said.

Before Roth could reply, Nailer spoke up and inquired if he might accompany them back to their ship because he wanted to stop off at his office and check on the situation with Ruth. Roth agreed and shaking Paxmire's hand and thanking him once again, the three of them made their way off the porch where they were greeted by the guards who led the way as they started towards the wharf.

The night was clear and warm and a full moon was out high overhead so it was easy to see the road that led from the administrator's house to the wharf where the *Galaunt* was docked.

As the men walked along, Nailer spoke up first. "Captain Roth, I would like to apologize for my actions this morning on the ship. You must understand that a man in my position must act the way I did or he would not be able to command the respect that is required to do the job that must be done every day. I hope you know that I was just doing my duty," he said.

"Think nothing of it. I would have done the same thing in your position and you had no way of knowing that I had received that pardon, heck I did not even know of it myself until just recently," Roth returned.

They walked on in silence again after that and Roth could see that they were nearing the Administration Building where Nailer had his office. As they came nearer to the building, they all suddenly heard, "Halt and hold where you stand!" The guards immediately stopped and raised their muskets to their shoulders and one of them called out, "Advance and be recognized."

They heard from the darkness of the side of the building, a man say, "Lower those muskets and stand at attention."

The guard that had spoken first started to say, "We have our orders." Before he could finish, however, several men moved from the shadows and made their way to the street and surrounded them. The obvious leader of this group was the officer that Roth had the incident with.

Upon recognition of the officer, the guards immediately lowered their muskets and snapped crisply to attention. The officer turned to the two guards and said, "Your service is no longer needed here. I will handle the situation. You are dismissed and you may return to your duties."

The officer watched as they walked away back towards the administrator's house. He then turned his attention to Nailer. "I am sure that you have better things to do than walk the streets at night with this sort of riff raff. Maybe you had better be off."

"Now see here. These men were guests of Administrator Paxmire and I was asked to see them safely to their ship. Who are you to tell me what it is that I should be doing?" Nailer asked.

"I am an officer in the British Army and it is my duty to see that order is maintained in this prison. That is who I am and I am ordering you off the streets," he said with a menacing scowl.

"You have no right to," Nailer started to say but was curtly cut off by the officer who sternly said, "I have every right to order you off the streets and if I were you, I would obey that order now."

Nailer had no choice but to comply and with a shrug, he turned towards the Administration Building and walked away.

The officer watched him until he had entered the building then turned towards Roth. "Now old man, I am going to teach you what it means to show disrespect to an officer in the British Military," he said in a low growl.

"I give respect where respect is due and you have shown me nothing that deserves my respect or for that matter my attention," Roth said in a quiet level tone. He started to turn towards his ship but was cut off by the others in the group.

"I am going to make you eat those words," the officer yelled.

Roth spun back around facing the young officer and without raising his voice said, "Then in that case, do not let anything but fear itself stop you from trying."

This infuriated the young man and he made a lunge at Roth as if he intended to wrestle him to the ground. Roth was ready for the attack and simply moved a little to the right and landed a left jab squarely on the bridge of the officer's nose. The nose erupted in a shower of blood but Roth did not hesitate and immediately drove a right punch into his midsection, doubling him over. Roth followed that with another left punch that knocked the younger man down and Roth was instantly on him pinning him to the ground with his right hand around the officer's throat. Behind him he heard Berkshire draw his sword from its scabbard and coldly say, "This is between those two. Let us just keep it that way."

Roth looked down at the man under his grasp and before he could say anything he heard the sound of many feet running their way from both directions. He realized that the guards must have alerted more soldiers of the impending trouble and the men from his ship were coming to his aid. Roth released his grasp and rose to his feet. He did not have to look very long to see what was about to happen as the two groups of armed men hastily approached each other. He held up his arms to both groups and yelled with all the authority he could muster, "That is far enough. This is over. There is no need for further violence." This caused both parties of converging men to stop and rethink their actions.

The young officer was being helped to his feet by a couple of his friends and as he was rising, he said. "If you think that this is over you are badly mistaken. We will meet again."

Roth looked back towards the man and coolly said, "It is over, here and now, for if we ever meet again in a situation such as this, I will kill you." Without another word, Roth turned and left the young man stunned with that oath and walked towards his men and they all left to reboard their ship.

Chapter 16
"Escape"

The next morning a great deal of noise and activity on the deck above him awakened Roth. He dressed quickly and made his way to the main deck. When he opened the door to the deck, the first thing he saw was that he was being surrounded by heavily armed British soldiers with their muskets shouldered and pointed directly at him. He glanced behind him up to the wheel deck and saw that there were more armed soldiers up there covering him with aimed muskets. Looking back at the soldiers in front of him, he could, over their shoulders, see that his crew had been herded onto the bow of the ship and they too were covered by more armed troops.

A colonel in full military dress was shouldering his way through the soldiers and when he stood in front of Roth he asked, "Are you Captain Roth?" Roth nodded and the colonel went on, "You and your crew are hereby placed under arrest for the attempted murder of an Officer of the Royal British Army and your ship is confiscated and is now the property of the British Navy. You are also hereby notified that you are commanded to accompany this officer to appear this morning before the Botany Bay Administrator for hearing and sentencing of the above mentioned crime."

Roth was stunned and could not believe what he was hearing. Before he could complain, or say anything for that matter, he was grabbed by both arms. The colonel turned and started to make his way towards the gangplank with Roth being hauled by soldiers behind him. He could hear protests from his crew and the soldiers shouting orders to keep them restrained. Roth shouted at them to stand down in the hopes that none of them would be harmed.

When he got to the gangplank, he saw there were many more armed soldiers lining the dock three abreast. It was obvious to him that the British were serious.

It was a short walk to the office of the administrator and when it was reached, he was ushered into the office where he saw General Willingham and a very angry looking Mister Paxmire. Looking around the office he also saw Mister Nailer, looking at him very intently, and the young officer that he had the run in with last night, was seated in the corner. The young man had a very swollen face and it was obvious that he had been in a fight, a fight that he had obviously lost.

The general spoke first. "Alright Ethan, here he is. I demand that you sentence him now and have that sentence carried out immediately. I still cannot believe that you allowed this pirate free access to run around the island anywhere he chose. If it were not for my precautions last night, one of my officers would surely have been murdered."

Ethan stood up and slammed his hand down upon the top of the desk. His face turned a very bright red and he looked like he was about to explode. He turned towards the general and yelled at him, "First of all, my good sir, in this office I will be addressed as Mister Administrator and secondly no one will make demands in this office except me. As I told you before, general, I received a report from Mister Nailer shortly after the incident. Also, I have statements from my guards as to what happened and I would like to remind you that they are my guards, under my command, and I will expect no further reprisals from you towards them." Paxmire visibly calmed down but still in a firm and menacing voice he continued. "As I told you this morning, you have no basis for your charges and if the truth be known, it is Captain Roth who should be making these charges." He paused for a moment, looking towards Roth, and then continued, "Now let me tell you what is to happen. First you will release this man and his crew. You will return his ship and you, your men and this sorry excuse of an officer will immediately vacate my office and hope that Captain Roth does not wish to push the issue. I can tell you now that if he does, I will prosecute the offending persons to the fullest extent of the law." Paxmire let this set in for a second and then said, "I thought I made it clear. Vacate this office at once! Rest assured that your conduct in this dismal affair, will be reported to your superiors in England at the soonest possible time. Now leave before I change my mind and have you replaced, something we both know, I have the authority to do."

A thoroughly chastised general stood there glaring at Paxmire before he turned and angrily moved towards the door. When he reached the door, he looked back at Roth with a very hateful stare and roared, "Don't think this is the end of it! You have not seen the last of me!" Shaking his fist at Roth, he swung open the door and left the room, followed by all of the other military personnel present.

Nailer could still hear him angrily yelling expletives as he moved to the door and closed it. He shook his head and chuckled to himself. Paxmire sat down, and with a handkerchief, he mopped his brow. He looked up at Roth, shook his head, and said, "It seems as if I am forever apologizing to you. I am sorry for what has happened and am in your debt for stopping what could have been a very ugly affair. I am also hoping that you do not pursue this issue any further because it would do no one any good, including yourself. Now my best advice to you would be for you to return to your ship and for your own safety stay aboard until it is time for you sail, which I hope is soon. Also, Mister Nailer and I have reviewed Ruth's case and have decided that we will honor your request and give her an early release." He paused here for a second and then added, "It is my hope that you will be able to afford her and her husband passage aboard your ship when you sail.

Roth, still a little stunned from all that had happened this morning, took a few moments before replying. When he did, he said, "There is no need for any further apologies for there was no harm done and as far as I am concerned this affair is over. I will respect your wishes and will stay aboard the *Galaunt* until we sail and of course, I will provide passage, at no expense, for Ruth and her husband."

Paxmire stood and offered Roth his hand as he said, "Thank you Captain Roth. You are an honorable man. Believe it or not, I hope we meet again."

Roth took Paxmire's hand in his and said, "Thank you for those kind words and if at all possible, we will meet again." With that, he shook Nailer's hand, walked out the door, and left the building, hoping never to return.

As Roth walked out the front door, he saw a column of soldiers marching down the street from the direction of the wharf. He took them to be the soldiers that had taken over his ship. As he watched the impromptu parade, he saw that the last two soldiers stopped and turned in his direction. He recognized them as the two guards that had been with him last night. As he watched, they both came to attention and gave him a crisp salute. Roth was surprised but still, he returned their salute with as much formality as was shown in theirs. They both gave him a nod of respect and then hurried away to catch up with the rest of the column. Roth watched them go until they caught up to the rest of the soldiers and then walked down the steps and returned to his ship.

As Roth climbed the gangplank, he was surprised to see the entire crew in a state of high activity. They looked as though they were preparing for war. Men were passing out muskets and pistols and the crew was making sure that they were primed and ready for use. Roth saw Mister Berkshire talking to a group of men and called out to him. The crew had apparently not noticed him come aboard and instantly stopped what they were doing. Berkshire quickly walked over to where Roth was standing and said, "Cap'n I am glad to see you. We were getting ready to come and rescue you."

Roth chuckled and said with smile, "Well I can see now that it was a good thing that they decided to release me. I do not think they would have been prepared for an invasion of thirty-one men."

Berkshire chuckled to himself as the thought it over and then asked, "Well what happened?"

"The general just had a bone to pick with me and he thought that what happened last night was cause enough. He was wrong though. Paxmire chewed him out pretty smartly and then he released me with his apologies," Roth answered.

"Good thing for them," was all that Berkshire said.

"Paxmire did, however, advise us to finish getting loaded and sail at the earliest possible moment to make sure that there would be no other trouble. The general is still very angry and I am sure that he has something else up his sleeve," Roth said.

"Aye, aye Cap'n," Berkshire said. "I will get the muskets stored and then we will go back to loading. It should not take more than today and we should be able to sail on the morning tide tomorrow."

Roth looked around and inquired, "Were you really going to storm the island in an attempt to rescue me?"

"Aye Cap'n and we would have fought to the last man if that was what it took," Berkshire answered proudly.

"I am glad that it did not come to that. Oh yes, there is one other thing. Send a couple of men to help the cobbler and his wife get their belongings packed and help them get it to the ship. They are coming with us when we sail," Roth added with notable pride in his crew.

"Aye, aye Cap'n and I will also get someone to clean out one of the storage cabins. It would not be wise to have a woman quartering with the crew," he said. Berkshire called two men over to him and Roth could hear him talking to them. He heard that he was giving the orders to leave the ship and help the cobbler. He then watched as the two walked down the gangplank and up the street.

Roth watched for a while as the crew began to return to their duties and finish with the loading of cargo. He walked over to the port side of the ship and gazed out over the water. His thoughts had turned to William and realized that he had not seen him since they first arrived in port. He figured that he was with his daughter and that got him to wondering where she was. He had only caught glimpses of her during the voyage from the island and he had not seen her at all since their arrival here in Botany Bay. He hoped that they were alright.

Roth spent the morning watching and sometimes helping the crew as the last of the cargo was being loaded and stored below in the holds. The cobbler, his wife and baggage were brought aboard and they were making their cabin livable for the long voyage ahead. They had thanked him for what he had obviously done for them and said they would try not to be a nuisance during the trip. He assured them that they would not be a problem and asked Ruth if she would be willing to help in the galley. She promptly agreed and seemed relieved that there would be something for her to do during the voyage. The cobbler also volunteered to work with the crew but Roth told him that he would probably be kept busy with repairing the works of leather aboard the ship and also repairing and possibly making boots and other items for the crew. The cobbler then made the suggestion that he be allowed to return to his home and gather a store of leather that he had there and bring back onboard. Roth readily agreed and sent the cobbler on his with two of his crew to help.

It was still early in the afternoon when Roth retired to his cabin to catch up on the never ending paperwork that came with his position. He had barely seated himself comfortably in his chair behind the desk when someone knocked loudly on his door. "Enter," he called out, somewhat perplexed. Berkshire stuck his head in the door and said, "Cap'n, Mister Nailer is out here and he says that he needs to talk to you about a matter of great urgency."

Roth knew that Nailer would not be here unless it was something very important. He stood up and walked around the desk and said to Berkshire, "Well, let us go and find out what is so important." He followed Berkshire down the short passageway and emerged on the main deck where he could see Nailer standing by the top of the gangplank. Walking up to the man he could see that there was something that had him very agitated.

"Mister Nailer, it is a pleasure having you on board once again," he said, and then added, "What can I help you with?"

Nailer immediately said, "It may not be a pleasure when you hear what I have to say. Administer Paxmire just got word that General Willingham has conspired with his fleet admiral to have you and your ship sunk once you reach open water. He knows that you are planning to sail on the tide in the morning and they are sending ships out to lay an ambush for you when you leave the mouth of the bay."

Roth did not hesitate for even a second before he said, "That is indeed something that I need to attend to. Thank you for bringing me that news and thank Mister Paxmire for me. I am in his debt." He did stop to see whether Nailer left the ship when he turned to Berkshire, "Is the cobbler back aboard?" he asked. Berkshire nodded affirmation. Roth then said, "Then get the ship ready, we sail immediately."

"Cap'n we are not fully loaded yet. It will take us the rest of the day to finish," Berkshire said knowing what was coming next.

"We are finished loadin' now. Cargo left on the docks is about as worthless as cargo on the bottom of the ocean," He said calmly adding, "Now get a move on it, we need to leave now." Roth watched with satisfaction as the crew moved to prepare for departure after receiving their orders.

It took less than an hour before the ship was rigged for sailing and untied from the dock. There was a good breeze coming up from aft and Roth ordered all canvas lowered. As the sails caught the breeze, the *Galaunt* leaped forward and she was not even halfway across the bay before she was moving as fast as she could with this wind.

"Berkshire, man the cannon and have the men prepare and be ready to fire on my command," he said as he worried about what was lying in wait on the other side of the cliffs that protected the mouth of the bay.

Roth's fears were justified as they shot past the cliffs on the south side of the entrance. He at once saw the two great Man O' War's that were coming up from the south, one less than 200 yards away. As the *Galaunt* neared the bow of the closer ship, he could see men running and could hear the shouts of orders being issued to prepare the cannon. But Roth was ready and as the *Galaunt* started to cross in front of the ship he yelled, "Port gunners find your targets and fire at will."

Almost before he had finished his order the guns roared to life. The damage to the other ship was devastating. The *Galaunt* was at point blank range and it seemed that none of her shots missed. Roth watched as two of its four masts came crashing down and a third mast lost its top half. Roth knew that this ship was out of the battle and now turned his attention to the other one.

This ship was way out of range but Roth knew the *Galaunt* would not stand a chance in a shooting battle with it and also knew he would not be able to run away from it either, for the other ship had twice the amount of sail surface that he did. The Galaunt was, however, much more maneuverable than the Man O' War but the British ship was faster and if Roth could not trick his way out of this mess then all hope would be lost.

Roth continued on the course they had been running, all the time watching the great ship as it changed course and came nearer. Roth knew that eventually it was going to have to turn or the *Galaunt* would start to pull away because of the angle. The other captain knew this too and Roth saw as the other ship started its slow turn to port. "Hard to starboard," he yelled, "Bring us about to a course of north northeast." Roth was thankful that the builders of the *Galaunt* had agility in mind when they built this ship. It was not long before the *Galaunt* was sailing straight away from the warship. The captain of the Man O' War realized his mistake and ordered his crew to bring the ship about, but because of it mammoth size, it took the ship a long time before they could resume the chase. In the meantime, the *Galaunt* was widening the gap between the two ships.

The warship finally was able to get on the same course as the *Galaunt* and again it was rapidly chewing away at the distance between the two ships. It was just a matter of time before the *Galaunt* would come into range of their guns.

Roth waited until he felt he could not stay out of range much longer when he gave the command to change course to due north. The warship started its turn and Roth gave another command to change course to east thus causing the great warship to once again, change its course. It was going to be close but it was rapidly approaching nightfall and Roth hoped that this time they would be able to stay far enough ahead that he could lose her in the dark.

The chase continued for another couple of hours and the warship had once again closed the gap to almost firing range but it was getting much darker. They were now close enough that Roth could hear the officers shouting orders and heard them give the orders to prepare the guns for firing.

Roth called for Berkshire to come to his side. When Berkshire appeared, Roth quietly said to him, "I am goin' to try and get that big gal out there to fire on us. If she does then I want you to turn us around so that we are heading east. Run on this course after she fires, until you hear me holler out an order, but regardless of what I say, I want you to turn the ship around and get us moving to the west, however, until she fires, do as I say, but after she does, you have your orders." Roth knew that his orders would be carried out and inside he hoped that this ploy would work.

After he was sure that his order had been relayed to the helmsman Roth yelled out, "Bring us to starboard, new bearing east." Sure enough as the ship started to turn the warship also turned, bringing her mighty array of guns to bear. Due to the growing darkness, Roth could only see the flashes followed by the thunderous roar as the mighty ship of war unleashed its deadly weapons of death and destruction upon the smaller *Galaunt*. Roth got a sickening feeling in the pit of his stomach because he knew that many of those balls would find their mark. He could only hope the deaths and the damage would be held to a minimum.

He held his breath as the first shots neared and was very shocked as he saw the shot fall short of their intended mark only to land harmlessly in the water off her stern. He could not even imagine how every shot had missed for the gunners on that ship were the best in the world, but now was not the time to dwell on it, Roth had other things to think about. Roth felt the ship turning to the west and waited until he could no longer see the warship because of the deepening darkness, but he knew they were out there, out there somewhere close on their port side. It was now or never so Roth barked out his final order, "Keep us runnin' on this course. We will make for the islands." Roth was gratified to feel his ship continue its turn to port and come to a heading of due west.

The *Galaunt* raced through the night, a dangerous thing to do when you are not sure where you are. Roth knew that he had to lose the great warship because if it found them in the morning then they would have to fight a fight they could not win. Sure, the *Galaunt* could out maneuver almost anything with sails and she had a sizable sting of her own but that sting was not nearly as deadly as that carried by the warship. So, they had no choice but to race through the night and pray that his trick had worked and the warship was now sailing in the opposite direction.

When dawn did eventually break the night, the lookouts where able to see in all directions and Roth could finally relax when they all shouted down that the seas around them were clear and no other ships were near. It had been a long night with everyone on deck prepared for any eventuality and it had definitely taken its toll. After the all clear was sounded, Roth could see those men that were not on actual duty, starting to fall asleep where they were. Roth himself would like nothing better than to find his rack and sleep through the day, but he knew that there were things that still had to be done and plans to be made. It was obvious, now that since they had fired on an English Man O' War, they would not be able to sail back to England.

Roth had spent the night on the wheel deck, along with Berkshire, the helmsman and those men that manned the rigging for the sails. Roth walked over to Berkshire and solemnly said, "Well Edward, it seems as I have made a mess of things once again."

"Cap'n, I cannot say that this is your fault. You did nothin' to provoke Willingham and certainly did nothin' to provoke the English

Navy. If you remember correctly, I was there at Paxmire's and I know what transpired. You have been pardoned by a king and that man was wrong for what he did." Berkshire shot back.

Roth, a little taken back by Berkshires forthrightousness, looked at his first mate before he spoke again, "Be that as it may, the English Navy is not goin' to look kindly on the fact that one of their ships was fired upon and damaged by us. I do not think that we should risk goin' home and the lot of us ending up in prison for somethin' that was not our fault," Roth replied after a little time for thought.

Berkshire paused here and found himself looking over the ocean with a wandering gaze wondering if he would ever be able to return home. "Yes Cap'n, that is true, but I cannot see myself ever again returnin' to my home and I am sure that many of the crew would feel the same."

Roth had many of the same feelings, but he knew that he did not have any choice. If he returned to England, he would be arrested and he would never see a free day again and would either be hung or returned to Australia as a real prisoner.

"Edward, as usual, you are right. I do not see why you and the crew could not return home. I will bear the blame for what has transpired. The ship and I are who the British will be looking for. I think that what we should do in the future is somethin' that we have to think about and right now is not the time for that kind of thought and it is definitely not somethin' that I should decide by myself for we are all in on this. We will let all the men get rested up and then we, as a group, will decide our future.

"In a couple of days, we will gather the entire crew on deck and let them know where we stand," Roth paused here for a few moments before he spoke again. "In the meantime, figure out where we are and then set course for the Cape."

Roth turned away from Berkshire and made his way to the stern of the ship and stood for quite a while looking out over that part of the ocean that lay astern before retiring to his cabin for some much needed rest.

The days that followed were filled with clear skies and a good wind at their backs. The men were able to get plenty of rest and Roth finally thought that it was time to gather the crew and let them know what lay in the future.

Roth and Berkshire stood by the wheel deck railing, behind them was the helmsman, the rest of the crew stood on the main deck facing them. Roth spoke first, "Men, as you all know by now, we cannot sail back to England. We could surely sail there before word of what has transpired would reach there, but as soon as word did arrive, we would all be arrested. I do not feel as though we were in the wrong, but I doubt that would do us any good. Also, this is not something that you should be punished for. I am the one that General Willingham has it in for, not you. It is our ship they will be huntin', but it is me they will really be after. Anyone caught onboard her, with me, will share a like punishment. So, I am asking for your thoughts of this matter."

Almost at once, one voice shouted, "We are with you Cap'n. Where you go, we all go." This was followed by the crewmembers shouting, AYE, AYE, AYE, while raising their fists to the captain.

Roth looked his crew over, making eye contact with every one of them. Finally, he spoke, "I do appreciate your loyalty and do wish that we could proceed on as if nothin' has happened." He paused here, gathering his next words. "I am an outlaw and, in their eyes, a pirate. There is not a danged thing that I can do to change that fact, but there is no reason, that I can see, for you to follow me on that path. It is not you that they will be huntin', it is me and this ship. We are the ones that they want. You have a chance to remain free and return to your homes and families."

"What choices do we have?" one of the crew asked.

Roth stood there, as if in thought, he already knew the answer but did not want the crew to think that he was making a snap reply. "As I see it, our options are very limited the way things stand now. We all know that we cannot return to England at this time. So, unless we all decide to turn to piracy, our only choice is to sneak into one of the American port towns," he stated.

One of the crewmen yelled out, "We would surely be arrested in America as quickly as we would in England."

"That could happen if word of what has transpired in the last few days were to reach wherever we land, but I doubt that will happen. America is not like an English port, where all the necessary paperwork has to be filled out, along with a cargo manifest and a list of the names of all crewmembers and passengers aboard, submitted and approved before a dock is even assigned. In America, they are happy to see any vessel come into their port and will immediately see to it that you have a docking site and will do their very best to get you unloaded and back on your way if that is what you choose to do. I think that it is entirely possible to get in there and out before word of what has happened reaches port. We could then set sail to another, larger, port town and man our long boats, scuttle the ship and then row ourselves into port and mix our way into the population. You could then make arrangements to get back to England. Or on the other hand, we could turn to piracy. This is not something that I am going to encourage because I, for one, do not wish to spend the rest of my life being hunted and hounded, with no place to call home, until that day when we are cornered or caught," he said before continuing. "Now it is up to you to decide which course we follow. I will go along with whatever you decide." he looked over at Berkshire who gave him an approving nod. They both then turned their attention back to the crew below.

The crew did not say anything to Roth but he could see that they were having a discussion amongst themselves and were breaking off into smaller groups as they talked. Gradually the smaller groups joined with others until it was one large group again, it appeared as if a consensus had been reached. Finally, the second mate turned towards Roth and Berkshire and said, "Cap'n, the crew thinks that you are right and as always, they will follow whatever course that you decide is best. However, they are not sure about the idea of scuttling the *Galaunt*. This is a fine ship that has gotten us through many times of trouble and she deserves a better end."

This took Roth by surprise. He had thought that they had been discussing what they should do and here they were more worried about the ship than themselves. He took a breath to keep from laughing and then spoke, "Well it is good to see that you are loyal to your ship, but there will be others that you would be able to secure passage and sail for home."

The second mate interrupted Roth and said, "With all due respect Sir, there is no choice other than America. We do not relish the idea of being 'hunted and hounded' either. We just do not *want* to see the *Galaunt* scuttled."

"Well, America has hundreds of miles of uncharted coastline, with several coves, inlets, waterways and rivers. We can surely find one that is large enough to hide a ship of this size. We will find one and there she can rest in peace. Is this agreeable with you?"

As one, the crew cheered acknowledgement to their captain.

"Then do we also agree that we sail to America?" he asked.

Once again the crew cheered, only this time the cheer was to America.

Roth turned to Berkshire and said, "You have heard the decision, plot and set the course to the America's and we will decide where to land when we get closer."

"Aye, aye Cap'n," he said and then added, "but first there is a matter of up most importance that needs to be attended to."

"What is that, Edward?"

"That cargo that we left on the dock in Australia consisted mostly of ships stores. We are very low on food and fresh water and other items that we will need for a long voyage," he answered.

"How many days' worth of food and water do you figure we have?" Roth asked.

"I figure that if we ration a little, then we might have two to three days' worth," Berkshire replied.

"How far from the Cape do reckon we are?"

Berkshire answered, "I would say about two to three days, but if I may, I would suggest that we make way for Madagascar. We could be there in less than two days if this wind holds out."

"Then that is what we will do. Plot the course."

"Aye, aye Cap'n," Berkshire answered.

Roth remained where he was at the railing of the wheel deck and watched as new orders were delivered and carried out by the crew on watch. As he stood there the thought suddenly came to his mind. What about Kathryn, did she know where they were? Would she be able to find them and what of William? Roth hated the thought that he had to leave him behind, but there was no time to look for him and anyway, he would not have known where to look.

Luck stayed with them and the *Galaunt* made port in Mahajanga, Madagascar before the sun set on the second day. Mahajanga is located on the northwestern side of Madagascar in the mouth of the Betsiboke River. Mahajanga was not the best place to lay over for supplies but it was safer than anything located along the east coast. Roth was able to negotiate a trade with local traders for a portion of his Australian lumber that was stored in the cargo holds for all the supplies that the ship and crew would need to round the Cape and make their way to the Americas.

On the second night that the ship was tied up alongside the wharf. Roth and Berkshire were alone in his cabin when a quiet knock was heard at the door. "Enter," he said. To both their surprise, William entered through the door, very wet and disheveled. It was Roth who reacted first. Leaping to his feet, he rushed over and took William's arm and guided him to an extra chair in front of his desk.

He asked with much concern, "My lord, son, pray tell what happened to you and for that matter, how did you come to be here?"

"That, sir, is a very long story and I have not had very much to eat or drink since you made your escape from Australia and I am very tired and would like to get some rest before I tell you everything that has transpired. Just know that Kathryn is safe and is at this moment resting just outside of the harbor." No sooner than it took him to say that short piece than he slumped over in the chair and fell fast asleep.

Roth and Berkshire just stared at each other for a few moments before Edward laughingly said, "That must be quite the story. I am surprised that he was able to say that much."

"Yes indeed, I will anxiously await him to wake up to hear it. In the meantime, we had better get him out of those wet clothes and onto my bunk before he catches a chill," Roth said.

After the two men had William changed and snuggly wrapped in a blanket on Roth's bunk they made their way out onto the deck to check on how the unloading and loading was progressing. Roth did not want to stay tied up alongside this dock any longer than they had to be. It was impossible to gauge how long it would be before news of the battle with the British Navy reached here. Roth hoped that they would be long gone before it did.

It turned out to be two more days before the ship was ready to set sail and as soon as she was, Roth ordered her back out to sea. Before Berkshire issued the sailing orders he walked over to Roth and said, "Cap'n, eight men have approached me and asked for permission to leave the ship."

"Did they tell you why?" Roth inquired curiously.

"Yes, they did, Cap'n. Four have found passage on another ship bound for England. Three have found berths aboard another ship bound for the islands to trade and for guidance to better trading spots, they will earn nice rewards. The last simply wants to stay here because he has found employment much to his liking," Berkshire answered.

"That is going to leave us very short handed in case of emergency, but we will have to make do. Give them permission and wish them luck. I will see them off at the gangplank," Roth said.

It was two days before William woke up from his slumber.

The *Galaunt* had just exited the mouth of the river when William made his way out onto the main deck. It was Berkshire that noticed him first and he nudged Roth in the side and pointed down to the deck at William. "Maybe now we might get to hear the rest of the story."

Roth nodded and turned to greet the youth on the main deck. When he approached William, he was startled to see what condition he was in. The youth appeared to be starved and undoubtedly dehydrated and was on the verge of collapse. Roth and Berkshire both rushed to his side and each taking an arm turned him around and started to make their way back to Roth's cabin. In the short hallway they passed Brian, the cabin boy. Roth told him to bring water and light provisions for three to his cabin on the double. They then got William back into the cabin and propped him up at the small table where, when food arrived, he would be able to eat. No one spoke a word until Brian arrived with the food and water. It was the water that William took first. Roth had to slow his drinking down so that he would not get sick and this reminded him of the first time he had given him water back on the island.

The water made a remarkable change in William and it was not long before he was able to take small bites of the food provided and from there it was not long before he was eating heartily. Neither Roth nor Berkshire had spoken while this was going on. "Are you beginning to feel better?" Roth finally asked.

"Much," William replied. "I did not realize how good salt pork could taste, but after not eating for several days, this is just about the best food I have ever had."

"Well enjoy your meal but know that you have a tale that we would very much like to hear," Roth said solemnly.

After a while, William looked up from his meal and faced Roth, then glanced at Berkshire. "There is really not that much to tell," he said.

Berkshire answered with, "Maybe you could start with how you came to be here."

"I guess I might as well start at the beginning," he said.

"That would be a very good place to start for sure and while you are at it, maybe you could explain where you were when we sailed and for that matter the whole time we were there," Roth said.

"When we first arrived in Australia, I found Kathryn and we immediately set out to explore the island. Australia is a very awesome place and there are many things to see in the waters around it. We found a small cove not far from where the *Galaunt* was docked and made it our base for exploration. We were keeping track of the *Galaunt* and could pretty well gauge how the loading was going so that I could be back on board when she was ready for sailing. It was when we were going back that we saw you sail out of the Bay and engage that British ship. We had no way of telling what was going on so we stayed out of harms way and watched the battle and the eventual chase by that other ship. There was not much we could do except follow and watch to see what unfolded. It was approaching nightfall when I guessed that you were not going to lose the warship before darkness set in, so I came up with a plan," he said.

"A plan? What was it that you thought you and my daughter could do to help us?" Roth asked.

"It was not what we thought we could do, it is what we did. Our plan was simple, we had to do something that would slow the warship down and give you the time you needed to escape into the darkness," he answered with a smug look.

"Young man, you now have our total attention. What was it that you did that gave us the time we needed?" Roth wondered, noticing the look on William's face.

"It really was quite simple. The warship was rapidly reaching the point where she could accurately use her cannon on you. I had Kathryn bring me up alongside the warship where it was an easy matter to climb up her side. I hid just over the railing at the stern of the ship right behind the helmsman. I saw that everyone's attention was focused on you, so I felt pretty secure in my position. I knew that the ship was going to have to make a turn soon to bring her whole array of guns to bear. I heard the captain give the order to prepare all starboard guns for a simultaneous assault. When all was ready, he gave the order to turn to port. That was my cue. As the helmsman started into the turn, I jumped over the rail, grabbed a belaying pin and gave him a sharp rap on the side of his head. His knees buckled and he slumped to the deck just as the captain gave the order to fire. The wheel was already spinning to starboard as the unsteered ship tried to right itself, so I hoped that the shot would fall short. I did not stay around to see what was going to happen and I raced back to the stern and dove over the railing back into the water where Kathryn was waiting. I am sure that no one saw me and they are probably still wondering what happened," William said with some pride.

Roth looked at Berkshire who was chuckling, then back at William before he said, "Well lad, it looks as though we owe you and Kathryn a great deal. I was wondering why experienced and practiced British gunners missed their mark by at least a hundred yards that night. William, that was indeed, well done. That was a very brave act. Now maybe you would tell us how it is that you are here."

"We could not find you again after it became dark. Kathryn was saying that the waters were very confused and she could not tell what direction you had gone, so we decided to follow the warship eastward. The next morning you were nowhere in sight and the warship must have decided that they had lost you and turned and started to make their way back to Australia. When Kathryn realized that you were not there, she said she knew that you had not sailed east but rather to the west. So that is what we did. We turned around and returned to the last place we had last seen you and then started to the west. It was not long before Kathryn told me that we were on the right track and you had sailed this way. I cannot explain it but Kathryn has this thing where she always knows where she is and also the ability to sense where you are. It is almost like she can smell the *Galaunt's* passage over the water. That is how we found you."

"That is quite the story young man and there is no reason not to believe it for here you are. You had better get some more rest, you have had quite the ordeal," Roth said and motioned for him and Berkshire to depart so William could return to bed.

"Do you believe everything he said?" Berkshire asked as they made their way to the main deck.

"There is no reason not to. We were indeed missed that night when by all rights we should have been shot to pieces and he is here to tell the story. I am inclined to believe what I have heard and will forever be grateful to him and my daughter for saving us from what could have been a devastating ruin," Roth replied.

The days passed quietly after that and the ship made an unimpressionable passage around a very calm Cape and was on their way north.

Roth had caught glimpses of Kathryn and he knew that she was out there keeping pace with the *Galaunt.*

Nothing of note happened during the next several days. The *Galaunt* had been sailing well to the west and far out to sea of normal sailing lanes and therefore had not encountered any other ships during this time.

Roth was on the wheel deck when he called out for Mister Berkshire to join him. It was only a few minutes until Roth saw his first mate climbing the ladder to join him.

"Edward, we are nearing the islands south of mainland America. There is much pirate activity in this area so we must be prepared for any eventuality. Keep double lookouts posted topside and have the crews prepare the cannon for instant use. I do not want to be caught by surprise by any ships that might think us easy prey," Roth told him.

Chapter 17
"Treasure"

"Smoke on the starboard beam," a lookout called down.

Roth grabbed his scope and began to survey the eastern horizon. His gaze stopped when he saw smoke. The smoke was heavy and black and that could only mean one thing, a ship was burning.

The lookout called down again, "Two ships forty-five degrees off the starboard bow, and they look to be under full sail and moving away from the area of the smoke."

Roth called back, "Keep those ships under watch and let me know straight away if they make any changes in their course or speed."

He turned to Berkshire and stated, "I have an uneasy feeling about this. That has to be a ship out there on fire and I am thinking' that it was probably caused by those other two ships. It would be prudent if we primed and readied all cannon just to be on the safe side."

"Aye Cap'n," Berkshire said as he moved off to give the orders to the crew.

"Helmsman, turn to starboard and make your course for the smoke on the eastern horizon," he said as he resumed his gaze towards the smoke.

Roth turned to William, "Do you think that you and Kathryn could make it to that smoke before we can?"

"Without any doubt sir, she is a very fast swimmer. I am sure that we could get there and back well before you could sail there," he said boastfully.

Roth stood there for a moment thinking over what he had in mind before he spoke. "Alright then, I will slow the ship so that you can get into the water. Here is what I want you to do," and he explained his thoughts to William.

Roth had the ship slow down enough that William could safely dive off the side of the ship. He then ordered Berkshire to raise sail and resume full speed and the *Galaunt* continued to fly towards the smoke.

Less than an hour had passed when the lookout called down, "I see Kathryn off our starboard bow about a quarter of a mile ahead."

Roth got Berkshire's attention and said, "Slow the ship and bring her to a stop so that we can bring William aboard."

"Aye Cap'n," he said and quickly gave the orders.

After the ship stopped, Roth saw William climb over the rail and make his way towards him. William climbed to the wheel deck and spoke, "You were right sir, it is a burning ship and there are two survivors in the water. We were also able to catch the fleeing ships and you were right again, they are making great haste to leave the scene. We did not get close enough to see who they were but we could see they were both flying the Black."

"Pirates huh, that would explain a lot. Good job William," Roth said and as an after thought he continued, "You had better dry off and get some dry clothing on, we might need Kathryn and you again.

It proved to be almost two hours before the burning ship came into view. Roth had moved to the bow for a better view. "Lookouts, can you still see those other ships?" he called out to the men above.

"Nay Cap'n, they have disappeared over the horizon," a lookout called back.

"Keep a good watch in all directions, I do not want them to circle back while we are occupied with the fire and looking for survivors, there should be two of them," he added.

Berkshire joined him at the bow and asked, "What do you make of it Cap'n?"

Not taking is eye from the scope, he answered, "From what I can see, it looks to be Spanish. I can still see that before she was set afire, cannon fire caused severe damage. I could not tell who those other ships might have been and it is anyone's guess as to why they were here or if they were the ones that even set her afire." he said in reply. He handed the scope to Berkshire and added, "Here, have a look and see what you can make of it."

While Berkshire was using the scope, Roth yelled, "Helmsman, bring us around to the upwind side, we do not want any burning ash to come our way."

He did not need to receive a reply because he felt a slight adjustment to the movement of the ship as the course changed to bring them upwind of the burning ship.

"Cap'n, I see survivors in the water dead ahead," Berkshire said. "There seems to be at least two of them."

"Slow the ship and let's get them aboard. Keep them under guard until we know for sure what it is that we are dealing with. After they are safely on board, move us off a safe distance and we will find out what they have to say," Roth said.

Berkshire immediately started giving orders to slow the ship and had an armed guard report to him near the port side longboat. Roth watched as the crew started to carry out those orders and then, after the ship had slowed to almost a stand still, he watched the longboat being lowered into the water to go get the two men. He was relieved to see that the men were recovered without any problems and as the longboat started to row back to the ship, he made his way to the port ladder.

The boat finally made it back to the ship where a couple of crewmembers reached out to help the survivors climb over the rail and onto the deck where they were immediately flanked by the armed guards.

Roth, who was standing nearby, saw that they were scratched and bruised. He surmised that their wounds were probably the result of them falling from the ship, while trying to escape from whoever attacked them.

The older of the two was looking around when his gaze settled on Roth, and must have recognized him to be the one in charge. He came to full attention and saluted. "I am Raphael Martinez, Chief Gunner formally of His Majesties Ship *Milan*," he said as he glanced over his shoulder at the burning hulk nearby. "This is Roberto Aragon, my assistant gunner," he continued with, "Do I have the pleasure of addressing the commander of this vessel?"

Roth spoke, "I am Captain Nathan Roth and you are correct, I command this ship."

Martinez, still at attention, spoke again, "I would like to express our gratitude for you coming to our aid and rescuing us from the water. I would also like to swear our loyalty to you and the ship for that kind act."

Roth, a little taken aback and still not fully accepting that loyalty yet, returned the salute and said, "You are welcome for the rescue, but the loyalty still needs to be proven. Before I question you further, are you in need medical services?"

"Our wounds are nothing sir and I will be only too happy to answer any questions that you might have," the man said as he visibly relaxed his posture.

"Very well then, the guards will take you to my cabin. I would very much like to hear your story." Turning to the guards he said, "Would you please escort these men to my cabin and see that they stay there. Keep your eyes on them and I will join you shortly."

Watching as they were escorted away he looked at Berkshire he said, "Well what do you think?"

"I do not see any reason not to believe him and they should be grateful that we plucked them from the water. However, before I would accept their loyalty at face value, there are many questions that remain to be answered before that determination can be given," He replied.

"I agree and I suppose we had better see what we can do to get those questions answered," He stated and then continued, "Would you arrange for some food and water to be delivered to my cabin and then join us there?"

As he entered his cabin, he saw that the guards had placed them in chairs facing his work desk and had taken positions on both sides and slightly behind them. As he was moving around to take the seat behind the desk, Berkshire entered with two flagons of water that he handed to the survivors. He found a seat for himself, sat down, and watched as the two men gulped down the water.

"Ah, that tastes very good, we thank you," Raphael said. "I suppose now is the time to relate what happened today."

"You can wait until you have had a bite to eat if you prefer," Roth said.

"I thank you for that but it is not a long story and I might just as well start it. We sailed on the morning tide three days ago from our port in Havana. We were docked about four days, loading up cargo to be carried back to Spain. On the fifth day, we were ordered below. As we were making our way to our berths, I saw a group of soldiers come aboard. I am not sure what they were doing there but we could hear the sounds of some additional cargo being loaded that we were not allowed to help with or see," he started with.

"Excuse me if you will. The army loaded the cargo? Is that not a little unusual?" Roth asked.

"Yes, it was. We were not even allowed out of our berths while this was taking place and there were armed guards in place to ensure that order was carried out and after we sailed those same guards where posted around the cargo holds. There were also many more official type people, than usual, on board so the talk was that we were carrying something of great value," Raphael said.

Roth looked at Berkshire with a very curious look. "Please continue," he said.

"During that first day of sailing all went on as usual until towards the evening when the lookouts reported sails on the horizon to our stern. They did, however, disappear before the sun set. Yesterday morning the lookouts reported all clear and the day was uneventful until once again in the late evening the lookout's reported sails on the stern horizon and, as before, they were gone before the sun set. This morning however, the lookouts reported a ship on our stern keeping pace with us. We did not like the idea of this ship following so close so the captain decided that we should take evasive actions and try to lose it. There was a fog bank to our starboard side and we turned to make our way towards it. We had plenty of time to lose ourselves in the fog so we did not prepare for trouble. As we neared the bank another ship shot out of it and ran a course directly in front of our bow. On passing, it opened up with its port side cannon and severely damaged the *Milan*. Almost everyone above deck was wounded or dead. Just as we were regaining our senses from that attack, the ship that had been following us came along side and gave us another full volley of cannon fire. Roberto and I were blown overboard during this second attack so I cannot tell you what transpired on board after that. The ship was dead in the water but not sinking and it seemed to me that both attacks were meant to disable but not sink the *Milan*. We hid back near the rudder and were there when one of the ships pulled up alongside and boarded. There was sporadic gunfire, probably killing off the poor souls left aboard that could possibly put up a fight. The ship alongside was there for quite some time and we heard many sounds that indicated that they were loading aboard their ship whatever it happened to be that we were carrying. We stayed hidden while this was going on and noticed that the other ship was slowly running patrol around us. Finally, they had whatever it was aboard their ship and sailed off. We started to smell smoke and knew that we had to get away or run the risk of being caught in a fire. We swam a short distance away to prevent being pulled under by the suction cause by the sinking ship and that is when we saw you approaching," he concluded.

"That is quite the story. You are lucky to be alive because I have received no reports that there are any other survivors to be found," Roth said.

A knock was heard at the door and Roth called out, "Enter."

It was Brian and Pots bringing with them two platters of food. Pots spoke, "I figured as long as I was comin' here I would care for their wounds."

"Good idea, Pots." Then to the guards he ordered, "After they have finished eatin', show them to a berth where they can get some rest. Continue to keep an eye on them until I am satisfied that they are of no danger." Looking back to Raphael he said, "After you are rested, we will talk again."

"That will be good, thank you sir," Raphael replied as he rose and gave a salute which was returned by Roth.

Roth and Berkshire left the cabin and made their way out onto the main deck. Berkshire spoke first, "Well, what do you think of that Cap'n? It is obvious that the *Milan* was probably carryin' something of value and maybe the pirates knew that or they just might have gotten lucky."

"Sounds to me like they probably already knew what the *Milan* was carryin' and just waited until the right circumstances to pull off that ambush and attack. I am also sure that if we saw them, then they saw us so we had better be ready for an encounter of our own with them. It is gettin' late and I do not prefer to run into them in the dark, so we will stay here for the night. After it gets dark, move us further away west where the glow of this fire will not mark us and make sure that all ship lighting is out. We do not need a light to signal our position," Roth returned then continued, "It also seemed to me that these two ships have used this form of attack before and look to be very good at it. We need to come up with a plan so we can be ready if we meet up with them."

After sailing a short distance, they held their position, watching the horizon, they saw the ship slowly burn away.

The sun had just set when a lookout called down from above, "Cap'n, I just spotted some sort of light on the horizon to the north, it flashed a couple of times then it was gone, but it was a long way off."

"Thank you. Keep your eyes open and watch for any more lights, not just to the north but all around us," Roth shouted back. He made his way down to the main deck and found Berkshire. "Edward, they are out there. Come to my cabin when you get us settled for the night, we need to plan. Bring the chief gunner and tomorrow mornin's helmsman."

"Aye Cap'n, I will not be long," Berkshire said.

"William, get back into the water and you and Kathryn go find those ships and let me know what they are up to," Roth said. William did not reply, he just eagerly ran to the rail and dove overboard. He had to laugh as he watched him do that and reflected back to when Kathryn had first brought him to the island. Roth chuckled to himself as he thought how much the boy, no not a boy, a man, had matured. He finally came out of the reverie and made his way down to his cabin.

Roth was busy looking over a chart that he had laid out on his desk when the knock came. "Enter," he said. When the door opened, he saw Berkshire, the chief gunner, the helmsman and William come in. He was surprised to see William and spoke to him first. "Were you able to locate the positions of those other ships?"

William answered, "Yes sir. When we left them, they were doubling back, slowly, under the cover of the darkness. I think they will be on us in the morning."

"Many thanks to you and Kathryn, you have told me what I needed to know. Now gather around here, I think that I have a plan." They stayed huddled like this through the night discussing the plan and making changes here and there. Eventually it started to get light. "Alright, let's get started and see how things turn out, we will only have one shot at it so let's get it right." Roth said with emphasis.

As the five men reached the main deck, Roth was glad to see that everyone was already in position. He and the helmsman climbed to the wheel deck where the helmsman relieved the night watch and took control of the helm. William, he saw, dived into the water.

Roth took up a position by the port railing. Berkshire already had his men in the rigging and they were preparing to get underway. The guns were the only part of the plan he was worried about. With the men that left the ship in Madagascar they were shorthanded and for the plan to work, Roth needed most of the men manning the sails. Roth noticed the gunner making his way towards him. "Sir, the two survivors say they know cannon and would like lend a hand," he offered.

Roth thought this over a short while before answering. "By all means, we can sure use them but keep an eye on them to make sure they do nothing to damage us." Now here is a lucky break, he thought to himself. Here was a chance to test their loyalty that they had pledged when first coming aboard and to give him the manpower he needed to man the guns.

Roth returned to his spot on the port rail and waited for a report from the lookouts above. That report was not long in coming. "Ship astern, two miles," was heard from above. Roth raised his scope and there it was, coming fast. He turned and then scoped the horizon to the east. Sure enough there was a fog bank, right about where he figured it would be. So, they were going to try the same ploy on them, he surmised, but if things went the way they had planned, the results would be different.

The *Galaunt* was already moving to the northeast, at about half speed when the lookouts called, "Signal." Roth had been waiting for this. It meant that Kathryn and William had found the ship hiding in the fog. "Helmsman, do you see the signal?"

"Aye Cap'n, I am changin' course now," he answered.

All Roth had to do now was watch and wait. The crew already had their orders so now it was just a matter of time.

As planned, the closer the ship got to them the more speed the *Galaunt* gained. This was just a simple matter of changing the setting of the sails slightly to give the sails more wind. They continued in this manner until the enemy was about two hundred yards off their stern, slightly to the port side and the *Galaunt* was about a quarter of a mile from the fog bank.

From above, the call that Roth had been waiting for, came. "Moving," shouted the lookout.

"Now," Roth yelled. The helmsman suddenly threw the ship hard to port and brought the port side guns to bear. No sooner had he started into his turn than Roth heard the roar of a cannon. He looked down to see who had fired early and saw that it was Raphael that had fired. Annoyed at what he considered a wasted shot, he looked back at the enemy ship and saw instantly that he was wrong, it had not been a wasted shot. The forward mast had been hit about ten feet above the deck and was already starting to topple over to the port side. As he watched the mast plunge into the water, he saw the ship list way over on its port side exposing the deck and everyone on it. The other cannon were now firing at the helpless ship and the devastation was total. Roth knew that he would have no more trouble with this ship. That was the easy part. He now had to deal with the second ship and it would be a matter of who fired first.

"Helmsman, bring us in line parallel with the fog bank," Roth ordered.

"Aye, aye Cap'n," the helmsman replied.

"Mister Berkshire, take whatever men you can spare from the sails and have them help with the starboard guns, we will need them shortly," Roth yelled to his first mate.

From somewhere below him he heard, "Aye Cap'n."

"Ship emerging from the fog abeam of us," A call came from the lookout.

Roth turned his focus to where the second ship was emerging from the fog just as the *Galaunt's* cannon came to life. He saw that it was trying to turn to bring its own guns to bear but it was too late. The *Galaunt's* shot proved to be very accurate and he watched as shot after shot brought masts down and wreaked havoc on the deck where the guns were. Roth knew that this ship was not going to be a problem either. It was dead in the water and had lost most of its sting, if not all.

"Lookouts, keep an eye on her to make sure she has no more fight left in her." To the helmsman he said, "Bring us about and let's go see how the first ship is farin'."

It did not take long to return to the sight of the first battle and Roth was glad to see that the ship was still afloat. She was still listing to port because of the mast dragging in the water but she did not look to be taking on much water. He could see that everyone on board was busy cutting away the rigging so that the mast could be shoved over the side and the ship righted. Roth also saw that the other mast had received considerable damage and knew that it would be quite some time before it would be seaworthy again.

"Helmsman, bring us within hailin' distance and then bring our port guns to bear," Roth ordered.

When the ship was where Roth wanted it, he called out, "One of two things are going to happen now. First, and this is the choice that I would take if you have any sense at all, you will lay down any weapons you have and move to the bow of the ship, or second, I will open fire and sink you."

Roth was not surprised when he saw those on board drop everything they had and move to the bow. "Good choice. You will now be boarded and if anything happens to my men, I will blow the bow of your ship off with you on it," Roth called out. Someone on board the stricken ship shouted out an order and Roth looked on as three more men that had been hidden, came into view and joined the others on the bow.

"Berkshire, take six armed men and board her. Let me know when you have things secured and I will send over more men," Roth commanded.

Roth watched as the longboat was lowered and rowed over to the wounded ship. The men left aboard the *Galaunt* were manning the guns ready for an order to fire.

Berkshire was able to board without any incidents. When he had all the crew under armed guard, he signaled to the *Galaunt* that all was secure.

Roth then ordered that the other longboat to be lowered and he and six other armed men rowed over to the other vessel.

Roth climbed aboard the captured ship and made his way to the bow. When he reached the men waiting there, he took Berkshire aside and whispered in his ear. When he had finished speaking, Berkshire just nodded, tapped two men, and moved off towards the stern. He turned back to the men under guard and said, "I am Captain Roth of the ship *Galaunt* and I am lookin' for the man in charge of this vessel."

One man, slightly smaller than Roth, stepped forward and angrily said, "I am Pierre Castille, Captain of the *Merci*, and on a mission for our government and I demand to know why you fired on my ship!"

Roth got a little smile on his face at the indignation of this man and said, "I fired on your ship because you were preparing to fire on us."

"That, sir, is a lie. We were trying to catch you to ask for help," Pierre screamed back.

"Help? What, pray tell, kind of help were you going to ask us for?" inquired Roth in a civil tone.

Pierre calmed down a little bit now that he thought Roth might be believing him, "We lost our sister ship, who I can see that you have also managed to damage, last night and all that I was going to ask you was if you had seen her. We were doing nothing and you fired on us."

Roth laughed at that. "Before we settle on whom it is that is lying, let me introduce you to Raphael Martinez and Roberto Aragon, survivors of the *Milan,* the ship that you and your friend over there," Roth pointed off to the North, "attacked yesterday."

"Survivors? There were no surv...," Pierre started to say but cut himself off.

"Oh, so now it seems that maybe it is you that is lying after all. I do not take kindly to someone that lies to me and then calls me the liar." Roth let this sink in before he spoke again, "Now that we have an understanding, perhaps you would come forth and tell me what it was that you took off the Spanish Galleon."

"We did not take anything from the Spaniard. We were just defending ourselves from them. They fired on us first," he said.

Roth slowly shook his head and looked at the deck. Finally, he said, "Here I was under the impression that you were through lying to me and yet you continue. Remember this, I have a Chief Gunner's Mate and his helper here with me aboard your ship and I have heard their story and personally, I find that I am inclined to believe them."

Just then Roth heard Berkshire holler at him from the stern of the ship. "Cap'n, I think you should come here and take a look at what we have found."

Roth gave the Frenchman one last look of disgust, ordered his men to keep watch over him until he returned, then made his way to the stern of the ship where Berkshire was waiting. Berkshire led him to a cabin adjacent to the captain's cabin and pointed inside. Roth first saw his two other crewmen and then looked further into the cabin. He immediately saw two chests lying against the far bulkhead. There was another long, narrow box lying on the other side of the room that was heavily fortified with three locks. It appeared to hold something that might be of great value. He turned and looked at Berkshire who just shrugged. Roth walked over to the chests and saw that they were identical and each was secured with a large metal lock. Each chest was about twelve inches wide, two feet long and twelve inches deep. Roth grabbed one of the locks, gave a hefty tug and was not surprised when nothing gave. He turned to one of the crewmen and said, "Find a pry bar so that we can break this lock and see what is inside." The crewman left and Roth turned back to the chests. He tried to pick one up but it was excessively heavy for him to lift by himself. The crewman returned with a pry bar, taking it from him, he applied it to the lock. This was a very well made lock and Roth no longer possessed the strength to break it. He stepped back and the younger of the two crewmen stepped forward. He was much younger than Roth and looked to be in much better shape also. He grasped the pry bar and with a fast hard jerk, broke the lock. Then he and Roth both grabbed the back of the chest and tugged it away from the wall. Roth removed the lock and opened the chest. There was a collective gasp as all four men peered inside and saw that it was crammed full of gold and silver coins, and many precious gems of all shapes and sizes.

"There is a fortune in this chest alone," Roth said. "This must have been what they took from the Spaniards. They must have known this was what they were transporting back to Spain and set out to capture her."

Berkshire answered, "I be agreein' there Cap'n, what are we gonna do with it?" he asked.

Roth thought about this for a few moments and finally said, "I am not sure what to do, but I certainly do not intent to let the French keep it. First, I guess it would be wise to remove it to the *Galaunt*. I will send you a few more men to help get it on the longboats. Take it over to the *Galaunt* and secure it in one of the holds then come back and get the rest of us."

"Aye, aye Cap'n," he replied.

Roth walked out of the cabin and back to where his men were holding the French sailors. He told five of his men to go and help Berkshire and then turned back to Pierre. "That is some horde that you have stowed away in that cabin. Is it something that you have been collecting or did you just come across it yesterday?" He asked. Pierre did not reply. Continuing he added, "Well, nevertheless, it is ours now. Is there any more on board that other ship?" he asked.

Pierre still did not say anything. Roth spoke again, "You might as well tell me, because I am going to search her anyway."

There was no more talking and everyone watched, except the three guards, as the chests were, one by one, brought out of the cabin and lowered into the longboats. Berkshire made short work of it and Roth saw the long boats being rowed over to the *Galaunt*. Soon Roth saw a single longboat being rowed back over. "We will be taking our leave now. Do not try anything heroic, I will still blow you out of the water if you do."

Roth and his remaining crewmembers moved over to the side of the ship, climbed down into the longboat, and returned to the *Galaunt*. Once aboard he found Berkshire and asked, "Is everything secured below?"

"Aye Cap'n,' he answered quietly.

"Very well then, let us go and see about that other ship," he ordered.

"The lookouts reported to me when I came back aboard that the other ship was able to raise enough sail to get headway and have moved back into the fog. We have no idea where they are," Berkshire said.

It was then that he noticed William leaning against the rail. He turned to William and asked, "Do you think that you and Kathryn can find her?"

"Yes, I do. If you will excuse me, we will go do just that," he said and went to the rail and vaulted himself into the water.

Roth moved over to the rail and saw as Kathryn swam up and with William on her back, disappeared into the fog.

"Mister Berkshire, my guess is that if they can make headway, they will stay in the fog as long as they can and then move to the northeast and try to make it back to the islands southwest of the mainland. I think that it will be wise if we make our course north along this fog bank but out of cannon range, and see if we can find the end," he said.

Roth took up a position on the wheel deck where he could watch the activities on the *Galaunt* and keep an eye out for Kathryn and William. The ship sailed to the north for about an hour when Roth caught sight of them emerging from the fog. It did not take Kathryn very long to catch up with the *Galaunt*. When they were matching speed and adjacent to Roth, William yelled up to him, "They are making their way north as you are. They are about a half mile in the fog and just about where you are now. They are not moving very fast but they are making headway."

"Good. Go back in there and keep following her and let me know if she makes any course changes. We will continue north and try to find the end of this and wait for her there," he yelled back.

With a wave Kathryn and William turned and Roth watched as once again they disappeared into the fog.

The *Galaunt* continued on its course to the north and sailed for another two hours before the fog finally broke up and they had a clear view to the west. Roth ordered the ship to be brought around broadside to the fog and then waited.

It was another couple of hours before the ship appeared. It came out of the fog and when it saw the *Galaunt,* it tried to turn and reenter but it was too late. Roth brought the *Galaunt* to within firing range and gave this ship the same ultimatum that he gave to the other. With noticeable reluctance, he saw the crewmembers either lay their weapons down or throw them over the side. He then ordered Berkshire to take both longboats and as many armed men, as he thought necessary, to the other ship and make a thorough search. He stayed on board the *Galaunt* this time and watched as his men climbed to the main deck of the wounded ship. William came back aboard while he was watching. It was not long before he saw Berkshire and a few of the other men loading what looked like identical chests on the longboats and begin to row back to the *Galaunt*.

"There were three more chests Cap'n. The captain and all of the officers are dead. I am not sure that the surviving crew, and that is not many, even knew what they had on board," he said when he reached Roth.

"Well then, we probably will not have any more trouble from them either. Unload the boats and get those chests stored below with the rest and we will be on our way."

Roth stayed where he was but was not really paying attention. He was deep in thought. He had a major decision that he had to make. In the hold of the *Galaunt,* he knew that he was carrying a very large fortune and he had to decide what he was going to do with it. He had a very good idea who the chests originally belonged to but he was not sure that he had to give it back, after all the Spanish had probably stolen it from the inhabitants of Mexico. And what if he was wrong and the chests did not come from the Spanish ship and he did take it to Spain. They would seize the treasure as soon as they learned of its existence. If that were to happen, what would they do with the *Galaunt* and her crew? What if an English ship spotted them, would they be able to escape or would they be captured and sent to prison. He made the decision that he would have to bring it up to the crew and let them know what the options were and then take a vote.

Before long he came out of his thoughts and saw that the other longboat had returned and Berkshire had the *Galaunt* back under sail and they were making a course north.

Roth made his way to the main deck and found Berkshire talking with a few men in the bow. "Make full speed on this course until the sun sets. After the ship is rigged for night sailing, gather all the men and we will tell them what has transpired and let them decide what course we should follow from here," he said in a passive tone. Roth returned to his cabin to collect his thoughts.

Roth must have fallen asleep because when he heard the knock on the door he had been dreaming about being home in England, in his cottage overlooking the river and hearing Kathryn happily laughing as she played in the front yard. He sat up, stretched, and thought to himself that he was getting too old for this life. Now all he wanted was to find his self a nice place to spend the rest of his life, one away from the sea and everything that came with it. The knocking continued. "Enter," he yelled out. The door opened and Berkshire stuck his head through and said, "Cap'n, as you ordered, the men are awaiting you on the main deck. Roth knew it was time to make the decision about what they were going to do and in some ways it troubled him. This was not one of his best days.

"Thank you, Edward. I will be there presently," he replied to his longtime friend. After the door was shut again, Roth stood up and walked over to the wash basin. He poured some water, dipped his hands in it and splashed it on his face a couple of times to get him fully awake. He grabbed a towel and wiped his face dry. He then made his way out to the main deck where he found the crew waiting and found a place to sit.

"Men, as you undoubtedly know by now, we have in our possession a veritable king's ransom stored in our hold. We must now decide what to do with it," he started.

"All that wealth belongs to Spain and I demand that you return it to its rightful owner," Raphael shouted out.

"Well now, that is where the dilemma comes into play. We do not know that it belongs to Spain," Roth countered.

Raphael returned with, "You know it belongs to Spain, it was taken off our ship yesterday when we were attacked by those pirates!"

Roth thought about this for a few seconds and then answered, "But do *we* know that? You yourself told me that you had no idea what it was that was being secretly held in your cargo hold and I did not hear from any of the pirates that it came from your ship. I might be willing to admit that it probably did come from your ship, but without proof we cannot know for sure." Raphael did not answer this. "Now men, I will put this question to you. What should we do with the newfound wealth that we have acquired? Should we concede that it does indeed belong to the Spanish or should we consider it plunder taken legally from ships that attacked us?"

Roth heard several replies of "Keep it" and one man yelled excitedly, "We risked our lives to get it, why should we give it up?"

"So, I see that the decision would be to keep it. Okay that is what we will do," Roth said.

Raphael spoke up again, "That is not right. You yourself admit that it probably came off our ship. It should be returned to Spain."

Roth looked straight at Raphael and Roberto and said bluntly, "The decision has been made. We are going to keep it as legal plunder. But let me ask you this. What would you rather do, return to Spain and turn this over to the government and return to your life as seamen or would you rather claim your share of the wealth and live the rest of your lives as wealthy men?" Raphael shrugged and said no more.

"Now as you know, the usual split of plunder is one quarter to the captain, one quarter to the officers and the rest divided amongst the remainder of the crew. However, seeing as this is our last voyage together and the last voyage of the *Galaunt*, I purpose that the loot be divided into twenty five equal parts and we all share together. Is that agreeable with you and the other officers Mister Berkshire?" he asked, observing the approving nods from the crew.

Berkshire looked to the other officers and seeing their nods of approval said to Roth, "We are in agreement with your suggestion. I for one have seen part of what is stored down there and know that there is more than can be spent by anyone that receives a share."

"Good, then we are in agreement. Here is how I propose we do this. Mister Berkshire will take three officers and one crewman of your choice, down into the hold and open all the chests. The gold and silver bars, coins and loose gems will be divided into twenty five equal shares. The artifacts will be brought up on deck and each man, according to rank, will each take an item of their choice until it is all gone. I will take two each time because I will choose for Kathryn, seeing, as she cannot choose for herself. Do we all agree to this?" he asked.

Every one of the men, even the Spaniards, shouted an affirmative.

"Mister Berkshire, you might as well get started. I do not think that you will be able to complete your task overnight. In the meantime, we will continue to sail north until we are well past the islands and, hopefully, safely out of pirate waters." He had been right, the dividing of the loot took several days but eventually, Berkshire had it completed.

Roth woke up one morning and immediately sensed that the ship was not moving. He hurried and got dressed and was on his way to the door when a knock was heard, "Enter," Roth called. It was Berkshire and two crewmen. The crewmen were carrying one of the chests between them, Berkshire was carrying the strange looking chest that Roth remembered seeing with the chests on the first ship. Berkshire spoke, "Here is Kathryn, William and your shares. There were two other items that I found that I think you should have. I asked around and every one of the crew agreed." They set the chest on the small table and Roth opened it. He was amazed to see that it was almost full.

There was enough wealth in there for several lifetimes. As the crewmen shut the chest, lifted it up off the table, and set it down on the floor, Berkshire lifted the odd chest and set it on the table, which he then opened. Inside was an ornately carved box with gold inlays. Roth lifted this box and upon opening it, saw that it revealed the most beautiful sword and matching dagger that he had ever seen. Roth lifted it to look it over and he was in awe. It looked to be made entirely of gold. The button was a round cut ruby as big as a man's thumb. The pommel had two more large rubies set on both sides and the outer edge had more rubies around it. The guard also had matching rubies set in it in a spiral pattern emanating from the center. The handle was wrapped with a filigree of finely braided gold threads. Rubies were also used around the top of the sheath with more lining the lower clasp. Roth pulled the blade from its sheath and was surprised to see that the blade was also made of gold. The fuller was covered with engravings of animals, some of which Roth had never seen before and the blade narrowed down to a fine point. Sheathing the sword and returning it to the box, Roth took up the dagger. It was almost identical except for the size. This sword and dagger were not meant to be used in combat but rather as a ceremonial piece to be worn by someone of great importance in fancy and great places. Roth did not think he was important enough to receive this gift. He turned to Berkshire and the crewmen, saying, "This is one fine piece of craftsmanship. I do not, however, think that I should wear it in the Spanish Court," he laughed. "Thank you very much. This will be cherished," he added humbly.

Berkshire grinned and patted his captain's shoulder and said, "It will look right smart on you Cap'n, but I agree with you, stay away from Spain." Berkshire went on to say, "We have all the artifacts laid out on the deck and the crew is waiting for you to take your picks."

Roth said with a smile, "Then let us be on our way, lest it be said that it was I that kept such a generous crew waiting." He turned to the door and led the way outside.

Reaching the deck he faced his men, "I would like to thank you all for that fine sword and dagger. A crew does not exist that is finer and more loyal than you. Once again, I thank you," he said with a big smile.

A crewman yelled out, "Three cheers for the captain."

"CAPTAIN ROTH! CAPTAIN ROTH! CAPTAIN ROTH!" suddenly rang out in the morning air.

"Now maybe we better get through with divvying this up," he said. "However, I feel like I have already received more than my fair share. So, I am going to give up my picks, but I would like to take a couple of pieces of jewelry for Kathryn seein' as she cannot make picks for herself," he said as he selected a couple of jeweled necklaces.

Next it was Berkshires turn. He chose a heavy gold and emerald broach and then turned to Roth. "Give this to Kathryn. She has earned it," he said with a bow. The Second Mate also chose a piece of jewelry and presented it to Roth for Kathryn. So, it went down the line, a piece of jewelry was taken and it was given to Kathryn until every man and woman (Ruth) had made their first choice. He stayed on the deck, watched until all the artifacts were gone, eventually Roth returned to his cabin, and placed all of Kathryn's presents in the chest. Before closing it, he took one more look inside and could not help but be proud of the men that made up his crew and the generosity they had shown towards Kathryn.

He had not been there for very long when he felt the *Galaunt* start to move. He went back above and made his way to the wheel deck. There he found Berkshire and William deep in conversation. Walking up to the two men he heard Berkshire say, "I know it is not a wise decision but it is the decision of the Cap'n and as long as he is on this ship, then his word is as an order and it will be carried out."

Not used to hearing his thoughts and decisions questioned by anyone he spoke up, "Well Mister Berkshire, what is it that you two are talking about and what decision have I made that you are not happy with?"

"Do not get me wrong Cap'n but the general feeling about sailing into Charles Town without knowing whether they know what we have done, could be very dangerous. The crew now stands to lose a lot if we go sailing into a trap," Berkshire stated.

Roth thought about this and it was true, they were all very rich men and woman now and to take a chance like that would be very unwise. "I think that I have a solution to that. When we get near, I will ask William here if it would be possible for him and Kathryn to make their way to Charles Town and find out if it will be safe for us dock there and unload what cargo we have. How about it William? Do you think that it is possible?" he asked.

"More than possible sir, that is what I was going to ask you later tonight. I thought about it several days ago but have not had the chance to say anything or talk to you about it. But yes sir, we can do it," William eagerly answered.

"Good. We still have a few more days before we get close to land, which will give us enough time to talk about it and make a plan, it will also give you a chance to discuss it with Kathryn," Roth said.

Chapter 18
"America"

The morning finally came when the lookouts above called out, "Land Ho!" Roth had been on the wheel deck since the sun rose watching to the west. He could make out the faint outline of land with his scope and knew that they were finally reaching the end of the voyage. Roth was nostalgic in his thoughts because he knew that this was to be the end of his life at sea and he was still not sure how he felt about that. It had been the only life that he had ever known, but he also knew what it had cost him. His new life was going to be very easy now that he was in possession of his share of the pirate's gold, but he wondered, would that be enough to make up for the life he had known being at sea in command of his own ship. It was going to be different to be sure. He would have to learn all the things that a person, land bound, would have to know and he was not young anymore.

He was deep into these thoughts when William came up to him and asked, "What do you think about Kathryn and me going into the harbor when we lay up for the night."

"I was thinking along those same lines. If we could find out if it will be safe for us and the ship, we can sail into port first thing in the morning," Roth said.

The day went by quickly and it was beginning to get dark. They were near enough to land now that with the scope, Roth could make out trees on the shoreline. He called out for Berkshire to join him. "Edward, we will lay up here for the night. I am going to send Kathryn and William into port to see what is going on and to find out if it is safe for us to enter the harbor," he said. He saw that William was making his way to the wheel deck and moved to meet him by the ladder. "William, maybe you had better call Kathryn and get on your way," he said to him.

"Way ahead of you Captain. I have already called her and she is waiting for me off the port side," he answered.

"All right then. You be careful and get back here as soon as you can. I would like to get in and out of that port as fast as we can. When you get back, I will have another job for you two," he said.

Roth watched as William made his way to the port side and climbed over the rail. He heard the splash as he dove in but it was too dark for him to see them swim away. He was worried but, in his heart, he knew that they would be safe.

The night passed slowly for Roth, there was not a lot that had to be done when the ship was lying over for the night. Edward had come to talk to him a couple of times but he saw that Roth was not very talkative so Berkshire left him alone throughout the night with his thoughts.

It would be dawn soon and Roth started to wonder where Kathryn and William were. It should not have taken that long for them to find out what he needed to know and the worry was starting to creep into his thoughts. It was beginning to get light and he was very relieved when he saw William climbing over the rail. Roth met him on the main deck and asked, "Well?"

"It was quiet in the port. There were only a couple of ships there and those were anchored out in the river. I got the impression from conversation I overheard at the only tavern in town that no ships had come into port for quite a while and there was no indication that a British ship has been in port for many months. I believe that it would be safe for you to sail into the harbor and get the cargo unloaded," he reported.

Roth called for Berkshire to join him and when he arrived, he gave the orders to get under way. Berkshire acknowledged him with a quick salute and moved away to give sailing orders.

Roth turned back to William and said, "Now I want you to go with Kathryn and explore the regions to the south. After we get through in Charles Town, then we are going to need a place to hide the *Galaunt* and I am goin' to need a place where I can settle down near there. I do not want to be too far away from her. The place that you are lookin' for must be near the sea because I must be able to visit with my daughter also. Do you understand what I am asking you?" he asked.

"Yes, sir I do. I know exactly what you are asking because it will be the place that I settle down also," he replied.

"All right then, be off and be careful," he said as William vaulted over the rail. He then returned to the wheel deck and observed as the crew raised the anchor and got the *Galaunt* underway.

The sun was just peeking over the horizon as the *Galaunt* made its way past a small island, to the north that sat in the middle of the harbor entrance. Roth had been here before, a long time ago, and knew that this was really the mouth of two great rivers that converged at this spot. The settlement was built on the tip of the peninsula that divided the two rivers and the port was located further up the river to the north and not far from the settlement. As they neared the port, Roth could see that William had been right, there were only two ships within sight and they were both moored out in the river away from the small dock that served the port. Roth had the helmsman sail to the north of the moored ships and come around so they would be pointed out to sea with the dock on the starboard side. He did not want to have to take the time to turn the ship in case something happened and they had to leave in a hurry. As the *Galaunt* passed the ships, Roth noticed that they seemed empty and unattended, something unusual due to the current of the river. If one broke loose, there would be nothing to stop it from either crashing into the other or being swept out to sea.

As they neared the dock, Roth saw several men run out to give assistance in tying up his vessel. This was a good indication that the port was eager to have a ship arrive. It would mean that they would be eager to trade and the ship would be off loaded in a short amount of time.

The *Galaunt* was neatly tied alongside the dock and the gangplank was just being lowered when two men on horseback rode up. They dismounted near the end of the gangplank and yelled up to the ship asking for permission to board. Roth, who was standing at the top of the gangplank, called back to come aboard. He had to think fast because he did not want anyone to know who he was or what the name of the ship was. He did not want the British to trace him here. He had made up his mind that this was where he was going to spend the last of his days and he wanted those days to be peaceful.

Roth saw that these men were not dressed in fancy clothes, but rather, dressed in functional clothes for the day. They looked like working men to him. As they neared him, the taller of the two extended his hand to Roth and said, "Welcome to Charles Towne Landing. I am the Harbor Master, John Wilson and this is Craig Thompson, the owner of the port and administer of the community and the surrounding areas."

Roth took his hand and shook it. "I am Daniel Horn, Captain of the Hampshire," he said as he waved his hand indicating the ship. Then turning to Berkshire he continued, "This is my First Mate, Michael Reed, it is our pleasure to make your acquaintance," he said as he shook the other man's hand.

John looked at him in a strange way before saying, "We have not had many ships come our way lately and hope that you are here to sell cargo that we can use. We can use just about any cargo around here so I am sure that we can make you a fine offer."

Roth replied, "We have just made our way up from Australia and have teak and mahogany lumber and leather in our holds. I hope that you can use it."

Thompson rubbed his chin and thought for just a moment before he said, "Ah yes, there is Ross Kragness, he has land up river a ways and he has a good start on a shipyard. I will contact him and I would be willing to bet that he will buy all your lumber. We do not have teak or mahogany here. The leather I will buy from you now. We can use that here and it is in short supply."

Roth suddenly had a thought and he said, "The lumber I can speak for but the leather, I am afraid, belongs to a passenger aboard the *Hampshire*. He is a cobbler, so you would have to speak with him,"

"A cobbler you say?" Craig said with a fair amount of excitement. "We could definitely use a cobbler."

"You may be in luck. I do believe that he has plans to maybe settle here. I know that he does not want to continue on with us," Roth replied. "Mister Thompson and Mister Wilson, if you would be so kind as to follow Mister Reed, he will show you to my cabin where we can discuss berthin' and off loadin'," he added.

He watched as Berkshire led the two men to his cabin and then made his way below decks to find the cobbler. He had a pretty good idea where he would be found and it turned out that he was right, he was in the galley talking to his wife, Ruth.

They talked for a few moments and Roth told him of his plan and made sure that he understood that he was now the owner of the leather and what was to be done with it. He also made him aware of the name changes. They then made their way to Roth's cabin. Once inside Roth said, "Mister Thompson, this is John Stark, the cobbler I was tellin' you about."

Thompson said as he was offering his hand, "Please call me Craig, and it is my pleasure to meet you. We sure could use a man with your skills in our community if you were willing to settle here. We are in need of footwear and a good saddler will find that he will get all the work that he would ever need."

John replied, "That is good news indeed, my wife and I were worried that we may not find a place that we could use our skills."

"Well, you have found that place if you so desire," Craig stated with a smile.

"Do you by chance have a place where I can store my leather until I can secure a place of my own where I can set up shop?" John asked.

"That warehouse directly across from the ship is empty and you can have what space you need for as long as you need it, free of charge. It will be good to have you amongst us," Wilson answered.

"Now that we have that taken care of, maybe we can get down to the cost of berthin' to your dock and what will it take to hire a crew to help with the off loadin'," Roth said.

Craig replied, "Same goes for you sir, the berthing is no charge and the crew will be paid for by me. I will recoup the cost through the sale of the lumber if you would allow me to be your broker."

"By all means, I would appreciate that. Now if our business is concluded here, there are several things that require my attention," Roth said as he stood and offered his hand.

Taking the offered hand, Craig said, "I will go and see about rounding up a crew for you and have them ready to go by morning."

Roth escorted them to the gangplank and saw them off. He then turned to Berkshire and told him to get the men together and have them store their riches amongst the leathers so that they could safely get them off the ship and tucked away in the warehouse until they could secure passage back home.

As Roth lounged around the wheel deck watching his crew prepare for unloading the next morning, he found that his attention was being drawn to the empty ships out on the river. He wondered what the story was about them. They appeared to be in reasonably good shape and he could not see any reason why they would be abandoned like they were. He decided that he should ask about them the first chance that he got. He was also concerned about William and Kathryn. He hoped that they would be able to find a resting place for the *Galaunt* where it would be safe and undiscovered by the British.

The next morning Roth was glad to see that Craig Thompson was a man of his word. There were men and wagons lined up on the dock and other men were already on board helping to make ready the rigging that would be needed to raise the cargo from the holds and lower it to the wagons that would haul it the short distance to the storage warehouse. He also saw that it was only his men that were moving the leather. This he was glad to see because he knew that the leather weighed more, much more, than it should and that would surely arouse suspicion. He glanced back out to the ships and he knew he needed some answers and now was as good as any other to find out the answers. He walked down the gangplank in search of the foreman of the crew. When he found him, he asked him if he knew anything about those ships out in the river. He was surprised at what he heard and he was finally able to put the final changes on the plan that was formulating in his head. Now the only thing that was missing was word from William and Kathryn.

Roth went back to the ship and was looking for Berkshire when he noticed Craig Thompson walking his way. "I have been in contact with the ship builder. He is willing to take the lumber but cannot afford to pay for it all at once. So, it is my idea that I take it off your hands and he can purchase it from me as he needs it and can afford it. He is just starting out and his funds are limited," he said.

"That sounds fine to me. Make an offer and we will go from there," Roth said.

They haggled over the price for a while until both sides were happy with the outcome. Little did Thompson know but Roth did not care about the sale because it meant little or nothing to him. For all he cared, he would have given the lumber away. He just did it for sake of appearances.

Later that evening he found Berkshire and together they made their way to his cabin and Brian brought some wine. Roth told him of his plan.

Berkshire listened intently until his captain finished outlining his thoughts. "That sounds to me like somethin' that could work. We would be outta here before anybody could put all the pieces together and know that we are not who we say we are," Berkshire stated. "It is all right here. We just need to hide the ship and all the other pieces will fall into place. Most of the crew wants to return to England anyway and this is a perfect way for that to happen."

Roth added, "Yes, but for it to happen, William and Kathryn have to find a place to hide the *Galaunt* or else we are going to have to scuttle her."

"Let us just hope that they will find a place because I do not want to see her go down like that either," Berkshire replied.

"How is the off loadin' goin'?" Roth asked.

Berkshire said, "It is goin' rather well. The leather is bein' handled by our men and taken right into the warehouse, so I do not think that anyone has noticed the extra weight. I do think that some of the hired crew is beginning to think that we are a little lazy and wastin' time by just takin' a small portion off the ship with each load. But there is nothing we can do about that because the riggin' can only hold so much weight and that leather is very heavy. Anyway, we should have it all off and safely stored away sometime tomorrow, and then we will help with the lumber."

Roth said, "Good, I do not want to stay in port with the *Galaunt* any longer than is required. It would not do us any good to have a ship of the British Navy come sailin' in here and recognize us."

The next day Roth could see that Berkshire had talked to the men and informed them of his plan. He could tell that by the extra energy that the men were putting into their work, they were in a hurry to finish. It was still before noontime that the last of the leather was off the ship and safely tucked away in the warehouse. It was good to see both crews now working to get the lumber unloaded. Roth thought that it might be possible to finish by nightfall and then they would be able to sail on the morning tide. Roth was getting nervous, they were too close to the end and he had a feeling that there was going to be trouble before they could get out of here.

He was still feeling nervous when Berkshire and Craig Thompson came up to him. It was Berkshire that spoke first. "Cap'n, we have the cargo unloaded and secured in the warehouse."

"Thank you, Mister Reed. Tell the men good job and let them spend the night in town but inform them that we are sailin' with the tide on the morrow so they have to be back on board and rested before daylight," Roth said to Berkshire.

"Aye, aye Cap'n and I think that I will be joinin' them just to make sure that they do not get too carried away that they cannot perform their duties tomorrow," he said to Roth with a wink of his eye.

"Do you really have to leave so soon?" Craig asked.

"Yes, we do. The men are gettin' anxious to be on their way home. It has been quite a while since any of them have been home and they long to see their families. We are goin' to try to find a cargo to take with us so that is goin' to take some time," Roth said to Thompson.

"I am sorry that we do not have anything that we can spare for a cargo, but we are growing and maybe next time you come to our port we will have something to trade," Craig said.

"Think nothin' of it and rest assured that if we return to this country, this is the port that we will seek out," Roth said.

"Good, then if I do not see you off in the morning, I bid you a safe journey," he said.

"Thank you and I hope that we can do business again," Roth said as he offered Thompson his hand.

Roth was alone on board the *Galaunt* and wandering around the main deck when he heard a noise behind him. Turning, he saw William climb over the port rail. Roth watched as the young man approached him. "We found the ideal spot sir. There is another river a few miles south of here and where it meets the ocean, it is lined with islands on both sides. On one of the larger islands there is an inlet to a cove. The inlet is wide enough for the *Galaunt* and about a quarter of a mile up this inlet, it opens up to a small cove. The cove is not big enough to turn a ship this size but it is big enough to safely hold her. It is quite deep and is lined with very tall pines. The island is nice also. It is bordered on the south by the river and on the west side there is a wide deep inland waterway that we followed all the way back here. It would be a very nice place to settle down. Kathryn had no difficulties because the water is very brackish around the island. The river has a slow current and that allows the sea water to back quite a way upriver," he said excitedly.

"That sounds very good indeed. I was beginnin' to think that I was goin' to have to scuttle her after all. You can lead us there when we sail in the morning. The crew is off in town, so you might as well get some rest, we sail at first light," Roth said.

The next morning when Roth walked from his cabin to the main deck, he was surprised see that he was the last man up. Berkshire had obviously aroused the men early and had gotten the ship ready for sailing. When Berkshire saw Roth, he said, "The ship is ready to set sail Cap'n, awaitin' your orders."

"Very well Mister Berkshire, let us lower some canvas and get us away from the dock," he ordered.

"Aye, aye Cap'n," his first mate said and then proceeded to give the instructions to the crew.

Roth made his way to the wheel deck. He found that William was already there and was conversing with the helmsman. Roth walked over to the wheel and asked William, "Have you given directions to Scotty?"

"Yes sir, I have. When we reach open water, we just need to sail southerly along the coast until we reach the other river. Then all there is left to do is sail up the river until we find the inlet to the cove. We should be there in a few hours. It will probably take most of the rest of the day to get the *Galaunt* into the cove but I do not see any major difficulties," he said.

"Have you also gone over this with Mister Berkshire?" Roth asked.

"Yes sir. I was still awake when he came back aboard last night and we discussed what was going to be needed to get the ship aligned and into the cove," he answered.

"Aligned?" Roth asked.

"The yards are too wide to fit through the opening of the inlet. They are going to have to be turned so that they are almost in line with the ship, or as near as we can get them, in order for the ship to be towed through the inlet to the cove. The tide should be coming back in at that time and the current is not that strong, so I think that we will be able to get the ship started in the right direction and the rest will be easy," he explained.

Roth thought to himself that it might not be as easy as William thinks to get a ship this size backed into a narrow inlet. It would take the entire crew most of the afternoon to accomplish the task, but if they were lucky the tide might be flowing into the inlet and that would help considerably.

Roth left the wheel deck and found Berkshire. He asked his first mate, "What do you think about this plan of William's."

"Cap'n, I am not sure. I had a long talk with him last night and he described everythin' to me, including the inlet and how we will have to move the ship. He makes it all sound pretty simple, but I am goin' to have to see the site myself afore I make any decisions on how easy it will all be," he answered with a slight chuckle.

"That is my thinkin' also, but I hope he is right. I would hate to have her beach her right out there in plain sight," he said as he turned away and started to walk around the ship. This would be the last time that he was going to sail on her and he was feeling a little sad.

The *Galaunt* made good time and they reached the river well before noon and turned into it. Roth was looking the shores over and saw that they were all lined with very tall pines that soared to a height much higher than the masts of the *Galaunt*. He could see, right away, that if the ship was behind those, it would be well hidden.

Roth's thoughts were interrupted when he heard William call out to him. He saw that William had moved his position to the bow. Joining him there he saw him pointing. "That is the island sir. It will not be long before we come to the site of the inlet. May I make a suggestion sir?" William asked.

"What do you have to say young man?" Roth asked.

"If we sail close to shore, as close as we safely can, just past the inlet, we can drop anchor and prepare the ship. I think that it will be much easier if we are upriver from the opening, then we can let the river itself, help us. The tide is in so we will be able to get closer to shore, but we have to be careful that we do not get too close. The bottom is very muddy and gets very shallow during low tide. The channel through the inlet is plenty deep enough so we do not have to worry about that, but we need to get the ship aligned with the channel," he said.

"Where is this inlet?" Roth asked.

"We should be coming up on it in another half mile or so," he replied.

"Mister Berkshire, after we pass the inlet, move the ship to the center of the channel. Make sure we have at least thirty feet of clear water below the keel and drop anchor," he said. Turning to William he added, "We do have the tide right now, but that will not last long before it starts goin' out. I am thinkin' that it will be best to wait until mornin' when the tide will be comin' in and with the current of the river, it should hold us steady enough. Also, it will give us a chance to look the site over a little and make sure that everythin' you have suggested will work."

It was not long before they were anchored in the middle of the river. Roth ordered a longboat into the water. Roth, Berkshire, William and six strong crewmen climbed into it and started to row towards the inlet. Roth noticed, as they neared the sight, the water was getting shallower along the shores of the island. They found the inlet and the channel leading through it. Roth asked Berkshire to take a sounding because he could not see the bottom. The water was about twenty-five feet in depth at this point and he thought that in the morning, with the tide coming in, it will be deeper. He ordered the boat into the channel and they started to make their way into the inlet. Berkshire continued to take soundings and relay the depth to Roth. He could see why William thought the yards should be as close to in line with the ship. The trees were very close to each other on either side and it would be a tight fit to squeeze the *Galaunt* through, but the more he looked the more confident he became that it could be done. The opening was slightly over thirty yards wide and the longboat was hugging the eastern bank where Berkshire was taking a constant reading of the depth. They found that at ten feet off the bank the water became much deeper with clearly enough depth to bring the *Galaunt* through, but they would have to take it slow and easy and make sure that they kept the ship in the center of the channel. Suddenly the inlet opened up to marsh grass and became much wider. The waterway was pretty straight for about a quarter of a mile and indeed, it ended at the cove that William said it would. The cove was not that large, as William had told them. Roth estimated that it was maybe two hundred feet long and one hundred feet wide. They rowed around the edge to make sure that the ship would be able to rest in deeper water. Roth was pleased with what he was seeing and ordered the boat back to the ship.

Once back on board the *Galaunt*, Roth asked Berkshire what he thought. Berkshire said, "It is going to be a tight fit for the first one hundred yards or so, but I think that we can do it safely. You were right about the tide, it will be much easier in the mornin' and we will not have to worry as much about gettin' stuck in the mud. If we stick her in the mud during high tide, we might just as well leave her because we will not get her off."

"Ok then, it is settled. Tomorrow mornin', we will take her in. Prepare the ship as much as you can tonight," he said.

"Aye, aye Cap'n," he said as he moved off to inform the crew of the decision.

The next morning, Roth and the crew rose early and began the arduous task of moving the *Galaunt* into the inlet. The first thing they did was bring the ship close to shore with the stern even with the inlet. They dropped anchor and secured all but one sail and then moved the yards into line with the ship.

They spent the rest of the morning and some of the afternoon slowly guiding the ship into the inlet and finally into the cove. It turned out to be not as hard as Roth had imagined. With the current from the rising tide and the wind blowing in from the ocean, the *Galaunt* seemed to want to go where they were taking her and everything went quite smoothly.

After they had her securely moored in the center of the cove and knew that she would be safe there, they all relaxed for a while before starting on the next part of the plan.

William had told Roth that the current in the inland waterway was flowing towards the harbor at Charles Towne, so he knew that this would be the easy part.

After the crew was rested, Roth gave the order to man the longboats. I was going to be a little crowded in the boats with eleven in one and ten in the other. With that many able seamen, everyone would be able to spell each other off so that no one had to row the entire distance. Roth was the only one that that did not row and that was only because the men in his boat would not allow him too.

With Kathryn leading the way, they rowed through the night and by morning they reached the river to the south of Charles Towne. William moved from Kathryn's back to one of the longboats. By noon they were nearing the dock. They must have been sighted because there seemed to be very many people lining the dock.

One of the crewmen, in each boat, threw a rope towards the dock and there it was caught by someone and the longboats were pulled up to the dock where they were securely tied. Many willing hands were offered to help the men aboard the boats climb up to the safety of the dock. As Roth was helped up, he saw that he was being approached by Mister Thompson who was already asking, "What happened? Where is your ship?"

Roth took a moment to gather his thoughts before he said, "We were attacked by pirates yesterday a few miles south of here and the ship was shot out from under us. It did not take long before she was gone and we were lucky that no one was hurt."

"Pirates you say. They have been a plague on us for quite some time. I think that is one of the reasons why there is not more shipping coming our way. Let us get you and your men into town and settled down so they can get some food into them and maybe some rest. If you would be so kind as to accompany me to my home, we will get you taken care of," Thompson said.

Roth and his crew went with Thompson and the rest of the people from the town to the buggies and wagons that had brought them to the harbor. It was a short ride and as they neared the community people started to move off in different directions to their homes where they could tend to their newly adopted crewmen.

The house that Roth, owned by Thompson, was taken too was one of a few houses that fronted a large park like area that comprised the tip of the peninsula. All the houses were similar in the fact that they were not very wide but tall, most had three stories. The houses were painted in a beautiful array of various colors, giving a personality to each. They all had a very good view of the rivers on both sides and the entrance to the ocean. When Roth was taken inside, he was surprised at the size.

From outside, it looked like the house was quite small and narrow, but on the inside, it was very large. It was long and very roomy. Roth was shown to an upstairs room and told that dinner would be along shortly. Roth took the opportunity to catch up on some rest.

Later that evening, after he had been fed, he and Thompson were sitting in a large and well appointed den, smoking cigars. It was Thompson that spoke first, "What are you going to do now that you have lost your ship?"

Roth thought for a moment before he spoke. "Well, I have not really had a lot of time to think about that. I guess the first thing that I have to consider is my men. They were looking forward to the voyage home. They have been gone from home for quite some time and are starting to miss their families. As for myself, I am not sure that I want to go back to England. On our way here, after the attack, I was looking over the land south of here and saw that there are many places that would be good to settle down on," Roth said.

"Oh yes, there is a lot of land south of here that would make very good places to start a plantation if you had the money to do so. I am, among other things, the governor of the Carolinas and it is one of my duties to sell land and grant patents. There is no end to the opportunities available here depending on how much time and money you have. As far as your men are concerned, I think that I have an answer to that also. We have two ships out in the harbor that were sailed here with colonists. My problem is we need to get them back to England so that they can be used again to bring more colonists here. I am sure that we can come to some sort of agreement to get you a ship if you think that there is someone that could captain it if you decide to stay," he said.

This was just what Roth was hoping he would say. "My first mate is more than qualified to captain a vessel. In fact, he was the captain of the Hampshire for several years while I was away on another mission. I just recently retook command of her before we made the voyage to Australia," he replied.

"Ah, that is good. Maybe he would be interested in sailing one of our ships back to England for us. He would be paid handsomely of course," Thompson said.

Roth replied, "I am not sure that you would have to pay him. He has family back in England and as I said before, wants to see them."

"Well then, I will approach him in the morning and make him an offer and see what he has to say. It is getting late and we have a lot to do tomorrow so I suggest that we get some sleep and get an early start in the morning," Craig said.

True to his word, Thompson was up early in the morning and after breakfast, he summoned his carriage. He and Roth made a short stop at another house and picked up Berkshire and the three of them made their way to the small harbor. Once there, he ordered two of his men to make a skiff ready and row them out to the nearest of the two ships moored in the river's mouth.

The ship was in surprisingly good shape and after a short inspection, Berkshire decided that it would make the sail back to England without any problems but said nothin until he had a chance to hear the terms of the deal.

"Well Mister Reed, what do you think?" Thompson asked after Roth and Berkshire rejoined him on the main deck.

Berkshire paused and looked over the rigging once again before answering, "She is a fine ship and it looks like she was well taken care of on her voyage from England."

"This is actually her second voyage. I was on her maiden voyage two years ago. Her name is Carolina I, that is her sister ship over there, the Carolina II. They were commissioned to be built by Lord Ashley Cooper for the sole purpose of transporting colonists from England to settle here in Charles Towne Landing. But unfortunately, the sailors from the last voyage decided, or most of them that they would rather settle here than sail back to their home country. So, as you can see we have somewhat of a dilemma here. I need to get both ships back to England as there are others that would like to make the voyage and settle here," Thompson said. "How many men do you think it would take to man each vessel for the voyage home?" he asked.

Berkshire thought for a few moments and then said, "I would reckon about eighteen per ship would make a reasonable crew, but twenty would be a lot better."

"How many of your men do you think would want to sail back with you?" Thompson asked.

Berkshire began to count off each man in his mind and finally he said, "I would be a thinkin that only fifteen or sixteen at the most."

"Is there someone amongst that group that could take over command of the other ship?" Thompson asked.

"Aye, there is a couple for sure," Berkshire replied.

Thompson pondered his next question and finally asked, "Would you be willing to split your crew between the two ships?"

"That would not be much of a problem, they are all experienced and know what has to be done," Berkshire answered back.

"Good, then I think that I can find another twenty or so men that would make up the rest of the crew," Thompson stated and then added, "However most of them would be between the ages of sixteen and twenty and probably not any sailing knowledge. Would that be satisfactory?"

"Aye," Berkshire responded.

"Then what say we head back to my house and we can discuss the details," Thompson suggested.

The discussion went on late in the night. They had picked up Roth's Second Mate, who would be commanding the Carolina II and between the four of them they ironed out most of the plan to take the ships back to England.

The next morning, Berkshire gathered all the men, seventeen in all, that would be taking part in the voyage and they rowed out into the river and brought the Carolina I up next to the dock. They immediately started the work that was needed to bring the ship up to standard for the voyage.

It was later in the day when Thompson and Captain Roth arrived with another ten men and introduced them to Berkshire. Berkshire first noticed the age of most of the men and realized that the majority of them were mere boys, maybe fourteen to sixteen at the most. He and Roth had both went to sea at about their age, but that was with a full crew of experienced crewmen. He knew it would be a difficult task before him but he was also sure that it could be done. Berkshire had already divided his old crew into two groups and new positions for both crews had already been assigned. Berkshire called his new First Mate to his side and told him to give them assignments.

Berkshire then turned his attention to Thompson and said, "We will need at least another ten if we are to properly crew both vessels."

"I have another twelve men lined up to start in the next two to three days, but they are older and have some other things to take care of before they can join your crew," Thompson stated.

"Just out of curiosity," Berkshire said. Then he asked, "Are any of them capable cooks?"

"I could not say for sure about cooks, but a couple of them have wives that I am sure would be willing to take on the task," Thompson replied.

"I am not sure if I want to have women on board. They are bad luck on a sailing ship making a long sea voyage if you get my meaning," Berkshire told him.

"Yes, I do get your meaning and you can rest assured that nothing will happen. Both the women I have in mind are advanced in age and can handle themselves well. Also, remember that their husbands, experienced sailors, will be along with them. Besides most of the men that I will bring you are friends of theirs and have known them for a long time and will also help to keep them safe," Thompson said with a chuckle.

Berkshire was still not happy about having a woman on board his ship but finally he said, "I guess you are right. If they can cook then they are welcome. That also frees up a couple of men to help the crew."

Over the course of the next few days, more and more crew members arrived and before long, Berkshire decided it was time to bring the Carolina II in from the river and start preparing her for the voyage ahead. With enough men to man both vessels, the work proceeded at a very fast pace. Arrangements had been made to load both ships with supplies that were required for the voyage and what little cargo could be scourged up. This consisted mostly of raw cotton, for there were no mills available, and furs that were to be taken back to England.

While the ships were being readied, Roth, having not much to do, decided, that he would pay a visit to the ship builder. He hired a horse and rode up river to where the ship builder had set up his operation. It did not take long for him to find the owner of the place and introduced himself as Captain Daniel Horn. The owner took his hand and said that his name was Ross Kragness and that he and his brother, Ken, were the co owners of the yard and that he was glad to make his acquaintance.

"Mister Kragness," Roth said and went on, "I would like to know if you could possibly build me a small sailboat that could be handled by one person while at the same time be large enough to handle a small amount of cargo if the need arises?"

"I could and I will. Thanks to you, I have enough lumber to build several small boats. But first, Captain Roth, I must tell you that we are in desperate need of sail cloth. I cannot put anything in the water until we acquire some and it might be a while until a ship comes in that has some they would like to sell," Mister Kragness said.

Roth was taken aback when he heard the man call him by his real name. "How is it that you know who I am? I know you were not here when I was here last, many years ago," Roth stated.

"No need to be worried captain, there are several here that know who you really are and none of them, I can assure you, would say anything until they know why you are hiding under an assumed name," he said. He then added, "The reason that I know who you are is because I was the principal designer of the *Galaunt* and any designer worth his salt would recognize their most prized creation when they saw it. My brother, Ken, was my assistant and many of my employees were part of the yard crew that built the ship. We were on the dock when you sailed in and heard you introducing yourself as Captain Horn and gave the *Galaunt* another name also. We decided that we would wait until we had a chance to talk to you before we said anything. Mister Wilson, the Harbor Master also knows who you are. He was a dock hand when you first took command of the *Galaunt*. We have talked often about you and the ship. The last that we knew was that you had taken to piracy and were captured off the coast of Ireland and the *Galaunt* wrecked on a beach. I knew that you were convicted and sent to the penal colony in Australia, but you never made it there and were presumed dead or drowned at sea. Would you be willing to tell me why you have a new name and the *Galaunt* shows up here?"

"It is really not much of a story," Roth said.

Worth said, "I am sure that it is a great story and I for one would very much like to hear it."

"Alright, but can we do our talking while we look over the design for the sailboat and discuss costs and sailcloth?" Roth asked.

"Yes sir. Let us go to the office," Ross replied.

Roth followed him to a small wooden building that he surmised was being used as the office. Once inside, Ross went to a shelf and pulled down a roll of drawings. Tom unrolled them on a table and began to tell Roth about the design that the drawings showed. They discussed them for a while with Roth making suggestions for slight changes here and there. Ross could not see any reason why those changes could not be made, in fact they could both see as to where they were actually improvements on the original design. After the discussion was over and Ross had made the changes to the drawings, he rolled them back up and replaced them on the shelf, and then he offered Roth a glass of wine. He led Roth to a small but comfortably furnished room where Roth was offered a seat and a glass of wine. "Now how about that story?" he asked.

Roth told him the entire story beginning with the voyage to Australia and ending when they sailed into the harbor. The only details he left out were those concerning Kathryn and the encounter with the pirates. "There you have it. As I said it is not very interesting," he said as he finished the tale.

Ross sat back in his chair and with a smile he said, "On the contrary, I found it to be quite interesting, especially the part about your stay on the island. I don't think that I could have survived that and the escape from the Royal Navy. I only wish that I could have been part of that. They think that they alone own the open seas. It is good to hear about them being bested like that and especially by a ship that I designed. It is too bad that she had to be destroyed by pirates." He paused here for a few moments and then said, "Earlier I believe that you said something about sailcloth. What did you have in mind?" he asked.

Roth said, "William and I have been thinking about returning to the sight and seein' if anything from the wreck may be washed ashore and salvage what we could. Never know what may be there. I remember seein' a couple of the masts, which were blown free, floating near us when we made our escape. Might be that they washed up somewhere and still have usable sail attached."

"That would be great if you could find them. It would, of course, be heavy sailcloth, much heavier than would be required for the boat we have in mind for you, but would still do the job," Ross said. "I might even be able to help you out. I have a small boat that you could use in your search. It is not made for ocean travel but would be ideal for use in the waterways and close to shore around the islands," he added.

"That will be just fine. A ship was all that was keeping us from going," Roth said even as he was thinking about the sailcloth stored in the locker next to the cargo holds of the *Galaunt*.

"Then it is settled," Ross said. "You just let us know when you need the boat and it will be made available."

They drank another glass of wine and talked about general things for a while longer and Roth finally left and rode back to town.

The next morning, he found William and told him of his plan. William readily agreed.

A few days later the ships were finally loaded and ready for departure. It was decided that they would set sail on the morning tide. The next morning Roth met with Berkshire and wished him a safe voyage. They shook hands knowing that this was the last time they would probably ever see each other. With neither saying what both knew, Berkshire finally turned away and climbed the gangplank of the Carolina I and started to give the orders to make way. The gangplank was hauled aboard and the lines were released from the dock. Roth watched as the ship slowly moved away from the dock. Berkshire was standing at the stern of the ship watching that everything was going correctly when he turned and faced Roth. He stood at attention and gave Roth one last crisp salute. Roth came to attention also and returned the salute as crisply as it was given. Both men held this position until the ship, with the Carolina II close behind, were well out into the river making way to the ocean and Roth saw Berkshire return his attention back to the ship under his command.

Roth remained where he was until the ships disappeared over the horizon and with a tear in his eye, quietly said, "Goodbye old friend."

Chapter 19
"Revelation"

The next morning, Roth found William and they both made their way to the shipyard. They found the Mister Kragness in the office and inquired into the use of the boat offered yesterday.

"I had a feeling that I would see you today after the ships sailed for England yesterday," Ross said.

Roth said, "Yes, I want to get to the wreck site as soon as possible to make sure that no one else beat us to the salvage. I also want to explore the islands in that area to see if there might be a place to settle. I am looking for a place that is out of the way where I can spend the rest of my days in relative seclusion."

"I don't know why you would want to live way out there, that far from town, but I guess you have your reasons. Anyway, the boat is ready and I have had it stocked with at least three days' worth of provisions. That should give you plenty of time to look around all you want," Ross replied.

"I do appreciate that. I was prepared to sail back to town and buy what we would need. How much do I owe you for the supplies?" Roth asked.

Ross did not hesitate in his reply, "You owe me nothing, if you can find some sail cloth and sell it to me for a fair price, then that will be payment enough. Now if you will follow me, I will take you out and show you the boat."

Both Roth and William followed him out of the office and across the yard where they entered a large warehouse. Upon entering Roth immediately knew that this was more than just a warehouse. There were several men working on various jobs and the entire back end was open to the air where there was a dock of sorts protected from the elements by a large overhang several feet above the water. There was a boat tied to this dock and Roth knew this must be the boat that they would be taking. It turned out that he was right. It was a fine looking craft and it was obvious that it was well constructed and well maintained. Ross and William, both, went over the boat with Ross showing where things were stored and other things that he thought they should know about the workings of the boat.

It was not long before they had the boat untied and were on their way out into the river. They found that the boat sailed rather well for a craft of its size and was very easy to handle, though it did take two men to operate the sails and navigate at the same time. It did not take them long to round the point of the peninsula and start their way across the river to the south, here they were joined by Kathryn who did not have any trouble keeping pace with the boat.

They made their way to the inland waterway and started down it going against the current. About noon, as far as Roth could reckon, they arrived at the opening of the inlet leading to the cove that held the *Galaunt*. Roth could not see the inlet and William explained to him that he and Kathryn had been back here several times hiding the opening. Roth thanked him and said that it was a very good job because if he had not known it was here, he would have sailed right by. Roth dropped the anchor and William began to lower the sails.

"Now watch this captain," William said.

Roth watched as William threw out a line to Kathryn and then raised the anchor. Kathryn began to tow the small boat into the inlet. William was at the tiller and kept the boat on a straight line. When they neared the tree line Roth was surprised to see Kathryn push what looked like a fallen tree aside revealing the way into the inlet. Once Kathryn had towed the boat past this obstruction, she swam back and pushed it back into place. Roth just shook his head thinking how industrious this pair had been while he was in town. Before he realized that they had even stopped, Kathryn was back to towing the boat through the trees until they reached the marshy area. Roth thought that it would not be that much trouble to just sail in from the river if he was careful because from there they were able to sail into the cove. He was glad to see the *Galaunt* and suddenly realized how much he missed her and the open sea. Kathryn pushed the smaller boat alongside the *Galaunt* and William tied it to the larger vessel.

Roth did not spend a lot of time looking around, he wanted to get the sail cloth loaded before nightfall. He and William made their way down to the locker where it was stowed and Roth selected the bundle of cloth nearest the hatchway. The bundle was about five feet by five feet and six feet in height and was very tightly compressed. They dragged it out to the middle of the cargo hold and then went back topside to prepare the rigging to lift it from the hold and lower it to the deck of the sailboat. This did not take nearly as much time as he had expected and before long, they had the bundle secured to the deck of the smaller boat. Roth looked at the bundle, saw that it was not more than the sailboat could handle and decided that it might be a good idea to bring along that large piece of cloth that was the remainder of a bundle that a sail had been made out of. Since the rigging was already in place this only took a few minutes.

It was still daylight and William suggested that they take a look around the island. Roth agreed and together they lowered the rowboat into the water and made their way to shore. Along the south side of the cove where the trees came right up to the water, the ground was firmer and they were able to row all the way to the shore.

William started running a monologue as soon as his feet touched the ground. He was telling Roth everything that they were going to see. It was obvious to him that William had been along this path before. He was amazed at how much detail William was able to remember. Everything he said was spot on and Roth felt like he had been here before.

As they walked through the trees, Roth looked at William's back. He thought that it had been a long time ago that Kathryn had rescued him and brought him to the island. William had just been eighteen at the time, so he had to be at least twenty eight now. He was no longer a boy but a mature man. Then the thought struck him, he must really be in love with Kathryn to still be here. How would they ever really have a relationship? They were so different, not in the way that they each thought, but in appearance and form. Would William wake up one morning and realize that he wanted more in life and he could not get that from Kathryn? He hoped not because Kathryn had already suffered enough. She seemed happy enough, but Roth knew that she missed her old life and longed for it to return.

Roth was deep into this thought and not paying attention to anything but William's back when he heard him say, "Here is the spot I was just telling you about."

Roth looked up at what William was showing him. He could not believe what he was seeing. They had climbed up a small rise and before him lay a big beautiful cove about two hundred yards away, it looked almost as if some giant animal had bitten the corner of the island off. There was a thin strip of marshland ringing it but for the most part, it looked like good firm land. There was another river on this side of the island that was much larger than the other side. He could see all the way to the ocean from where he stood. The view was spectacular to say the least. The clearing, with the rise in the center, was large and was lined with tall pines. Roth knew that this was the spot that he would build a house and spend the rest of the time that he had left in this life.

Roth heard splashing and looked out into the cove. He saw Kathryn and the ever present dolphins playing the game they liked so much, leaping into the air and splashing back down into the water. Out of the corner of his eye, he saw William race off towards the water and make a dive into the cove. He watched them play for a while and then started to make his way back to the boat. He was surprised at how far they had come through the trees. It had to have been at least a quarter of a mile. He reflected again on what he had been thinking about and became saddened with the thought. Oh well, he thought, there is nothing that he could do about it and only time would tell what was going to happen.

He found the rowboat without any trouble and rowed back to the *Galaunt*. He hauled the boat back on board and made his way to his cabin. Here he found a small satchel which he filled with gold and silver coins from the larger chest that he had hidden under his desk. He then carried the satchel out to the deck and climbed down to the small sailboat. He stowed the satchel away and seeing as it was starting to get a little darker, he started to prepare a meal in the small galley below deck. He was just finishing when he felt, rather than heard, William climb onto the deck. He stuck his head out and asked if he was hungry. William said that he was starved, so Roth told him to come and join him, the meal was just about ready. They talked a little while they were eating and Roth told him of his decision to build on the island and settling there. William told him that he knew that he would like it and he agreed with him on the decision.

After dinner was eaten and cleaned up, they both decided that it would probably be more comfortable to spend the night aboard the *Galaunt*. They both climbed back aboard the larger ship and then sat for a while discussing plans for building a house. Roth wanted to ask William what he thought about the future, but he decided that this was not the time that he wanted to broach the subject. After a while they both retired to their cabins where they sought much needed sleep because in the morning they would sail back to Charles Towne.

The sun had not risen yet, but it was light enough to see what they were doing when they departed the *Galaunt* the next morning. Roth decided that they would not sail directly to Charles Towne. He wanted to sail around the island and see the place that he wanted to build, from the water, so that is what they did. It did not take long to reach the cove cut into the island and Roth was happy to see that the water in the cove was very deep. He could anchor the *Galaunt* here if he so desired. They moved closer to the shore and could get to within a few yards of the thin strip of marshland before the water got to shallow for them to proceed any further. This was good because Roth had decided to build a small dock here in the cove. After a short sail around the cove to find the best spot for the dock, they left the island and sailed up the southerly river and started the journey back to Charles Towne.

They arrived back at the shipyard a little after noon and tied up to the dock inside the warehouse. Ross was in the warehouse when they sailed in so he helped them dock the small boat. It was Ross that spoke first, "I see that you were successful. That much sailcloth will go a long way." He jumped onto the sailboat and started to inspect the cloth. Almost immediately, Ross turned and looked at Roth very suspiciously. After a short inspection Ross, "Yes, this will be ideal. There is enough here to make several sails the size that we will need."

Roth instantly knew his mistake. This cloth was not water stained and it was obvious to anyone that knew anything about ships, that this cloth had never seen water, not even rain. There was nothing that he could do now so he just remained quiet and waited to see if Ross would say anything about it. He didn't and went on to say, "What would like for this?"

Roth thought for a moment and then asked, "How long do you think it will take you to build the boat that we discussed?"

"It will only take a few weeks, I think. We have already begun the construction," he said and pointed to the far end of the warehouse where several men were working. Ross called a few men over to the dock and asked them to offload the cloth and then climbed back on the dock. He then led Roth and William over to the area where the other men were working. "As you can see the keel is already laid and we are in the process of attaching the ribs," he said as he pointed to the ribs that were already attached. "This is our priority job. We do not have any other orders and we want to get this one finished so that others, that might like one of their own, will see it. I am sure that after it is finished, we will get more orders. It is a unique design and can be made very economically, so it will sell. Yours, of course, will have everything that could possibly be built on it, but it can be built with less."

"That is good news. Now as far as the price of the cloth is concerned, I will let you have it in exchange for the use of your sailboat until mine is completed. I explored the area around where we got the cloth and have decided that it is an ideal place for me to build a house and retire," he stated.

"That is very generous indeed, but you do not need to be that generous. The cloth is worth a great deal of money and, even without the cloth, you would be welcome to use our boat whenever you want," Ross stated.

"No, I insist that you take the cloth. I am not in need of money as I also found most of my belongin's in the same area as the cloth and with them were my savin's," Roth said and immediately knew he had made another mistake.

Ross, picking up on this, said, "I suppose that if you are thinking of settling there then there is no reason to haul your possession's back here."

Roth was grateful that Ross had not pressed the subject but he also knew now that Ross was sure that he was not telling him everything.

"In that case, would it be alright with you if we sailed the boat back to town? I want to get started on a dock on a cove near to where

I have decided to build my home, as soon as I can. I want it to be ready when I get my own boat and I want to start work on the house. I want a place of my own. The room that I am occupyin' is not very big and I need space to move around in," Roth stated.

"I can see no problem with that. I very seldom use the boat anyway with the town so close," Ross replied.

Roth said, "Then it is settled. The cloth is yours and I promise that I will treat your boat as if it were mine. Now I think that I had better get back to town and find Mister Thompson and make arrangements to purchase the land I have in mind."

"You will not have any trouble with getting the land. All land is free around here as long as you settle on it and build a house or business," Ross told him.

"That is more good news. I will check in with you from time to time to see how my boat is comin' and to see if you need yours. Thank you again for your generosity," Roth said as he shook his hand.

William and Roth made their way back to the sailboat and sailed it back to town. Once they had the boat safely tied to the small dock in town, Roth and William walked across the park to Thomson's house. Roth knocked on the door and it was quickly answered by Thomson. After the initial greetings were concluded, Roth said, "I just got back from the wreck site where we were able to salvage a few things. While I was there, I had a chance to look the islands over and wonder what it would take to get possession of one of them."

Thomson looked at him and said, "Land is free. The only thing that we require is that the land that is taken into private ownership is improved within the first year and not left to sit idle. Are you sure that you want to live way out there by yourself? That is a long way from town and I am sure you would not get many visitors."

"I would not be out there by myself, William here will be there also. I am a solitary man by nature and am used to being by myself for long periods of time," Roth said.

"Alright then, just meet me at my office in the morning and you can show me the island that you are talking about and we will fill out the required paperwork and the island will be yours. Do you mind my asking what improvements you are going to make?" Thompson inquired.

"I do not mind at all. First, I have made arrangements with the Kragness Brothers to build me a sailboat that I can handle alone. I want to build a dock to tie her up to. Next, I plan on building a house on a small rise overlookin' a cove and with a grand view of the ocean," Roth stated.

Thompson said, "That sounds fine." Thompson then added, "Is there any land on the island that you could grow crops?"

"There is some open area around where I plan on buildin' the house, but I will probably only use it to grow the things that I need," Roth answered.

"Well keep in mind that this community is in need of supplies and if you so desire and find arable land on surrounding islands, you could start a plantation and help to fill the needs of our growing community," Thompson informed him.

"I will definitely keep that in mind, but for now I will be content with what I have and maybe after I have built what I need, I will consider expanding my holdings," he replied.

"There is a great opportunity in this new land for people of means and vision. In the morning then," Thompson said as he led them to the door.

"In the mornin'," Roth said as they left the house.

Roth left his room early the next morning and made his way to town. As he was making his way to Thompson's office, he noticed a smell in the air, a smell of rotting fish. It was coming from down an alley and was vaguely familiar to him so he decided to check it out. The further into the alley he went, the stronger the smell. Suddenly it struck him where he had last smelled this strong odor and at the same time, he saw the old man sitting there surrounded by piles of garbage. It was definitely the same old man, there was no mistaking the rags that he wore and the eyes that peered out from behind all the hair covering his face were that unmistakable blue that was like the blue of the ocean at high noon of a clear day. And the smell, there was no forgetting that smell. Yes ,there was no doubt in Roth's mind.

"Ah, it is you again. I thought that our paths would cross again, but I am afraid that I have nothing more that might interest you," the old man said in his croaking voice. "However, it is possible that I could have some information that you could find interesting."

"What information would that be, old man?" Roth asked.

"Do I freely give information away for nothing?" the old man asked.

Roth thought about this for a minute before he replied, "I think that I would have to hear what you have to say before I would consider paying you anything."

"Then listen well for I will not repeat it," he said, and then continued. "The pendant that you bought from me all those years ago has more properties than you are undoubtedly unaware about."

"What other properties are you talking about? It has already done what you said it would do. Thanks to the pendant, my daughter is still alive," Roth said with a slight tone of remorse.

"You sound a little sad that it worked as I said it would," the old man remarked.

"Not sad that it worked, sad that my daughter has not been able to enjoy life as it was intended. She will never be able to experience the things that normal women her age have been able to enjoy," Roth replied.

"Then listen well for this is the part of my story that you will want to pay close attention to. The other properties that the pendant holds are the ability to reverse other actions," the old man stated.

This peaked Roth's attention and he had a hard time believing what he had heard. "Am I to believe that there is a chance that she might be able to return to a normal life?"

"That depends on what you would consider to be normal, but yes, if she desires then she can indeed return to her life as a land dweller," the old man commented.

Roth was definitely excited now when he asked, "What is it that she must do?"

"It is simple. All that needs to be done is for her to remove the pendant and drop it back into the sea," he returned. Then he added, "But it must be returned to the place of where it was used."

"That means sailing halfway around the world, but that is a small price to pay if she wants to be normal again. The decision will be hers however," Roth said.

"Well do you think the information is worth a small fee?" the old man inquired.

Without hesitation, Roth removed the satchel from his shoulder and handed it to the old man and said, "Indeed it does and I hope that this is enough to earn it."

The old man held up his hand and stopped Roth, then said, "From the looks of that, it is far more than my story is worth. A simple coin would be all the payment that I would require."

Roth looked at the old man for a moment and then reached inside the satchel and grabbed the first coin that he touched and handed it to the old man.

The old man took the coin and looking at it said, "You are very generous indeed. May you have a safe voyage and I hope you obtain what everyone concerned, desires."

Roth thanked him again and turned to walk out of the alley. He had not gone very far when he turned his gaze back and was surprised when he saw that the old man was no longer seated there amongst the garbage. He looked around but could not see him anywhere. He began to wonder if he had really seen him at all.

Thinking about what had just happened he made his way back to the street and once again started towards Thompson's office. Craig was there and had the maps of the areas to the south already spread out on the top of a layout table situated to the side of his office. Roth found the proper map and showed him the island that he wished to own. Thompson then sat behind his desk and started on the paperwork. While Craig was busy, Roth busied himself looking at the maps of the surrounding areas around his island. Right off he saw that directly across the southern river was a large island dividing two rivers. This was a very large island that probably comprised many square miles. Roth's mind went to work and he began to consider the possibilities of what could be if he were to own that island.

Roth's thoughts, on that matter, were interrupted when Thompson said, "Alright then, all that is needed now is your signature and my stamp and you will be the proud owner of your own land."

Roth walked over to Thompson's desk and he was shown where to sign the two documents on the desk in front of Thompson. Roth dipped the quill into the inkwell and commenced to write his name on the two documents. Thompson then took the documents and placed them, one at a time, on a piece of soft leather with one hand and with the other he slammed his heavy seal upon the paper embossing them. He then took one of the documents and placed it in a cabinet behind his desk and the other he rolled up and handed it to Roth saying, "Here is your copy of the patent granting you ownership. Do not lose it."

"You need not worry about that. Now if you would be so kind as to tell me where I can procure the material that I will need to get started on the improvements and the construction of my home," Roth said as he slipped the paper into his satchel.

"You will find a sawmill about five miles inland, that will furnish everything that you require. Just follow the westerly road out of town and it will lead you right to it," Thompson said. Roth thanked him, shook his hand and left the office.

Once outside he made his way to the stable where he was able to rent a horse and then upon finding the westerly road, he started out to find the sawmill.

He rode through the morning and eventually found what he was seeking. He knew that he was getting close by the smell. A sawmill has a very distinctive smell, a smell that is pleasant to the nostrils. The smell of freshly sawn wood was something that Roth had always appreciated.

He rode into the yard and asked the first man that he saw where he would be able to find the owner. The man pointed toward the mill, itself, and said that in the rear, he would find the office. The owner should be there. Roth thanked the man and continued his way to the mill. It was a large two story building that was situated next to a quick flowing stream. It was the stream that supplied the power to run the saws. Roth rode around the building and saw that there was a smaller one story building attached to the side of the mill. He rode to the front of this building and secured his horse and stepped inside. The smell of sawn wood was much stronger here and there was dust in the air. Roth stifled a sneeze.

"May I help you?" a man on his right said.

"Yes, I am looking for the owner. I would like to purchase some lumber to build a house and a dock," Roth replied.

The man said, "Well you most certainly have come to the right place. I am Jason Byrnes, the owner and operator of this mill. What is it that you have in mind?" Roth proceeded to tell Byrnes what he had in mind. Byrnes then said, "Well we can certainly supply you with all the materials that you will need, but would you mind if I made a suggestion? There is a man located on the outskirts of Charles Town, by the name of Ken Kragness. He is a house designer and builder. He has designed and built most of the houses and buildings in town. You should seek him out first and then decide on what you will need as far as lumber goes. First go find him and have a talk. He will tell you what you will need and I can certainly supply it."

"Kragness, you say. Is he by any chance related to the ship builder, Ross Kragness," Roth inquired.

Byrnes replied, "Why yes, he is, they are brothers. Have you met Ross?"

"I have met him and I have contracted him to build a small sailboat for me," he answered.

"You will not be disappointed with his work, I can assure you of that. He and his brother built that shipyard together, hence the name. It was not long after that, people started inquiring into the possibility of them designing and building homes for them. Ross was not that interested in anything other than the building of boats, so he assumed control of the yard and Ken started designing and building homes. I supply him with all his needs."

"Then I will most certainly seek him out," Roth said.

Roth thanked the man and rode back to town. He wished that Thompson would have told him about this Kragness man first, it would have saved him a long ride and Roth was not used to riding a horse.

After a few inquiries, when he reached town, Roth was directed to the house where Kragness lived. He dismounted in front of the house and tied the horse to a post that was provided for that purpose. He stretched his weary legs before he approached the house. He knocked on the door and did not have to wait very long before it was opened by a very tall man with wide shoulders. Roth introduced himself and asked if he was Ken Kragness. The man said that he was and invited him into his house. He entered and was led to a room that was obviously an office. Kragness asked him what is was that he could help him with. Roth then briefly outlined what he had in mind for the building of the dock and house. Kragness listened intently and when Roth had finished, he asked, "That is quite the undertaking, it will cost a considerable amount of money. Are you prepared to pay that price?"

Roth did not hesitate and replied, "The money is no problem. My question to you is can you, do it?"

"Oh yes, I can do it. The only problem that I see is getting the material and men to the site. Your island is quite a ways from here. I do not think that it would be cost effective to ferry back and forth every day. I would need a place for me and my men to stay until the job is finished," Kragness said.

"What would you suggest?" Roth inquired.

"I would suggest that the dock be built first. That can be done with a few men in a few days and they could just camp on the island until that is completed. Next, I would build a smaller house that would contain a kitchen and bunks for the men to use during the construction of the main house. The main house is going to take some time and the men will be on the island for quite some time. It will probably take at least three months to build, depending on what you have in mind," Kragness said.

"That does not sound unreasonable. When can you start?" Roth asked.

Kragness laughed aloud at this question. When his mirth subsided, he said, "You are in a hurry, but you will have to be a little patient. There are quite a few things that need to be taken care of first."

"Such as?" Roth asked.

Kragness looked at Roth and chuckled to himself again and said, "Well, I will need to see the land to find out if it is even possible to build on and then we are going to have to sit down and find out what you want. If it turns out that it is feasible, then plans are going to have to be made, materials ordered and a schedule will have to be made. Not to mention finding the right men that will be willing to take on such a project."

"Are you free in the mornin'?" Roth asked.

Kragness laughed out loud and then answered, "You definitely are in a hurry, however, I have a few things that need to take care of, but I think that I can be ready by , lets say, mid morning,".

"Good, then I will meet you at the dock shortly after sunrise tomorrow and William and I will take you to the island," Roth said. He then reached inside of his satchel and withdrew two heavy gold coins and handed them to Kragness. "This should compensate you for your time," he said.

Kragness noticed the satchel for the first time and saw how it hung heavily on Roth's shoulder and the bulge from the contents inside. It was then that he realized that this man before him must be very well off indeed.

"That is far more than enough. I will be at the dock in the morning," he stated matter of factly. They shook hands and Kragness escorted him to the door.

Roth remounted his horse and rode him back to the stable where he thanked the owner for its use. He walked to a place where he could get some dinner and then returned to his room near the dock. Before he retired for the night, he pulled back the curtain on his window overlooking the dock and harbor. It was the signal that he and William had agreed upon informing William that he would be needed in the morning. He left a candle burning inside the window to make sure that William would see it.

Roth rose early the next morning and dressed for the day. He walked to the dock where the small sailboat was tied up and saw that William was already there. He told William about his encounter with the old man yesterday and said that he had some things that he needed to discuss with him and Kathryn as soon as possible then went on to tell him what they were going to do today. He and William started to ready the boat and while they were doing this, Kragness arrived. He was not alone. With him was another man not quite as big as Kragness but tall, nevertheless. Kragness introduced him as Steve Miller and told him that Steve was a furniture and cabinet maker and that he would be doing the interior portion of the house. Kragness also said that he knew it was not important for Steve to be along on the trip, but yesterday when Kragness had talked to him, he showed a desire to come along if it was alright with Roth. Roth could find no reason for him not to come and told them both to climb aboard. With both men seated, William untied the boat and pushed it away from the dock and then started to raise the sails. The boat started to make headway and Roth brought it around heading towards the tip of the peninsula.

The trip did not take that long and they arrived at the island in just a few hours. Roth had already decided not to sail into the inlet and expose the *Galaunt*, but rather he would sail to the cove where the construction was to take place. Taking the boat as near the shore that he felt was safe, he showed the men where he thought would be the best place for the dock. Both men agreed and Kragness told Roth that he needed to see the place where Roth would like to build his house. They then jumped into the water and waded the short distance to the shore. William stayed with the boat. Roth knew why he was staying but made no mention of it to the others.

Soon they were all standing on the rise that Roth wanted to build his home. Kragness immediately found several sturdy sticks that he proceeded to jam into the ground. He walked and jammed over a large area and finally stopped, proclaiming, "I find this to be a fine area for a house. It has good firm soil and with a splendid view. It would be an honor to build here."

The three then proceeded back to the edge of the marsh where Kragness produced a coil of light cord that had knots tied along its entire length. He then found a spot where he jammed his stick into the ground and said, "It is high tide right now. I need to know how long the walkway to the dock will be so that the proper number of materials can be ordered. Steve, if you would be so kind as to hold onto the end of my measuring cord, I will wade back into the water and see what we need." He handed the end of the cord to Miller and proceeded to wade back to the boat. Roth was happy to see that this man was very efficient and he knew that Kragness would be the right man for this job.

When Kragness reached the boat, he pulled the cord tight and then wrote the results down on a piece of paper he had in his pocket. He then called too Roth and Miller that he had what he needed for the dock and they could go back to town.

It was not a quiet sail back to the town. Kragness was asking all sorts of questions concerning the home that Roth would like to have built. Roth already knew that it would be patterned after the cottage that he had owned in England but it would be larger and have more windows facing out towards the sea. Kragness was taking in everything that Roth was saying and interrupting on occasion to ask a question, all the while taking notes on the paper he had.

By the time they reached the dock in town, Kragness had a very good idea as to what Roth wanted. After they tied the boat to the dock, Kragness said, "I will design the dock tonight and determine the materials that we will need. If you can spare the time in the morning, can you come to my house and we will go over what I have and make any changes you want and then ride out to the mill and put in an order for the materials. Steve and I are going to get something to eat would you and William care to join us?"

Roth accepted but William declined saying he had some things to take care of on board. Kragness, followed by Miller and Roth, left the dock to go eat.

When Roth returned to the dock, he found William waiting for him. They did not waste any time before they set sail towards the small island that sat in the middle between the two points of land that comprised the mouth of the harbor. There they found Kathryn waiting for them. There was a group of rocks on the west side of the island that made a natural dock to which they tied up the boat and climbed out onto the rocks. Kathryn had already found a place where they could sit and talk.

As soon as they were settled, Roth told them both the entire conversation that he had with the old man. Both were growing more excited as he got further into the story. When he finished, it was Kathryn that spoke first, "I can get there is just a few days. I will leave immediately."

Roth held up his hand and said, "Slow down there a bit, young lady. You cannot go swimming off in the middle of the night like that. There are some things that need to be done first."

Kathryn said, "What things. I do not need anything, I can make it in no time."

Roth chuckled at his daughter's enthusiasm and knew in his heart she had already made up her mind as to what she wanted to do. He said, "What are you going to do when you get there? Are you simply going to throw away the pendant? What are you going to do if you lose that tail of yours and grow your legs back? How long do you think you would survive out there in the ocean if you can no longer swim like you can now?" He saw the look of disappointment come over both of their faces at the realization that she could not leave now. He went on to say, "But we do, however, have the means to accomplish what needs to be done and we can get started on that right away."

It was William that asked, "What do we have that will make this possible?"

"The *Galaunt*," Roth answered.

Roth went on to discuss his plan for getting Kathryn where she needed to go and then safely return her back here. They talked and made plans for a couple more hours then Roth and William left a very happy Kathryn on the island and made their way back to town.

True to his word, when Roth arrived at Kragness's home the next morning, he had plans for a dock spread out on his layout table. Kragness pointed out to Roth a new idea he had for a floating dock. It consisted of the dock itself, being built on three large floating tree trunks. The dock itself was connected by a loop of iron on both ends that was wrapped around two poles firmly embedded into the mud allowing the dock to raise and lower with the tide and kept it in the same position. The walkway itself ended with a hinged ramp that could slide on the dock as it raised and lowered maintaining the necessary connection. Roth liked the idea and told him so. Kragness was very pleased with being able to try out his new innovation. After a few minor changes were made, Roth and Kragness left the house and started out for the mill.

Kragness presented his plans to Byrnes and they discussed the materials that would be needed for the construction. After a while Byrnes informed them that most of the materials was already available and the rest would be ready before they could use up what he had. Roth made arrangements with Byrnes to have the materials delivered to the dock where it could be loaded on the small boat and taken to the island. Byrnes told him that he would have most of the lumber on the dock by morning and the rest shortly after that. Roth knew that the boat would only carry so much so he readily agreed with this plan. He thanked Byrnes and gave him enough gold coins to pay for the lumber. He then asked if either one of the men knew of anyone that he could hire to help him load the boat and unload it at the island. Byrnes told him that he would have the necessary men at the dock in the morning to both load and unload and also to build the dock under Ken's supervision.

The next morning, when Roth arrived at the dock, he was surprised to find that the boat was already loaded and everyone was waiting for him. William must have brought it up at first light. He also noticed six other young men that must be the building crew. Kragness came up to him and said, "It turns out that Byrnes already hired a crew for you. I have talked to them all and they appear to know their business. They also brought along camping gear and enough supplies to stay on the island until the job is finished."

Roth introduced himself to the men. They were all young men ranging in ages from twenty-two to twenty-seven, but they were all strong and fit. Roth then got into the boat and found a place for himself amongst the stowed supplies, it seemed that his help was not required for this trip. He was glad for that because he was getting a little tired and this would be a great opportunity to just relax and enjoy the trip.

They made good time and got to the island before noon. Roth was glad to see that the building crew wasted no time getting the boat unloaded and the material dragged to shore. While they were at that, Kragness headed to the trees that outlined the clearing and started making selections of the trees that would be used for the pilings and the floating dock.

They all pitched in when it came time to fell the trees and prepare them for their various needs. Kragness pointed out to Roth that they needed long, sturdy pines to make up the pilings that were long enough to be driven into the mud down to and into solid ground.

Roth helped as much as he could but soon found himself to be more in the way than being of help, so he amused himself wondering around the island instead. He soon found himself on the banks of the cove where the *Galaunt* was moored. He sat down and stared at his ship and started to think back on the days that he was at sea with her. His reverie was broken by a loud splash, he looked back down at the water and immediately saw his daughter treading water in front of him.

"Well, what do you think of the site that I have decided to build our new home?" he asked.

"I think that it is a wonderful place. The water in the cove is also brackish so I will be able to go there as often as I want," she replied.

He was glad that she approved but was saddened inside knowing that even with the information they had, she still might never be able to enjoy this place as much as he. He so wished that there was something that he could do to make sure things turned out the way that they all hoped that they would. He also thought that he could see it in her face that she was probably thinking along the same lines. It was not long before they said their goodbyes and she swam off, leaving him alone once again with his thoughts.

Roth sat there for a while longer before making his way back to the building site. Here he was surprised to see that the men, including William had cut several trees and had prepared them for use as pilings. He also saw that they had rigged a contraption that would be used as a pile driver and they were already driving piles into the mud. Kragness came up to him and told him that the men knew their business and that he thought they would make better time than he had planned on.

It was getting into midafternoon when Kragness came to him again and told him that they had probably better get started back to town while they still had enough light to do so. Kragness gave the leader of the crew some more instructions and he, William and Roth made their way back to the boat for the sail home.

On the way home, Roth and Kragness talked about plans for the house. Kragness thought it would be a good idea if he and Roth could sit down and put those thoughts on paper.

And so it went for the next few weeks with Roth and William ferrying men and materials back and forth from town to the building site. When William was not needed, he would sneak off to meet with Kathryn at the cove that held the *Galaunt*, from there they would explore the other islands surrounding the work site. William was paying particular attention to the island to the south across the river. He found that it contained much arable land and would be ideal for crops. So, whenever they had a chance to be alone they started to make plans for their futures.

Finally, the day arrived when Kragness declared the building complete. Roth and Kragness made the final inspection and Roth declared that he was very happy with the final results. While they had been making their walkthrough, the men that compiled the construction crew loaded up their tools and prepared the sailboat for the last trip back to Charles Towne. It was a quiet trip and Roth contemplated his future. He had some ideas and was going to go talk them over with Thompson while he was in town.

When they arrived at the town docks, there was a message awaiting him that informed him that the Ross Kragness would like him to stop by the yard at his earliest convenience. He was pretty sure that they had his sailboat ready so he decided to go see Thompson first and take care of that business before heading to the boat builders.

When he arrived at Thompson's office, he was glad to find that Craig was there. Craig rose from his desk when he saw Roth and said, "Ah, Mister Horn, it is good to see you again. Are you getting everything settled on your land?"

"Indeed I am. In fact, Mister Kragness finished my home today and that is one of the reasons why I am in town today. I was wondering if perhaps I could lay claim to an additional piece of land directly south and across the river from my island." Roth said.

Thompson looked at him curiously and then asked, "Would you please step over to the map and show me what piece you are inquiring about?"

Roth did just that and Thompson said, "That is a very large piece of land you are looking at. Would it be too presumptuous to ask you what you have in mind for it?"

"Not at all," Roth replied. "I am going to build a plantation and grow cotton and tobacco."

"That is quite an undertaking and it will require a large workforce. Do you know where you are going to acquire those workers?" Thompson asked.

"I plan on parceling it and hiring anyone that is willing to work hard as a sharecropper," Roth replied.

Thompson was still skeptical and said, "You know of course that there is the requirement of improvements within the first year. Are you prepared to fulfill that obligation?"

"Of course, William has already been working the land. He has already located a spot where he plans on building a house and has looked over most of the rest of the island and has a pretty good idea as to how he plans on dividing it up for sharecropping," Roth stated proudly.

Thompson laughed and said, "All right then, it sounds as if you have a fairly good grasp on what it is that you desire to do. Come by my office in a few days and I will have the papers ready for you to sign."

"You will not be sorry. I have decided to make this area my home and I plan on investing in the community so that we both can grow and prosper," Roth said.

They made a little more small talk and finally Roth bid Thompson farewell for now and made his way back to the town dock where he met William. He told him what he had done as they launched the boat to make their way to the Kragness yard.

As they made their way around to the open side of the construction shed, the first thing that Roth noticed was a new sailboat tied alongside the dock. It looked to have a sturdy oak hull with teak trim and shiny brass fittings. It was almost as large as the boat they were in. Roth was very happy with what he saw. He also saw Ross Kragness standing on the dock next to the boat, talking to a group of men. One of the men noticed them coming their way, tapped Kragness on the arm, and pointed in their direction. Roth saw Kragness smile and start to walk to where they were going to dock.

"Well, what do you think of her," he asked even before they had a chance to tie up.

Roth threw a line out to one of the hands and watched as he tied it to a cleat bolted into the dock.

Roth was stepping from the boat to the dock as he said, "She looks really good. Does she sail as well as she looks?" he asked.

Ross looked a little affronted at that and said curtly, "I had her out earlier and she handles like a dream."

Roth looked at him with a smile and chuckled as he said, "Of that there is no doubt in my mind. As you well know, I have been sailing on a ship and a boat of your design for quite some time now and have had nothing but admiration for their capabilities and the utmost respect for their designer."

"Then take her out and see if she lives up to those standards," he said somewhat embarrassed by his previous remark.

"There is time enough for that later, Ross. Right now, there are a couple of things that I would like to discuss with you in your office if you don't mind. Maybe William would like to take her out," Roth said.

"By all means let us retire to my office and discuss what it is that you have on your mind. I will have my foreman go over the things that William will have to know in order to sail the boat by himself," Ross answered in return.

On the way to the office Ross found his foreman working with a group of men outside the shed, organizing some lumber for what was probably their next project and asked him to go help William. After that they made their way to the office. Once inside Ross offered Roth a seat and asked him if he would like a glass of wine. Roth declined and said, "Before I get into what I would like to ask of you, I would like to tell you a little of what I am planning for the future." Roth then began to outline the ideas that he had and then said, "So, as you can see, I am going to be in need of ocean going ships and I cannot very well go to England to purchase them. So, I would like to have you build them for me."

"You flatter me with your trust in my building capabilities. Of course, I would be willing to build them for you but right now I do not have the facilities to take on a venture such as you suggest. It would take a great deal of capital to construct the berths necessary to even start construction not to mention the materials that they would require," Ross said solemnly.

Roth looked at him and said, "If it is money that is the problem, then do not even give that a second thought. I am prepared to pay you whatever is required as a down payment and more if it is required. I will need to have everything in place within three years and for that to happen, things need to be started now."

"We can go over that in time, but you made mention that there is something else that you wanted to discuss with me," he said.

"Yes, there is. You have probably surmised that the *Galaunt* was not really lost at sea," Roth stated.

"It is good to know for sure that she has not been lost," he answered.

Roth went on to say, "And you are probably aware that she is a hunted ship and would never be able to safely sail the open seas without always running the risk of being found by the British and possibly sunk. I need her for one more voyage, a voyage of the utmost importance. With your previous knowledge of the *Galaunt*, I am hoping that you would be able to work on her and change her appearance enough so that without close inspection she would not be recognized."

Ross settled back into his chair and gave Roth a long hard look before he replied. "That should not be too difficult, but I will need to have her here in the yard to be able to make the changes. Is that a possibility?"

Roth did not hesitate and answered, "The only problem that I can see is finding a trustworthy crew to bring her out of her place of hiding and sail her here. I was hoping that maybe you would be able to help me out there. You are undoubtedly more familiar with the experienced sailors in this area."

"You leave that to me. You are right, I do know the sailors around here and I know who is to be trusted and who is not. Come back in a couple of days and I should have everything ready," Ross said.

Roth sighed and said, "It is good to know that there are still men like you in the world. It is good to do business with someone that does not ask a lot of questions."

Ross chuckled and said, "Do not get me wrong here, I am very curious to know what this is all about but I know you to be an honorable man so I am not worried about any repercussions."

"Thank you so much for that. I will tell you that it concerns my daughter and I must make sure that things will be safe for me to go get her and bring her here," Roth said quietly.

Ross looked at him again, only this time there was more respect on his face. "I appreciate your trust and it will be my pleasure to do everything within my power to make sure that she can arrive here safely," he said as he rose from his seat and offered Roth his hand.

Roth knew that he had a friend here that he could trust as he took Ross's hand and firmly shook it saying, "I will return two days hence to see how you are coming along."

Chapter 20
"Reunion"

Roth was alone and in deep thought as he sailed up the waterway during his return to town. He had left Kathryn and William behind to open up the inlet to the *Galaunt* just in case the Kragness's were able to gather a crew together. If so, they would be going for the *Galaunt* today.

As he neared the open end of the construction shed, he was surprised to see that many men were gathered there. He hoped they were the crew. As he was pulling up alongside the dock, several hands reached out and helped pull the boat in and tie it up.

He saw Ross Kragness approaching as he climbed out of his boat. As they got to where he was, it was Ross that spoke first, "It is good to see you. I was getting a little worried that you might not make it today. As you can see, I have a crew ready to go get the *Galaunt* and bring her here."

"I can see that," Roth replied. "Where were you able to find this many men?" he asked.

"They all work for me. Not everyone that is employed by me works here in the yard. There is much that goes on in shipbuilding and many parts that are used in the construction are manufactured at other sites around the community. They are all men that I know and I am sure that they can be trusted to keep quiet about what we are doing," he answered with a mischievous wink.

"I will trust you with your decisions. Now is there somewhere that we can talk for a few minutes? I have some other stuff that I need to take care of in town today and I have to tell you where to find the *Galaunt*," Roth stated.

"You can say whatever you need to say right here if you want. As I mentioned before, I trust these men and I am sure that you will come to trust them also. They are very eager to work with you and will do whatever you ask of them, within reason. I have placed John Wilson, whom I am sure that you remember, in charge of them. John has had several years of experience with ocean going sailing ships and is familiar with the *Galaunt*. He is also very familiar with the waters around here and seeing as the *Galaunt* will be arriving in the dark, he will get her here safely. I will remain behind to put up the lighting that will guide the *Galaunt* to a safe anchorage just upriver from here, to a place where we can begin the work," Ross said.

There were about fifteen men altogether and Roth had them gather around him as he explained where the ship was and what would be needed to get her out of the cove. After he was sure that they knew what was going to be required of them, he took Wilson aside and told him that he had an appointment in town that should not take that long and then he would meet him at the cove. Wilson then chose the men that would be sailing with him in the Kragness Brother's boat and told the others that they were to wait for Roth to return from town and they would sail with him in his boat. Roth bode him farewell and climbed back into his boat for the short sail to the town dock.

When he arrived, he hurried to Thompson's office. It was a short way to the office and Roth was glad to find Craig there and even happier to find that he had the documents ready for his signature. His business with Thompson did not take long and he soon found himself back in his boat returning to the Kragness's yard.

The men that were waiting for him did not take long to board his boat and Roth set sail for his island and the cove where the *Galaunt* was moored.

It was late in the afternoon when they finally arrived at their destination. Roth was surprised to find the *Galaunt* riding at anchor in the middle of the river. As they approached the vessel, Roth could see many of the men high in the rigging preparing the ship to set sail and he could hear orders being given. Roth and the men with him tied the sailboat alongside the *Galaunt* and scrambled aboard where Wilson and William met them.

"It proved to be rather easy to pull the *Galaunt* from that cove," Wilson said. "The channel was wide enough to sail right in with our boat and as it turned out, we carried just enough sail to pull her out."

"That was indeed a break in our favor," William added. "And along with it being high tide there was plenty of room on both sides so she was able to slip right out. These men know their business for sure and it will only be a short while longer before the *Galaunt* will be able to set sail for the harbor."

It turned out that William was right for it was not long before Wilson came up to Roth and said, "She is ready and we are going to depart soon. Are you going to sail with us or are you going to stay here?"

"Seeing as this could very easily be the last time I will be able to sail on her, I think that I would very much like to make this trip," Roth replied.

"Ok then, the command is yours. Just give us enough time to secure the two boats to the stern and we will get under way," Wilson said with a salute.

"No, no. You are in command. You seem to know what you are about and I can see no reason why you should not sail her to the yard," Roth exclaimed.

"As you wish. It will be a few more minutes and we will be under way," he said. He then started issuing orders to get the two sailboats tied off to the stern. When that task was completed, he issued the necessary orders to get the *Galaunt* under way and before Roth knew it, they were on their way to the open sea.

They were sailing northward along the coast but well out to sea to prevent any accidents as the sun had set a few hours before. It seemed to Roth that they had been sailing for a long time before they spotted a fire off the port side. Wilson then explained the fire was set as a marker to show where the point of land was that comprised the south side of the entrance to the harbor. Wilson gave the necessary orders to change course and set a westerly heading. He made sure that they steered clear of the fire but not too far out so there would not be a possibility of running into the island that lay in the middle of the entrance. After they had cleared the harbor entrance, Wilson changed the course a few degrees northward to make sure they were sailing up the Cooper River and would clear the peninsula where the town was located. Roth was very impressed by the manner that Wilson maintained control over the situation and how the men responded to him. Roth knew that this man must have spent many years on sailing ships and wondered why he had given up the sea.

It was not long before Roth noticed another fire burning on the shore ahead of them and once again Wilson told him that this fire marked the spot on shore across from where they would anchor the *Galaunt*. As they got nearer to the fire, Roth was able to make out another light, this one appeared to be a lantern. When it came into sight, Wilson gave the orders to secure all sails except the topsail which he would need to maintain forward momentum. They approached the lantern light and Roth could now make out a man standing in a small boat slowly waving it back and forth. Wilson brought the *Galaunt* right up next to it and ordered the anchor dropped and the topsail secured.

When the ship was anchored and the sailboats had been brought alongside, Roth sought out Wilson to thank him. "You handled that quite well for it being as dark as it was," Roth said.

"I have been sailing around this area for quite some time now and got to know the rivers when I first came here. I was a captain on the first trip here to start this community," Wilson answered back.

"Do you mind me asking why you are not still in command of a ship?" Roth inquired.

"I had a ship shot out from under me a few years back and have not been on another until tonight," he answered. "It was good to be back on board a fine sailing ship like you have here. The *Galaunt* is as fine a ship as I have ever seen. It was an honor to be in command of her even if it was just for a short time. I would like to thank you for the opportunity," he added.

"It is I that should be thanking you for bringing her here safely." With that, Roth offered his hand.

It was beginning to grow light in the East by the time Roth, William, Wilson and the rest of the crew finally made it back to the construction shed where they were met by Ross.

Roth made his way over to him and asked, "How long do you think it will take to make the changes necessary to disguise her?"

He replied, "That is hard to say. We will need to look her over and decide what should be done and make sure that what we do will not change the way that she handles."

Ross added, "I will do the actual work but I do not foresee a long time passing before she is out on the ocean once again."

"That is good. I need her back as soon as possible. I have an important matter that I must undertake and time is of the essence," Roth replied with an air of urgency.

"You need not worry on that score. We will get the job done as fast and as soon as we can," Ross said.

"There is something else that I would like to discuss with you if have the time," Roth said.

Ross answered, "Then maybe we should go up to the house. Everyone has had a long night and maybe we can get some coffee and maybe even a little breakfast while we talk."

"I have not had anything to eat since yesterday morning, so you will get no argument from me," Roth said with a hearty laugh.

Roth, William and Ross left the shed and made their way to Ross's house.

It was only a short walk to where Ross lived and when they arrived, Ross asked his housekeeper if she would please inform the cook that there was going to be three for breakfast and if they could get some coffee while they were waiting.

Once settled in the dining room Ross asked, "You have twice made mention of an important voyage that you have to make. Would it be appropriate for me to ask what the voyage consists of?"

"I think that you have the right to know since you are going to make it possible. But I must ask you for your promise that you will keep it to yourself. After hearing what it consists of, I am sure you will understand why I am acting with such secrecy. I am going to bring my daughter here to live with me and since my ship and I are both wanted I have to make sure that it can be done safely. I am not ready, nor willing, to put my daughter in harm's way, so you can see why things are being done as they are," Roth proceeded to tell him.

Ross replied, "That is as good a reason as I have ever heard and you can be assured that your secret is safe with me. As far as my crew goes, they know to keep their mouths quiet anyway. They know that they would lose their jobs if word about the doings of our yard were to be bandied about."

Roth went on to say, "Then that is settled. Now if you do not mind, I would like to ask you the story behind John Wilson. It was obvious to me that he knows a lot about ships and it seemed to me that he should be in command of his own ship. Why is it that he has settled for a land job like the one that he now holds?"

Ross answered. "That is a tragic tale. John was indeed in command of his own ship, in fact he was in command of the whole fleet that was commissioned to settle this community. It was he that brought the first settlers to this place, me included. But unfortunately for him, on his second voyage here with more settlers, including his wife, son and daughter, his ship was attacked by a pair of Spanish Galleons right out there in the mouth of the harbor. The other two ships turned to help him but could not get there in time to save his ship, but they were able to rescue a number of the passengers. Unfortunately, his wife, son and daughter were not amongst them. John took it very hard and lost himself to drink. It was Craig Thompson that brought him out of it by offering him the job of harbormaster. Since that time, he has cleaned himself up and made something of himself, but I often wonder if he does not wish that he could return to his life at sea."

The cook came in with the breakfast and the conversation changed to small talk. After they had eaten their fill, Roth thanked Ross but said that he and William had better get back to the island and get a little rest. Ross told him that he would get the men started on the ship and would let them know when it was completed. Roth thanked him and then he and William made their way back to the shed, retrieved their boat and set sail for home.

On their way home, Roth outlined what he had on his mind for the island, which he had acquired, to William. William was asking all sorts of questions and was also inserting comments on how it would be possible to improve on Roth's ideas. By the time they reached Roth's island home, they had a plan all worked out and William was anxious to get started.

The days passed slowly for Roth. William was busy with the things necessary to bring their plans together, but for Roth, his only thoughts were for his daughter and what needed to be done to get her back to the way he remembered her. He had been spending a lot of his time talking with her. She was getting very anxious to get underway. William and she were making a lot of plans also. Roth did not want to point out to her that there was still a possibility that what the old man had said might not really do what he had said it would do.

The three of them were sitting out on the dock one morning talking about the eventuality of the voyage before them. Roth said, "Kathryn, how would you feel about the idea of me not making the voyage with you?"

Kathryn, surprised, looked at her father, "Why would you think about not making the trip. I need you there. William is not prepared to command the *Galaunt* and there is no one else that could do it."

Roth replied, "Kathryn, I have been giving this much thought and I do not believe that I can make it through another voyage like this one will be. I am getting too old to be able to handle the rigors of sea life and if something were to happen to me then how would the trip end? I am afraid that I just cannot risk it."

"Then what are we to do?" Kathryn asked frightfully.

"I have an idea on that, but I have to talk with Ross Kragness before I can make any final decisions," Roth answered.

Kathryn suddenly perked up and said that someone was coming just before she slipped into the water and out of sight. Roth and William both looked out towards the water but could not see anything or anyone out there. They were still looking when a boat came into view from the riverside of the island. Roth wondered how Kathryn had known that, but this was definitely not the first time she had done things that surprised him.

They watched as the boat came closer and it was not long before they were able to make out that it was occupied by Ross Kragness and John Wilson. After William helped them tie up the boat, it was Kragness that was the first to step out onto the dock. Roth said with a chuckle, "It is strange that you should show up. We were just talking about you and I was going to prepare to come into town to look you up."

"Well now, it seems that we both have to talk to each other, why not take me up to your house and show me around while we talk. I have heard a lot about it and would very much like to see it."

Roth led the way up the rock walkway from the dock and towards his home. The house was amazingly like the cottage that he had owned in Liverpool but much larger. He felt a sense of pride as he was showing them around. Kragness told him that he had come today to tell him that the modifications on the *Galaunt* were completed. The only thing that he required now was a new name and he would be able to finish the paperwork so that the *Galaunt* would be able to be christened as a new ship. Roth had not given any thought to a name change but when asked he knew that it was something that had to be done in order to completely hide her identity.

Roth did not have to think long about a new name and he said, "We will name her Mary Elizabeth."

Kragness smiled and asked, "Is that name someone of importance to you?"

"She was my wife, she died in childbirth," he answered sadly.

Kragness, in a serious tone replied, "You have my deepest condolences. Then it is a proud name to put on a proud ship. I will complete the paperwork tonight when I return to my office and the ship will be ready when you are."

"There is something else that I wish to discuss with you in private if I may," Roth said.

Roth asked William if he would show John the unique design of the dock. When they left, he turned to Ross and said, "I have come to the conclusion that my ocean sailing days are over. William does not have enough experience to command a ship on a voyage like the one that I am planning. What I would like to know is if you have anyone that you would recommend to take command of the *Galaunt*?"

Kragness did not even hesitate when he replied, "I think we both know the answer to that. John Wilson would be my only choice. He has both the knowledge and the experience to accomplish the mission set before him. It would only be a matter of whether or not he would be willing to take on such a task."

"Well then, let us go and see if he is willing," Roth said. They left the house and made their way down to the dock where they could see William pointing out various things around it.

Roth walked up to them and to John he said, "John, I would like to ask if you would be interested in commanding the *Galaunt* on the voyage that I need her to make?"

John thought about it for a few minutes before he replied, "First I would need to know what the voyage entails."

"It will require sailing around the Cape of Good Hope and getting my daughter and bringing her back here. There will be no other requirements," he said.

John smiled and said, "That is nothing that sounds too awfully difficult. Here I was thinking that with all the secrecy of late, that it would be very dangerous or a very illegal voyage. Of course, I would take command and be very much honored to do it. I must tell you that I was going to approach you anyway to see if there was any way that I could get on the crew. My days on land have come to be something that I was hoping I would get a chance to end."

"Then that is settled. I will of course let you select your own crew and I hope that I can trust you to make sure that they also have the trust of Ross here. This is very important to me," Roth said with an air of hope about him. He then added, "I think it is time for you to meet the object of my concern."

William jumped up from where he had been sitting and exclaimed, "Sir, do you think that is wise? I will be there and I can take care of her."

"William, I know that you would be more than capable of caring for her, but I am sorry to have to tell you that you are not going on the voyage either. I need you here," Roth said with authority.

"But sir, I have to be there. She will not know anyone and she will be scared," he said sadly.

"William, I think that you underestimate Kathryn. She is a Roth and my blood flows through her veins. That is why I think that it is important for her to meet the man that will bring her back to us," Roth said. He then turned back to the two men and saw that they were quite perplexed at what they had just heard. "I know that you have no idea as to what just took place and are probably wondering whether I have lost my mind, but if you will be patient for just a bit longer, all will become clear. But I must ask for your silence on what you are about to see. I am sure that after you see what I am about to show you, you will understand why I ask that of you. William, will you please call for Kathryn."

William hesitated and looked at Roth one more time before he walked over to the edge of the dock. He knelt down and cupping his hand, he patted the water three times. It did not make much noise but Roth knew that if Kathryn were near, as he knew she would be, she would hear it without any problem. They did not have to wait long. Kathryn slowly rose until her head and shoulders were above the water. Roth was looking at the two men and saw the look of incredulous astonishment come over both of their faces.

"Gentlemen, may I please introduce my daughter, Kathryn?" Roth said.

It was Wilson that was able to regain his composure first and he stammered to say, "I-I am very glad to meet you I think."

Kathryn laughed and said, "I am very glad to meet you also."

Kragness finally was able to say, "What is this? Is it some kind of a joke? How can this be?"

William started to react at this, but with a restraining glance Roth stopped him, then spoke up and said, "I assure you that this is no joke. She is real and is definitely as she appears to be." He went on to tell the story of how she had become what she was and went on to enumerate the story of how he had met the old man again in town and what he had told him about how to reverse the change that had overcome her. "So now you know the whole story and I hope that you can see why it is so important to both of us that she is able to return to where all this happened and change back to a normal woman once again."

Kragness said, "That is some story and I can definitely see why you would want us to remain silent. You can rest assured that I will never speak of this to another soul. I doubt that anyone would believe me anyway."

"Well John, are you still willing to take on this voyage now that you know everything?" Roth asked Wilson.

Wilson did not even hesitate when he answered, "If the young lady would allow me, I would be honored to help in any way that I can and take her anywhere she needs to be."

"What say you then Kathryn? It seems as if the final decision is yours," Roth said.

"I can see no reason why we should not proceed. I am anxious to find out whether this will work," she replied.

They talked for a while longer about what needed to be procured and what still needed to be accomplished. Finally with a reassurance from Roth that he would be in town in the morning, Kragness and Wilson climbed back into their boat and set sail for town.

It was barely light enough the following morning when Roth and William set sail for town. William was still angry at not being allowed to make the voyage and they had argued long into the night. Kathryn had sided with her father and between the two of them, they had convinced him that it was better for him to stay and do what was necessary to secure their future. William finally capitulated but was still not happy about his situation. This made for a very quiet ride into town.

They made their way straight to the Kragness's yard. The *Galaunt* was now anchored closer to the open end of the construction shed and Roth saw immediately that Ross Kragness had, indeed, done what they said they would do. If Roth had not known that the ship anchored in the river was the *Galaunt,* he would never have recognized it. He saw right away that a low forecastle had been added and she now had a longer bowsprit that was rigged to hold three sails whereas she only had one before. Looking towards the stern of the ship, he saw that the wheel deck had been widened and extended to give it an overhang on three sides. Swing booms had also been added above the wheel deck and rigged to hold a large square sail. She also had new railings, trimmed and painted, he doubted that anyone would recognize her now even with a close inspection.

They tied off at the dock inside the construction shed and sought out Ross. When he was located, they all walked back out to the dock and Ross immediately started to tell Roth about the changes. "As you can see, she now carries more sail and I am sure that they will increase her speed and possibly her maneuverability as well. There is room for two more guns on the forecastle but we do not have those here so we could not install them."

"With any luck they will not need them on this voyage," Roth said. "I would like to talk to John about a few more things. Is he around today?" Roth inquired.

Kragness answered, "I have not seen him today. I would imagine that he is out looking for crew and ordering supplies. He started as soon as he returned from your island yesterday. He is anxious to get going. Seems that he was quite impressed with what he was shown. I told you that you could not do better than having him lead."

"That is a good thing. I think that I made the right choice also," Roth said. "I am going to sail to the town and see if I can find him." As

Roth was stepping onto his boat, he saw Wilson enter the shed through a side door. "Ah, just the man we were looking for," he said.

"I was told that you had sailed this way and I thought that you would be here. I have an update for you," Wilson returned. "I have been able to hire most of the crew. I was surprised at how many men wanted to get back to the sea. Most of them are single and they stated that they were tired of being here on land. I still have a few to find, but I have enough to move the ship to the deepwater dock in town so that we can get her loaded for the voyage," he said.

"Good, the sooner the better." He then turned to Ross and asked, "How soon before she will be ready to move from here?"

"She will be ready in just a couple of days. The only thing that still remains to be completed is the carving of her new name and attaching it to her stern," Ross answered.

"Those are the type of answers that I like to hear. John, have you started to arrange for supplies?" Roth asked.

"Yes. I just left from a meeting with the merchants around town and they assured me that they would be able to supply me with almost everything that I will need. What they do not have on hand, I am assured, will be gathered from the local farmers who seem more than willing to give what they have for a reasonable price. From what I have been told, I should be able to set sail within two weeks," John replied.

Those two weeks passed very slowly. William and Kathryn were spending as much time together as was possible. William was becoming more despondent by the day but Kathryn was getting more and more excited about the prospect of departing. Roth had been spending most of his time in town helping with arrangements and obtaining needed supplies. Finally sailing day arrived and William and Roth were on hand to see them off. Roth found Wilson talking to Thompson on the dock and walked up to them.

"I was hoping that you would show up. We are just about ready to set sail, just waiting for the tide to turn," Wilson said.

"That should be within the hour. Have you got everything that you think you will need?" Roth asked.

Wilson chuckled and said, "Oh heavens yes. This ship is stocked with enough supplies for us to sail around the world and still have leftovers. We are not going to lose any weight, that is for sure. That man that you got as our cook is the finest cook I have ever had the pleasure of being fed by." They talked for a while longer and finally Wilson said, "Well the tide is going out. We might just as well go out with it."

"Yes, you should. Just remember what the mission is and take your time getting there but hurry back," Roth said as he gave Wilson a farewell handshake.

Wilson turned and walked up the gangplank and before the gangplank could be hauled up and secured, he began to issue orders that got the ship moving away from the dock and out into the river. Roth and William stood on the dock and watched her sail away until they could not see her any longer. It reminded Roth of another time he had watched another ship do the same thing, only this time he had hopes of seeing it return.

It has been over a year since the *Galaunt* had set sail. Roth had not received any word about where the ship might be or what her fate could possibly be. William had already grown quite dejected and he hardly ever came to visit anymore, which greatly disappointed Roth. William had built a very large home on the big island that he had hoped he would be able to share with Kathryn when she returned home but he was sure now that he would never see her again. Roth was sure that William somehow felt that he was responsible because he had not allowed him to accompany her on the voyage. Roth was even starting to second guess himself on that decision even though he knew that it would probably not have changed whatever had happened to the *Galaunt* and his daughter. He knew that he had made the right choice. William had been needed here to make sure that everything that he had planned for had come into being and, for the most part, they had.

Over the course of the year that had passed, more colonists had arrived at the settlement. Several of them, had left England because of persecution rather than a desire for a new start. Most of them had taken Roth up on his offer of sharecropping. He had offered them a fair size tract of land and a house for half of the profits made from that land. It was more than a fair deal for those that arrived with nothing more than the clothes that they were wearing.

Most of the people that had settled on the island did not have the means to make it into Charles Towne, so he opened a general store and hired a married couple to run it. Now those that lived there could get the materials they needed without having to go all the way into town to obtain them. Because almost everyone on the island was starting out with nothing, Roth had given them a line of credit at the store that they would be able to pay off when they sold the crops that they raised.

The Kragness's yard had completed one of the ships that Roth had ordered and were well on their way to completing the second. The ship, which Roth had named the *Carolina*, had already made one voyage back to England where it had sold a cargo made up of goods grown or manufactured entirely in America. The profits were not exactly what they had hoped for but they were still substantial and everyone profited. Roth had decided that the next load would be sent to the colonies to the north. His thoughts were that it would bring a better profit because the cargo consisted mostly of cotton. In the north they were building textile mills in the hopes they could compete with England. Goods shipped from England were very expensive and all colonies up and down the coast were starting to manufacture what they needed and cotton could only be grown in the south. He was also hoping that he could drive up the price of cotton in England so that if he did ship there, it would be much more profitable. England could not grow its own cotton and thereby had to rely on others to bring it to them. All of his plans were starting to bear fruit but it all meant nothing if he could not have Kathryn back. Everything that he had done was for her and William and if she was not to return then it was all for naught.

Roth awoke early in the morning. He was planning on sailing over to the big island to have a talk with William. In Roth's mind, it was time for William to move on with his life. He had plenty of money as well as a share in everything that Roth had.

Roth stepped out of his front door and was greeted by his groundskeeper Sean Duffy. "A wee bit of a nip in the air this mornin' sir. I hope ye have donned your warm woolens," Sean said with a large smile.

Roth liked this young man. Sean and his wife, Linda, arrived from Ireland and had nothing when Roth had found them looking very lost on the town dock. He talked to them and instantly found them to his liking. He immediately offered them jobs as a groundskeeper and his housekeeper. Linda turned out to be an excellent cook also.

"I think that I will be all right today. I am just going to go over and see William," Roth answered back.

"I be thinkin' ye may want to hang back a bit afore ye be settin' sail sir," Sean said as he pointed out towards the cove.

Roth saw right away what he was pointing at. There was a boat coming into the cove from the river and Roth recognized it as being the Kragness Brothers' yard boat. His eyesight was not what it used to be but he could see that it contained at least four people. As he watched it approach, he made his way down to the dock accompanied by Sean. It was not long before he was able to recognize Ross and Ken Kragness along with another man that he thought resembled John Wilson. There was also a lady on board with long dark auburn hair that looked like it could be Kathryn. Could this really be true? Is this the day that he has longed so soulfully for? His heart started to race in anticipation of seeing his beloved daughter after all this time. That is the dream that he had lived for over this past year and now was it possible that it was going to happen?

Kathryn could hardly see her father but she felt his closeness as she had so many times when he neared her at sea. Wilson pointed to the area where her father may be sighted. Kathryn immediately saw him and started to cry with tears flowing freely down her cheeks from a great feeling of happiness. She immediately withdrew her handkerchief from a small bag to dry the tears from her face. She did not want her father to see her in such disarray.

As the boat neared the dock, Sean ran over to catch a lanyard that John threw towards him as Roth caught a second lanyard thrown by Ross. Both were then tied to the dock securing the boat. Kathryn stood up in the boat and looked at her father. Neither of them could speak nor move. After this moment of realization, they both started talking at the same time. They started to laugh and then he took her hand and helped her step onto the dock. They embraced in a warm clinging hug, now they were both shedding tears of joy. Roth was very reluctant to let her go after all these years of not being able to hold her like this and found to his delight, she was hugging him just as tightly. Eventually he released her from the tight hold and grasping her by the shoulders, held her at arm length and gazed into her eyes. The first thing that he noticed was the color of her eyes. They were a liquid blue, as blue as the ocean depths. They were now the same color as the old mans had been.

"Where have you been? We had almost given up hope that you would ever return. Oh darlin', I am so glad to see you," Roth said fighting a losing battle to hold back his emotions.

"We had our doubts about whether or not we would return also," Wilson said. "It has been quite the adventure for sure."

Still holding on to his daughter, Roth said, "Let's go up to the house so you can rest and tell me all about it." He turned to Sean and said, "Sean, would you take the boat over to the big island and get William. Do not tell him why but tell him that I need to see him right away."

Sean did not say anything as he ran to where Roth's boat was tied off and immediately cast off and started to make his way over to the island.

The rest of them walked up the walkway and crossed the lawn to the house. Once on the porch, Roth called to his housekeeper and asked her if she would be so kind and bring them all something cool to drink. Roth then told everyone to take a seat on the porch. Looking at his daughter, he said, "Well now that we have settled, how about letting me hear the story of the voyage."

Kathryn said, "I will let Captain Wilson tell it, he knows more about the voyage than I do."

Roth looked over at Wilson and asked, "Why did it take so long? You should have been back months ago."

Linda, the housekeeper, brought them their drinks and when she reentered the house, John started his tale. "We did not have any problems reaching the area that you told us to sail too, but when we arrived there, Kathryn was nowhere to be found. I had not seen her for the entire voyage, except for when we first sailed, so we just sailed around there looking for her."

Roth looked at Kathryn and asked, "Why were you not there young darlin'?"

"I am not sure that anyone would believe me if I told them what I was doing," Kathryn answered.

Roth laughed, looked around at the other men on the porch and said, "Kathryn, I am sure that at this point, we would believe just about anything. Why not tell us and let us decide what is to be believed."

"Alright, I will tell you but you have to promise not to call me a liar," she said with a slight tone of amusement.

Roth laughed again and said, "There is no need for you to fear that."

Kathryn paused for a while before she finally started to talk. "I was following the ship, a short distance behind, as I had always done, usually playing with the dolphins, as you know I like to do. After we had rounded the Cape and proceeded to the area where we encountered the storm, they, the dolphins, were not there. This was very strange as they were always there. I looked around for them but they were nowhere to be found. I was beginning to get a little worried and maybe even a little afraid. It was just a while after noon that a merman appeared and started to swim alongside me. I stopped and so did he. He was old, older than anyone that I had ever seen. He was bigger than me and his face was mostly covered with hair but he had the most intense blue eyes that I noticed right away, they matched the color of the ocean. When he spoke, his voice was clear and deep and sounded as if he was very old and wise. He told me that there was nothing for me to be afraid of and introduced himself as Ophius. He told me that he had been watching me for several years and that now was the time that he had to teach me a few things before I made the decision to change back into a human form. He told me that we were the last of our kind and that he did not have much more time left and that I, shortly, would be the last of our kind. We swam around for a few days while he told me his story. He was very old indeed, he told me of a time when mermaids and mermen roamed the seas and were as many as humans are today. He told me of the great disease that came and killed all of them except for a very few. Those few soon died also until there was only him that was still here, but now it was quickly approaching the time when he was to also join his ancestors. So, he knew that he must finally come to me and let me know what it was to be a mermaid and what would happen to me if I were to change back to a human form. I told him then it was going to be my decision to change back to human form and that brought a strange look on his face. He seemed to grow sadder. Anyway, we swam around together for several days until we found a large piece of what looked to me like a part of a hull from a ship that had broken up. He said that we were going to need this if I was determined to change, so we pushed it until we caught sight of the *Galaunt*. It was becoming night when we got closer to the ship and he told me to climb on top of the wood and take off the pendant and throw it into the sea. I did as he said and then fell asleep. When I awoke, the first thing that I saw was a rowboat coming over to where I was floating on the wood. Captain Wilson and two others manned it. The old merman was nowhere in sight and I wondered if maybe I had imagined it all. They had brought along some clothes that I was very grateful for, I had changed back to human form and was completely naked. After I got the clothes on and climbed into the rowboat, they took me back to the *Galaunt*. The rest of the story Captain Wilson can tell you. I do not remember all of it for I was very tired and slept through most of it."

Wilson picked up the story where Kathryn had left off saying, "After we got Kathryn safely on board, we turned and set sail for home. It was turning to evening as we were rounding the Cape once again. All seemed well so we decided to leave the sails up and make some time. Around midnight, we were beset by a freak wave that we had no idea was anywhere near us. It hit us abeam the port side, so hard and so high that if we had not been tacking to the port, it would have probably rolled us over. As it was the main mast snapped like a twig and crashed through the main deck and crew deck nearly to the waterline. We had to scramble for the next few hours to save the ship and we barely made it. After we had cut loose the sail and hacked away the wreckage of the main mast the gash was now safely above the waterline and we stopped shipping water. We now had time to assess the damage and found that we had lost five men. Three must have been thrown overboard and the falling mast crushed the other two. We limped into a large bay on the tip of the Africa's where we could drop anchor and see what we could do about repairs. The ship was in no condition to make the trip home. There was not a lot that we could do from the bay, so we patched the side as best we could and decided to try and make it to Madagascar where we could have the ship repaired to where it would be able to make the trip back home. We had lost a lot of sail that we could not replace and with the main mast gone, it took us a long time to get there. Once we got there, we were able to get the necessary repairs done and soon set sail for home. It took us a lot longer than we had planned but we made it early this morning. I left the *Galaunt* at the shipyard, borrowed their boat and immediately set sail for here with your daughter."

Roth was about to say something when he heard his daughter let out a shriek of joy. He looked up and then in the direction that she was looking. No one had noticed that Sean and William had sailed into the cove and were now tying up the boat. William spun around when he heard the shriek and immediately saw Kathryn. Kathryn jumped up and started running down to the dock as William started to run towards her. They met each other at the end of the walkway and William grabbed her, raised her off the ground and spun her around. Roth could see that they were excitedly talking to one another, but he could not hear what they were saying. William finally stopped twirling her around and set her down. They embraced and held each other for a long time. Roth looked at them sadly for now he knew that he had regained his daughter in one way but had lost her in another.

Epilogue

Roth sat alone in his old rocker, covered with a shawl, on the upper porch that encircled his house where his housekeeper, Linda, had helped him to earlier. Many years had passed since Kathryn had come home in her human form and Roth was now a very old man. Some had said that it was unusual for a man to live as long as he had. Roth was sitting there thinking about his life. He had grandchildren now. William and Kathryn had blessed him with two children, a girl named Elizabeth and a boy named Nathan. They were the love of his life. Almost everything that he had dreamed and planned for had turned out to be a reality. He had a thriving plantation on the big island and his shipping company was flourishing. William had built the big island into the pride of the Carolinas. In fact, there was even a small town located on the island. John Wilson was in charge of the shipping company and he had expanded it to eight ships that were constantly under sail delivering cargo everywhere up and down the coast and sometimes even to England when the need arose.

Roth remembered the old days also. The days he had spent on the island with Kathryn as his constant and only companion. He also remembered his days at sea with his old friend Edward Berkshire. Eventually his thoughts returned to his daughter and it was with the thought of her in his mind that he leaned his head back, smiled and closed his eyes for the last time.

Linda found him some time later and knew right away that he was gone from this life. She left him as he was and went to find Sean to send him over and bring Kathryn and William here.

When they arrived, Kathryn rushed to her father's side and hugged him, laid her head on his chest and told him for the last time that she loved him. She sobbed and when William tried to move her away, she resisted, telling him that she needed more time to spend alone with her father. William was very concerned but followed her will. He wished that there was some way that he could help her to relieve her pain.

As Kathryn knelt down alongside her father, she brushed back his hair and kissed him on his forehead. "Oh father, I will always carry you in my heart and I will share with your grandchildren all of the sea stories that you shared with me as a child. I will always remember the love and excitement of you returning home from a voyage. No other man could be a better father than you have been to me. My only regret was all the years we had to be apart while I was a mermaid. Yet if that had not happened it would be you mourning your loss of me and I am glad that you were spared that." She lingered there until William came and gently pulled her away, saying, "Come Kathryn, the children and I need you and I think you need us also. You must rest, we have much to do."

The funeral was a quiet affair with only close personal friends in attendance. Roth was to be buried at sea, the one place where he had been truly the happiest. As it turned out, the *Galaunt* happened to be tied up alongside the town dock when the news reached John Wilson. He arranged for her to be the ship that would take Roth to his final place of rest.

It was not a long sail from Roth's island out to the sea. After the ceremony and a short prayer, his body was commended to the sea. There was a small gathering at Roth's house when the ship returned to the island where everyone could share their thoughts before the *Galaunt* and most of the mourners returned to town.

Kathryn and William decided to spend the night at Roth's house. During the night, when Kathryn was sure that everyone was asleep, she arose from the bed, dressed and made her way out to the dock. Once there, she stripped off all her clothes and dove into the water. The change happened quickly and now she was able to make good time underwater. She swam out to the point where they had commended her father's body to the sea. She quickly found the shroud wrapped around the body of her father. Gently she took him into her arms and carried him to a sandy place on the bottom of the ocean. There, she proceeded to cover him with nearby rocks to protect his body from scavenger fish. When she had completed this task, she gathered more rock and constructed a monument at his head. On this monument she placed the pendant that he had given her so long ago. The very same pendant that had started it all. This was the one thing that she had left out from her story. She did not tell anyone that the old merman had told her that he was going to die and it was now her responsibility to be the last of her kind and everything that went along with that duty. She would live for an exceptionally long time and someday she would need to find someone to take her place, ensuring that there would always be a line that would never be broken. Until that time, she would leave the pendant, on the monument, to watch over her father. Turning to swim away, she paused and floated a short distance from the site, recalling the life she had had with her father. After a short time, tearfully, she bid him a final farewell. Her tears changed into a smile as she thought about all the wonderful adventures and tales that she would be able to share with Nathan and Elizabeth, about her hero, their grandfather.